Trace

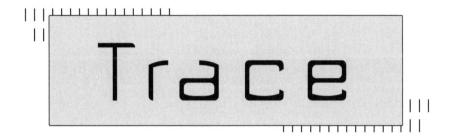

patricia cornwell

G. P. PUTNAM'S SONS

NEW YORK

This is a work of fiction. Names, characters, places, and incidents
either are the product of the author's imagination or are used fictitiously,
and any resemblance to actual persons, living or dead, businesses,
companies, events, or locales is entirely coincidental.

G. P. Putnam's Sons
Publishers Since 1838
a member of
Penguin Group (USA) Inc.
375 Hudson Street
New York, NY 10014

Library of Congress Cataloging-in-Publication Data

Cornwell, Patricia Daniels.
Trace / Patricia Cornwell.
p. cm.
ISBN 0-399-15219-9
1. Scarpetta, Kay (Fictitious character)—Fiction.   2. Teenage girls—
Crimes against—Fiction.   3. Forensic pathologists—Fiction.
4. Women physicians—Fiction.   5. Virginia—Fiction.   I. Title.
PS3553.O692T73   2004   2004042190
813'.54—dc22

Printed in the United States of America
1   3   5   7   9   10   8   6   4   2

This book is printed on acid-free paper. ∞

BOOK DESIGN BY AMANDA DEWEY

Trace

1.

||| YELLOW BULLDOZERS hack earth and stone in an old city block that has seen more death than most modern wars, and Kay Scarpetta slows her rental SUV almost to a stop. Shaken by the destruction ahead, she stares at the mustard-colored machines savaging her past.

"Someone should have told me," she says.

Her intention this gray December morning was innocent enough. All she wanted was to indulge in a little nostalgia and drive past her old building, not having a clue that it was being torn down. Someone could have told her. The polite and kind thing would have been to mention it, at least say, Oh, by the way, that building where you used to work when you were young and full of hopes and dreams and believed in love, well, that old building you still miss and feel deeply about is being torn down.

A bulldozer lurches, its blade raised for the attack, and the noisy mechanical violence seems a warning, a dangerous alert. I should have listened, she thinks as she looks at the cracked and gouged concrete. The front of her old building is missing half of its face. When she was asked to come back to Richmond she should have paid attention to her feelings.

"I've got a case I'm hoping you might help me with," explained Dr. Joel Marcus, the current chief medical examiner of Virginia, the man who took her place. It was just yesterday afternoon when he called her on the phone and she ignored her feelings.

"Of course, Dr. Marcus," she said to him over the phone as she moved around in the kitchen of her South Florida home. "What can I do for you?"

"A fourteen-year-old girl was found dead in bed. This was two weeks ago, about noon. She'd been sick with the flu."

Scarpetta should have asked Dr. Marcus why he was calling her. Why her? But she wasn't paying attention to her feelings. "She was home from school?" she said.

"Yes."

"Alone?" She stirred a concoction of bourbon, honey, and olive oil, the phone tucked under her chin.

"Yes."

"Who found her and what's the cause of death?" She poured the marinade over a lean sirloin steak inside a plastic freezer bag.

"Her mother found her. There's no obvious cause of death," he said. "Nothing suspicious except that her findings, or lack of them, indicate she shouldn't be dead."

Scarpetta tucked the plastic bag of meat and marinade inside the refrigerator and opened the drawer of potatoes, then shut it, changing her mind. She'd make whole-grain bread instead of potatoes. She couldn't stand still, much less sit, and she was unnerved and trying very hard not to sound unnerved. Why was he calling her? She should have asked him.

"Who lived in the house with her?" Scarpetta asked.

"I'd rather go over the details with you in person," Dr. Marcus replied. "This is a very sensitive situation."

At first Scarpetta almost said that she was leaving for a two-week trip to Aspen, but those words never came out and they are no longer true. She isn't going to Aspen. She'd been planning on going, for months she had, but she wasn't going and she isn't going. She couldn't bring herself to lie about it, and instead used the professional excuse that she couldn't come to Richmond because she is in the midst of reviewing a difficult case, a very difficult death by hanging that the family refuses to accept as a suicide.

"What's the problem with the hanging?" asked Dr. Marcus, and the more he talked, the less she heard him. "Racial?"

"He climbed a tree, put a rope around his neck, and handcuffed himself behind his back so he couldn't change his mind," she replied, opening a cabinet door in her bright, cheerful kitchen. "When he stepped off the branch and dropped, his C-2 fractured and the rope pushed up his scalp in back, distorting his face, so it looked like he was frowning, as if he were in pain. Try explaining that and the handcuffs to his family in Mississippi, deep down there in Mississippi, where camouflage is normal and gay men are not."

"I've never been to Mississippi," Dr. Marcus said blandly, and maybe what he really meant was he didn't care about the hanging or any tragedy that had no direct impact on his life, but that wasn't what she heard, because she wasn't listening.

"I'd like to help you," she told him as she opened a new bottle of unfiltered olive oil, even though it wasn't necessary to open it right that minute. "But it's probably not a good idea for me to get involved in any case of yours."

She was angry but denied it as she moved about her large, well-equipped kitchen of stainless-steel appliances and polished granite countertops and big bright views of the Intracoastal Waterway. She was angry about Aspen but denied it. She was just angry, and she didn't want to bluntly remind Dr. Marcus that she was fired from the same job he now enjoys, which is why she left Virginia with no plans for ever coming back. But a long silence from him forced her to go on and say that she didn't leave Richmond under amicable conditions and certainly he must know it.

"Kay, that was a long time ago," he replied, and she was professional and respectful enough to call him Dr. Marcus, and here he was calling her Kay. She was startled by how offended she was by his calling her Kay, but she told herself he was friendly and personal while she was touchy and overly sensitive, and maybe she was jealous of him and wished him failure, accusing herself of the worst pettiness of all. It was understandable that he would call her Kay instead of Dr. Scarpetta, she told herself, refusing to pay attention to her feelings.

"We have a different governor," he went on. "It's likely she doesn't even know who you are."

Now he was implying that Scarpetta is so unimportant and unsuccessful that the governor has never heard of her. Dr. Marcus was insulting her. Nonsense, she countered herself.

"Our new governor is rather much consumed with the Commonwealth's enormous budget deficit and all the potential terrorist targets we've got here in Virginia . . ."

Scarpetta scolded herself for her negative reaction to the man who succeeded her. All he wanted was help with a difficult case, and why shouldn't he track her down? It's not unusual for CEOs fired from major corporations to be called upon later for advice and consultation. And she's not going to Aspen, she reminded herself.

". . . nuclear power plants, numerous military bases, the FBI Academy, a not-so-secret CIA training camp, the Federal Reserve. You

4

won't have any problem with the governor, Kay. She's too ambitious, actually, too focused on her Washington aspirations, the truth be told, to care about what's going on in my office." Dr. Marcus went on in his smooth southern accent, trying to disabuse Scarpetta of the idea that her riding back into town after being ridden out of it five years earlier would cause controversy or even be noticed. She wasn't really convinced, but she was thinking about Aspen. She was thinking about Benton, about his being in Aspen without her. She has time on her hands, she was thinking, so she could take on another case because she suddenly has more time.

Scarpetta drives slowly around the block where she was headquartered in an early stage of her life that now seems as finished as something can be. Puffs of dust drift up as machines assault the carcass of her old building like giant yellow insects. Metal blades and buckets clank and thud against concrete and dirt. Trucks and earthmoving machines roll and jerk. Tires crush and steel belts rip.

"Well," Scarpetta says, "I'm glad I'm seeing this. But someone should have told me."

Pete Marino, her passenger, silently stares at the razing of the squat, dingy building at the outer limits of the banking district.

"I'm glad you're seeing it, too, Captain," she adds, although he isn't a captain anymore, but when she calls him Captain, which isn't often, she is being gentle with him.

"Just what the doctor ordered," he mutters in a sarcastic tone that is his most common tone, like middle C on a piano. "And you're right. Someone should have told you, that someone being the prickless wonder who took your place. He begs you to fly here when you haven't set foot in Richmond for five years and can't bother to tell you the old joint's being torn down."

"I'm sure it didn't cross his mind," she says.

"The little prick," Marino replies. "I hate him already."

This morning Marino is a deliberate, menacing mixture of messages in black cargo pants, black police boots, a black vinyl jacket, and an LAPD baseball cap. Obvious to Scarpetta is his determination to look like a tough big-city outsider because he still resents the people in this stubborn small city who mistreated him or dissed him or bossed him around when he was a detective here. Rarely does it occur to him that when he was written up, suspended, transferred, or demoted, usually he deserved it, that when people are rude to him, usually he provokes them.

Slouched in the seat with sunglasses on, Marino looks a bit silly to Scarpetta, who knows, for example, that he hates all things celebrity, that he especially hates the entertainment industry and the people, including cops, who are desperate to be part of it. The cap was a wise-guy gift from her niece, Lucy, who recently opened an office in Los Angeles, or Lost Angeles, as Marino calls it. So here is Marino, returning to his own lost city, Richmond, and he has choreographed his guest appearance by looking exactly like what he's not.

"Huh," he muses in a lower pitch of voice. "Well, so much for Aspen. I guess Benton's pretty pissed."

"Actually, he's working a case," she says. "So a few days' delay is probably a good thing."

"A few days my ass. Nothing ever takes a few days. Bet you never get to Aspen. What case is he working?"

"He didn't say and I didn't ask," she replies, and that's all she intends to say because she doesn't want to talk about Benton.

Marino looks out the window and is silent for a moment, and she can almost hear him thinking about her relationship with Benton Wesley, and she knows Marino wonders about them, probably constantly and in ways that are unseemly. Somehow he knows that she has been distant from Benton, physically distant, since they got back together, and it angers and humiliates her that Marino would detect such a thing. If anyone would figure it out, he would.

"Well, that's a damn shame about Aspen," Marino says. "If it was me, it would really piss me off."

"Take a good look," she says, referring to the building being knocked down right before their eyes. "Look now while we're here," she says, because she does not want to talk about Aspen or Benton or why she isn't there with him or what it might be like or what it might not be like. When Benton was gone all those years, a part of her left. When he came back, not all of her did, and she doesn't know why.

"Well, I guess it's about time they tore the place down," Marino says, looking out his window. "I guess because of Amtrak. Seems I heard something about it, about needing another parking deck down here because of them opening Main Street Station. I forget who told me. It was a while ago."

"It would have been nice if you had told me," she says.

"It was a while ago. I don't even remember who I heard it from."

"Information like that is a good thing for me to know."

He looks at her. "I don't blame you for being in a mood. I warned you about coming here. Now look what we find right off. We haven't even been here an hour, and look at this. Our old joint's being smashed up with a wrecking ball. It's a bad sign, you ask me. You're going maybe two miles an hour. Maybe you ought to speed up."

"I'm not in a mood," she replies. "But I like to be told things." She drives slowly, staring at her old building.

"I'm telling you, it's a bad sign," he says, staring at her, then out his window.

Scarpetta doesn't speed up as she watches the destruction, and the truth sinks in slowly, as slowly as her progress around the block. The former Office of the Chief Medical Examiner and Division of Forensic Science Laboratories is well on its way to becoming a parking deck for the restored Main Street railway station, which never saw a train during the decade she and Marino worked and lived here. The hulking Gothic station is built of stone the hue of old blood and was dormant for long years until, with but a few agonal twitches, it was transformed into shops, which soon failed, and then state offices, which soon closed. Its tall clock tower was a constant on the horizon, watching over sweeping bends of I-95 and train overpasses, a ghostly white face with filigree hands frozen in time.

Richmond has moved on without her. Main Street Station has been resurrected and is a hub for Amtrak. The clock works. The time is sixteen minutes past eight. The clock never worked all those years it followed Scarpetta in her mirrors as she drove back and forth to take care of the dead. Life in Virginia has moved on and no one bothered to tell her.

"I don't know what I expected," she says, glancing out her side window. "Maybe they would gut it, use it for storage, archives, state surplus. Not tear it down."

"Truth is, they ought to tear it down," Marino decides.

"I don't know why, but I never thought they would."

"It ain't exactly one of the architectural wonders of the world," he says, suddenly sounding hostile toward the old building. "A 1970s piece of concrete shit. Think of all the murdered people who been through that joint. People with AIDS, street people with gangrene. Raped, strangled, and stabbed women and kids. Wackos who jumped off buildings and in front of trains. There ain't a single kind of case that joint ain't seen. Not to mention all those pink rubbery bodies in the floor vats of the Anatomical Division. Now that creeped me out worse than anything. 'Member how they'd lift 'em out of those vats with chains and hooks in their ears? All naked and pink as the Three Little Pigs, their legs hitched up." He lifts his knees to demonstrate, black-cargo-pants-covered knees rising toward the visor.

"Not so long ago, you couldn't lift your legs like that," she says. "You could hardly even bend your legs not even three months ago."

"Huh."

"I'm serious. I've been meaning to say something about how fit you're getting."

"Even a dog can lift its leg, Doc," he jokes, his mood obviously improved by the compliment, and she feels bad that she hasn't complimented him before now. "Assuming the dog in question's male."

"I'm serious. I'm impressed." She has worried for years that his atrocious health habits were going to drop him dead, and when he finally makes an effort, she doesn't praise him for months. It requires her old building to be torn down for her to say something nice to him. "I'm sorry I haven't mentioned it," she adds. "But I hope you're not just eating protein and fat."

"I'm a Florida boy now," he says cheerfully. "On the South Beach Diet but I sure as hell don't hang out in South Beach. Nothing but fags down there."

"That's an awful thing to say," she replies, and she hates it when he talks like that, which is why he does it.

"Remember the oven down there?" Marino continues his reminiscing. "You always knew when they was burning up bodies down there, because smoke would be coming out the chimney." He points to a black crematorium smokestack on top of the battered old building. "When I used to see ol' smoky going, I didn't particularly want to be driving around down here breathing the air."

Scarpetta glides past the rear of the building, and it is still intact and looks exactly the way it did last time she saw it. The parking lot is empty except for a big yellow tractor that is parked almost exactly where she used to park when she was chief, just to the right of the massive closed bay door. For an instant, she hears the screeching and complaining of that door cranking up or down when the big green and red buttons inside were pressed. She hears voices, hearses and ambulances rumbling, doors opening and slamming shut, and the clack and clatter of stretcher legs and wheels as shrouded bodies were rolled up and down the ramp, the dead in and out, day and night, night and day, coming and going.

"Take a good look," she says to Marino.

"I did the first time you went around the block," he replies. "You plan on us driving around in circles all day?"

"We'll circle it twice. Take a good look."

Turning left on Main Street, she drives a little faster around the demolition site, thinking that pretty soon it will look like an amputee's raw stump. When the back parking lot comes into view again, she notices a man in olive-green pants and a black jacket standing close to the big yellow tractor, doing something to the engine. She can tell he is having a problem with his tractor, and she wishes he wouldn't stand in front of the huge back tire, doing whatever he's doing to the engine.

"I think you might want to leave the cap in the car," she says to Marino.

"Huh?" Marino asks, and his big weathered face looks at her.

"You heard me. A little friendly advice for your own good," she says as the tractor and the man recede behind her and are gone.

"You always say something's friendly and for my own good," he answers. "And it never is." He takes off the LAPD cap and looks at it thoughtfully, his bald head glistening with sweat. The scant quota of gray hair nature is kind enough to allot him is gone by his design.

"You never did tell me why you started shaving your head," she says.

"You never asked."

"I'm asking." She turns north, heading away from the building toward Broad Street and going the speed limit now.

"It's the in thing," he replies. "Point is, if you ain't got hair, may as well get rid of it."

"I suppose that makes sense," she says. "As much sense as anything."

2.

||| EDGAR ALLAN POGUE stares at his bare toes as he relaxes in the lawn chair. He smiles and contemplates the reactions of people should they find out he now has a home in Hollywood. A second home, he reminds himself. He, Edgar Allan Pogue, has a second home where he can come for sun and fun and privacy.

No one is going to ask which Hollywood. At the mention of Hollywood, what immediately comes to mind is the big white Hollywood sign on the hill, mansions protected by walls, convertible sports cars, and the blessed beautiful ones, the gods. It would never enter anyone's mind that Edgar Allan Pogue's Hollywood is in Broward County, about an hour's drive north of Miami, and does not attract the rich and famous. He will tell his doctor, he thinks with a trace of pain. That's right, his doctor will be the first to know, and next time he won't run out of the flu shot, Pogue thinks with a trace of fear. No doctor would ever deprive his Hollywood patient of a flu shot, no matter the shortage, Pogue decides with a trace of rage.

"See, Mother Dear, we're here. We really are here. It's not a dream," Pogue says in the slurred voice of someone who has an object in his mouth that interferes with the movement of his lips and tongue.

His even, bleached teeth clamp down harder on a wooden pencil.

"And you thought the day would never come," he talks around the pencil as a bead of saliva drips from his lower lip and slides down his chin.

You won't amount to anything, Edgar Allan. Failure, failure, failure. He talks around the pencil, mimicking his mother's mean-spirited, slurred, drunken voice. You're a thin soup, Edgar Allan, that's what you are. Loser, loser, loser.

His lawn chair is exactly in the middle of the airless, stinking living room, and his one-bedroom apartment is not quite exactly in the middle of the second level of units that face Garfield Street, named after the U.S. president and running east-west between Hollywood Boulevard and Sheridan. The pale yellow stucco two-level complex is called Garfield Court for reasons unknown, beyond the obvious one of false advertising. There is no courtyard, not even a blade of grass, just a parking lot and three spindly palm trees with ragged fronds that remind Pogue of the tattered wings of the butterflies he pinned to cardboard as a boy.

Not enough sap in the tree. That's your problem.

"Stop it, Mother. Stop it right now. It's unkind to talk like that."

When he rented his second home two weeks ago, Pogue didn't argue about the price, although nine hundred and fifty dollars a month is outrageous compared to what that amount of money would get him in Richmond, assuming he paid rent in Richmond. But proper accommodations aren't easy to find around here, and he didn't know where to start when he finally arrived in Broward County after a sixteen-hour drive, and in an exhausted but exhilarated mood began cruising, getting himself oriented, looking for a place and unwilling to rest in a motel room, not even for one night. His old white Buick was packed with his belongings, and he didn't want to take the chance that some juvenile delinquent might smash out the car windows and steal his VCR and TV, not to mention his clothing, toiletries, laptop computer and wig, the lawn chair, a lamp, linens, books, paper, pencils, and bottles of red, white, and blue touch-up paint for his cherished tee ball bat, and a few other vitally important personal possessions, including several old friends.

"It was terrifying, Mother," he retells the tale in an effort to distract her from her drunken nagging. "Mitigating circumstances dictated that I leave our lovely little southern city immediately, although not permanently, certainly not. Now that I have a second home, of course I'll be back and forth between Hollywood and Richmond. You and I have always dreamed about Hollywood, and like settlers on a wagon train, we set out to find our fortunes, didn't we?"

His ploy works. He has redirected her attention along a scenic route that avoids thin soup and not enough sap.

"Only I didn't feel too fortunate at first when I somehow got off North Twenty-fourth Street and ended up in a godforsaken slum called Liberia where there was an ice cream truck."

He talks around the pencil as if it is a bit in his mouth. The pencil substitutes for a smoke, not that tobacco is a health concern or a bad habit, but rather an expense. Pogue indulges in cigars. He indulges in very little else, but he has to have his Indios and Cubitas and A Fuentes, and most of all, Cohibas, the magic contraband of Cuba. He is smitten with Cohibas and he knows how to get them, and it makes all the difference when Cuban smoke touches his stricken lungs. Impurities are what kill the lungs, but the pure tobacco of Cuba is healing.

"Can you possibly believe it? An ice cream truck with its sweet, innocent jingle playing and these little Negro children coming forward with coins to buy treats, and here we are in the middle of a ghetto, a war zone, and the sun has gone down. I'll just bet there are lots of gunshots fired at night in Liberia. Of course I got out of there and miraculously ended up in a better part of town. I got you to Hollywood safe and sound, didn't I, Mother?"

Somehow he found himself on Garfield Street, driving slowly past tiny one-story stucco houses with wrought-iron railings, jalousie windows, carports, and patches of lawn that couldn't possibly accommodate a swimming pool, sweet little abodes probably built in the fifties and sixties that spoke to him because they have survived decades of horrendous hurricanes and jolting demographic changes and relentless increases in property taxes that drive out old-timers and replace them with new-timers who probably don't speak English or try. And yet, the neighborhood has survived. And then, just as he was thinking all this, the apartment complex filled his front windshield like a vision.

The building has a sign posted out front that reads GARFIELD COURT and lists the telephone number, and Pogue responded to the vision by pulling into the parking lot and writing down the number, then he went to a gas station and used the pay phone. Yes, there was one vacancy, and within the hour he had his first and hopefully only encounter with Benjamin P. Shupe, the landlord.

Can't do it, can't do it. Shupe wouldn't stop saying that as he sat across the desk from Pogue downstairs in the office, which was warm and stuffy and poisoned by the offensive scent of Shupe's overpowering cologne. If you want air conditioning, you gotta buy your own window unit. That's up to you. But this is the primo time of year, what they call the season. Who needs air conditioning?

Benjamin P. Shupe brandished white dentures that reminded Pogue of bathroom tiles. The gold-encrusted slum sovereign tap-

tap-tapped the desktop with a fat index finger and flashed a diamond cluster ring. And you're lucky. Everybody wants to be here this time a year. I got ten people waiting in line to take this apartment. Shupe the slum king gestured in a way that was to his gold Rolex watch's best advantage, unaware that Pogue's dark tinted glasses were nonprescription and his shaggy long black curly hair was a wig. Two days from now, it will be twenty people. In fact, I really shouldn't let you have this apartment at this price.

Pogue paid cash. No deposits or other sorts of security were required, no questions or proof of identification were requested or desired. In three weeks, he has to pay cash again for the month of January should he decide to maintain his second home during Hollywood's primo season. But it is a bit early for him to know what he'll do come the New Year.

"Work to do, work to do," he mumbles, thumbing through the magazine for funeral directors that falls open to a collection of urns and keepsakes, and he rests the magazine on his thighs and studies colorful pictures he knows by heart. His favorite urn is still the pewter box shaped like a stack of fine books with a pewter quill on top, and he fantasizes that the books are old volumes by Edgar Allan Poe, for whom he was named, and he wonders how many hundreds of dollars that elegant pewter box would cost were he of a mind to call the toll-free number.

"I should just call it and place the order," he says playfully. "I should just do it, shouldn't I, Mother?" He teases her as if he has a phone and can call right this minute. "Oh, you'd like it, would you?" He touches the picture of the urn. "You'd like Edgar Allan's urn, would you? Well, tell you what, not until there's something to celebrate, and right now my work isn't going as planned, Mother. Oh yes, you heard me. A little setback, I'm afraid."

Thin soup, that's what you are.

"No, Mother Dear. It's not about thin soup." He shakes his head, flipping through the magazine. "Now let's not start that again. We're in Hollywood. Isn't it pleasant?"

He thinks of the salmon-colored stucco mansion on the water not too far north of here and is overwhelmed by a confusion of emotions. He found the mansion as planned. He was inside the mansion as planned. And everything went wrong and now there is nothing to celebrate.

"Faulty thinking, faulty thinking." He flicks his forehead with two fingers, the way his mother used to flick him. "It wasn't supposed to happen like that. What to do, what to do. The little fish that got away." He swims his fingers through the air. "Leaving the big fish." He swims both arms through the air. "The little fish went some-where, I don't know where, but I don't care, no I do not. Because the Big Fish is still there, and I ran off the little fish and the Big Fish can't be happy about that. Can not. Soon there will be something to celebrate."

Got away? How stupid was that? You didn't catch the little fish and think you'll catch the big one? You're such thin soup. How can you be my son?

"Don't talk that way, Mother. It's so impolite," he says with his head bent over the magazine for funeral directors.

She gives him a stare that could nail a sign to a tree, and his fa-ther had a label for her infamous stare. The hairy eyeball, that was what he called it. Edgar Allan Pogue has never figured out why a stare as scary as his mother's is called a hairy eyeball. Eyeballs do not have hair. He has never seen or heard of one that does, and he would know. There isn't much he doesn't know. He drops the magazine to the floor and gets up from the yellow and white lawn chair and fetches his tee ball bat from the corner where he keeps it propped. Closed venetian blinds blot out sunlight from the living room's one window, casting him into a comfortable gloom barely pushed back by a lonely lamp on the floor.

"Let's see. What should we do today?" he continues, mumbling around the pencil, talking out loud to a cookie tin beneath the lawn chair and gripping the bat, checking its red, white, and blue stars and stripes that he has touched up, let's see, exactly one hundred and eleven times. He lovingly polishes the bat with a white handkerchief, and rubs his hands with the handkerchief, rubs and rubs them. "We should do something special today. I believe an outing is in order."

Drifting to a wall, he removes the pencil from his mouth and holds it in one hand, the bat in the other, cocking his head, squinting at the early stages of a large sketch on the dingy, beige-painted sheetrock. Gently, he touches the blunt lead tip to a large staring eye and thickens the lashes. The pencil is wet and pitted between the tips of his index finger and thumb as he draws.

"There." He steps back, cocking his head again, admiring the big, staring eye and the curve of a cheek, the tee ball bat twitching in his other hand.

"Did I happen to mention how especially pretty you look today? Such a nice color you'll soon have in your cheeks, very flushed and rosy, as if you've been out in the sun."

He tucks the pencil behind an ear and holds his hand in front of his face, splaying his fingers, tilting and turning, looking at every joint, crease, scar, and line, and at the delicate ridges in his small, rounded nails. He massages the air, watching fine muscles roll as he imagines rubbing cold skin, working cold, sluggish blood out of subcutaneous tissue, kneading flesh as he flushes out death and pumps in a nice rosy glow. The bat twitches in his other hand and he imagines swinging the bat. He misses rubbing chalky dust in his palms and swinging the bat, and he twitches with a desire to smash the bat through the eye on the wall, but he doesn't, he can't, he mustn't, and he walks around, his heart flying inside his chest, and he is frustrated. So frustrated by the mess.

The apartment is bare but a mess, the countertop in the kitchenette scattered with paper napkins and plastic plates and utensils, and canned foods and bags of macaroni and pasta that Pogue hasn't bothered to store inside the kitchenette's one cupboard. A pot and a frying pan soak in a sink full of cold, greasy water. Strewn about on the stained blue carpet are duffel bags, clothing and books, pencils, and cheap white paper. Pogue's living quarters are beginning to take on the stale aroma of his cooking and cigars, and his own musky, sweaty scent. It is very warm in here and he is naked.

"I believe we should check on Mrs. Arnette. She's not been well, after all," he says to his mother without looking at her. "Would you like to have a visitor today? I suppose I should ask you that first. But it might make both of us feel better. I'm a bit out of sorts, I must confess." He thinks of the little fish that got away and he looks around at the mess. "A visit might be just the thing, what do you think?"

That would be nice.

"Oh, it would, would it?" His baritone voice rises and falls, as if he is addressing a child or a pet. "You would like to have a visitor? Well, then! How splendid."

His bare feet pad across the carpet and he squats by a cardboard box filled with videotapes and cigar boxes and envelopes of photographs, all of them labeled in his own small, neat handwriting. Near the bottom of the box, he finds Mrs. Arnette's cigar box and the envelope of Polaroid photographs.

"Mother, Mrs. Arnette is here to see you," he says with a contented sigh as he opens the cigar box and sets it on the lawn chair. He looks through the photographs and picks out his favorite. "You remember her, don't you? You've met before. A true-blue old woman. See her hair? It really is blue."

Why, it sure enough is.

"Whyyyit-shorrre-nuffffis," he echoes his mother's deep drawl and the slow, thick way she swims through her words when she's in the vodka bottle, way deep inside the vodka bottle.

"Do you like her new box?" he asks, dipping his finger inside the cigar box and blowing a puff of white dust into the air. "Now don't be jealous, but she's lost weight since you saw her last. I wonder what her secret is," he teases, and he dips in his finger again and blows more white dust into the air for his enormously fat mother's benefit, to make his disgustingly fat mother jealous, and he wipes his hands on the white handkerchief. "I think our dear friend Mrs. Arnette looks wonderful, divine really."

He peers closely at the photograph of Mrs. Arnette, her hair a blue-tinted aura around her pink dead face. The only reason he knows her mouth is sutured shut is because he remembers doing it. Otherwise, his expert surgery is impossible to discern, and the uninitiated would never detect that the round contour of her eyes is due to the caps beneath the lids, and he remembers gently setting the caps in place over the sunken eyeballs and overlapping the lids and sticking them together with dabs of Vaseline.

"Now be sweet and ask Mrs. Arnette how she's feeling," he says to the cookie tin beneath the lawn chair. "She had cancer. So many of them did."

3.

|||DR. JOEL MARCUS gives her a stiff smile, and she shakes his dry, small-boned hand. She feels she might despise him given a chance, but other than that premonition, which she pushes down into a dark part of her heart, she feels nothing.

About four months ago, she found out about him the same way she has found out about most things that have to do with her past life in Virginia. It was an accident, a coincidence. She happened to be on a plane reading *USA Today,* and happened to notice a news brief about Virginia that read, "Governor appoints new chief medical examiner after long search . . ." Finally, after years of no chief or acting chiefs, Virginia got a new chief. Scarpetta's opinion and guidance were not requested during the endless ordeal of a search. Her endorsement was not necessary when Dr. Marcus became a candidate for her former position.

Had she been asked, she would have confessed that she had never heard of him. This would have been followed by her diplomatic suggestion that she must have run into him at a national meeting or two and just didn't recall his name. Certainly he is a forensic pathologist of note, she would have offered, otherwise he would not have been recruited to head the most prominent statewide medical examiner system in the United States.

But as she shakes Dr. Marcus's hand and looks into his small cold eyes, she realizes he is a complete stranger. Clearly, he has been on no committees of significance, nor has he lectured at any pathology or medico-legal or forensic science meetings she has attended, or she would remember him. She may forget names, but rarely a face.

"Kay, at last we meet," he says, offending her again, only now it is worse because he is offending her in person.

What her intuition was reluctant to pick up over the phone is unavoidable now that she is in his presence inside the lobby of the building called Biotech II where she last worked as chief. Dr. Marcus is a small thin man with a small thin face and a small thin stripe of dirty gray hair on the back of his small head, as if nature has been trifling with him. He wears an outdated narrow tie, shapeless gray trousers and loafers. A sleeveless undershirt is visible beneath a cheap white dress shirt that sags around his thin neck, the inside of the collar dingy and rough with cotton picks.

"Let's go in," he says. "I'm afraid we've got a full house this morning."

She is about to inform him that she isn't alone when Marino emerges from the men's room, hitching up his black cargo pants, the LAPD cap pulled low over his eyes. Scarpetta is polite but all business as she makes introductions, explaining Marino, as much as he can be explained.

"He used to be with the Richmond Police Department and is a very experienced investigator," she says as Dr. Marcus's face hardens.

"You didn't mention you were bringing anyone," he says curtly in her former spacious lobby of granite and glass blocks, where she has signed in, where she has stood for twenty minutes, feeling as conspicuous as a statue in a rotunda, while she waited for Dr. Marcus, or someone, to come get her. "I thought I made it clear this is a very sensitive situation."

"Hey, not to worry. I'm a real sensitive guy," Marino says loudly.

Dr. Marcus doesn't seem to hear him, but he bristles. Scarpetta can almost hear his anger displace air.

"My senior superlative in high school was Most Likely to Be Sensitive," Marino adds loudly. "Yo, Bruce!" he yells to a uniformed guard who is at least thirty feet away, having just stepped out of the evidence room and into the lobby. "What'cha know, man? Still bowling on that sorry team The Pin Heads?"

"I didn't mention it?" Scarpetta is saying. "I apologize." She didn't mention it, and she isn't sorry. When she is called into a case, she'll bring who and whatever she wants, and she can't forgive Dr. Marcus for calling her Kay.

Bruce the guard looks puzzled, then amazed. "Marino! Holy smoke, that you? Talk about a ghost from the past."

"No, you didn't," Dr. Marcus reiterates to Scarpetta, momentarily off balance, his confusion palpable, like the flapping of startled birds.

"The one and only, and I ain't no ghost," Marino says as obnoxiously as possible.

"I'm not sure I can allow it. This hasn't been cleared," Dr. Marcus says, flustered and inadvertently exposing the ugly fact that someone he answers to not only knows Scarpetta is here but may indeed be the reason she is here.

"How long you in town?" The yelling between old friends goes on.

Scarpetta's inner voice warned her and she didn't listen. She is walking into something.

"Long as it takes, man."

This was a mistake, a bad one, she thinks. I should have gone to Aspen.

"When you get a minute, stop by."

"You got it, buddy."

"That's enough, please," Dr. Marcus snaps. "This is not a beer hall."

He wears a master key to the kingdom on a lanyard around his neck, and he stoops to hold the magnetic card close to an infrared scanner next to an opaque glass door. On the other side is the chief medical examiner's wing. Scarpetta's mouth is dry. She is sweating under the arms and her stomach feels hollow as she walks into the chief medical examiner's section of the handsome building she helped design and find funding for and moved into before she was fired. The dark blue couch and matching chair, the wooden coffee table, and the painting of a farm scene hanging on the wall are the same. The reception area hasn't changed, except there used to be two corn plants and several hibiscus. She was enthusiastic about her plants, watering them herself, picking off the dead leaves, rearranging them as the light changed with the seasons.

"I'm afraid you can't bring a guest," Dr. Marcus makes a decision as they pause before another locked door, this one leading into administrative offices and the morgue, the inner sanctum that once was hers rightfully and completely.

His magnetic card does its magic again and the lock clicks free. He goes first, walking fast, his small wire-rimmed glasses catching fluorescent light. "I got caught in traffic, so I'm running late, and we have a full house. Eight cases," he continues, directing his comments to her as if Marino doesn't exist. "I have to go straight into staff meeting. Probably the best thing is for you, Kay, to get coffee. I may be a while. Julie?" he calls out to a clerk who is invisible inside a cubicle, her fingers tapping like castanets on a computer keyboard. "If you could show our guest where to get coffee." This to Scarpetta,

"If you'll just make yourself comfortable in the library. I'll get to you as soon as I can."

At the very least, as a matter of professional courtesy, a visiting forensic pathologist would be welcomed at staff meeting and in the morgue, especially if she is providing expertise pro bono to the medical examiner's office that she once headed. Dr. Marcus could not have insulted Scarpetta more had he asked her to drop off his dry cleaning or wait in the parking lot.

"I'm afraid your guest really can't be in here." Dr. Marcus makes that clear once again as he looks around impatiently. "Julie, can you show this gentleman back out to the lobby?"

"He's not my guest and he's not waiting in the lobby," Scarpetta says quietly.

"I beg your pardon?" Dr. Marcus's small thin face looks at her.

"We're together," she says.

"Perhaps you don't understand the situation," Dr. Marcus replies in a tight voice.

"Perhaps I don't. Let's talk." It is not a request.

He almost flinches, his reluctance is so acute. "Very well," he acquiesces. "We'll duck into the library for a minute."

"Will you excuse us?" She smiles at Marino.

"No problem." He walks inside Julie's cubicle and picks up a stack of autopsy photographs and starts going through them like playing cards. He snaps one out between forefinger and thumb like a blackjack dealer. "Know why drug dealers got less body fat than let's say you and me?" He drops the photograph on her keyboard.

Julie, who can't be more than twenty-five and is attractive but a bit plump, stares at a photograph of a muscular young black male, as naked as the day he was born. He is on top of an autopsy table, chest cut open wide, hollowed out, organs gone except for one very conspicuously large organ, probably his most vital organ, at least to him, at least when he was alive enough to care about it. "What?" Julie asks. "You're kidding me, right?"

"I'm serious as a heart attack." Marino pulls up a chair and sits next to her, very close. "See, darling, body fat directly correlates to the weight of the brain. Witness you and me. Always a struggle, ain't it?"

"No kidding. You really think smarter people get fat?"

"A fact of life. People like you and me gotta work extra hard."

"Don't tell me you're on one of those eat-all-you-want-except-white-stuff diets."

"You got it, babe. Nothing white for me except women. Now me? If I was a drug dealer, I wouldn't give a shit. Eat whatever the hell I wanted. Twinkies, Moon Pies, white bread and jelly. But that's because I wouldn't have a brain, right? See, all these dead drug dealers are dead because they're stupid, and that's why they ain't got body fat and can eat all the white shit they want."

Their voices and laughter fade as Scarpetta follows a corridor so familiar she remembers the brush of the gray carpet beneath her shoes, the exact feel of the firm low-pile carpet she picked out when she designed her part of the building.

"He really is most inappropriate," Dr. Marcus is saying. "One thing I do require in this place is proper decorum."

Walls are scuffed, and the Norman Rockwell prints she bought and framed herself are cockeyed and two are missing. She stares inside the open doorways of offices they pass, noticing sloppy mounds of paperwork and microscopic slide folders and compound microscopes perched like big tired gray birds on overwhelmed desks. Every sight and sound reaches out to her like needy hands, and deep down she feels what has been lost and it hurts much more than she ever thought it could.

"Now I'm making the connection, regrettably. The infamous

Peter Marano. Yes indeed. Quite a reputation that man has," Dr. Marcus says.

"Marino," she corrects him.

A right turn and they do not pause at the coffee station but Dr. Marcus opens a solid wooden door that leads into the library, and she is greeted by medical books abandoned on long tables and other reference books tilted and upended on shelves like drunks. The huge horseshoe-shaped table is a landfill of journals, scraps of paper, dirty coffee cups, even a Krispy Kreme doughnut box. Her heart pounds as she looks around. She designed this generous space and was proud of the way she budgeted her funds because medical and scientific textbooks and a library to hold them are exorbitantly expensive and beyond what the state considers necessary for an office whose patients are dead. Her attention hovers over sets of Greenfield's *Neuropathology* and law reviews that she donated from her own collection. The volumes are out of order. One of them is upside down. Her anger spikes.

She fastens her eyes on Dr. Marcus and says, "I think we'd better lay down some ground rules."

"Goodness, Kay. Ground rules?" he asks with a puzzled frown that is feigned and annoying.

She can't believe his blatant condescension. He reminds her of a defense attorney, not a good one, who hoodwinks the courtroom by stipulating away the seventeen years she spent in postgraduate education and reduces her on the witness stand to Ma'am or Mrs. or Ms. or, worst of all, Kay.

"I'm sensing resistance to my being here . . ." she starts to say.

"Resistance? I'm afraid I don't understand."

"I think you do . . ."

"Let's don't make assumptions."

"Please don't interrupt me, Dr. Marcus. I don't have to be here."
She takes in trashed tables and unloved books and wonders if he is

this contemptuous with his own belongings. "What in God's name has happened to this place?" she asks.

He pauses as if it requires a moment of divining to understand what she means. Then he comments blandly, "Today's medical students. No doubt they were never taught to pick up after themselves."

"In five years they've changed that much," she says, dryly.

"Perhaps you're misinterpreting my mood this morning," he replies in the same coaxing tone that he used with her over the phone yesterday. "Granted, I have a lot on my mind, but I'm quite pleased you're here."

"You seem anything but pleased." She keeps her eyes steadily on him while he stares past her. "Let's start with this. I didn't call you. You called me. Why?" I should have asked you yesterday, she thinks. I should have asked you then.

"I thought I'd made myself clear, Kay. You're a very respected forensic pathologist, a well-known consultant." It sounds like an ingenuous endorsement for someone he secretly can't stand.

"We don't know each other. We've never even met. I'm having a hard time believing you called me because I'm respected or well known." Her arms are folded and she is glad she wore a serious dark suit. "I don't play games, Dr. Marcus."

"I certainly don't have time for games." Any attempt at cordiality fades from his face and pettiness begins to glint like the sharp edge of a blade.

"Did someone suggest me? Were you told to call me?" She is certain she detects the stench of politics.

He glances toward the door in a not so subtle reminder that he is a busy, important man with eight cases and a staff meeting to run. Or perhaps he is worrying that someone is eavesdropping. "This is not productive," he says. "I think it's best we terminate this discussion."

"Fine." She picks up her briefcase. "The last thing I want is to be a pawn in some agenda. Or shut off in a room, drinking coffee half the day. I can't help an office that isn't open to me, and my number-one ground rule, Dr. Marcus, is that an office requesting my assistance must be open to me."

"All right. If you want candor, indeed you shall have it." His imperiousness fails to hide his fear. He doesn't want her to leave. He sincerely doesn't. "Frankly, bringing you here wasn't my idea. Frankly, the health commissioner wanted an outside opinion and somehow came up with you," he explains as if her name were drawn from a hat.

"He should have called me himself," she replies. "That would have been more honest."

"I told him I would do it. Frankly, I didn't want to put you on the spot," he explains, and the more he says "frankly," the less she believes a word he says. "What happened is this. When Dr. Fielding couldn't determine a cause or manner of death, the girl's father, Gilly Paulsson's father, called the commissioner."

The mention of Dr. Fielding's name stings her. She didn't know whether he was still here and she hasn't asked.

"And as I said, the commissioner called me. He said he wanted a full-court press. Those were his words."

The father must have clout, she thinks. Phone calls from upset families are not unusual, but rarely do they result in a high-ranking government official's demanding an outside expert.

"Kay, I can understand how uncomfortable this must be for you," Dr. Marcus says. "I wouldn't relish being in your position."

"And what is my position as you see it, Dr. Marcus?"

"I believe Dickens wrote a story about that called *A Christmas Carol*. I'm sure you're familiar with the Ghost of Christmas Past?" He smiles his trifling smile, and perhaps he doesn't realize he is plagiarizing Bruce, the guard who called Marino a ghost from the past. "Going back is never easy. You have guts, I'll give you that. I don't believe I would have been so generous, not if I perceived that my former office had been somewhat uncharitable to me, and I can well understand your feeling that way."

"This isn't about me," she replies. "It's about a dead fourteen-year-old girl. It's about your office—an office that, yes, I'm quite familiar with, but . . ."

He interrupts her, "That's very philosophical of . . ."

"Let me state the obvious," she cuts him off. "When children die, it's federal law that their fatalities are thoroughly investigated and reviewed, not only to determine cause and manner of death, but whether the tragedy might be part of a pattern. If it turns out that Gilly Paulsson was murdered, then every molecule of your office is going to be scrutinized and publicly judged, and I would appreciate it if you wouldn't call me Kay in front of your staff and colleagues. Actually, I would prefer that you didn't call me by my first name at all."

"I suppose part of the commissioner's motivation is preventive damage control," Dr. Marcus replies as if she said nothing about his calling her Kay.

"I didn't agree to participate in some media relations scheme," she tells him. "When you called yesterday, I agreed to do what I could to help you figure out what happened to Gilly Paulsson. And I can't do that if you aren't completely open with me and whoever I bring in to assist me, which in this case is Pete Marino."

"Frankly, it didn't occur to me that you would have a strong desire to attend staff meeting." He glances at his watch again, an old watch with a narrow leather wristband. "But as you wish. We have no secrets in this place. Later, I'll go over the Paulsson case with you. You can re-autopsy her if you want."

He holds open the library door. Scarpetta stares at him in disbelief.

"She died two weeks ago and her body hasn't been released to her family yet?" she asks.

"They're so distraught, they haven't made arrangements to claim her, allegedly," he replies. "I suppose they're hoping we'll pay for the burial."

4.

||| IN THE CONFERENCE ROOM of the OCME, Scarpetta rolls out a chair at the foot of the table, an outer reach of her former empire that she never visited when she was here. Not once did she sit at the foot of the conference table in the years she ran this office, not even if it was to have a casual conversation over a bagged lunch.

It registers somewhere in her disturbed thoughts that she is being *contraire* by choosing a chair at the foot of the long dark polished table when there are two other empty seats midway. Marino finds a chair against the wall and sets it next to hers, so he is neither at the foot of the table nor against the wall but somewhere in between, a big grumpy lump in black cargo pants and an LAPD baseball cap.

He leans close to her and whispers, "Staff hates his guts."

She doesn't respond and concludes that his source is Julie the clerk. Then he jots something on a notepad and shoves it toward her. "FBI involved," she reads.

Marino must have made phone calls while Scarpetta was with Dr. Marcus in the library. She is baffled. Gilly Paulsson's death is not federal jurisdiction. At the moment it's not even a crime, because there is no cause or manner of death, only suspicion and sticky politics. She subtly pushes the notepad back in Marino's direction and senses Dr. Marcus is watching them. For an instant, she is in grammar school, passing notes and about to be scorched by one of the nuns. Marino has the nerve to slip out a cigarette and begin tapping it on top of his notepad.

"This is a nonsmoking building, I'm afraid," Dr. Marcus's authoritative voice punctures the silence.

"And it oughta be," Marino says. "Secondary smoke will kill ya." He taps the filtered end of a Marlboro on top of the notepad that bears his secret message about the FBI. "I'm happy to see the Guts Man is still around," he adds, referring to the male anatomical model on a stand behind Dr. Marcus, who sits at the head of the table. "Now that's a thousand-yard stare if I ever saw one," Marino says of the Guts Man, whose removable plastic organs are present and primly in place, and Scarpetta wonders if he has been used for teaching or explaining injuries to families and attorneys since she was here. Probably not, she decides. Otherwise Guts Man would be missing organs.

She does not know anyone on Dr. Marcus's staff except Assistant Chief Jack Fielding, who so far has avoided eye contact with her and has developed a skin disorder since she saw him last. Five years have passed, she thinks, and she can scarcely believe what has become of her vain bodybuilding former forensic pathology partner. Fielding was never supremely useful in administrative matters or necessarily respected for having a searing medical mind, but he was loyal, respectful, and caring during the decade he worked for her. He never tried to undermine her or take her place, and he never came to her defense, either, when detractors far bolder than he decided to banish her and succeeded. Fielding has lost most of his hair and his once attractive face is puffy and blotchy, his eyes runny. He sniffs a lot. He would never touch drugs, and she is sure of that, but he looks like a drinker.

"Dr. Fielding," she says, staring at him. "Allergies? You didn't used to have them. Perhaps you have a cold," she suggests, although she seriously doubts he has a cold or the flu or any other contagious disease.

Possibly, he is hungover. Probably, he is suffering from a histamine reaction to something or perhaps to everything. Scarpetta detects the raw edge of a rash peeking out from the v-neck collar of his surgical scrubs, and she follows the white sleeves of his unbuttoned lab coat, over the contours of his arms, to his raw, scaly hands. Fielding has lost considerable muscle mass. He is almost skinny and is suffering from an allergy or allergies. Dependent personality types are thought to be more susceptible to allergies, diseases, and dermatological complaints, and Fielding isn't thriving. Maybe he shouldn't thrive, and for him to do well without her would seem to confirm that the Commonwealth of Virginia and humankind in general are better off since she was fired and publicly degraded half a decade ago. The small nasty beast inside her that finds relief in Fielding's misery instantly crawls back into its dark place, and she is stung by upset and concern. She gives Fielding her eyes again. He won't complete the connection.

"I hope we'll have a chance to catch up before I leave," she says to him from her green upholstered chair at the foot of the table, as if nobody else is in the room, just Fielding and her, the way it used to be when she was chief and so well respected that now and then naive medical students and rookie cops asked for her autograph.

She feels Dr. Marcus watching her again, his stare as palpable as thumbtacks driven into her skin. He wears neither lab coat nor any other medical mantle, and she isn't surprised. Like most passionless chiefs who should have left the profession years ago and probably never loved it, he's not the sort to perform autopsies unless there is no one else to do them.

"Let's get started," he announces. "I'm afraid we have a full house this morning, and we have guests. Dr. Scarpetta. And her friend Captain Marino . . . Or is it Lieutenant or Detective? Are you with Los Angeles now?"

"Depends on what's going on," Marino says, his eyes shadowed by the brim of his baseball cap as he fiddles with the unlit cigarette.

"And where are you working now?" Dr. Marcus reminds him that he has not fully explained himself. "I'm sorry. I don't recall Dr. Scarpetta mentioning she was bringing you." He has to remind Scarpetta again, this time before an audience.

He is going to take swipes at her in front of everyone. She can see it coming. He will make her pay for confronting him inside his slovenly library, and it occurs to her that Marino made phone calls. Someone he talked to might have alerted Dr. Marcus.

"Oh, of course." He suddenly remembers. "She did mention you work together, I believe?"

"Yes," Scarpetta confirms from her lowly spot at the foot of the table.

"So we're going to get through the cases quickly," he informs Scarpetta. "Once again, if you and, uh, I guess I'll just call you Mr. Marino, if the two of you want to get coffee? Or smoke as long as it's outside. You're welcome to sit through our staff meeting but you certainly don't have to."

His words are for the benefit of those not privy to what has already transpired in less than one rude hour, and she detects a warning in his tone. She wanted to intrude and now she may get an exposure she will find decidedly unpleasant. Dr. Marcus is a politician and not a good one. Perhaps when he was appointed, those in power had deemed him malleable and harmless, the antithesis of what they thought of her, and maybe they were wrong.

He turns to the woman directly on his right, a big, horsey woman with a horsey face and closely shorn gray hair. She must be the administrator, and he nods at her to proceed.

"Okay," says the administrator, and everyone looks at the yellow photocopies of today's turndowns, views, and autopsies. "Dr. Ramie, you were on call last night?" she asks.

"I sure was. 'Tis the season," Dr. Ramie replies.

No one laughs. A pall hangs over the conference room. It has nothing to do with the patients down the hall who await the last and most invasive physical examination they'll ever have with any doctor on earth.

"We have Sissy Shirley, ninety-two-year-old black female from Hanover County, history of heart disease, found dead in bed," Dr. Ramie says, looking at her notes. "She was a resident of an assisted living facility and she's a view. In fact, I already viewed her. Then we have Benjamin Franklin. That really is his name. Eighty-nine-year-old black male, also found dead in bed, history of heart disease and nerve failure . . ."

"What?" Dr. Marcus interrupts. "What the hell is nerve failure?"

Several people laugh and Dr. Ramie's face heats up. She is an overweight, homely young woman and her face is glowing like a halogen heater on high.

"I don't believe nerve failure is a legitimate cause of death," Dr. Marcus plays off his deputy chief's acute embarrassment like an actor playing off his captive audience. "Please don't tell me we've brought some poor soul into our clinic because he allegedly died of nerve failure."

His attempt at humor is not meant kindly. Clinics are for the living and poor souls are people in hard times, not victims of violence or random, senseless death. In three words, he has managed to completely deny and mock the reality of people down the hall who are pitifully cold and stiff and zipped inside vinyl and fake fur funeral home pouches, or naked on hard steel gurneys or on hard steel tables, ready for the scalpel and Stryker saw.

"I'm sorry," Dr. Ramie says with glowing cheeks. "I misread my notes. Renal failure is what I have here. Even I can't read my writing anymore."

"So old Ben Franklin," Marino starts in with a serious face as he plays with the cigarette, "he didn't die of nerve failure after all? Like maybe when he was out there tying a key to his kite string? Anybody on that list of yours happen to die of lead poisoning? Or are we still calling it gunshot wounds?"

Dr. Marcus's stare is flat and cold.

Dr. Ramie goes on in a monotone, "Mr. Franklin also is a view. I did view him already. We have Finky . . . uh, Finder . . ."

"Not Finky, oh Lordy," Marino keeps up the straight-man charade in that huge voice of his. "You can't find her? I hate it when Finky does that, damn her."

"Is that the proper name?" Dr. Marcus's voice has the thin ring of a metal triangle, several octaves higher than Marino's voice.

Dr. Ramie's face is so red that Scarpetta worries the tortured woman is going to burst into tears and flee from the room. "The name I was given is what I just stated," Dr. Ramie woodenly replies. "Twenty-two-year-old black female, dead on the toilet, needle still in her arm. Possible heroin O.D. That's the second in four days in Spotsylvania. This was just handed to me." She fumbles with a call sheet. "Right before staff meeting we got a call about a forty-two-year-old white male named Theodore Whitby. Injured while working on a tractor."

Dr. Marcus blinks behind his small wire-rimmed glasses. Faces blank out. Don't do it, Scarpetta silently says to Marino. But he does.

"Injured?" he asks. "He's still alive?"

"Actually," Dr. Ramie stammers. "I didn't take this call. Not personally. Dr. Fielding . . ."

"No, I didn't," Fielding interrupts like a gun hammer clicking back.

"You didn't? Oh. Dr. Martin did. This is his note," Dr. Ramie goes on, her hot and humiliated head bent low over the call sheet. "No one seems to be real clear on what happened, but he was on or near the tractor one minute and then his coworkers suddenly saw him badly injured in the dirt. Around half past eight this morning, not even an hour ago. So, somehow, he ran over himself, fell off or something, you know, and ran over himself. Was dead when the squad got there."

"Oh. So he killed himself. A suicide," Marino decides, slowly twirling the cigarette.

"Well, it's an irony that this occurred at the old building, the one they're tearing down at Nine North Fourteenth Street," Dr. Ramie adds tersely.

This catches Marino. He drops his not-so-funny act, his silent reaction nudging Scarpetta while she remembers the man in olive-green pants and a dark jacket standing in front of the tractor's back tire on the pavement near the bay door. He was alive then. Now he's dead. He should not have been standing in front of the tire, doing whatever he was doing to the engine. She thought that at the time, and now he's dead.

"He's a post," Dr. Ramie says, her composure and authority somewhat restored.

Scarpetta remembers turning the corner as she drove around her old building, and the man and his tractor vanished from sight. He must have gotten his tractor started within minutes of her seeing him, and then he died.

"Dr. Fielding, I suggest you do the tractor death," Dr. Marcus says. "Make sure he didn't have a heart attack or some other underlying problem before he was run over. The inventory of his injuries is going to be extensive and time-consuming. I don't need to remind you of how thorough we need to be in cases like this. Somewhat ironical, in light of our guest." He looks at Scarpetta. "A bit before my time, but I believe Nine North Fourteenth Street was your old building."

"It was," says she, the ghost from the past as she recalls Mr. Whitby from a distance in black and olive green, now a ghost too. "I started out in that building. A bit before your time," she repeats. "Then I moved to this one." She reminds him that she worked in this building too, and then feels slightly foolish for reminding him of a fact that is indisputable.

Dr. Ramie continues going through the cases: a prison death that isn't suspicious, but by law, all prison deaths are medical examiner cases; a man found dead in a parking lot, possibly hypothermia; a woman who was a known diabetic died suddenly while climbing out of her car; an unexpected infant death; and a nineteen-year-old found dead in the middle of a street, possibly a drive-by shooting.

"I'm on call for court in Chesterfield," Dr. Ramie concludes. "I'm going to need a ride, my car's in the shop again."

"I'll drop you off," Marino volunteers, winking at her.

Dr. Ramie looks terrified.

Everyone makes moves to get out of their chairs, but Dr. Marcus stops them. "Before you go," he says, "I could use your help and you could probably use a little mental stretching. As you know, the Institute is running another death investigation school, and as usual I've been prevailed upon to lecture about the medical examiner system. I thought I'd try out a few test cases on the group, especially since we are fortunate enough to have an expert in our midst."

The bastard, Scarpetta thinks. So this is what it's going to be like. The hell with their talk in the library. The hell with his making the office open to her.

He pauses, looking around the table. "A twenty-year-old white female," he begins, "seven weeks pregnant. Her boyfriend kicks her in the belly. She calls the police and goes to the hospital. Hours later she passes the fetus and placenta. The police notify me. What do I do?"

No one answers him. It's obvious that they aren't accustomed to his mental stretches and just stare at him.

"Come on, come on," he says with a smile. "Let's say I just got such a phone call, Dr. Ramie."

"Sir?" She turns red again.

"Come, come. Tell me how to handle it, Dr. Ramie."

"Process it like a surgical?" she guesses as if some alien force has just sucked away her long years of medical training, her very intelligence.

"Anybody else?" Dr. Marcus asks. "Dr. Scarpetta?" He says her name slowly, making sure she notices that he didn't call her Kay. "Ever had a case like this?"

"I'm afraid so," she replies.

"Tell us. What's the legal impact?" he asks quite pleasantly.

"Obviously, if you beat up a pregnant woman, it's a crime," she answers. "On the CME-1, I'm going to call the fetal death a homicide."

"Interesting." Dr. Marcus looks around the table as he takes aim at her again. "So your initial report of investigation would say homicide. Perhaps a bit bold of you? Intent is for the police to determine, not us, correct?"

The sniping son of a bitch, she thinks. "Our job as mandated by code is to determine cause and manner of death," she says. "As you may recall, in the late nineties the statute changed after a man shot a woman through the belly and she lived but her unborn child died. In the scenario you've put before us, Dr. Marcus, I suggest you have the fetus brought in. Autopsy it and give it a case number. There's no place on a yellow-bordered death certificate for manner of death, so you include that with cause, an intrauterine fetal demise due to an assault on the mother. Use a yellow-bordered death certificate since the fetus wasn't born alive. Keep a copy with the case file because a year from now that certificate won't exist anymore, after the Bureau of Vital Records compiles its statistics."

"And what do we do with the fetus?" Dr. Marcus asks, not quite so pleasantly.

"Up to the family."

"It's not even ten centimeters," he says, his voice getting tight again. "There's nothing left for the funeral home to bury."

"Then fix it in formalin. Give it to the family, whatever they want."

"And call it a homicide," he says coldly.

"The new statute," she reminds him. "In Virginia, an assault with the intent of killing family members, born or unborn, is a capital crime. Even if you can't prove intent and the charge is malicious wounding of the mother, that carries the same penalty as murder. From there it tracks down through the system as manslaughter and so on. The point is, there doesn't have to be intent. The fetus doesn't even have to be viable. A violent crime has occurred."

"Any debate?" Dr. Marcus asks his staff. "No comments?"

No one responds, not even Fielding.

"Then we'll try another one," Dr. Marcus says with an angry smile.

Go ahead, Scarpetta thinks. Go ahead, you insufferable bastard.

"A young male in a hospice program," Dr. Marcus begins. "He's dying of AIDS. He tells the doctor to pull the plug. If the doctor withdraws life support and the patient dies, is it an ME case or not? Is it a homicide? How about our guest expert again? Did the doctor commit homicide?"

"It's a natural death unless the doctor put a bullet through the patient's head," Scarpetta answers.

"Ah. Then you're an advocate of euthanasia."

"Informed consent is murky." She doesn't answer his ridiculous charge. "The patient is often dealing with depression, and when people are depressed, they can't make informed decisions. This is really a societal question."

"Let me clarify what you're saying," Dr. Marcus replies.

"Please do."

"You have this man in hospice who says, 'I think I'd like to die today.' Should you expect your local doc to do it?"

"The truth is, the patient in hospice already has that capacity. He can decide to die," she replies. "He can have morphine when he wants it for pain, so he asks for more and goes to sleep and dies from an O.D. He can wear a Do Not Resuscitate bracelet and a squad doesn't have to resuscitate him. So he dies. Chances are there will be no consequences to anyone."

"But is it our case?" Dr. Marcus insists, his thin face white with rage as he glares at her.

"People are in hospices because they want pain control and want to die in peace," she says. "People who make informed decisions to wear DNR bracelets basically want the same thing. A morphine O.D., a withdrawal of vital support in a hospice, a person wearing a DNR bracelet isn't resuscitated. These are not our issues. If you get called about a case like that, Dr. Marcus, I hope you turn it down."

"Any comment?" Dr. Marcus asks tersely, shuffling paperwork and ready to leave.

"Yeah," Marino says to him. "You ever thought of writing Q-and-A's for *Jeopardy*?"

5.

| | | BENTON WESLEY paces from window to window inside his three-bedroom town home at the Aspen Club. The signal of his cell phone surges in and out, and Marino's voice is clear, then broken.

"What? I'm sorry, say that again." Benton backs up three steps and stands still.

"I said that's not the half of it. A hell of a lot worse than you thought." Marino's voice comes through intact. "It's like he brought her in to kick the shit out of her in front of an audience. Or try. I emphasize *try.*"

Benton stares out at snow caught in crooks of aspen trees and piled on the stubby needles of black spruce. The morning is sunny and clear for the first time in days, and magpies frolic from branch to branch, landing in a flutter and then flitting off in small white bursts of snow. A part of Benton's mind processes the activity and tries to determine a reason, perhaps a biological cause and effect that might explain the long-tailed birds' gymnastics, as if it matters. His mental probing is as conditioned as the wildlife and as relentless as the gondolas swinging up and down the mountain.

"Try, yes. Try." Benton smiles a little as he imagines it. "But you need to understand he didn't invite her because it was a choice. It was an order. The health commissioner's behind it."

"And you know that how?"

"It took me one phone call after she told me she was going."

"It's too bad about Asp—" Marino's voice fractures.

Benton moves to the next window, flames snapping and wood popping in the fireplace at his back. He continues to stare out the floor-to-ceiling glass, his attention fixing on the stone house across the street as the front door opens. A man and a boy emerge dressed for the weather, their breath streaming out in a frozen vapor.

"By now she's aware of it," Benton says. "Aware she's being used." He knows Scarpetta well enough to make predictions that undoubtedly are true. "I promise she knows the politics or simply that there are politics. Unfortunately, there's more, a lot more. Can you hear me?"

He looks out at the man and the boy shouldering their skis and poles, walking sluggishly in half-buckled ski boots. Benton will not ski or snowshoe today. He doesn't have time.

"Huh." Marino has started saying that a lot of late, and Benton finds it annoying.

"Can you hear me?" Benton asks.

"Yeah, I'm copying now," Marino comes back, and Benton can tell he's moving around, roaming for a better signal. "He's trying to blame everything on her, like he brought her here to do that. I don't know what else to tell you until I get into it more. The kid, I mean."

Benton is aware of Gilly Paulsson. Her mysterious death may not be national news, not yet, but details from Virginia media sources are on the Internet, and Benton has his own ways of accessing information, very confidential information. Gilly Paulsson is being used, because it is not a requirement to be alive if certain people want to use you.

"Did I lose you again? Dammit," Benton says, and communication would be immensely improved if he could use the land line in his own home, but he can't.

"I'm copying you, boss." Marino's voice is suddenly strong. "Why don't you use your land line? That would solve half our problem," he says, as if reading Benton's thoughts.

"Can't."

"You think it's bugged?" Marino isn't joking. "There are ways to detect that. Get Lucy to do it."

"Thanks for the suggestion." Benton doesn't need Lucy's help with countersurveillance, and his concern isn't that his line is bugged.

He follows the progress of the man and the boy as he contemplates Gilly Paulsson. The boy looks about Gilly's age, the age Gilly was when she died. Thirteen, maybe fourteen, only Gilly never got to ski. She never visited Colorado or anywhere else. She was born in Richmond and that's where she died, and during her short life, mostly she suffered. Benton notices that the wind is picking up. Snow blowing off trees fills the woods like smoke.

"This is what I want you to tell her," Benton says, and his emphasis on the word "her" indicates he means Scarpetta. "Her successor, if I must call him that," he says, and he doesn't want to say Dr. Marcus's name either or engage in any specifics, and he can't stomach the thought of anyone, least of all this worm Dr. Joel Marcus, succeeding Scarpetta. "This person is of interest," Benton continues, talking cryptically. "When she gets here," he adds, referring to Scarpetta again, "I'll go over all of it in person with her. But for now, use caution, extreme caution."

"What do you mean, 'when she gets here'? I'm assuming she might be stuck here for a while."

"She needs to call me."

"Extreme caution?" Marino complains. "Shit, you would have to say something like that."

"While she's there, you stay with her."

"Huh."

"Stay with her, am I clear?"

"She won't like it," Marino says.

Benton looks out at the harsh slopes of the snow-laced Rockies, at a beauty shaped by cruel, scouring winds and the brute force of glaciers. Aspens and evergreens are a stubble on the faces of mountains that surround this old mining town like a bowl, and to the east, beyond a ridge, a distant gray shroud of clouds is slowly spreading across the intense blue sky. Later today, it will snow again.

"No, she never does," Benton says.

"She said you got a case."

"Yes." Benton can't discuss it.

"Well, it's too bad, being in Aspen and all, and you got a case and now she does. So you'll just stay there and work your case, I guess."

"For now I will," Benton says.

"Must be something serious if you're on it during your vacation in Aspen," Marino fishes.

"I can't get into it."

"Huh. These damn phones," Marino says. "Lucy ought to invent something that can't be tapped into or picked up on a scanner. She could make a fortune."

"I believe she's already made a fortune. Maybe several fortunes."

"No kidding."

"Take care," Benton says. "If I don't talk to you in the next few days, take care of her. Watch your back and hers, I mean it."

"Tell me something I don't already do," Marino says. "Don't hurt yourself out there playing in the snow."

Benton ends the call and returns to a couch that faces the windows near the fire. On the wormy chestnut coffee table is a legal pad filled with his almost indecipherable scrawl and near that is a Glock .40-caliber pistol. Slipping a pair of reading glasses out of the breast pocket of his denim shirt, he settles against the armrest and begins flipping through the legal pad. Each lined page is numbered and in the upper right-hand corner is a date. Benton rubs his angular jaw, remembering that he hasn't shaved in two days, and his rough, graying beard reminds him of the bristly trees on the mountains. He circles the words "shared paranoia" and tilts his head up as he peers through the reading glasses on the tip of his straight, sharp nose.

In the margin he scribbles, "Will seem to work when fills in gaps. Serious gaps. Can't last. L is real victim, not H. H is narcissist," and he underlines "narcissist" three times. He jots "histrionic" and underlines it twice, and he turns to a different page, this one with the heading "Post Offense Behavior," and he listens for the sound of running water, puzzled that he hasn't heard it yet. "Critical mass. Will reach no later than Xmas. Tension unbearable. Will kill by Xmas if not sooner," he writes, quietly looking up as he senses her before he hears her.

"Who was that?" asks Henri, which is short for Henrietta. She stands on the stairway landing, her delicate hand resting on the railing. Henri Walden stares across the living room at him.

"Good morning," Benton says. "You usually take a shower. There's coffee."

Henri pulls a plain red flannel robe more tightly around her thin body, her green eyes sleepy and reticent as she takes in Benton, studying him as if a preexisting argument or encounter stands between them. She is twenty-eight and attractive in an off-tilt way. Her features aren't perfect, because her nose is strong and, according to her own warped beliefs, too big. Her teeth aren't perfect either, but right now nothing would convince her that she has a beautiful smile, that she is disturbingly alluring even when she doesn't try to be. Benton hasn't tried to convince her and won't. It is too dangerous.

"I heard you talking to someone," she says. "Was it Lucy?"

"No," he replies.

"Oh," she says and disappointment tugs her lips and anger flashes in her eyes. "Oh. Well. Who was it then?"

"It was a private conversation, Henri." He takes off his reading glasses. "We've talked a lot about boundaries. We've talked about them every day, haven't we?"

"I know," she says from the landing, her hand on the railing. "If it wasn't Lucy, who was it? Was it her aunt? She talks too much about her aunt."

"Her aunt doesn't know you're here, Henri," Benton says very patiently. "Only Lucy and Rudy know you're here."

"I know about you and her aunt."

"Only Lucy and Rudy know you're here," he repeats.

"It was Rudy then. What did he want? I always knew he liked me." She smiles and the look on her face is peculiar and unsettling. "Rudy is gorgeous. I should have gotten with him. I could have. When we were out in the Ferrari I could have. I could have with anybody when I was in the Ferrari. Not that I need Lucy to have a Ferrari."

"Boundaries, Henri," Benton says, and he refuses to accept the abysmal defeat that is a dark plain in front of him, nothing but darkness that has spread wider and deeper ever since Lucy flew Henri to Aspen and entrusted her to him.

You won't hurt her, Lucy said to him at the time. Someone else will hurt her, take advantage of her, and find out things about me and what I do.

I'm not a psychiatrist, Benton said.

She needs a post-incident stress counselor, a forensic psychologist. That's what you do. You can do it. You can find out what happened. We have to know what happened, Lucy said, and she was beside herself. Lucy never panics, but she was panicking. She believes Benton can figure out anyone. Even if he could, that doesn't mean all people can be fixed. Henri is not a hostage. She could leave anytime. It profoundly unsettles him that she seems to have no interest in leaving, that she just might be enjoying herself.

Benton has figured out a lot in the four days he has spent with Henri Walden. She is a character disorder and was a character disorder before the attempted murder. If it wasn't for the scene photographs and the fact that someone really was inside Lucy's house, Benton might believe there was no attempted murder. He worries that Henri's personality now is simply an exaggeration of what it was before the assault, and that realization is extremely disturbing to him and he can't imagine what Lucy was thinking when she met Henri. Lucy wasn't thinking, he decides. That's the likely answer.

"Did Lucy let you drive her Ferrari?" he asks.

"Not the black one."

"What about the silver one, Henri?"

"It's not silver. It's California blue. I drove it whenever I wanted." She looks at him from the landing, her hand on the railing, her long hair messy and her eyes sultry with sleep as if she is posing for a sexy photo shoot.

"You drove it by yourself, Henri." He wants to make sure. A very important missing piece is how the perpetrator found Henri, and Benton does not believe the attack was random, the luck of the draw, a pretty young woman in the wrong mansion or in the wrong Ferrari at the wrong time.

"I told you I did," Henri says, her face pale and lacking in expression. Only her eyes are alive and the energy in them is volatile and unsettling. "But she's selfish with the black one."

"When was the last time you drove the California blue Ferrari?" Benton asks in the same mild, steady voice, and he has learned to get information when he can. It doesn't matter if Henri is sitting or walking or standing on the other side of the room with her hand on the railing, if something comes up, he tries to dislodge it from her before it is out of sight again. No matter what happened or happens to her, Benton wants to know who went inside Lucy's house and why. The hell with Henri, he is tempted to think. What he really cares about is Lucy.

"I'm something in that car," Henri replies, her eyes bright and cold in her expressionless face.

"And you drove it often, Henri."

"Whenever I wanted." She stares at him.

"Every day to the training camp?"

"Whenever I damn well wanted." Her impassive pale face stares at him and anger shines in her eyes.

"Can you remember the last time you drove it? When was that, Henri?"

"I don't know. Before I got sick."

"Before you got the flu, and that was when? About two weeks ago?"

"I don't know." She has become resistant and will not say anything else about the Ferrari right now, and he doesn't push her because her denials and avoidance have their own truths to tell.

Benton is quite adept at interpreting what isn't said, and she has just indicated that she drove the Ferrari whenever she pleased and was aware of the attention she attracted and enjoyed it because she has to be the eye of the storm. Even on her best days, Henri has to be the center of chaos and the creator of chaos, the star of her own crazy drama, and for this reason alone most police and forensic psychologists would conclude that she faked her own attempted murder and staged the crime scene, that the attack never happened. But it did. That's the irony, this bizarre, dangerous drama is real, and he worries about Lucy. He has always worried about Lucy, but now he is really worried.

"Who were you talking to on the phone?" Henri gets back to that. "Rudy misses me. I should have gotten with him. I wasted so much time down there."

"Let's start the day with a reminder of our boundaries, Henri," Benton patiently says the same thing he said yesterday morning and the morning before that, when he was making notes on the couch.

"Okay," she replies from the landing. "Rudy called. That's who it was," she says.

6.

| | | WATER DRUMS in sinks and x-rays are illuminated on every light box as Scarpetta leans close to a gash that almost severed the dead tractor driver's nose from his face.

"I'd do a STAT alcohol and CO on him," she says to Dr. Jack Fielding, who is on the other side of the stainless-steel gurney, the body between them.

"You noticing something?" he asks.

"I don't smell alcohol, and he's not cherry-pink. But just to be on the safe side. I'm telling you, cases like this are trouble, Jack."

The dead man is still clothed in his olive-green work pants, which are dusted with red clay and ripped open at the thighs. Fat and muscle and shattered bones protrude from split skin. The tractor ran over the middle of his body, but not while she was watching. It could have happened one minute, maybe five minutes, after she turned the corner, and she is certain that the man she saw was Mr. Whitby. She tries not to envision him alive but every other minute he is there in her mind, standing in front of the huge tractor tire, poking at the engine, doing something to the engine.

"Hey," Fielding calls out to a young man whose head is shaved, probably a soldier from Fort Lee's Graves Registration Unit. "What's your name?"

"Bailey, sir."

Scarpetta picks out several other young men and women in scrubs, shoe and hair covers, face masks and gloves who are probably interns from the Army and here to learn how to handle dead bodies. She wonders if they are destined for Iraq. She sees the olive green of the Army and it is the same olive green of Mr. Whitby's ripped work pants.

"Do the funeral home a favor, Bailey, and tie off the carotid," Fielding says gruffly, and when he worked for Scarpetta, he wasn't so unpleasant. He didn't boss people around and loudly find fault with them.

The soldier is embarrassed, his muscular tattooed right arm frozen midair, his gloved fingers around a long crooked surgical needle threaded with #7 cotton twine. He is helping a morgue assistant suture up the Y incision of an autopsy that was begun prior to staff meeting, and it is the morgue assistant and not the soldier who should know about tying off the carotid. Scarpetta feels sorry for the soldier, and if Fielding still worked for her, she would have a word with him and he would not treat anyone rudely in her morgue.

"Yes, sir," the soldier says with a stricken look on his young face. "Just getting ready to do that, sir."

"Really?" Fielding asks, and everyone in the morgue can hear what he is saying to the poor young soldier. "You know why you tie off the carotid?"

"No, sir."

"It's polite, that's why," Fielding says. "You tie string around a major blood vessel such as the carotid so funeral home embalmers don't have to dig around for it. It's the polite thing to do, Bailey."

"Yes sir."

"Jesus," Fielding says. "I put up with this every day because he lets everyone and their brother in here. You see him in here?" He resumes making notes on his clipboard. "Hell no. He's been here almost four damn months and hasn't done one autopsy. Oh. And in case you haven't figured it out, he likes to make people wait. His favorite thing. Obviously, nobody gave you the rundown on him. Excuse the pun." He indicates the dead man between them who managed to run himself down with a tractor. "If you'd called me, I'd have told you not to bother coming here."

"I should have called you," she says, watching five people struggle to roll an enormous woman off a gurney onto a stainless-steel table. Bloody fluid trickles from her nose and mouth. "She's got a huge panniculus." Scarpetta refers to the fold or drape of fat that people as obese as the dead woman have over their bellies, and what Scarpetta is really saying to Fielding is that she won't engage in comments about Dr. Marcus when she is standing in his morgue and surrounded by his staff.

"Well, it's my fucking case," Fielding says, and now he is talking about Dr. Marcus and Gilly Paulsson. "The asshole never even stepped foot in the morgue when her body came in, for Christ's sake, and everyone knew the case was going to cause a stink. His first big stink. Oh, don't give me one of your looks, Dr. Scarpetta." He never could stop calling her that, even though she encouraged him to call her Kay because they respected each other and she considered him a friend, but he wouldn't call her Kay when he worked for her and he still won't. "No one here is listening, not that I give a damn. You got dinner plans?"

"With you, I hope." She helps him remove Mr. Whitby's muddy leather work boots, untying the filthy laces and pulling out the dirty cowhide tongues. Rigor mortis is in the very early stages, and he is still limber and warm.

"How the hell do these guys run over themselves, can you tell me that?" Fielding says. "I never can figure it out. Good. My house at seven. I still live in the same place."

"I'll tell you how they often do it," she says as she remembers Mr. Whitby standing in front of the tractor tire, doing something to the engine. "They're having some sort of mechanical problem and get off the seat and stand right in front of that huge back tire and fool with the starter, possibly trying to jump it with a screwdriver, forgetting the tractor's in gear. It's their bad luck it starts. In his case, running him over midsection." She points at the dirty tire tread pattern on Mr. Whitby's olive work pants and his black vinyl jacket that is embroidered with his name, T. Whitby, in thick red thread. "When I saw him, he was standing in front of the tire."

"Yeah. Our old building. Welcome back to town."

"Was he found under the tire?"

"Went right over him and kept going," Fielding pulls off mud-stained socks that have left the impression of their weave on the man's large white feet. "Remember that big yellow painted metal pole sticking up from the pavement near the back door? The tractor ran into it and that's what stopped it, otherwise it might have busted right through the bay door. I guess it wouldn't matter since they're tearing the place down."

"Then he's not likely to be an asphyxia. A diffuse crush injury the width of that tire," she says, looking at the body. "Exsanguination. Expect an abdominal cavity full of blood, ruptured spleen, liver, bladder, bowels, crushed pelvis, my guess. Seven o'clock it is."

"What about your sidekick?"

"Don't call him that. You know better."

"He's invited. He looks pretty goofy in that LAPD cap."

"I warned him."

"What do you think cut his face? Something underneath or in back of the tractor?" Fielding asks, and blood trickles down the side of Mr. Whitby's stubbly face as Fielding touches the partially severed nose.

"It may not be a cut. As the tire progressed over his body, it pulled his skin with it. This injury," she points at the deep, jagged wound over his cheeks and the bridge of his nose, "may be a tear, not a cut. If it's really an issue, you should be able to see rust or grease under the scope, and significant tissue bridging from the shearing effect as opposed to cutting. One thing I would do if I were you is answer all questions."

"Oh yeah." Fielding glances up from his clipboard, from the clothing and personal effects form he is filling out with a ballpoint pen tied to the steel clamp.

"A very good chance this man's family is going to want relief for their suffering," she says. "Death at the workplace, a notorious workplace."

"Oh yeah. Of all places to die."

Fielding's latex-gloved fingers are stained red as he touches the wound on the man's face, and warm blood drips freely as he manipulates the nearly severed nose. He flips up a page on the clipboard and begins to draw the injury on a body diagram. He leans close to the face, peering intensely through plastic safety glasses. "Don't see any rust or grease," he says. "But that doesn't mean it's not there."

"Good idea." She agrees with the direction of his thoughts. "I'd swab it, get the labs to check it out, check everything. I wouldn't be surprised if someone says this man was run over or pushed off the tractor or in front of it, or was slammed in the face with a shovel first. You never know."

"Oh yeah. Money, money, money."

"Not just money," she replies. "Lawyers make it all about money. But at first, it's all about shock, pain, loss, about its being somebody else's fault. No family member wants to believe this was a stupid death, that it was preventable, that any experienced tractor driver knows better than to stand in front of a back tire and fool with the starter, bypassing the default safety of a normal ignition, which allows the tractor to start only in neutral, not in gear. But what do people do? They get too comfortable, are in a hurry and don't think. And it's human nature to deny the probability that someone we care about caused his or her own death, intentionally or inadvertently. But you've heard my lectures before."

When Fielding was starting out, he was one of her forensic fellows. She taught him forensic pathology. She taught him how to perform not just competent but meticulous and aggressive medicolegal scene investigations and autopsies, and it saddens her to remember how unabashedly eager he was to work across the table from her and take it all in, to go with her to court when time allowed and listen to her testify, to sit down in her office and go over his reports, to learn. Now he is worn out and has a skin condition and she is fired and both of them are here.

"I should have called you," she says, and she unbuckles Mr. Whitby's cheap leather belt and unbuttons and unzips his torn olive pants. "We'll work on Gilly Paulsson and figure her out."

"Oh yeah," Fielding says, and he didn't used to say "Oh yeah" so often, either.

7.

||| HENRI WALDEN wears fleece-lined suede slippers that make no sound on the carpet as she drifts like a black apparition toward the tan leather wing chair across from the couch.

"I took my shower," she says, perching on the chair and drawing her slender legs under her.

Benton catches the deliberate flash of young flesh, the pale recesses of high inner thighs. He does not look or react the way most men would.

"Why do you care?" she asks him, and she has asked him this every morning since she got here.

"It makes you feel better, doesn't it, Henri?"

She nods, staring at him like a cobra.

"Little things are important. Eating, sleeping, being clean, exercise. Regaining control."

"I heard you talking to someone," she says.

"That's a problem," he replies, his eyes steady on hers over the rim of his glasses, the legal pad in his lap as before, but there are more words on it, the words "Black Ferrari" and "without permission" and "was followed from the camp, likely" and "point of contact, the black Ferrari."

He says, "Private conversations are supposed to be just that. Private. So we need to go back to our original agreement, Henri. Do you remember what it was?"

She pulls off her slippers and drops them on the carpet. Her delicate bare feet are on the chair cushion, and when she bends over to study them, the red robe falls open slightly. "No." Her voice is barely audible and she shakes her head.

"I know you remember, Henri." Benton repeats her name often to remind her who she is, to personalize what has been depersonalized and, in some regards, irrevocably damaged. "Our agreement was respect, remember?"

She bends more deeply and picks at an unpainted toenail, her stare fixed on what she is doing, her nakedness beneath her robe offered to him.

"Part of having respect is allowing each other privacy. And modesty," he says, quietly. "We've talked about boundaries a lot. Violating modesty is a violation of boundaries."

Her free hand crawls up to her chest and gathers the robe together while she continues to study and manipulate her toes. "I just woke up," she says, as if this explains her exhibitionism.

"Thank you, Henri." It is important for her to believe that Benton does not want her sexually, not even in his fantasies. "But you didn't just get up. You got up, came in, and we talked, and then you took a shower."

"My name isn't Henri," she says.

"What would you like me to call you?"

"Nothing."

"You have two names," he says. "You have the name you were christened at birth and the name you used in your acting career and still use."

"Well, I'm Henri, then," she says, looking down at her toes.

"So I'll call you Henri."

She nods, looking at her toes. "What do you call her?"

Benton knows who she means but he doesn't answer.

"You sleep with her. Lucy's told me all about it." She emphasizes the word "all."

Benton feels a flash of anger but he doesn't show it. Lucy would not have told Henri all about his relationship with Scarpetta. No, he reminds himself. This is Henri goading him again, testing his boundaries again. No, crashing through his boundaries again.

"How come she's not here with you?" Henri asks. "It's your vacation, isn't it? And she's not here. A lot of people don't have sex after a while. That's one reason I don't want to be with anyone, not for long. No sex. Usually after six months, people stop having sex. She's not here because I am." Henri stares at him.

"That's correct," he replies. "She's not here because you are, Henri."

"She must have been mad when you told her she couldn't come."

"She understands," he says, but now he isn't being entirely honest.

Scarpetta understood and she didn't. You can't come to Aspen right now, he told her after he got Lucy's panicked phone call. I'm afraid a case has come up and I have to deal with it.

You're leaving Aspen, then, Scarpetta said.

I can't talk about the case, he replied, and for all he knows, she thinks he is anywhere but in Aspen right now.

This really isn't fair, Benton, she said. I set aside these two weeks for us. I have cases too.

Please bear with me, he replied. I promise I'll explain later.

Of all times, she said. This is a very bad time. We needed this time.

They do need this time, and instead he is here with Henri. "Tell me about your dreams last night. Do you remember them?" he is saying to Henri.

Her nimble fingers fondle her left big toe, as if it is sore. She frowns. Benton gets up. Casually, he picks up the Glock and walks across the living room to the kitchen. Opening a cupboard, he places the pistol on a top shelf, and pulls out two cups and pours coffee. He and Henri drink it black.

"May be a little strong. I can make more," and he sets her cup on an end table and returns to his place on the couch. "Night before last you dreamed about a monster. Actually, you called it 'the beast,' didn't you?" His keen eyes find her unhappy ones. "Did you see the beast again last night?"

She doesn't answer him, and her mood has dramatically altered from what it was earlier this morning. Something happened in the shower, but he'll get to that later.

"We don't have to talk about the beast if you don't want to, Henri. But the more you tell me about him, the more likely I am to find him. You want me to find him, don't you?"

"Who were you talking to?" she asks in the same hushed, child-like voice. But she is not a child. She is anything but innocent. "You were talking about me," she persists as the sash of her robe loosens and more flesh shows.

"I promise I wasn't talking about you. No one knows you're here, no one but Lucy and Rudy. I believe you trust me, Henri." He pauses, looking at her. "I believe you trust Lucy."

Her eyes get angry at the mention of Lucy's name.

"I believe you trust us, Henri," Benton says, sitting calmly, his legs crossed, his fingers laced and in his lap. "I would like you to cover yourself, Henri."

She rearranges her robe, tucking it between her legs and tightening the sash. Benton knows exactly what her naked body looks like, but he does not imagine it. He has seen photographs, and he will not look at them again unless it is necessary to review them with other professionals and eventually with her, when she is ready or if she is ready. For now, she represses the facts of the case either unwillingly or willingly, and acts out in ways that would seduce and infuriate weaker human beings who neither care about nor understand her ploys. Her relentless attempts to sexually arouse Benton are not simply about transference but are a direct manifestation of her acute and chronic narcissistic needs and her desire to control and dominate, degrade and destroy anyone who dares to care about her. Henri's every action and reaction are about self-hate and rage.

"Why did Lucy send me away?" she asks.

"Can you tell me? Why don't you tell me why you're here?"

"Because . . ." She wipes her eyes on the sleeve of her robe. "The beast."

Benton's eyes are steady on her from his safe position on the couch, the words on the legal pad unreadable from where she sits and well beyond her reach. He does not encourage her conversation. It is important that he be patient, incredibly patient, like a hunter in the woods who stands perfectly still and barely breathes.

"It came into the house. I don't remember."

Benton watches her in silence.

"Lucy let it into the house," she says.

Benton will not push her, but he will not allow misinformation or outright lies. "No. Lucy did not let it into the house," Benton corrects her. "No one let it into the house. It came in because the back door was unlocked and the alarm was off. We've talked about this. Do you remember why the door was unlocked and the alarm was off?"

She stares at her toes, her hands still.

"We've talked about why," he says.

"I had the flu," she replies, staring at a different toe. "I was sick and she wasn't home. I was shivering and went out in the sun, and I forgot to lock the door and reset the alarm. I had a fever and forgot. Lucy blames me."

He sips his coffee. Already, it has gotten cold. Coffee doesn't stay hot in the mountains of Aspen, Colorado. "Has Lucy said it's your fault?"

"She thinks it." Henri is staring past him now, out the windows behind his head. "She thinks everything is my fault."

"She's never told me she thinks it's your fault," he says. "You were telling me about your dreams," he goes back to that. "The dreams you had last night."

She blinks and rubs her big toe again.

"Is it hurting?"

She nods.

"I'm sorry. Would you like something for it?"

She shakes her head. "Nothing would help."

She isn't talking about her right big toe, but is making the connection between its having been broken and her now finding herself in his protective care more than a thousand miles from Pompano Beach, Florida, where she almost died. Henri's eyes heat up.

"I was walking on a trail," she says. "There were rocks on one side, this sheer wall of rocks very close to the trail. There were cracks, this crack between the rocks, and I don't know why I did it, but I wedged myself into it and got stuck." Her breath catches and she shoves blond hair out of her eyes, and her hand shakes. "I was wedged between rocks . . . I couldn't move, I couldn't breathe. I couldn't get free. And nobody could get me out. When I was in the shower I remembered my dream. The water was hitting my face, and when I held my breath I remembered my dream."

"Did someone try to get you out?" Benton doesn't react to her terror or pass judgment on whether it is real or false. He doesn't know which it is. With her, there is so little he knows.

She is motionless in her chair, struggling for breath.

"You said nobody could get you out," Benton goes on, calmly, quietly, in the unprovocative tone of the counselor he has become for her. "Was another person there? Or other people?"

"I don't know."

He waits. If she continues to struggle for breath, he will have to do something about it. But for now, he is patient, the hunter waiting.

"I can't remember. I don't know why, but for a minute I thought someone . . . it occurred to me in my dream, maybe, that someone could chip away at the rocks. Maybe with a pickax. And then I thought, no. The rock is way too hard. You can't get me out. No one can. I'm going to die. I was going to die, I knew it, and then I couldn't take it anymore, so the dream stopped." Her rambling rendition stops as abruptly as the dream apparently did. Henri takes a deep breath and her body relaxes. Her eyes focus on Benton. "It was awful," she says.

"Yes," he says. "It must have been awful. I can't think of anything more frightening than not being able to breathe."

She flattens her hand against her heart. "My chest couldn't move. I was breathing very shallowly, you know? And then I just didn't have the strength."

"No one would be strong enough to move the rocky face of a mountain," he replies.

"I couldn't get air."

Her assailant may have tried to smother or asphyxiate her, and Benton envisions the photographs. One by one he holds up the photographs in his mind and examines Henri's injuries, trying to make sense of what she has just said. He sees blood trickling from her nose and smeared across her cheeks and staining the sheet beneath her head as she lies on her belly on the bed. Her body is naked and uncovered, her arms stretched out above her head and palms down on the bed, her legs bent, one more bent than the other.

Benton examines another photograph, focusing on it in his memory as Henri gets up from her chair. She mutters that she wants more coffee and will get it herself. Benton processes what she says and the fact that his pistol is in the kitchen cabinet, but she doesn't know which cabinet because her back was to him when he tucked the pistol out of sight. He watches her, reading what she is doing in the moment while he reads the hieroglyphics of the injuries, the peculiar marks on her body. The tops of her hands were red because he or she, and Benton will not assume the gender of her assailant, bruised her. She had fresh contusions on the tops of her hands, and she had several reddish areas of contusion on her upper back. Over the next few days, the redness from subcutaneous broken blood vessels darkened to a stormy purple.

Benton watches Henri pour more coffee. He thinks about the photographs of her unconscious body in situ. The fact her body is beautiful is of no importance beyond Benton's consideration that all details of her appearance and behavior may have been violent triggers to the person who tried to murder her. Henri is thin but most assuredly not androgynous. She has breasts and pubic hair and would not appeal to a pedophile. At the time of the assault, she was sexually active.

He watches her return to the leather chair, both hands cupping the mug of coffee. It doesn't bother him that she is inconsiderate. A polite person would have asked if he would like more coffee too, but Henri is probably one of the most selfish, insensitive people Benton has ever met and was selfish and insensitive before the attack and will always be selfish and insensitive. It would be a good thing if she were never around Lucy again. But he has no right to wish that or make it happen, he tells himself.

"Henri," Benton says, getting up for more coffee, "are you up for doing a fact-check this morning?"

"Yes. But I can't remember." Her voice follows him into the kitchen. "I know you don't believe me."

"Why do you think that?" He pours more coffee and returns to the living room.

"The doctor didn't."

"Oh yes, the doctor. He said he didn't believe you," Benton says as he sits back down on the couch. "I think you know my opinion of that doctor, but I'll express it again. He thinks women are hysterical and doesn't like them, certainly he has no respect for them, and that's because he is afraid of them. He's also an ER doctor, and he knows nothing about violent offenders or victims."

"He thinks I did this to myself," Henri replies angrily. "He thinks I didn't hear what he said to the nurse."

Benton is careful how he reacts. Henri is offering new information. He can only hope that it is true. "Tell me," he says. "I would very much like to know what he said to the nurse."

"I should sue the asshole," she adds.

Benton waits, sipping his coffee.

"Maybe I will sue him," she adds, spitefully. "He thought I didn't hear him because I had my eyes shut when he walked into the room. I was lying there half asleep and the nurse was in the doorway and then he showed up. So I pretended I was out of it."

"Pretended you were asleep," Benton says.

She nods.

"You're a trained actor. You used to be a professional actor."

"I still am. You don't just stop being an actor. I'm just not in any productions right now because I have other things to do."

"You've always been good at acting, I would imagine," he says.

"Yes."

"At pretending. You've always been good at pretending." He pauses. "Do you pretend things often, Henri?"

Her eyes get hard as she looks at him. "I was pretending in the hospital room so I could hear the doctor. I heard every word. He said, 'Nothing like being raped if you're mad at someone. Payback's hell.' And he laughed."

"I don't blame you for wanting to sue him," Benton says. "This was in the ER?"

"No, no. In my room. Later that day when they moved me to one of the floors, after all the tests. I don't remember which floor."

"That's even worse," Benton says. "He shouldn't have come to your room at all. He's an ER doctor and isn't assigned to one of the floors. He stopped by because he was curious, and that's not right."

"I'm going to sue him. I hate his guts." She rubs her toe again, and her bruised toe and the bruises on her hands have faded to a nicotine-yellow. "He made some comment about Dextro Heads. I don't know what that is, but he was insulting me, making fun of me."

Again, this is new information, and Benton feels renewed hope that with time and patience, she will remember more or be more truthful. "A Dextro Head is someone who abuses allergy and flu remedies or cough syrups that have opiates. It's popular among teenagers, unfortunately."

"The asshole," she mutters, picking at her robe. "Can't you do something to get him into trouble?"

"Henri, do you have any idea why he indicated you were raped?" Benton asks.

"I don't know. I don't think I was."

"Do you remember the forensic nurse?"

She slowly shakes her head, no.

"You were wheeled into an examination room near the ER, and a physical evidence recovery kit was used. You know what that is, don't you? When you got tired of acting, you were a police officer before Lucy met you in L.A. this fall, just a few months ago, and hired you. So you know about swabs and collecting hair and fibers and all the rest."

"I didn't get tired of it. I just wanted time off from it, to do something else."

"Okay. But you remember the PERK?"

She nods.

"And the nurse? She was very nice, I'm told. Her name is Brenda. She examined you for sexual assault injury and evidence. The room is also used for children and was filled with stuffed animals. The wallpaper was Winnie the Pooh, bears, honeypots, trees. Brenda wasn't wearing a nurse's uniform. She had on a light blue suit."

"You weren't there."

"She told me over the phone."

Henri stares at her bare feet, which are up on the chair cushion. "You asked her what she had on?"

"She's got hazel eyes, short black hair." Benton tries to dislodge what Henri is repressing or pretends to be repressing, and it is time to discuss the physical evidence recovery kit. "There was no seminal fluid, Henri. No evidence of sexual assault. But Brenda found fibers adhering to your skin. It appears you had on some sort of lotion or body oil. Do you remember if you put on lotion or body oil that morning?"

"No," she quietly replies. "But I can't say I didn't."

"Your skin was oily," Benton says. "According to Brenda. She detected a fragrance. A nice fragrance like a perfumed body lotion."

"He didn't put it on me."

"He?"

"It must have been a he. Don't you think it was a he?" she says in a hopeful tone that rings off-key, the way voices sound when people are trying to fool themselves or others. "It couldn't have been a she. A woman. Women don't do things like that."

"Women do all sorts of things. Right now we don't know if it was a man or a woman. Several head hairs were found on the mattress in the bedroom, black curly ones. Maybe five, six inches long."

"Well, we'll know soon enough, right? They can get DNA from the hair and find out it's not a woman," she says.

"I'm afraid they can't. The kind of DNA testing they're doing can't determine gender. Possibly race, but not gender. And even race will take at least a month. Then you think you might have put on the body lotion yourself."

"No. But he didn't. I wouldn't have let him do it. I would have fought him if I'd had a chance. He probably wanted to do it."

"And you didn't put the lotion on yourself?"

"I said he didn't and I didn't and that's enough. It's none of your business."

Benton understands. The lotion has nothing to do with the attack, assuming Henri is telling the truth. Lucy enters his thoughts, and he feels sorry for her and is angry with her at the same time.

"Tell me everything," Henri says. "Tell me what you think happened to me. You tell me what happened and I'll agree or disagree." She smiles.

"Lucy came home," Benton says, and this is old information now. He resists revealing too much too soon. "It was a few minutes past noon, and when she unlocked the front door, she noticed immediately that the alarm wasn't armed. She called out to you, you didn't answer, and she heard the back door that leads out to the pool bang against the doorstop, and she ran in that direction. When she got into the kitchen, she discovered the door leading out to the pool and the seawall was wide open."

Henri stares wide-eyed past Benton, out the window again. "I wish she'd killed him."

"She never saw whoever it was. It's possible the person heard her pull up in the driveway in her black Ferrari and ran . . ."

"He was in my room with me and then had to go down all those stairs," Henri interrupts, staring off with wide eyes, and at this moment, it feels to Benton that she is telling the truth.

"Lucy didn't park in the garage this time because she was only stopping by to check on you," Benton says. "So she was in the front door quickly, came in the front door as he was running out the back door. She didn't chase him. She never saw him. At that moment, Lucy's focus was you, not whoever had gotten into the house."

"I disagree," Henri says, almost happily.

"Tell me."

"She didn't drive up in her black Ferrari. It was in the garage. She had the California blue Ferrari. That's the one she parked out front."

More new information, and Benton remains calm, very easygoing. "You were sick in bed, Henri. Are you sure you know what she drove that day?"

"I always know. She wasn't driving the black Ferrari because it got damaged."

"Tell me about the damage."

"It got damaged in a parking lot," Henri says, studying her bruised toe again. "You know, the gym up there on Atlantic, way up there in Coral Springs. Where we go to the gym sometimes."

"Can you tell me when this happened?" Benton asks, calmly, not showing the excitement he feels. The information is new and important and he senses where it leads. "The black Ferrari got damaged while you were in the gym?" Benton prods her to tell the truth.

"I didn't say I was in the gym," she snaps, and her hostility confirms his suspicions.

She took Lucy's black Ferrari to the gym, obviously without Lucy's permission. No one is allowed to drive the black Ferrari, not even Rudy.

"Tell me about the damage," Benton says.

"Someone scratched it, like with a car key, something like that.

Scratched a picture on it." She stares down at her toes, picking at her big yellowish toe.

"What was the picture?"

"She wouldn't drive it after that. You don't take out a scratched Ferrari."

"Lucy must have been angry," Benton says.

"It can be fixed. Anything can be fixed. If she'd killed him, I wouldn't have to be here. Now I'll have to worry the rest of my life that he's going to find me again."

"I'm doing my best to make sure you'll never have to worry about that, Henri. But I need your help."

"I may never remember." She looks at him. "I can't help it."

"Lucy ran up three flights of stairs to the master bedroom. That's where you were," Benton says, watching her carefully, making sure she can handle what he is saying, even though she has heard this part before. All along, he has feared that she might not be acting, that none of what she says and does is an act. What if it isn't? She could break with reality, become psychotic, completely decompensate and shatter. She listens, but her affect isn't normal. "When Lucy found you, you were unconscious, but your breathing and heart rate were normal."

"I didn't have anything on." She doesn't mind that detail. She likes reminding him of her naked body.

"Do you sleep in the nude?"

"I like to."

"Do you remember if you'd taken off your pajamas before you got back into bed that morning?"

"Probably I did."

"So he didn't do it? The attacker didn't. Assuming it's a he."

"He didn't need to. I'm sure he would have, though."

"Lucy says that when she saw you last, at about eight A.M., you were wearing red satin pajamas and a tan terry-cloth robe."

"I agree. Because I wanted to go outside. I sat in a lounge chair by the pool, in the sun."

More new information, and he asks, "What time was this?"

"Right after Lucy left, I think. She drove off in the blue Ferrari. Well, not right after," she corrects herself in a flat tone, and stares out at the snow-covered, sun-dazzled morning. "I was mad at her."

Benton slowly gets up and places several logs on the fire. Sparks fly up the chimney and flames greedily lick the bone-dry pine. "She hurt your feelings," he says, drawing the mesh curtain shut.

"Lucy isn't nice when people get sick," Henri replies, more focused, more poised. "She didn't want to take care of me."

"What about the body lotion?" he asks, and he has figured out the body lotion, he's pretty sure he has, but it is smart to make absolutely sure.

"So what? Big deal. That's a favor, now isn't it? You know how many people would love to do that? I let her as a favor. She'll only do so much, only what suits her, then she gets tired of taking care of me. My head hurt and we were arguing."

"How long did you sit out by the pool?" Benton says, trying not to get distracted by Lucy, trying not to wonder what the hell she was thinking when she met Henri Walden, and at the same time he is all too aware of how impressive and bewitching sociopaths can be, even to people who should know better.

"Not long. I didn't feel good."

"Fifteen minutes? Half an hour?"

"I guess half an hour."

"Did you see any other people? Any boats?"

"I didn't notice. So maybe there weren't any. What did Lucy do when she was in the room with me?"

"She called nine-one-one, continued checking your vital signs while she waited for the rescue squad." Benton says. He decides to add another detail, a risky one. "She took photographs."

"Did she have a gun out?"

"Yes."

"I wish she'd killed him."

"You keep saying 'he.' "

"And she took pictures? Of me?" Henri says.

"You were unconscious but stable. She took pictures of you before you were moved."

"Because I looked like I had been attacked?"

"Because your body was in an unusual position, Henri. Like this." He straightens out his arms and holds them over his head. "You were facedown with your arms stretched out in front of you, palms down. Your nose was bleeding, and you had bruises, as you know. And your right big toe was broken, although that wasn't discovered until later. You don't seem to remember how it got broken."

"I might have stubbed it going down the stairs," she says.

"You remember that?" he asks, and she has remembered nothing or admitted nothing about her toe before now. "When might this have happened?"

"When I went out by the pool. Her stone stairs. I think I missed a step or something, because of all the medicine and my fever and everything. I remember crying. I remember that. Because it hurt, really hurt, and I thought about calling her but why bother. She doesn't like it when I'm sick or hurt."

"You broke your toe going down to the pool and thought of calling Lucy but didn't." He wants to make this clear.

"I agree," she says, mockingly. "Where were my pajamas and robe?"

"Neatly folded on a chair near the bed. Did you fold them and put them there?"

"Probably. Was I under the covers?"

He knows where she is going with this, but it is important that he tell her the truth. "No," he replies. "The covers were pulled down to the bottom of the bed, were hanging off the mattress."

"I didn't have anything on and she took pictures," Henri says, and her face is expressionless as she looks at him with hard, flat eyes.

"Yes," Benton says.

"That figures. She would do something like that. Always the cop."

"You're a cop, Henri. What would you have done?"

"She would do something like that," she says.

8.

||| "WHERE ARE YOU?" Marino asks when he sees Lucy's number in the display of his vibrating cell phone. "What's your location?" He always asks her where she is, even if the answer isn't relevant.

Marino has spent his adult life in policing, and one detail a good cop never overlooks is location. It doesn't do a damn bit of good to get on your radio and scream Mayday if you don't know where you are. Marino considers himself Lucy's mentor, and he doesn't let her forget it even if she forgot it long years back.

"Atlantic," Lucy's voice returns in his right ear. "I'm in the car."

"No joke, Sherlock. You sound like you're in a damn garbage disposal." Marino never misses an opportunity to give her a hard time about her cars.

"Jealousy is so unattractive," she says.

He walks several steps away from the OCME coffee area, looking around, seeing no one and satisfied that his conversation isn't over-heard. "Look, it ain't going so good up here," he says, peeking through the small glass window in the shut library door, seeing if anyone is inside. No one is. "This joint's gone to hell." He keeps talk-ing into his tiny cell phone, moving it back and forth between his ear and mouth, depending on whether he's listening or speaking. "I'm just giving you a heads-up."

After a pause, Lucy replies, "You're not just giving me a heads-up. What do you want me to do?"

"Damn. That car is loud." He paces, his eyes constantly moving beneath the brim of the LAPD baseball cap Lucy gave him as a joke.

"Okay, so now you're starting to worry me," she says above the roar of her Ferrari. "I should have known when you said this was no big deal, it was going to turn out to be a big deal. Dammit. I warned you, I warned both of you not to go back there."

"There's more to it than this dead girl," he replies quietly. "That's what I'm getting at. It ain't about that, not entirely. I'm not saying she ain't the main problem. I'm sure she is. But there's something else going on here. Our mutual friend," he refers to Benton, "is making that loud and clear. And you know her." Now he means Scarpetta. "She's gonna end up right in the middle of shit."

"Something else going on? Like what? Give me an example." Lucy's tone changes. When she turns very serious, her voice gets slow and rigid, reminding Marino of drying glue.

If there is trouble here in Richmond, Marino thinks, he's stuck, all right. Lucy will be all over him like glue, all right. "Let me tell you something, Boss," he goes on, "one of the reasons I'm still walk-ing around is 'cause I got instincts."

Marino calls her Boss as if he is comfortable with her being his boss, when of course he is anything but, especially if his remarkable instincts warn him that he is about to earn her disapproval. "And my instincts is screaming bloody murder right about now, Boss," he is saying, and a part of him knows damn well that Lucy and her aunt Kay Scarpetta see his insecurity when he starts trotting out bravado or bragging about his instincts or calling powerful women Boss or Sherlock or other less polite appellations. But he just can't help himself. So he makes matters worse. "And I'll add this to the mix," he continues, "I hate this stinking city. Goddamn, I hate this stinking place. You know what's wrong with this stinking place? They ain't got respect, that's what."

"I'm not going to say I told you so," Lucy tells him so. Her voice is setting like glue very quickly now. "Do you want us to come?"

"No," he says, and it gripes him that he can't tell Lucy what he thinks without her assuming she should do something about it. "Right now, I'm just giving you a heads-up, Boss," he says, wishing he hadn't called Lucy and told her anything. It was a mistake to call her, he thinks. But if she finds out her aunt is having a hard time and he didn't say a word, Lucy will be all over him.

When he first met her she was ten years old. Ten. A pudgy little runt with glasses and an obnoxious attitude. They hated each other, then things changed and she hero-worshipped him, and then they became friends, and then things changed again. Somewhere along the line, he should have put a stop to progress, to all the changing, because about ten years ago things were just right and he felt good teaching her to drive his truck and ride a motorcycle, how to shoot, how to drink beer, how to tell if someone's lying, the important things in life. Back then he wasn't afraid of her. Maybe fear isn't the right word to describe what he feels, but she has power in life and he doesn't, and half the time when he gets off the phone after talking to her, he feels down in the dumps and bad about himself. Lucy can do whatever she likes and still have money and order people around, and he can't. Not even when he was a sworn police officer could he flaunt power the way she does. But he's not afraid of her, he tells himself. Hell no, he's not.

"We'll come if you need us," Lucy says over the phone. "But it's not a good time. I'm into something down here and it's not a good time."

"I told you I don't need you to come," Marino says grumpily, and being grumpy has always been the magic charm that forces people to worry more about him and his moods than about themselves and their moods. "I'm telling you what's going on and that's it. I don't need you. There's nothing for you to do."

"Good," Lucy says. Grumpy doesn't work with her anymore. Marino keeps forgetting that. "I've got to go."

9.

| | | LUCY TOUCHES the paddle shift with her left index finger and the engine kicks up a thousand rpm's with a roar as she slows down. Her sonaradar chirps and the front alert flashes red, indicating police radar somewhere up ahead.

"I'm not speeding," she says to Rudy Musil, who sits in the passenger's seat, near the fire extinguisher, and he is looking at the speedometer. "Only going six miles over."

"I didn't say anything," he replies, glancing in his side-view mirror.

"Let me see if I'm right." She keeps the car in third and just a little over forty miles per hour. "The cop car's going to be at the next intersection looking for us yahoos who can't wait to hit the coast and haul ass."

"What's going on with Marino? Let me guess," Rudy says. "I need to pack a suitcase."

Both of them keep up their constant scans, checking mirrors, noting other cars, aware of every palm tree, pedestrian, and building on this flat stretch of strip malls. Traffic is moderate and relatively polite at the moment on Atlantic Boulevard in Pompano Beach, just north of Fort Lauderdale.

"Yup," Lucy says. "Tally ho." Her sunglasses are fixed straight ahead as she passes a dark blue Ford LTD that has just turned right off Powerline Road, an intersection with an Eckerd's drugstore and the Discount Meat Market. The unmarked Ford slides in behind her in the left lane.

"You got him curious," Rudy says.

"Well, he's not paid to be curious," she says aggressively as the unmarked Ford follows her, and she knows damn well the cop is hoping she'll do something that gives him cause to turn on his lights and check out the car and the young couple in it. "Look at that. People passing me in the right lane, and that guy over there's got an expired inspection sticker." She points. "And the cop's more interested in me."

She stops checking on him in the rearview mirror and wishes that Rudy would lighten his mood. Ever since she opened an office in Los Angeles, he has been out of sorts. She's not sure how, but clearly she's miscalculated his ambitions and needs in life. She assumed that Rudy would love a highrise on Wilshire Boulevard with a view so immense that on a clear day one can see Catalina Island. She was wrong, terribly wrong, as wrong as she has ever been about anything she has ever assumed about him.

A front is rolling in from the south, the sky divided into layers that vary between thick smoke to sunlit pearly gray. Cooler air pushes away rain that at times today was pounding, leaving puddles that blast the undercarriage of Lucy's low-slung car. Just ahead, a flock of migrating seagulls swirl over the road, flying low and in crazy directions, and Lucy drives on, the unmarked car dogging her rear.

"Marino doesn't have much to say," she answers Rudy's question from a moment ago. "Just that something's up in Richmond. As usual, my aunt is stepping into a mess."

"I heard you volunteer our services. I thought she was just going to consult about something. What's up?"

"I don't know if we need to do anything. We'll see. What's up is the chief, I can't remember his name, asked her help in a case, some kid, a girl, who suddenly died and he can't figure out why. His office can't, so no big surprise. He's not even been there four months, and he washes his hands of the first big problem and calls my aunt. Hey, how about you coming on up and stepping in this shit so I don't have to. Right? I told her not to touch it and now it seems there are other problems. Huge surprise. I don't know. I told her not to go back to Richmond, but she doesn't listen to me."

"Listens to you about like you listen to her," Rudy says.

"You know something, Rudy. I don't like this guy." Lucy looks in her rearview mirror, at the unmarked Ford.

It is still on her bumper, and its driver is a dark-skinned person, perhaps a man, but Lucy can't tell and she doesn't want to seem interested in him or even aware of him, and then something else occurs to her.

"Damn, I'm stupid," she says, incredulous. "My radar's not going off. What am I thinking? It hasn't made a chirp since that car pulled in behind us. It's not a police car with radar. It can't be. And he's following us."

"Easy," Rudy says. "Just drive and ignore him. Let's see what he does. Probably just some dude looking at your car. That's what you get for driving cars like this. I've told you and told you. Shit."

Rudy didn't used to lecture her. When they first met years ago at the FBI Academy, they became colleagues, then partners, then friends, and then he thought enough of her personally and professionally to leave law enforcement not long after she did and come work for her company, which might be described as an international private investigation firm for lack of a better definition of what The Last Precinct or its employees do. Even some of the people who work for TLP don't know what it does and have never met its founder and owner, Lucy. Some employees have never met Rudy, or if they have, they don't know who he is or what he does.

"Run the plate," Lucy says.

Rudy has his palm-size computer out and he is logging on, but he can't run the plate number because he can't see it. The car has no license plate in front, and Lucy feels stupid for ordering him to run a number he can't see.

"Let him get in front of you," Rudy says. "I can't see his plate unless he gets in front."

She touches the left paddle and drops to second gear. Now she is going five miles below the speed limit, and the driver stays behind her. He doesn't seem interested in passing her.

"Okay, let the games begin," she says. "You're fucking with the wrong chicken, asshole." She suddenly turns a hard right into a strip mall parking lot.

"Oh shit. What the hell . . . ? Now he knows you're messing with him," Rudy says in annoyance.

"Get the plate now. You should be able to see it."

Rudy twists around in the seat, but he's not going to get the plate because the Ford LTD has turned off too, and is still on their tail, following them through the parking lot.

"Stop," Rudy says to Lucy. He is disgusted with her, completely disgusted with her. "Stop the car right now."

She eases on the brake and shifts the car into neutral, and the Ford stops right behind her. Rudy gets out and walks toward it as the driver's window rolls down. Lucy has her window open, her pistol in her lap, and she watches the activity in her side-view mirror and tries to chase away her feelings. She feels stupid and embarrassed and angry and slightly afraid.

"You got a problem?" she hears Rudy say to the driver, definitely a Hispanic male, a young one.

"Me have a problem? I was just looking."

"Maybe we don't want you looking."

"It's a free country. I can fucking look. You have the problem, fuck you!"

"Go look somewhere else. Now get the hell out of here," Rudy says without raising his voice. "You follow us one more time, you're going to jail, you fucking piece of shit."

Lucy has the bizarre urge to laugh out loud as Rudy flashes his fake credentials. She is sweating and her heart is beating wildly, and she wants to laugh and get out of the car and kill the young Hispanic male, and she wants to cry, and because she understands nothing about her feelings, she sits behind the wheel of her Ferrari and doesn't move. The driver says something else that she can't make out and angrily drives off, squealing rubber. Rudy walks back to the Ferrari and climbs in.

"Way to go," he says as she slips back into the traffic on Atlantic. "Just some punk interested in your car, and you have to turn it into an international incident. First you think some cop's following you because the car's a black Crown Vic. Then you notice that your radar detector isn't detecting a damn thing, so next you think . . . what? What did you think? The Mafia? Some hit man who's going to take us out in the middle of a busy highway?"

She doesn't blame Rudy for losing his temper with her, but she can't allow it. "Don't yell at me," she says.

"You know what? You're out of control. You're unsafe."

"This is about something else," she says, trying to sound sure of herself.

"You're damn right it is," he retorts. "It's about her. You let someone stay in your house and look what happens. You could be dead.
She sure as hell should be dead. And something worse is going to
happen if you don't get a grip."

"She was being stalked, Rudy. Don't make it my fault. It's not
my fault."

"Stalked, you're damn right. She sure as hell was being stalked,
and it sure as hell is your fault. If you would drive something like a
Jeep . . . or drive the Hummer. We have company Hummers. Why
don't you drive one of those once in a while? If you hadn't let her
drive your damn Ferrari. Showing off, Miss Hollywood. Jesus. In
your damn Ferrari."

"Don't get jealous. I hate . . ."

"I'm not jealous!" he yells.

"You've been acting jealous since we hired her."

"This isn't about your hiring her! Hired her to do what? She's
going to protect our L.A. clients? What a joke! So you hired her to
do what? To do what?"

"You can't talk to me like this," Lucy says quietly, and she is
surprisingly calm, but she has no choice. If she fires back at him,
then they'll really have a fight and he might do something terrible like quit.

"I won't be run out of my own life. I'll drive what I want and live
where I want." She stares fiercely straight ahead, at the road, at the
cars turning off on side streets and into parking places. "I'll be generous to whoever I want. She wasn't allowed to drive my black Ferrari. You know that. But she took it out and that's what started
everything. He saw her, followed her, and then look what happens.
It's nobody's fault. Not even hers. She didn't invite him to vandalize
my car and follow her and try to kill her."

"Good. You live your life the way you want," Rudy replies. "And
we'll just keep pulling into parking lots and maybe next time I'll beat

up some innocent stranger who was just looking at your damn Ferrari. Hell, maybe I'll get to shoot someone. Or maybe I'll get shot. That would be even better, right? Me get shot over a stupid car."

"Calm down," Lucy says as she stops at a red light. "Please, calm down. I could have handled that better. I agree."

"Handled? I didn't notice you handling anything. You just reacted like an idiot."

"Rudy, stop it. Please." She doesn't want to get so angry with him that she makes a mistake. "You can't talk to me like this. You can't. Don't make me pull rank."

She turns left on A1A, driving slowly along the beach, and several teenaged boys almost fall off their bicycles as they turn around to stare at her car. Rudy shakes his head and shrugs, as if to say, I rest my case. But talk about the Ferrari is no longer about the Ferrari. For Lucy to change the way she lives is to allow him to win, and she thinks of the beast as a him. Henri called him a beast, and he is a male beast, Lucy believes that. She has no doubt of that. The hell with science, the hell with evidence, the hell with everything. She knows damn well the beast is a him.

He is either a cocky beast or a stupid beast because he left two partial fingerprints on the glass-covered bedside table. He was stupid or careless to leave prints, or maybe he doesn't care. So far, the partial prints aren't matching up with any prints in any Automated Fingerprint Identification System, so maybe he doesn't have a ten-print card in any database because he's never been arrested or his prints have never been taken for some other reason. Maybe he didn't care when he left three hairs on the bed, three black head hairs, and why should he care? Even when a case is high priority, mitochondrial DNA analysis can take thirty to ninety days. There is no certainty that the results will be worth a damn because there is no such thing as a centralized and statistically significant mitochondrial DNA database, and unlike the nuclear DNA of blood and tissue, the mitochondrial DNA of hair and bones isn't going to tattle on the perpe-trator's gender. The evidence the beast left doesn't matter. It may never matter unless he becomes a suspect and direct comparisons can be made.

"All right. I'm rattled. I'm not myself. I'm letting it get to me," Lucy says, concentrating hard on her driving, worried that maybe she is losing control, that maybe Rudy is right. "What I did back there shouldn't have happened. Never. I'm too careful for that kind of shit."

"You are. She's not." Rudy's jaw is set stubbornly, his eyes blacked out by nonpolarized sunglasses that have a mirrored finish. Right now he refuses to give Lucy his eyes, and that bothers her.

"I thought we were talking about the Hispanic guy back there," Lucy replies.

"You know what I told you from day one," Rudy says. "The dan-ger of someone living in your house. Someone using your car, your stuff. Someone flying solo in your airspace. Someone who doesn't know the same rules you and I do and sure as hell doesn't have our training. Or care about the same things we do, including us."

"Not everything in life should be about training," Lucy says, and it is easier to talk about training than whether someone you love re-ally cares. It's easier talking about the Hispanic than Henri. "I should never have handled it like that back there, and I'm sorry."

"Maybe you've forgotten what life is really like," Rudy replies.

"Oh, please don't go into your Boy Scout Be Prepared shit," she snaps at him, and speeds up, going north, getting close to the Hills-boro neighborhood where her salmon-colored stucco Mediterranean mansion overlooks an inlet that connects the Intracoastal Waterway to the ocean. "I don't think you can be objective. You can't even say her name. Someone-this and Someone-that."

"Ha! Objective? Ha! You should talk." His tone is dangerously ap-proaching cruel. "That stupid bitch has ruined absolutely everything.

And you didn't have a right to do that. You didn't have a right to drag me along for the ride. You didn't have a right."

"Rudy, we've got to stop fighting like this," Lucy says. "Why do we fight like this?" She looks at him. "Everything isn't ruined."

He doesn't answer her.

"Why do we fight like this? It's making me sick," she says.

They didn't used to fight. Now and then he sulked but he never turned on her until she opened the office in Los Angeles and recruited Henri from the LAPD. A deep horn blares out a warning that the drawbridge is about to go up, and Lucy downshifts and stops again, this time getting a thumbs-up from a man in a Corvette.

She smiles sadly and shakes her head. "Yeah, I can be stupid," she says. "Genetic wiring, bad wiring. From my crazy Latino biological father. Hopefully, not from my mother, although it would be worse to be like her. Much worse."

Rudy says nothing, staring at the rising bridge giving way to a yacht.

"Let's don't fight," she says. "Everything isn't ruined. Come on." She reaches over and squeezes his hand. "A truce? Start all over? Do we need to call in Benton for hostage negotiation? Because you're not just my friend and partner these days. You're my hostage, and I guess I'm yours, right? Here because you need the job or at least want the job, and I need you. That's just the way it is."

"I don't have to be anywhere," he says, and his hand doesn't move. His hand is dead under hers, and she lets go of it and moves away.

"How well I know," she replies, hurt that he wouldn't touch her, and she places her rejected hand back on the steering wheel. "I live with that fear all the time these days. You're going to say, I quit. Good-bye. Good riddance. Have a good life."

He stares at the yacht sailing through the open bridge, heading out to sea. The people on the deck of the yacht are dressed in Bermuda shorts and loose shirts, and move with the ease of the rare very rich. Lucy is very rich. But she has never believed it. When she looks at the yacht, she still feels poor. When she looks at Rudy, she feels poorer.

"Coffee?" she asks. "Will you have a coffee with me? We can sit out by that pool I never use and look out at the water I never notice in that house I wish I didn't have. I can be stupid," she says. "Have a coffee with me."

"Yeah, I guess." He stares out the window like a sulking little boy as Lucy's mailbox comes into view. "I thought we were taking that thing down," he says, indicating the mailbox. "You don't get mail at your house. The only thing you might get in that thing is something you don't want. Especially these days."

"I'll get the landscaper to take it down next time he comes," she says. "I haven't been here much. Opening the office down here and everything else. I feel like the other Lucy. The Lucy of *I Love Lucy*. Remember that one when she's working in the candy factory and can't keep up because the candy's coming off the belt so fast?"

"No."

"You probably never watched *I Love Lucy* even once in your entire life," Lucy says. "My aunt and I used to sit around watching Jackie Gleason, *Bonanza, I Love Lucy,* the shows she watched when she was growing up down here in Miami." She slows almost to a stop at the offending mailbox at the end of her driveway. Scarpetta lives simply compared with how Lucy lives, and she warned Lucy about the house.

For one thing, it's too opulent for the neighborhood, Scarpetta told her. It was a foolish decision to buy the house and Lucy has turned on the house and calls the three-story eleven-thousand-square-foot mansion her nine-million-dollar townhouse because it is built on a third of an acre. There isn't enough grass to feed a rabbit, just stonework and a small disappearing-edge pool, a fountain and a few palms and plants. Didn't her aunt Kay nag her about moving here? No privacy or security, and accessible to boaters, Scarpetta said when

Lucy was too busy and preoccupied to give a part-time domain the appropriate attention, when she was obsessed with making Henri happy. You'll be sorry, Scarpetta said. Lucy moved here not even three months ago and she's as sorry as she's ever been in her life.

Lucy presses one remote control to open her gate and another one to open her garage.

"Why bother?" Rudy is talking about her gate. "The damn driveway's ten feet long."

"Tell me about it," Lucy says angrily. "I hate this goddamn place."

"Before you know it, someone's on your ass and inside your garage," Rudy says.

"Then I have to kill them."

"This isn't a joke."

"I'm not joking," Lucy says as the garage door slowly shuts behind them.

10.

| | | LUCY PARKS the Modena next to the black Ferrari, a twelve-cylinder Scaglietti that will never realize its power in a world that regulates speed. She won't look at the black Ferrari as she and Rudy climb out of the Modena. She looks away from the damaged hood, from the crude sketch of the huge eye with eyelashes that is etched into the beautiful glossy paint.

"Not that it's a pleasant subject," Rudy says, walking between the two Ferraris, toward the door that leads inside the mansion. "But is it possible she did it?" He indicates the scratched hood of the black Scaglietti, but Lucy won't look. "I'm still not sure she didn't, that she didn't stage the whole thing."

"She didn't do it," Lucy says, refusing to look at the damaged hood. "I had to wait on a list for more than a year to get that car."

"It can be fixed," Rudy says, and he digs his hands into his pockets as Lucy lets them in and deactivates an alarm system that has every detection device imaginable, including cameras inside the house and out. But the cameras don't record. Lucy decided she didn't want to record her private activities inside her house and on her property, and Rudy can understand up to a point. He wouldn't want hidden cameras recording him all over his house either, but these days there wouldn't be much to record in his life. He lives alone. When Lucy decided she didn't want her cameras to record what went on in and around her house, she wasn't living alone.

"Maybe we should change your cameras over to ones that record," Rudy says.

"I'm getting rid of this place," Lucy replies.

He follows her into the huge granite kitchen and looks around the magnificent dining and living area, and out at the panoramic view of the inlet and the ocean. The ceiling is twenty feet high and has been hand-painted with a Michelangelo-like fresco that is centered by a crystal chandelier. The glass dining room table looks carved out of ice and is the most incredible thing he has ever seen. He doesn't try to figure out what she paid for the table and the buttery soft leather furniture and the African wildlife art, the huge canvases of elephants, zebras, giraffes, and cheetahs. Rudy couldn't begin to afford a single light fixture in Lucy's part-time Florida house, not a single silk rug, probably not even some of the plants.

"I know," she says as he looks around. "I fly helicopters and can't even work the movie theater in this place. I hate this place."

"Don't ask for sympathy."

"Hey." She arrests the conversation with a tone he recognizes. She has had enough bickering.

He opens one of the freezers, in search of coffee, and says, "What you got to eat in this place?"

"Chili. Homemade. Frozen, but we can zap it."

"Sounds like a plan. Want to go to the gym later? Like maybe five-thirty or so?"

"Got to," she replies.

It is just now that they notice the back door leading out to the pool, the same door he, whoever he is, used to enter and leave her house not even a week ago. The door is locked but something is stuck to the outside glass, and Lucy is already walking quickly that way before he realizes what has happened. She stares at a sheet of un-lined white paper hanging by a single strip of tape.

"What is it?" Rudy asks, shutting the freezer and looking at her. "What the hell is it?"

"Another eye," Lucy says. "A drawing of another eye, the same eye. In pencil. And you thought Henri did it. She's not even within a thousand miles of here, and you thought she did it. Well, now you know." Lucy unlocks the door and opens it. "He wants me to know he's watching," she says angrily, and she steps outside to get a better look at the drawing of the eye.

"Don't touch!" Rudy yells at her.

"What do you think, I'm stupid?" she yells back at him.

11.

| | | "EXCUSE ME," says a young man who is suited up in purple scrubs, face shield and mask, and hair and shoe covers, and double pairs of latex gloves. He looks like a parody of an astronaut as he moves closer to Scarpetta. "What do you want us to do with her dentures?" he asks.

Scarpetta starts to explain that she doesn't work here, but words vanish before they leave her brain and she finds herself staring at the obese dead woman as two people, also suited up as if expecting a plague, tuck her inside a body pouch on a gurney sturdy enough to bear her enormous weight.

"She has dentures," the young man in purple scrubs says, this time to Fielding. "We put them in a carton and then forgot to put them inside the bag before we sewed her up."

"You don't want them inside the bag." Scarpetta decides to handle this amazing problem herself. "They need to go back inside her mouth. The funeral home, the family, will want them inside her mouth. She would probably appreciate being buried with her teeth."

"So we don't need to open her up and get the bag," says the soldier in purple. "Whew, that's good."

"Forget the bag," Scarpetta tells him. "You never want to put dentures in the bag," she says of the sturdy transparent plastic bag that is sewed up inside the obese dead woman's empty chest cavity, the bag that contains her sectioned organs, which were not returned to their original anatomical positions, because it isn't the forensic pathologist's job to put people back together again, nor is it possible, but it would be rather much like returning a stew to the condition of a cow. "Where are her dentures?" Scarpetta asks.

"Right over there." The young man in purple scrubs points to a countertop on the other side of the autopsy suite. "With her paperwork."

Fielding wants nothing to do with this lobotomized problem and completely ignores the man in purple, who looks too young to be a rotating medical student and likely is another soldier from Fort Lee. He might have a high school education and is spending time at the OCME because his military duty requires that he learn to handle the war dead. Scarpetta is inclined to say, but doesn't, that even soldiers blown up by grenades would like their dentures to go home with them, preferably inside their mouths, if they still have mouths.

"Come on," she says to the Fort Lee soldier in purple. "Let's go take a look."

She accompanies him across the tile floor, passing another gurney that was rolled out moments earlier, this one bearing a gunshot victim, a young black man with strong arms that are covered with tattoos and folded stiffly across his chest. He has goose bumps, a postmortem reaction of his erector pili muscles to rigor mortis that makes him look cold or frightened or both. The Fort Lee soldier picks up the plastic carton from the countertop and starts to hand it to Scarpetta, then notices that she isn't wearing gloves.

"I guess I'd better get dressed again," she says, passing on green Nitrile gloves, opting instead for a pair of old-fashioned latex ones that she whips out of a box on a nearby surgical cart. She works her hands into the gloves and takes the dentures out of the container.

She and the soldier walk back across the tile floor, toward the toothless dead woman.

"You know, next time you have a problem," Scarpetta says to the young soldier in purple, "you can just place the dentures with the personal effects and let the funeral home deal with them. Don't ever put them in the bag. This lady's awfully young for dentures."

"I think she was on drugs."

"Based on what?"

"Someone said so," the soldier in purple replies.

"I see," Scarpetta considers, leaning over the enormous sutured-up body on the gurney. "Vasoconstrictor drugs. Like cocaine. And out fall the teeth."

"I always wondered why drugs do that," says the soldier in purple. "You new here?" He looks at her.

"No, just the opposite," Scarpetta replies, working her fingers into the dead woman's mouth. "Very old around here. Just visiting."

He nods, confused. "Well, you look like you know what you're doing," he says awkwardly. "I sure am sorry about not putting her dentures back in. I feel real stupid. I hope nobody tells the chief." He shakes his head and blows out a loud breath. "That's all I need. He don't like me anyway."

Rigor mortis has come and gone, and the obese dead woman's jaw muscles do not resist Scarpetta's prying fingers, but the gums don't want the dentures for the simple reason that they don't fit.

"They aren't hers," Scarpetta says, placing the dentures back into the carton and returning it to the soldier in purple. "They're too big, much too big. Maybe a man's? Was there someone else just in here with dentures and maybe there's been a mix-up?"

The soldier is baffled yet happy with the news. This isn't his fault. "I don't know," he says. "Sure have been a lot of people in and out of here. So these aren't hers? Just a good thing I didn't try to cram them in her mouth."

Fielding has noticed what is going on and suddenly is there, staring down at the bright pink synthetic gums and white porcelain teeth inside the plastic carton that the soldier in purple is holding. "What the hell?" Fielding blurts out. "Who mixed this up? You put the wrong case number on this carton?"

He glares at the soldier in purple, who can't be more than twenty years old, his short light-blond hair peeking out from under the blue surgical cap, his wide brown eyes unnerved behind scratched safety glasses.

"I didn't label it, sir," he addresses Fielding, his superior officer. "I just know it was here when we started working on her. And she didn't have no teeth in her mouth, not when we started on her."

"Here? Where is here?"

"On her cart." The soldier indicates the cart bearing the surgical instruments for table four, also known as the Green Table. Dr. Marcus's morgue still uses the Scarpetta system of keeping track of instruments with strips of colored tape, ensuring that a pair of forceps or rib cutters, for example, don't end up elsewhere in the morgue. "This carton was on her cart, then somehow it got moved over there with her paperwork." He looks across the room to the countertop where the dead woman's paperwork is still neatly spread out.

"There was a view on this table earlier," Fielding says.

"That's right, sir. An old man who died in bed. So maybe the teeth are his?" says the soldier in purple. "So it was his teeth on the cart?"

Fielding looks like an angry blue jay flapping across the autopsy suite and yanking open the enormous stainless-steel door of the cooler.

He vanishes inside a rush of cold dead-smelling air and reemerges almost instantly with a pair of dentures that he apparently removed from the old man's mouth. Fielding holds them in the palm of a gloved hand stained with the blood of the tractor driver who ran over himself.

"Anybody can see these are too damn small for that guy's mouth," Fielding complains. "Who stuck these in that guy's mouth without checking that they fit?" he asks the noisy, crowded epoxy-sealed room with its four bloody wet steel tables, and x-rays of projectiles and bones on bright light boxes, and steel sinks and cabinets, and long countertops covered with paperwork, personal effects, and streamers of computer-generated labels for cartons and test tubes.

The other doctors, the students, soldiers, and today's dead have nothing at all to say to Dr. Jack Fielding, second in command to the chief. Scarpetta is shocked in a sick, disbelieving way. Her former flagship office is out of control and so is everybody in it. She glances at the dead tractor driver, half undressed on his red-clay-stained sheet, on top of a gurney, and she stares at the dentures in Fielding's bloodstained gloved hands.

"Scrub those things before you put them in her mouth," she can't help but say as Fielding hands the misplaced dentures to the soldier in purple. "You don't need another person's DNA, or other people's DNA, in her mouth," she tells the soldier. "Even if this isn't a suspicious death. So scrub her dentures, his dentures, everybody's dentures."

She snaps off her gloves and drops them in a bright orange biohazard trash bag. As she walks off, she wonders what has become of Marino, and she overhears the soldier in purple saying something, asking something, apparently wanting to know exactly who Scarpetta is and why she is visiting and what just happened.

"She used to be the chief here," Fielding says, failing to explain that the OCME wasn't run anything like this back then.

"Holy shit!" the soldier exclaims.

Scarpetta hits a large wall button with her elbow, and stainless-steel doors swing open wide. She walks into the dressing room, past cabinets of scrubs and gowns, then through the women's locker with its toilets and sinks and fluorescent lights that make mirrors un-kind. She pauses to wash her hands, noticing the neatly written sign, one she posted herself when she was here, that reminds people not to leave the morgue with the same shoes on that they wore in it. Don't track biological menaces onto the corridor carpet, she used to re-mind her staff, and she feels sure nobody cares about that or anything else anymore. She takes off her shoes and washes the bottoms of them with antibacterial soap and hot water and dries them off with paper towels before walking through another swinging door to the not-so-sterile grayish-blue-carpeted corridor.

Directly across from the women's locker room is the glass-enclosed chief medical examiner's suite. At least Dr. Marcus exerted the energy to redecorate. His secretary's office is an attractive col-lection of cherry-stained furniture and colonial prints, and her com-puter's screensaver shows several tropical fish swimming endlessly on a vivid blue screen. The secretary is out, and Scarpetta knocks on the chief's door.

"Yes," his voice faintly sounds from the other side.

She opens the door and walks into her former corner office, and avoids looking around but can't help taking in the tidiness of the bookcases and the top of Dr. Marcus's desk. His work space looks sterile. It is only the rest of the medical examiner's wing that is in chaos.

"Your timing is perfect," he says from his leather swivel chair be-hind the desk. "Please sit and I'll brief you on Gilly Paulsson before you take a look at her."

"Dr. Marcus, this isn't my office anymore," Scarpetta says. "I re-alize that. It's not my intention to intrude, but I'm concerned."

"Don't be." He looks at her with small, hard eyes. "You weren't brought here as some sort of accreditation team." He folds his hands on top of the ink blotter. "Your opinion is sought in one case and one case only, the Gilly Paulsson case. So I strongly encourage you not to overtax yourself with how different you might find things here. You have been gone a long time. What? Five years. And during most of that period of time, there was no chief, just an acting chief. Dr. Fielding, as a matter of fact, was the acting chief when I got here just a few months ago. So yes, of course, things are very different. You and I have very different management styles, which is one of the reasons the Commonwealth hired me."

"It's been my experience that if a chief never spends time in the morgue, there will be problems," she says, whether he wants to hear it or not. "If nothing else, the doctors sense a lack of interest in their work, and even doctors can get careless, lazy, or dangerously burned out and undone by the stress of what they see every day."

His eyes are flat and hard like tarnished copper, his mouth fixed in a thin line. Behind his balding head, the windows are as clean as air and she notices that he has replaced the bulletproof glass. The Coliseum is a brown mushroom in the distance, and a dreary drizzle has begun to fall.

"I can't turn a blind eye to what I see, not if you want my help," she says. "I don't care if it is one case and one case only, as you put it. Certainly you must know all things are used against us in court and elsewhere. Right now, it's the elsewhere that worries me."

"I'm afraid you're talking in riddles," Dr. Marcus replies, his thin face staring coldly at her. "Elsewhere? What is elsewhere?"

"Usually scandal. Usually a lawsuit. Or worst of all, a criminal case that is destroyed by technicalities, by evidence that is ruled inadmissible because of impropriety, because of flawed procedures, so there is no court. There is no trial."

"I was afraid this was going to happen," he says. "I told the commissioner what a bad idea this was."

"I don't blame you for telling him that. No one wants a former chief reappearing to straighten up . . ."

"I warned the commissioner that the last thing we needed was a disgruntled former employee of the Commonwealth dropping by to fix things," he says, picking up a pen and setting it down again, his hands nervous and angry.

"I don't blame you for feeling . . ."

"Especially crusaders," he says coldly. "They're the worst. Nothing worse than a crusader unless it is a wounded one."

"Now you're getting . . ."

"But here we are. So let's make the best of it, shall we?"

"I would appreciate your not interrupting me," Scarpetta says. "And if you're calling me a wounded crusader, then I'll choose to accept that as a compliment and we'll move along to the subject of dentures."

He stares at her as if she has gone mad.

"I just witnessed a mix-up in the morgue," she says. "The wrong dentures with the wrong decedent. Carelessness. And too much autonomy for young Fort Lee soldiers who have no medical training and in fact are here to learn from you. Suppose some family gets their loved one returned to the funeral home, and there's an open casket and the dentures are missing or don't fit, and you have the beginning of a disintegration that is hard to stop. The press loves stories like that, Dr. Marcus. You mix up those dentures in a homicide case, and you've just given the defense attorneys quite a gift, even if the dentures have absolutely nothing to do with anything."

"Whose dentures?" he asks, scowling. "Fielding is supposed to be supervising."

"Dr. Fielding has too much to do," she replies.

"So now we get to that. Your former assistant." Dr. Marcus rises from his chair. He does not tower over the desk, not that Scarpetta ever did because she isn't tall either, but he seems small as he erupts from behind the desk and moves past the table with a microscope shrouded in plastic. "It's already ten o'clock," he says, opening his office door. "Let's get you started on Gilly Paulsson. She's in the decomp fridge and it's best you work on her in that room. No one will bother you there. I suppose you've decided to re-autopsy."

"I'm not doing this without a witness," Scarpetta says.

12.

||| LUCY DOESN'T SLEEP in the third-floor master suite any-
more but locks herself into a much smaller bedroom downstairs. She
tells herself she has sound investigative reasons for not sleeping in
that bed, the one Henri was attacked in, that huge bed with the
hand-painted headboard in the center of a palatial suite that overlooks
the water. Evidence, she thinks. No matter how fastidious she and
Rudy are, it is always possible that evidence was missed.

Rudy has driven off in her Modena to gas it up, or at least this was
his excuse when he plucked the keys off the kitchen counter. He has
another agenda, Lucy suspects. He is cruising. He wants to see who
follows him, assuming anybody does, and probably nobody in his
right mind would follow someone as big and strong as Rudy, but the
beast who drew the eye, two eyes now, is out there. He is watching.
He watches the house. He might not realize Henri is gone, so he con-

tinues to watch the house and the Ferraris. He might be watching the house right now.

Lucy walks across tawny carpet, past the bed. It is still unmade, the soft, expensive covers pulled over the foot of the mattress and spilled onto the floor in a silk waterfall. Pillows are shoved to one side, exactly where they were when Lucy ran up the flights of stone steps and found Henri unconscious on the bed. At first Lucy thought she was dead. Then she didn't know what to think. She still doesn't know what to think. But at the time she was frightened enough to call 911, and what a mess that has caused. They had to deal with the local police, and the last thing Lucy ever wants is the police involved in her secret lives and activities, many of them illegal means to just ends, and of course, Rudy is still furious.

He accuses Lucy of panicking, and she did. She should never have called 911, and he's right. They could have handled the situation themselves and should have. Henri isn't Suzy-Q citizen, Rudy said. Henri is one of their agents. It didn't matter if she was out cold and naked. She was breathing, wasn't she? Her pulse and blood pressure weren't dangerously fast or low, were they? She wasn't bleeding, was she? Just a little bit of a bloody nose, right? It wasn't until Lucy flew Henri on a private jet to Aspen that Benton offered an explanation that unfortunately makes sense. Henri was attacked and may have been unconscious briefly, but after that she was faking.

"No way," Lucy argued with Benton when he told her that. "She was completely unresponsive."

"She's an actor," he said.

"Not anymore."

"Come on, Lucy. She was a professional actor half her life before she decided to change careers. Maybe becoming a cop was simply another acting role for her. It may be that she can't do anything but act."

"But why would she do something like that? I kept touching

her, talking to her, trying to make her wake up, why would she do it? Why?"

"Shame and rage, who knows why, exactly?" he said. "She may not remember what happened, may have repressed it, but she has feelings about it. Maybe she was ashamed because she didn't protect herself. Maybe she wants to punish you."

"Punish me for what? I didn't do anything. What? She's practically been murdered and it occurs to her, oh, I'll punish Lucy while I'm at it?"

"You'd be surprised what people do."

"No way," Lucy told Benton, and the more adamant she was, the more he probably knew he was right.

She walks across the bedroom to a wall of eight windows that are so high it isn't necessary to cover the top half of them with shades. The shades are drawn over the lower half of the windows, and she presses a button on the wall and the shades electronically retract with a soft whir. She stares out at the sunny day, scanning her property to see if anything is different. She and Rudy were in Miami until very early this morning. She hasn't been back to her home in three days, and the beast had plenty of time to wander and spy. He came back looking for Henri. He walked right across the patio to the back door and taped his drawing on it to remind Henri, to taunt her, and no one called the police. People are vile in this neighborhood, Lucy thinks. They don't care if you're beaten to death or burglarized as long as you don't do anything that might make life unpleasant for the rest of them.

She gazes at the lighthouse on the other side of the inlet and wonders whether she should dare go next door. The woman who lives next door never leaves her house. Lucy doesn't know her name, only that she is nosy and takes photographs through the glass whenever the yard man trims the hedges or cuts the grass in back by the pool. Lucy supposes the neighbor wants proof should Lucy allow anything done to the yard that might alter the nosy neighbor's view or somehow cause her emotional distress. Of course, had Lucy been allowed to top off her three-foot walls with another two feet of wrought iron, the beast might not have had such an easy time getting onto her patio and into her house and up to the bedroom where Henri was sick with the flu. But the nosy neighbor fought the variance and won, and Henri was almost murdered, and now Lucy finds a drawing of an eye that is like the eye scratched on the hood of her car.

Three stories down, the pool disappears over its edge, and beyond is the deep blue water of the Intracoastal Waterway, then a spit of beach and the dark blue-green ruffled water of the ocean. Maybe he came by boat, she thinks. He could tie up at her seawall and climb up the ladder and there he would be, right on her patio. Somehow she doesn't think he arrived by boat or even has a boat. She doesn't know why she thinks that. Lucy turns around and walks closer to the bed. To the left of it in the top drawer of a table is Henri's Colt .357 Magnum revolver, a lovely stainless-steel gun that Lucy bought for her because it is a piece of art with the sweetest action on earth. Henri knows how to use a gun, and she isn't a coward. Lucy believes without a doubt that had Henri heard the beast inside the house, flu or not, she would have shot him dead.

She pushes the button on the wall and closes the shades. She turns off the lights and walks out of the bedroom. Just off it is a small gym, then two master closets and a huge bathroom with a Jacuzzi built into agate the color of tiger's eye. There has been no reason at all to suspect that Henri's attacker entered the gym, closets, or bathroom, and each time Lucy has walked into them, she stands still to see what she feels. Each time, she feels nothing inside the gym and closets, but she feels something inside the bathroom. She looks at the tub and the windows behind it that open onto the water and the Florida sky, and she sees through his eyes. She doesn't know why, but when she looks at that huge, deep tub built into agate, she feels that he looked at it, too.

Then something occurs to her and she backs up to the archway that leads into the bathroom. Maybe when he came up the stone steps to the master floor, he turned left instead of right and ended up in the bathroom instead of the bedroom. That morning it was sunny, and light would have filled the windows. He could see. He might have hesitated and looked at the tub before turning around and heading silently into the bedroom, where Henri was clammy and miserable with a high fever, the blinds down and the room dark so she could sleep.

So you came into my bathroom, Lucy says to the beast. You stood right here on the marble floor and looked at my tub. Maybe you never saw a tub like that. Maybe you wanted to imagine a woman naked in it, relaxing, minding her own business before you murdered her. If that's your fantasy, she says to him, then you're not very original. She walks out of the bathroom and back down the steps to the second floor, where she sleeps and has her office.

Past the cozy movie theater is a large guest bedroom that she has converted into a library with built-in bookcases, the windows covered by black-out shades. Even on the sunniest day, this room is dark enough to develop film. She turns on a light, and hundreds of reference books and loose-leaf binders and a long table bearing laboratory equipment materialize. Against one wall is a desk that is centered by a Krimesite imager that looks like a stubby telescope mounted on a tripod stand. Next to it is a sealed plastic evidence bag, and inside is the drawing of the eye.

Lucy plucks examination gloves out of a box on the table. Her best hope for fingerprints is the Scotch tape, but she'll save that for testing later because it involves chemicals that will alter the paper and the tape. After brushing Magnadust over her entire back door and

the windows nearest it, she lifted not a single print with ridge detail, not one, just smudges. Had she found a print, chances are it
would be the yard man's, Rudy's, hers, or that of whoever washed the
glass last, so there isn't much point in feeling discouraged. Prints
outside a house don't mean much, anyway. What matters is what she
finds on the drawing. Gloves on, Lucy unsnaps the clasps of a hard
black briefcase lined with foam rubber and gently lifts out the
SKSUV30 Puissant lamp. She carries it to the desk and plugs it into
a surge protector power strip. Pressing the rocker switch, she turns
on the high-intensity short-wave ultraviolet light, and then turns on
the Krimesite imager.

Opening the plastic bag, she grips the sheet of white paper by a
corner and pulls it out. She turns it over, and the eye drawn in pencil stares at her as she holds it up to the overhead light. The white
paper lights up and there is no watermark, just millions of cheap
paper pulp fibers. The pencil-drawn eye dims as she lowers it, placing the sheet of paper in the center of the desk. When the beast
taped the drawing to her door, he attached the tape to the back of it
so the eye would be staring through the glass, into her house. She
puts on a pair of orange-tinted protective goggles and centers the
drawing under the imager's military-grade ocular lens, and peers
into the eyepiece, opening the UV aperture all the way while slowly
rotating the focus barrel and focus ring until the honeycomb viewing screen is visible. With her left hand, she directs the UV light at
her target, adjusting it to just the right angle, and begins moving
the sheet of paper, scanning for prints, hoping the scope will pick
them up so she doesn't have to resort to destructive chemicals such
as ninhydrin or cyanoacrylate. In the UV light, the paper is a ghostly
greenish-white beneath the lens.

With her fingertip, she moves the paper until the piece of Scotch
tape is in the field of view. Nothing, she thinks. Not even a smudge.
She could try rosaniline chloride or crystal violet, but now is not the

time for that. Maybe later. Sitting down at the desk, she stares at the drawing of the eye. That's all it is, just an eye, the pencil outline of an eye, iris and pupil, fringed in long lashes. A woman's eye, she thinks, drawn with what looks like a number-two pencil. Mounting a digital camera to a coupler, she takes photographs of magnified areas of the drawing, then makes photocopies.

She hears the garage door go up and turns off the UV lamp and the scope and places the drawing back inside the plastic bag. A video screen on the desk shows Rudy backing the Ferrari into the garage. Lucy tries to decide what to do about him as she shuts the library door and quickly skips down the stone steps. She imagines him walking out the door and never coming back and has no idea what would become of her and the secret empire she has created. First there would be the blow, then numbness, then pain, and then she would get over it. This is what she tells herself when she opens the door off the kitchen and he is there, holding up her car keys as if he is holding up a dead mouse by the tail.

"I guess we should go ahead and call the police," she says, taking the keys from him. "Since technically this is an emergency."

"I guess you didn't find prints or anything else important," Rudy says.

"Not with the scope. I'll do the chemicals if the police don't take the drawing. I'd rather they didn't take it. Actually, we won't let them take it. But we should call. See anybody while you were out?" She walks across the kitchen and picks up the phone. "Anybody besides all the women who ran off the road when they saw you coming?" She looks at the key pad and enters 9-1-1.

"No prints so far," Rudy says. "Well, it ain't over 'til it's over. What about indented writing?"

She shakes her head and says, "I want to report a prowler."

"Is the person on the property now, ma'am?" the operator asks in her calm, capable voice.

"Doesn't appear to be," Lucy said. "But I think this might be related to a B-and-E your department already knows about."

The operator verifies the address and asks the complainant's name because the name of the resident showing up on her video screen is whatever limited liability corporate name Lucy happened to have selected for this particular property. She can't remember what it is. She owns a number of properties and all of them are in different LLC names.

"My name's Tina Franks." Lucy uses the same alias she used last time she called the police, the morning Henri was attacked and Lucy panicked and made the mistake of dialing 911. She tells the operator her address, or more specifically, Tina Franks's address.

"Ma'am, I'm dispatching a unit to your home right now," the operator says.

"Good. You happen to know if CSI John Dalessio is on duty?" Lucy talks to the operator easily and with no fear. "He might want to know about this. He responded to my house the other time, so he's familiar." She picks out two apples from a bowl of fruit in the kitchen's center island.

Rudy rolls his eyes and indicates that he can get hold of CSI Dalessio a lot more quickly than the 911 operator can. Lucy smiles at the joke and shines an apple on her jeans and tosses it to him. She buffs the other apple and bites into it as if she's on the phone with a take-out restaurant or the dry cleaner or Home Depot and not the Broward County Sheriff's Department.

"Do you know which detective worked your breaking and entering, originally?" the 911 operator asks. "Normally, we don't contact the crime scene investigator, just the detective."

"All I know is I dealt with CSI Dalessio," Lucy replies. "I don't think a detective ever came to the house, just to the hospital, I guess. When my houseguest went to the hospital."

"He's marked off, ma'am, but I can get him a message," the 911

operator says, and she sounds a bit uncertain, and she should be uncertain since CSI John Dalessio is someone the operator has never
talked to or ever met or heard on the air. In Lucy's world, a CSI is a
Cyber Space Investigator who exists only in whatever computer Lucy
or those who work for her hacked into, which in this case is the
Broward County Sheriff's Department computer.

"I've got his card. I'll call him. Thanks for your help," Lucy says,
disconnecting the line.

She and Rudy stand in the kitchen, eating their apples, looking
at each other.

"Kind of a funny thing when you think about it," she says, hoping Rudy will start seeing the situation with the local cops as funny.
"We call the police as a formality. Or worse, because it entertains us."

He shrugs his muscular shoulders, crunching into the apple and
wiping juice off his mouth with the back of a hand. "Always good
to include the local cops. In a limited way, of course. You never know
when we might need them for something." Now he's turning the
local cops into a game, his favorite game. "You asked for Dalessio, so
it's on record. Not our fault he's hard to track down. They'll spend
the rest of their careers trying to figure out who the hell Dalessio is
and did he quit or get fired or what? Did anyone ever meet him?
He'll become a legend, give them something to talk about."

"Him and Tina Franks," Lucy says, chewing a piece of apple.

"Fact is," he replies, "you'd have a hell of a lot harder time proving you're Lucy Farinelli than Tina Franks or whoever else you decide to be on any given day. We've got birth certificates and all the
other paper shit for our fake IDs. Hell, I can't tell you where my real
birth certificate is."

"I'm not sure I know who I am anymore," she says, handing him
a paper towel.

"Me, either." He takes another big bite out of the apple.

"I'm not sure I know who you are, now that you mention it. So you'll answer the door when the cop shows up and have him call CSI Dalessio to pick up the drawing."

"That's the plan." Rudy smiles. "Worked like a charm last time."

Lucy and Rudy keep jump-out bags and crime scene kits at strategic locations, such as residences and vehicles, and it is amazing what they manage to get away with by virtue of ankle-high black leather boots, black polo shirts, black cargo pants, dark windbreakers with FORENSICS on the back in bold yellow letters, the usual camera and other basic equipment, and most important of all, body language and attitude. The simple plan is usually the best one, and after Lucy found Henri and panicked and called 911 for an ambulance, she called Rudy. He changed his clothes and simply walked in her front door after the police had been there a few minutes, and he said he was new with the crime scene unit and the officers didn't have to hang around while he processed the house, and that was fine with them, because to hang around with the crime scene technicians amounts to babysitting in the eyes of cops.

Lucy, or Tina Franks, as she identified herself on that terrible day, offered her own lies to the police that morning. Henri, also given a false name, was a guest visiting from out of town, and while Lucy was in the shower, Henri, who was sleeping off a hangover, heard the intruder and fainted, and because she tends to get hysterical and hyperventilate and may very well have been attacked, Lucy called for an ambulance. No, Lucy never saw the intruder. No, nothing was taken as far as Lucy could tell. No, she doesn't think Henri was sexually assaulted but she ought to be checked at the hospital because that's what people do, right? That's what they do on all those cops shows on television, right?

"Wonder how long it will take them to figure out that CSI Dalessio never seems to show up anywhere except your house," Rudy says, amused. "Damn good thing their department's taken over most of Broward. It's as huge as Texas and they don't know who the hell is coming or going."

Lucy looks at her watch, timing the marked unit that should be headed this way now. "Well, what matters is we included Mr. Dalessio so he doesn't get his feelings hurt."

Rudy laughs, his mood much improved. He can't stay irritable for long when the two of them swing into motion. "Okay. The po-lice will be here any minute. Maybe you should scram. I won't give the uniform guy the drawing. I'll give him Dalessio's number, tell him I'd be more comfortable talking to the CSI since I met him last week when you called about the B-and-E. So he'll get Dalessio's voice mail, and after he leaves, yours truly, the legendary Dalessio, will call him back and tell him I'll take care of things."

"Don't let the cops in my office."

"The door's locked, right?"

"Yes," she says. "If you're worried about your Dalessio cover being blown, call me. I'll come right back and deal with the cops myself."

"Going somewhere?" Rudy asks.

"I think it's time I introduce myself to my neighbor," Lucy says.

13.

| | | THE DECOMPOSED ROOM is a small mortuary with a walk-in cooler and double sinks and cabinets, all in stainless steel, and a special ventilation system that sucks noxious odors and microorganisms out through an exhaust fan. Every inch of walls and floor is painted with nonslip gray acrylic that is nonabsorbent and can withstand scrubbing and bleach.

The centerpiece of this special room is a single transportable autopsy table, which is nothing more than a cart frame with casters equipped with swivel wheels that have brakes, and a body tray that rolls on bearings, all of which is supposed to eliminate the need for human beings to lift bodies in the modern world, but in reality doesn't. People in the morgue still struggle with dead weight and always will. The table is sloped so it can drain when it is attached to the sink, but that won't be necessary this morning. There is nothing left to drain. Gilly Paulsson's body fluids were collected or washed down the drain two weeks ago when Fielding autopsied her the first time.

This morning, the autopsy table is parked in the middle of the acrylic painted floor, and Gilly Paulsson's body is inside a black pouch that looks like a cocoon on top of the shiny steel table. There are no windows in this room, none that open onto the outside, only a row of observation windows that were installed too high for anyone to see through them, a design flaw that Scarpetta didn't complain about when she moved into the building eight years ago because no one needs to observe what goes on in this room, where the dead are bloated and green and covered with maggots or burned so badly they look like charred wood.

She has just walked in, having spent a few minutes in the women's locker room to suit up in the appropriate biohazard gear. "I'm sorry to interrupt your other case," she says to Fielding, and in her mind she sees Mr. Whitby in olive-green pants and his black jacket. "But I believe your boss really thought I was going to do this without you."

"How much did he brief you?" he asks from behind his face mask.

"Actually, he didn't," she says, working her hands into a pair of gloves. "I know nothing more than what he told me yesterday when he called me in Florida."

Fielding frowns and he has started to sweat. "I thought you were just in his office."

It occurs to her that this room might be bugged. Then she remembers when she was chief and tried out a variety of dictating equipment in the autopsy suite, all to no avail because there is too much background noise in the morgue and it tends to foil even the best transmitters and recorders. With that in mind, she moves to the sink and turns on the water, and it drums loudly and hollowly against steel.

"What's that for?" Fielding asks, unzipping the pouch.

"I thought you might like a little water music while we work."

He looks up at her. "It's safe to talk in here, I'm pretty sure. He's not that smart. Besides, I don't think he's ever been in the decomp room. He probably doesn't know where it is."

"It's easy to underestimate people you don't like," she says, helping him open the flaps of the pouch.

Two weeks of refrigeration have retarded decomposition, but the body is desiccating, or drying out, and on its way to being mummified. The stench is strong but Scarpetta doesn't take it personally. A bad smell is just another way the body speaks, no offense intended, and Gilly Paulsson can't help herself, not the way she looks or stinks or the fact that she is dead. She is pale and vaguely green and bloodless, her face emaciated from dehydration, her eyes open to slits, the sclera beneath the lids dried almost black. Her lips are dried brown and barely parted, her long blond hair tangled around her ears and under her chin. Scarpetta notes no external injuries to the neck, including any that might have been introduced at autopsy, such as the deadly sin of a buttonhole, which should never happen but does when someone inexperienced or careless is reflecting back tissue inside the neck to remove the tongue and larynx and accidentally pokes through the surface of the skin. An autopsy-induced cut to the neck is not easily explained to distraught families.

The Y incision begins at the ends of the clavicle and meets at the sternum, and travels down, taking a small detour around the navel and terminating at the pubis. It is sutured with twine that Fielding begins to cut with a scalpel, as though he is opening the seams of a hand-stitched rag doll, while Scarpetta picks up a file folder from a countertop and glances through Gilly's autopsy protocol and the initial report of investigation. She was five-foot-three and weighed a hundred and four pounds and would have turned fifteen in February had she lived. Her eyes were blue. Repeatedly on Fielding's autopsy report are the words "within normal limits." Her brain, her heart, her liver, and her lungs, all of her organs were just what they should have been for a healthy young girl.

But Fielding did find marks that should now be even more apparent because the blood is drained from her body and any blood trapped in tissue due to bruising is vivid against her very pale skin. On a body diagram, he has drawn contusions on the tops of her hands. Scarpetta places the file back on the counter while Fielding lifts out the heavy plastic bag of sectioned organs from the chest cavity. She gets close to look at her and lifts out one of her small hands. It is shriveled and pale, cold and damp, and Scarpetta holds it in her gloved hands and turns it over, looking at the bruise. The hand and arm are limp. Rigor mortis has come and gone, the body no longer stubborn, as if life is too far gone to resist death anymore. The bruise is deep red against the pallor of her ghostly white skin and is precisely on the top of her slender, shrunken hand, the redness spreading from the knuckle of her thumb to the knuckle of her little finger. A similar bruise is also on her other hand, her left hand.

"Oh yeah," Fielding says. "Weird, right? Like someone held her, maybe. But to do what?" He untwists a tie around the top of the bag, opening it, and the stench from the tan mush inside is horrific. "Shewww. Don't know what you're going to accomplish by going through this. But be my guest."

"Just leave it on the table and I'll pick through it in the bag. Somebody may have restrained her. How was she found? Describe the position of her body when she was found," Scarpetta says, walking over to the sink and finding a pair of thick rubber gloves that will reach almost to her elbows.

"Not sure. When Mom got home she tried to revive her. She says she can't remember whether Gilly was facedown, on her back, on her side, whatever, and she hasn't a clue about her hands."

"What about livor?"

"Not a chance. She wasn't dead long enough."

When the blood is no longer circulating, it settles according to gravity and creates a pattern of deep pinkness and blanching where the surfaces of the body touch whatever is pressing against them. As much as one always hopes to get to the dead in a hurry, there are advantages with delays. A few hours will do, and livor mortis and rigor mortis set in and reveal the position the body was in when it died, even if the living come along later and move things around or change their stories.

Scarpetta gently pulls open Gilly's bottom lip, checking for any injuries that might have been caused by someone pressing a hand over her mouth to silence her or by pushing her face into the bed to smother her.

"Help yourself, but I looked," Fielding says. "No other injuries that I could find."

"And her tongue?"

"She didn't bite herself. Nothing like that. I hate to tell you where her tongue is."

"I think I can guess," she says, dipping her hands inside the bag of frigid, soupy organ sections and feeling her way through them.

Fielding is rinsing his gloved hands in the vigorous stream of water thundering into the metal sink. He dries them with a towel. "I notice Marino didn't come along for the ride."

"I don't know where he is," she says, not particularly happy about it.

"He never was much for decomposed bodies."

"I would worry about anybody who likes them."

"And kids. Anybody who likes dead kids," Fielding adds, leaning against the edge of the counter, watching her. "I hope you find something, because I can't. Frustrates the hell out of me."

"What about petechial hemorrhages? Her eyes are in grim shape, too grim for me to tell anything at this point."

"She was pretty congested when she came in," Fielding replies. "Hard to tell if she had petechial hemorrhages, but I didn't notice any."

Scarpetta envisions Gilly's body when it first arrived at the morgue, when she had been dead only hours, her face congested red, her eyes red. "Pulmonary edema?" she asks.

"Some."

Scarpetta has found the tongue. She walks over to the sinks and rinses it, patting it dry with a small white terry-cloth towel from an especially cheap batch purchased by the state. Rolling a surgical lamp close, she turns it on and bends it near the tongue. "You got a lens?" she asks, patting the tongue again with the towel and adjusting the light.

"Coming up." He opens a drawer, finds a magnifying glass, and gives it to her. "See anything? I didn't."

"Does she have any history of seizures?"

"Not according to what I've been told."

"Well, I don't see any injury." She is looking for evidence that Gilly might have bitten her tongue. "And you swabbed her tongue, the inside of her mouth?"

"Oh yeah. I swabbed her everything," Fielding says, returning to the counter and leaning against it again. "I didn't find anything obvious. Preliminarily, the labs haven't found anything to indicate sexual assault. I don't know about whatever else they've found, if anything yet."

"It says in your CME-1 that her body was clothed in pajamas when it came in. The top was inside out."

"That sounds right." He picks up the file and starts flipping through it.

"You photographed the hell out of everything." She doesn't ask, simply verifies what should be accepted as routine.

"Hey," he says, laughing. "Who taught my sorry ass?"

She gives him a quick look. She taught him better than this, but she doesn't say it. "I'm happy to report you didn't miss anything on the tongue." She drops it back into the bag, where it rests on top of the other tan pieces and parts of Gilly Paulsson's rotting organs. "Let's turn her over. We're going to have to take her out of the pouch."

They do this in stages. Fielding grips the body under the arms and lifts while Scarpetta pulls the pouch out from under it, and then he rolls the body over on its face as she works the pouch out of the way, its heavy vinyl complaining in heavy rumbles as she folds it up and sets it back on the gurney. She and Fielding see the bruise on Gilly's back at the same time.

"I'll be damned," he says, unnerved.

It is a faint blush, somewhat round, and about the size of a silver dollar on the left side of the back, just below the scapula.

"I swear that wasn't here when I posted her," he says, leaning close, adjusting the surgical light to get a better look. "Shit. I can't believe I missed it."

"You know how it is," Scarpetta replies, and she doesn't tell him what she thinks. There is no point in criticizing him. It's too late for that. "Contusions always show up better after the body's been autopsied," she says.

She plucks a scalpel off the surgical cart and makes deep linear incisions in the reddish area, checking to see if the discoloration might be a postmortem artifact, and therefore superficial, but it's not. Blood in the underlying soft tissue is diffuse, usually meaning some trauma broke blood vessels while the body still had a blood pressure, and that's all a bruise or contusion is, just lots of little blood vessels that get smashed and leak. Fielding places a six-inch plastic rule next to the incised area of reddish flesh and starts taking photographs.

"What about her bed linens?" Scarpetta asks. "You checked them?"

"Never seen them. The cops took them, handed them over to the labs. Like I said, no seminal fluid. Damn, I can't believe I missed this bruise."

"Let's ask if they see any pulmonary edema fluid on the sheets, the pillow, and if so, have the stain scraped for ciliated respiratory epithelium. You find that, it supports a death by asphyxia."

"Shit," he says. "I don't know how I missed that bruise. Then you're thinking this is a homicide, for sure."

"I'm thinking someone got on top of her," Scarpetta says. "She's facedown and the person has a knee in her upper back, leaning on her with all his weight and holding her hands up and out above her head, palms down on the bed. That would explain the bruises on the tops of her hands and on her back. I'm thinking she's a mechanical asphyxia, a homicide, absolutely. Someone sits on your chest or back, and you can't breathe. It's a horrible way to die."

14.

||| THE LADY NEXT DOOR lives in a flat-roofed house of curved white concrete and glass that interacts with nature and reflects the water, earth, and sky, and reminds Lucy of buildings she has seen in Finland. At night her neighbor's house looks like an immense lantern lit up.

There is a fountain in the front courtyard, where tall palms and cacti have been wound with strands of colorful lights for the holidays. An inflated green Grinch scowls near the soaring double glass doors, a festive touch that Lucy would find comical if someone else lived inside. In the upper left side of the door frame is a camera that is supposed to be invisible, and as she presses the doorbell she imagines her image filling a closed-circuit video screen. No response, and she presses the button again. Still there is no answer.

Okay. I know you're home because you picked up your newspaper and the flag is up on your mailbox, she thinks. I know you're watching me, probably sitting right there in the kitchen staring at me on your video screen, got the Aiphone up to your ear to see if I'm breathing or talking to myself, and it just so happens I'm doing both, idiot. Answer your damn door or I'll stand out here all day.

This goes on for maybe five minutes. Lucy waits in front of the heavy glass doors, imagining what the lady is seeing on the video screen and deciding she can't look threatening in jeans, t-shirt, fanny pack, and running shoes. But she has to be annoying as she keeps pressing the bell. Maybe the lady is in the shower. Maybe she isn't looking at the video monitor at all. Lucy rings once more. She's not going to come to the door. I knew you wouldn't, idiot, Lucy silently says to the lady. I could be standing out here having a heart attack on camera and you couldn't be bothered. I guess I'm going to have to make you come to the door. She envisions Rudy pulling out his fake ID to scare the hell out of the Hispanic not even two hours earlier, and she decides, All right then, let's try this and see what you do now. Slipping a thin black wallet out of the back pocket of her tight-fitting jeans, she flashes a badge up close to the not-so-secret camera.

"Hello," she says out loud. "Police. Don't be alarmed, I live next door, but I'm a cop. Please come to the door." She rings the bell again and continues holding up her fake credentials directly in front of the pinhole camera.

Lucy blinks in the sunlight, sweating. She waits and listens but doesn't hear a sound. Just when she is about to flash her fake badge again, suddenly there is a voice, as if God is a bitchy woman.

"What do you want?" asks the voice through an invisible speaker near the so-called invisible camera on the upper door frame.

"I've had a trespasser, ma'am," Lucy replies. "I think you might want to know what's happened next door at my house."

"You said you're the police," the unfriendly voice accuses, and the accent is deeply southern.

"I'm both."

"Both what?"

"Both the police and your neighbor, ma'am. My name's Tina. I wish you'd come to the door."

Silence, then in less than ten seconds, Lucy sees a figure floating toward the glass doors from the inside, and that figure becomes a woman in her forties dressed in a tennis warm-up suit and jogging shoes. It seems to take her forever to get all the locks undone, but the neighbor does and deactivates the alarm and opens one of the glass doors. At first, she doesn't seem to have any intention of inviting Lucy in, but stands in the doorway, staring at her without a trace of warmth.

"Make this quick," says the lady. "I don't like strangers and have no interest in knowing my neighbors. I'm here because I don't want neighbors. In case you haven't figured it out, this isn't a neighborhood, anyhow. It's where people come to be private and left alone."

"What isn't?" Lucy warms up to her task. She recognizes the tribe of the self-consumed, curdled rich and plays a little naive. "Your house isn't or the neighborhood isn't?"

"Isn't what?" The woman's hostility is briefly supplanted by bewilderment. "What are you talking about?"

"What's happened next door at my house. He was back," Lucy replies, as if the woman knows exactly what she means. "Could have been early this morning, but I'm not sure because I was out of town most of yesterday and last night and just landed in Boca on the helicopter. I'm sure I know who he's after but I'm worried about you. It certainly wouldn't be fair if you got caught in the wake, if you know what I mean."

"Oh," she says, and she has a very nice boat docked off the seawall behind her house and knows exactly what wake is and how unfortunate and possibly destructive it is to be caught in it. "How can you be police and live in a house like that?" she asks without looking in the direction of Lucy's salmon-colored Mediterranean mansion. "What helicopter? Don't tell me you have a helicopter too."

"Lord, you're getting warm," Lucy says with a resigned sigh. "It's a long story. It's all connected to Hollywood, you know. I just moved here from L.A., you know. I should have stayed in Beverly Hills where I belong, but this damn movie, excuse my French. Well, I'm sure you've heard all about what happens when you make a movie deal, and all that goes into it when they plan on filming on location."

"Next door?" Her eyes open wide. "They're filming a movie next door at your house?"

"I really don't think it's a good idea for us to have this conversation out here." Lucy looks around cautiously. "Do you mind if I come in? But you've got to promise this is all between us chickens. If word got out . . . well, you can imagine."

"Ha!" The woman points a finger at Lucy and gives her a toothy smile. "I knew you were a celebrity."

"No! Please don't tell me I'm that transparent!" Lucy says with horror as she walks into a minimally furnished living room, all in white, with a two-story-high glass wall that overlooks the granite-paved patio, the pool, and the twenty-seven-foot speedboat that she seriously doubts her spoiled, vain neighbor knows how to start, much less sail. The name of the boat is *It's Settled*, the port of call supposedly Grand Cayman, a Caribbean island that has no income tax.

"That's quite a boat," Lucy says as they sit on white furniture that seems suspended between the water and sky. She sets a cell phone on the glass coffee table.

"It's Italian." The woman smiles a secretive, not-so-nice smile.

"Reminds me of Cannes," Lucy says.

"Oh yes! The film festival."

"No, not that so much. The Ville de Cannes, the boats, oh the yachts. Just past the old clubhouse you turn on Quai Number One, very near the Poseidon and Amphitrite boat rentals out of Marseilles.

Nice fellow who works there, Paul, drives this bright yellow old Pontiac, a strange sight to see in the South of France. You just keep walking past the storage units, turn on Quai Number Four, and go to the end toward the lighthouse. I've never seen so many Mangustas and Leopards in my life. I once had a Zodiac with a pretty muscular Suzuki engine, but a big boat? Who has the time? Well, maybe you do." She gazes at the dry-docked speedboat. "Of course, the sheriff's department and Customs will nail you good if you go more than ten miles an hour in that thing through here."

The lady is clueless. She is pretty but not in a way that Lucy finds appealing. She looks very rich and pampered and addicted to Botox, collagen, thermal treatments, whatever new magic is offered by the dermatologist. It may have been years since she was able to frown. But then, she doesn't need negative facial gestures. For her face to look angry and mean would be redundant.

"As I said, I'm Tina. And you are . . . ?"

"You can call me Kate. That's what my friends call me," the spoiled rich lady replies. "I've been in this house for seven years and never once has there been a problem, except with Jeff, who I am happy to report is off living his life in the Cayman Islands, among other places. I guess what you're telling me is you're not really a police officer."

"I really apologize if I slightly misled you, but I didn't know what else to do to get you to come to the door, Kate."

"I saw a badge."

"Yes, I held it up so you would. It's not real—not really. But when I'm in training for a part, I live it as much as I can, and my director suggested that I not only move into the house where we're shooting, but go ahead and carry a badge and drive the same cars the special agent does, and all the rest."

"I knew it!" Kate shoots that finger at her again. "The sports cars.

Ah! It's all part of your role, isn't it?" She settles her long-legged thin body back into the depths of her big white chair and plumps a pillow in her lap. "You don't look familiar, though."

"I try not to."

Kate attempts a frown. "But I would think you would look at least a little familiar. And I can't think who you are, anyway. Tina who?"

"Mangusta." She offers the name of her favorite boat, fairly certain the neighbor won't directly connect Mangusta with earlier comments about Cannes, but rather will think that Mangusta sounds familiar, somewhat familiar.

"Actually, yes, I have heard the name. It seems. Maybe," Kate says, encouraged.

"I haven't been in much, not big roles although some of the films have been big. This is my break, you might say. I started out on off-off-Broadway and then made the jump to off-off-movies, whatever I could get. And I just hope it won't drive you crazy when all the trucks and everything roll in, but fortunately that's not until summer, and it may not happen at all because of this crazy person who seems to have followed us here."

"What a pity." She leans forward in the big white chair.

"Tell me about it."

"Oh dear." Kate's eyes darken and she looks worried. "From the West Coast? That's where he followed y'all from? You said you have a helicopter?"

"I'm pretty sure," Lucy answers. "If you've never been stalked, you can't really understand what a nightmare it is. I would never wish it on anyone. I thought coming here would be the best thing we ever did. But somehow he found us and followed us. I'm sure it's him, pretty sure. God help me if we now have two stalkers, so I hope it's him, oddly. And yes, I travel in helicopters when needed, but not all the way from the West Coast."

"At least you don't live alone," Kate comments.

"My roommate, another actress, just moved out and went back west. Because of the stalker."

"What about that good-looking boyfriend of yours? Actually, I wondered early on if he might be an actor, someone famous. I've been trying to figure out who he is." She smiles wickedly. "Hollywood is written all over that one. What's he been in?"

"Trouble mostly."

"Well, if he does you wrong, darling, you just come see Kate, here." She pats the pillow in her lap. "I know what to do about some things."

Lucy looks out at *It's Settled* shining long, sleek, and white in the sun. She wonders if Kate's ex-husband is boatless and hiding from the IRS in the Cayman Islands. She says, "Last week the wacko came on my property, or at least I assume it was him. I'm just wondering . . ."

Kate's unlined tight face registers a blank. "Oh," she then says. "The one stalking y'all? Why no, I didn't see him, not that I'm aware of, but then there are a lot of people roaming about, all these yard men, pool people, construction workers, and so on. But I did notice all the police cars and the ambulance. It scared me to death. That's just the sort of thing that ruins an area."

"You were home then. My roommate, former roommate, was in bed with a hangover. She may have gone out to sit in the sun."

"Yes. I saw her do that."

"You did?"

"Oh yes," Kate replies. "I was upstairs in the gym and just happened to look down and I saw her come out the kitchen door. I do remember she had on pajamas and a robe. And now that you tell me she had a hangover, that explains it."

"Do you remember what time?" Lucy asks as her cell phone on the coffee table continues to record their conversation.

"Let me see. Nine? Or close enough." Kate points behind her, toward Lucy's house. "She sat by the pool."

"And then what?"

"I was on the elliptical machine," she says, and in Kate's way of thinking everything is about Kate. "Let me see, I believe I was distracted by something on one of the morning shows. No, I was on the phone. I do remember looking out and she was gone, apparently had gone back into the house. She wasn't out there long, my point is."

"How long were you on the elliptical machine, and do you mind showing me your gym so I can see exactly where you were when you saw her?"

"Sure, come right on, darling." Kate gets up from her big white chair. "How about something to drink? I believe I could use a little mimosa right about now, with all this talk about stalkers and big noisy movie trucks rolling in and helicopters and all. I usually do the elliptical machine for thirty minutes."

Lucy picks up her cell phone from the coffee table. "I'll have whatever you're having," she says.

15.

||| THE HOUR is half past eleven when Scarpetta meets Marino by the rental car in the parking lot of her former building. Dark clouds remind her of angry fists flailing across the sky, and the sun ducks in and out of them and sudden gusts of wind snatch at her clothing and hair.

"Is Fielding coming with us?" Marino asks, unlocking the SUV. "I'm assuming you want me to drive. Some son of a bitch held her down and smothered her. Goddamn son of a bitch. Killing a kid like that. Had to be somebody pretty big, don't you think, to hold her down and she can't move?"

"Fielding's not coming. You can drive. When you can't breathe, you panic and struggle like hell. So her assailant didn't have to be huge, but he did have to be big and strong enough to keep her down, to pin her down. More than likely, she's a mechanical asphyxiation, not a smothering."

"And that's what ought to be done to his ass when he gets caught. Let a couple uh huge prison guards pin him down and sit on his chest so he can't breathe, see how he likes it." They climb in and Marino starts the engine. "I'll volunteer. Let me do it. Jesus, doing that to a kid."

"Let's save the 'Kill 'em all, let God sort 'em out' part for later," she says. "We have a lot to handle. What do you know about Mama?"

"Since Fielding's not coming, I assume you called her."

"I told her I want to talk to her and that was about the extent of it. She was a little strange on the phone. She thinks Gilly died of the flu."

"You going to tell her?"

"I don't know what I'm going to tell her."

"Well, one thing's for sure. The Feds will be thrilled when they hear you're making house calls again, Doc. Nothing thrills them more when they get their hooks in a case that ain't any of their business and then you show up making your damn house calls." He smiles as he drives slowly through the crowded lot.

Scarpetta doesn't care what the Feds think, and she looks out at her former building called Biotech II, at its clean gray shape trimmed with deep red brick, at the covered morgue bay that reminds her of a white igloo sticking out to one side. Now that she's back, she may as well have been here all along. It doesn't feel strange that she is headed to a death scene, most likely a crime scene, in Richmond, Virginia, and she doesn't care what the FBI or Dr. Marcus or anyone else thinks about her house calls.

"Got a feeling your pal Dr. Marcus will be thrilled too," Marino adds sarcastically, as if he is following her thoughts. "Did you tell him Gilly's a homicide?"

"No," she replies.

She didn't bother looking for Dr. Marcus or telling him anything after she finished with Gilly Paulsson and cleaned up and changed back into her suit and looked at some microscopic slides. Fielding could give Dr. Marcus the facts and pass on that she would be happy to brief him later and can be reached on her cell phone, if necessary, but Dr. Marcus won't call. He wants as little to do with the Gilly Paulsson case as possible, and Scarpetta now believes he decided long before he contacted her in Florida that he wasn't going to benefit from this fourteen-year-old girl's death, that nothing but trouble was headed his way if he didn't do something to deflect it, and what better deflection than calling in his controversial predecessor, Scarpetta the lightning rod? He's probably suspected all along that Gilly Paulsson was murdered and for some reason decided not to dirty his hands with the case.

"Who's the detective?" Scarpetta asks Marino as they wait for traffic rolling off I-95 to pass on 4th Street. "Anyone we know?"

"Nope. He wasn't here when we was." He finds an opening and guns the engine, rocketing them into the right lane. Now that Marino's back in Richmond, he's driving the way he used to drive in Richmond, which is the way he used to drive when he started out as a cop in New York.

"Know anything about him?"

"Enough."

"I suppose you're going to wear that cap all day," she says.

"Why not? You got a better cap for me to wear? Besides, Lucy will feel good knowing I'm wearing her cap. Did you know police headquarters moved? It ain't on Ninth Street anymore, is down there near the Jefferson Hotel in the old Farm Bureau Building. Aside from that, the police department hasn't changed except for the paint job on the marked units and they let them wear baseball caps too, like they're NYPD."

"I guess baseball caps are here to stay."

"Huh. So don't be griping about mine anymore."

"Who told you the FBI's gotten involved?"

"The detective. His name's Browning, seems all right but he's not been doing homicides long and the cases he has worked are of the urban renewal variety. One piece of shit shooting another piece of shit." Marino flips open a notepad and glances at it as he drives through town toward Broad Street. "Thursday, December fourth, he gets a call for a DOA and responds to the address where we're now heading in the Fan, over there near where Stuart Circle Hospital used to be before they turned it into high-dollar condos. Or did you know that? It happened after you left. Would you want to live in a former hospital room? No thank you."

"Do you know why the FBI is involved, or do I have to wait for that part?" she asks.

"Richmond invited them. That's just one of many pieces that doesn't make sense. I got no idea why Richmond P.D. invited the Feds to stick their noses in or why the Feds want to."

"What does Browning think?"

"He's not particularly revved up about the case, thinks the girl probably had a seizure or something."

"He thinks wrong. What about the mother?"

"She's a little different. I'll get to that."

"And the father?"

"Divorced, lives in Charleston, South Carolina, a doctor. An irony, ain't it? A doctor would know damn well what a morgue is like, and here's his little girl inside a body bag in the morgue for two damn weeks because they can't decide on who's making the arrangements or where she's going to be buried and God knows what else they're fighting about."

"What I'd do pretty soon is take a right on Grace," Scarpetta says. "And we'll just follow it straight there."

"Thank you, Magellan. All those years I drove in the city. How'd I do it without you navigating?"

"I don't know how you function at all when I'm not around. Tell me more about Browning. What did he find when he got to the Paulsson house?"

"The girl was in bed, on her back, pajamas on. Mother was hysterical, as you might imagine."

"Was she under the covers?"

"The covers were thrown back, in fact they were mostly on the floor, and the mother told Browning they were like that when she got home from the drugstore. But she's having memory problems, as you probably know. I think she's lying."

"About what?"

"Not sure. I'm basing everything on what Browning told me over the phone, meaning as soon as I talk to her, I start all over again."

"What about evidence someone might have broken into the house?" Scarpetta asks. "Anything to make us think that?"

"Nothing to make Browning think that, apparently. Like I said, he's not revved up about it. Never a good thing. If the detective's not revved up about it, then the crime scene techs probably aren't revved up either. If you don't think anyone broke in, where the hell do you start dusting for prints, for example?"

"Don't tell me they didn't even do that."

"Like I said, when I get there, I start all over again."

They are now in an area called the Fan District, which was annexed by the city soon after the Civil War and was eventually dubbed the Fan because it is shaped like one. Narrow streets wind and wend and dead-end without cause and have fruity names like Strawberry, Cherry, and Plum. Most homes and row houses have been restored to an earlier charmed state of generous verandas and classical columns and fancy ironwork. The Paulsson home is less eccentric and ornate than most, a modest-sized dwelling with simple lines, a flat brick facade, a full front porch, and a false mansard slate roof that reminds Scarpetta of a pillbox hat.

Marino pulls in front near a dark blue minivan and they get out. They follow a brick walkway that is old and worn smooth and slick in spots. The late morning is overcast and cold, and Scarpetta would not be surprised to see a little snow, but she hopes there will be no freezing rain. The city has never adapted to adverse winter weather, and at the mere mention of snow, Richmonders raid every grocery store and market in town. Power lines are above ground and don't last long when grand old trees get uprooted or snapped off by blasting winds and heavy sleeves of ice, so Scarpetta sincerely hopes there will be no freezing rain while she's in town.

The brass knocker on the black front door is shaped like a pineapple, and Marino raps three times. The loud, sharp clank of it is startling and seems insensitive because of the reason for this visit. Footsteps sound, moving quickly, and the door swings open wide. The woman on the other side is small and thin, and her face is puffy, as if she doesn't eat enough but drinks plenty and has been crying a lot. On a better day, she might be pretty in a rough, dyed-blond way.

"Come in," she says, her nose stopped up. "I have a cold but I'm not contagious." Her bleary eyes touch Scarpetta. "Then who am I to tell a doctor that? I assume you're the doctor, the one I just talked to." It is a safe assumption since Marino is a man and is wearing black fatigues and an LAPD baseball cap.

"I'm Dr. Scarpetta." She offers her hand. "I'm so very sorry about Gilly."

Mrs. Paulsson's eyes brighten with tears. "Come in, won't you? I've not been much of a housekeeper of late. I just made some coffee."

"Sounds good," Marino says, and he introduces himself. "Detective Browning's talked to me. But I thought we'd start from square one, if that's all right."

"How do you take your coffee?"

Marino has the good sense not to offer his usual line: like my women, sweet and white.

"Black is fine," Scarpetta says, and they follow Mrs. Paulsson along a hallway of old pine planking, and off to their right is a comfortable small living room with dark green leather furniture and brass fireplace tools. To the left is a stiff formal parlor that doesn't look used, and the chill of it reaches out to Scarpetta as she walks past.

"May I take your coats?" Mrs. Paulsson asks. "There I go asking about coffee when you're at the front door and asking about your coats when we get to the kitchen. Don't mind me. I'm not right these days."

They slip out of their coats and she hangs them on wooden pegs in the kitchen. Scarpetta notices a bright red handknit scarf on one of the pegs and for some reason wonders if it might have been Gilly's. The kitchen has not been remodeled in recent decades and has an old-fashioned black-and-white-checkered floor and old white appliances. Its windows overlook a narrow yard with a wooden fence, and behind the back fence is a low roof of slate that is missing tiles and piled with dead leaves in the eaves and patched with moss.

Mrs. Paulsson pours coffee and they sit at a wooden table by a window that offers a view of the back fence and the mossy slate roof beyond. Scarpetta notices how clean and orderly the kitchen is, with its rack of pots and pans hanging from iron hooks over a butcher's block and the drain board and sink empty and spotless. She notices a bottle of cough syrup on the counter near the paper-towel dispenser, a bottle of nonprescription cough syrup with an expectorant. Scarpetta sips her black coffee.

"I don't know where to start," Mrs. Paulsson says. "I don't really know who you are for that matter, except when Detective Browning called me this morning, he said you were experts from out of town and would I be home. Then you called." She looks at Dr. Scarpetta.

"So Browning called you," Marino says.

"He's been nice enough." She looks at Marino and seems to find something interesting about him. "I don't know why all these people are . . . Well, I guess I don't know much." Her eyes fill up again. "I should be grateful. I can't imagine having this happen and no one cares."

"People certainly care," Scarpetta says. "That's why we're here."

"Where do you live?" Her eyes are fixed on Marino, and she lifts her coffee, taking a sip, looking carefully at him.

"Based down in South Florida, a little north of Miami," Marino replies.

"Oh. I thought maybe you were from Los Angeles," she says, her eyes moving up to his cap.

"We got L.A. connections," Marino says.

"It's just amazing," she says, but she doesn't look amazed, and Scarpetta begins to see something else peek out from Mrs. Paulsson, some other creature that coils within. "My phone hardly stops ringing, a lot of reporters, a whole lot of those people. They were here the other days." She turns around in her chair, indicating the front of the house. "In a big TV truck with this tall antenna or whatever it is. It's indecent, really. Of course, this FBI agent was here the other day and she said it's because no one knows what happened to Gilly. She said it's not as bad as it might be, whatever that means. She said she's seen a whole lot worse, and I don't know what could be worse."

"Maybe she meant the publicity," Scarpetta says kindly.

"What could be worse than what happened to my Gilly?" Mrs. Paulsson asks, wiping her eyes.

"What do you think happened to her?" Marino asks, his thumb stroking the rim of his coffee cup.

"I know what happened to her. She died of the flu," Mrs. Paulsson replies. "God took her home to be with Him. I don't know why. I wish someone would tell me."

"Other people don't seem to be so sure she died of the flu," Marino says.

"That's the world we live in. Everybody wants drama. My little girl was in bed with the flu. A lot of people have died of the flu this year." She looks at Scarpetta.

"Mrs. Paulsson," Scarpetta says, "your daughter didn't die of the flu. I'm sure you've been told this already. You talked to Dr. Fielding, didn't you?"

"Oh yes. We talked on the phone right after it happened. But I don't know how you can tell if someone died of the flu. How could you possibly tell that after the fact when they're not coughing and don't have a fever and can't complain about how they're feeling?" She begins to cry. "Gilly had a temperature of one hundred degrees and was about to choke from coughing when I went out to get more cough syrup. That's all I did, drove to the CVS on Cary Street to pick up some more cough syrup."

Scarpetta glances at the bottle on the counter again. She thinks of the slides she looked at in Fielding's office just before she left for Mrs. Paulsson's house. Microscopically, there were remnants of fibrin and lymphocytes and macrophages in sections of lung tissue, and the alveoli were open. Gilly's patchy bronchopneumonia, a common complication of the flu, especially in the elderly and the young, was resolving and wasn't severe enough to impair lung function.

"Mrs. Paulsson, we could tell if your daughter died of the flu," Scarpetta says. "We could tell from her lungs." She doesn't want to go into graphic detail about how uniformly hard or consolidated and lumpy and inflamed Gilly's lungs would have been had she died of acute bronchopneumonia. "Was your daughter on antibiotics?"

"Oh yes. The first week she was." She reaches for her coffee. "I really thought she was getting better. I just sort of thought she had a cold left, you know."

Marino pushes back his chair. "You mind if I let the two of you talk?" he asks. "I'd like to look around if that's okay with you."

"I don't know what there is to look at. But go ahead. You're not the first one to come in here and want to look around. Her bedroom's in the back."

"I'll find it." He walks off, his boots heavy on the old wooden floor.

"Gilly was getting better," Scarpetta says. "The examination of her lungs shows that."

"Well, she was still weak and puny."

"She didn't die from the flu, Mrs. Paulsson," Scarpetta tells her firmly. "It's important you understand that. If she had died of the flu I wouldn't need to be here. I'm trying to help and I need you to answer some questions for me."

"You don't sound like you're from around here."

"From Miami originally."

"Oh. And that's where you still live, real near it anyway. I've always wanted to go to Miami. Especially when the weather's like this, so gloomy and all." She gets up to pour more coffee, and she moves with difficulty, her legs stiff as she walks across to the coffeemaker near the bottle of cough syrup. Scarpetta imagines Mrs. Paulsson restraining her daughter facedown on the bed and doesn't rule it out as a possibility, but finds it an unlikely one. Mother doesn't weigh much more than her daughter did, and whoever restrained Gilly was sufficiently heavy and strong to prevent her from struggling enough to suffer more injuries than she has. But Scarpetta doesn't rule out that Mrs. Paulsson murdered Gilly. She can't rule that out as much as she might like to.

"I wish I could have taken Gilly to Miami or Los Angeles or someplace special," Mrs. Paulsson is saying. "But I'm afraid to fly and I get carsick, so I never have gone much of anywhere. And now I wish I'd tried harder."

She slides out the coffeepot and it trembles in her small, slender hand. Scarpetta keeps looking at Mrs. Paulsson's hands and wrists and any areas of exposed skin, checking for any evidence of old scratches or abrasions or other injuries, but two weeks have passed. She jots a note on her notepad to find out if Mrs. Paulsson might have had any injuries when the police responded to the scene and interviewed her.

"I wish I had, because Gilly would have liked Miami, all those palm trees and pink flamingos," Mrs. Paulsson says.

At the table, she refills their cups, and coffee sloshes in the glass pot as she returns it to the drip coffeemaker, ramming it in a little too hard. "This summer she was going to travel with her father." She sits down wearily in the straight-back oak chair. "Maybe just stay with him in Charleston, if nothing else. She's never been to Charleston either." She rests her elbows on the table. "Gilly's never been to the beach, never seen the ocean except in pictures and now and then on TV, although I didn't let her watch much TV. Can you blame me?"

"Her father lives in Charleston?" Scarpetta asks, although she knows what she's been told.

"Moved back there last summer. He's a doctor there, lives in a grand house right there on the water. He's on the tour route, you know. People pay good money to walk in and look at his garden. Of course, he doesn't do a thing to that garden, can't be bothered with such things as that. He hires whoever he wants to help him with things he can't be bothered with, like the funeral. He has lawyers screwing that all up, let me tell you. Just to get me, you know. 'Cause I want her here in Richmond and for that reason he wants her in Charleston."

"What kind of doctor is he?"

"A little of everything, a general practitioner, and he's a flight surgeon too. You know they have that big Air Force base in Charleston, and Frank has a line out his door every day, so he's told me. Oh, he brags about it enough. All these pilots dropping by to get their flight physicals for seventy dollars each. So he does all right, Frank does," she talks on, scarcely catching her breath between sentences and slightly rocking in her seat.

"Mrs. Paulsson, tell me about Thursday, December fourth. Start with your getting up that morning." Scarpetta can see where this will go if she doesn't do something about it. Mrs. Paulsson will talk in convolutions forever, sidewinding her way around questions and details that really matter and obsessing about her estranged husband. "What time did you get up that morning?"

"I'm always up at six. So I was up at six, don't even need an alarm clock because I've got one built in." She touches her head. "You know I was born at exactly six A.M. and that's why I wake up at six A.M., I'm sure of that . . ."

"And then what?" Scarpetta hates to interrupt, but if she doesn't, this woman will talk in tangled digressions the rest of the day. "Did you get out of bed?"

"Why, of course I got out of bed. I always do, come right here in the kitchen, fix my coffee. Then I go back to my bedroom and read the Bible for a while. If Gilly has school, I have her out the door by seven-fifteen with her little lunch packed and all the rest, and one of her friends gives her a ride. For that I'm lucky. She has a friend whose mother doesn't mind driving every morning."

"Thursday, December fourth, two weeks ago," Scarpetta steers her back where she needs her. "You got up at six, made coffee, and returned to your room to read your Bible? Then what?" she asks as Mrs. Paulsson nods affirmatively. "You sat in your bed and read the Bible? For how long?"

"A good half hour."

"Did you check on Gilly?"

"I prayed for her first, just let her sleep in while I prayed for her. Then around quarter of seven I went in, and she was lying in bed all wadded up in the covers, just sleeping to beat the band." She starts crying. "I said, 'Gilly? My little baby Gilly? Wake up and let's get you some hot Cream of Wheat.' And she opened those pretty blue eyes of hers and said, 'Mama, I was coughing so much last night, my chest hurts.' That's when I realized we were out of cough syrup." She stops suddenly, staring with wide runny eyes. "Funny thing about it is the dog was barking and barking. I don't know why I never thought of that until now."

"What dog? Do you have a dog?" Scarpetta makes notes but doesn't make a big production out of it. She knows how to look and listen and lightly jot a few words in a scrawl that few people can read.

"That's the other thing," Mrs. Paulsson says, and her voice jumps and her lips tremble as she cries harder. "Sweetie ran off! Dear God in Heaven." She cries harder and rocks harder in her seat. "Little Sweetie was out in the yard when I was in talking to Gilly, and then later she was gone. The police or ambulance didn't shut the gate. As if it wasn't bad enough. As if everything wasn't bad enough."

Scarpetta slowly closes the leather notebook and sets it and the pen on the table. She looks at Mrs. Paulsson. "What kind of dog is Sweetie?"

"She was Frank's and he couldn't be bothered. He walked out, you know, not even six months ago on my birthday. How's that for a fine thing to do to another human being? And he said, 'You keep Sweetie unless you want her to end up at the Humane Society.' "

"What kind of dog is Sweetie?"

"He never cared for that dog, and you know why? Because he doesn't care about anybody but himself, that's why. Now Gilly loves that dog, oh my, does she. If she knew . . ." Tears run down her cheeks and her tongue is small and pink as it rolls out and licks her lips. "If she knew, it would just break her little heart."

"Mrs. Paulsson, what kind of dog is Sweetie and have you reported her missing?"

"Reported?" She blinks, her eyes focusing for an instant and she almost laughs when she blurts out, "To who? To the police who let her out? Well, I don't know that you'd call it reporting exactly, but I did tell one of them, I can't say who, one of them, anyway. I said, My dog's missing!"

"When was the last time you saw Sweetie? And Mrs. Paulsson, I know how upset you are, I really do. But if you could please try to answer my questions."

"What's my dog got to do with you anyway? Seems like a missing dog isn't any of your concern unless maybe it's dead, and even then, I don't think doctors the type you are do much about dead dogs."

"I'm concerned about everything. I want to hear everything you can tell me."

Just then, Marino is in the kitchen doorway. Scarpetta didn't hear his heavy feet. She is startled that he can carry his formidable mass on those big-booted feet and she doesn't hear a thing. "Marino," she says, looking right at him. "You know anything about their dog? Their dog's missing. Sweetie. She's a . . . What kind is she?" She looks to Mrs. Paulsson for help.

"A basset hound, just a baby," she sobs.

"Doc, I need you for a minute," Marino says.

16.

|||LUCY LOOKS AROUND at the expensive weight machines
and at the windows in the third-floor gym. Her neighbor Kate has
all she needs to stay fit while she enjoys a spectacular view of the Intracoastal Waterway, the Coast Guard station and lighthouse, and the
ocean beyond, and much of Lucy's private property.

The window in the gym's southern exposure overlooks the back
of Lucy's house, and it is more than a little unnerving to realize that
Kate can see just about everything that might go on inside Lucy's
kitchen, dining area, and living room, and also on the patio, in the
pool, and along the seawall. Lucy looks down at the narrow path
that runs along the low wall between the two houses, and it is this
cedar-chip-covered passageway that she believes he, the beast, followed to get into the door off the pool, the door Henri left unlocked.
Either that, or he arrived by boat. She doesn't believe he did, but has

to consider it. The ladder on the seawall is folded up and locked, but if someone was determined to dock at her wall and climb onto her property, certainly it was possible. The locked ladder is deterrent enough for normal people, but not for stalkers, burglars, rapists, or killers. For those people there are guns.

On a table next to the elliptical machine is a cordless phone that plugs into a jack in the wall. Next to the jack is a standard wall socket, and Lucy unzips her fanny pack and removes a transmitter that is disguised as a plug adapter. She plugs it into the wall socket. The small, innocuous piece of spy equipment is off-white, the same bland color as the wall socket, and not something Kate is likely to notice or care about if she does. Should she decide to plug something into the adapter, that is fine. It is functional when connected to AC power. She stands still for an instant, then walks back out of the gym, listening. Kate must still be in the kitchen or somewhere down on the first floor.

In the south wing is the master bedroom, an enormous space with a huge canopied bed, and a massive flat-screen TV on the wall opposite the bed. The walls overlooking the water are glass. From this perch, Kate has a perfect view of the back of Lucy's house and also into Lucy's upstairs windows. This isn't good, she thinks as she looks around and notices an empty champagne bottle on the floor next to a bedside table where there is a dirty champagne flute, a phone, and a romance novel. Her rich, nosy neighbor can see far too much of what might go on at Lucy's house, assuming the shades are open, and usually they're not. Thank God, usually they're not.

She thinks about the morning Henri was almost murdered and tries to remember whether the shades were open or shut, and she spots the telephone jack beneath the bedside table and wonders if she has time to unscrew the plate and replace it. She listens for the elevator, for footsteps on the stairs, and hears not a sound. She gets down on the floor as she pulls a small screwdriver out of the fanny pack. The screws in the plate aren't tight and there are only two of them, and she has them off in seconds as she listens for Kate. She replaces the generic beige wall plate with one that looks just like it but is a miniature transmitter that will allow her to monitor any telephone conversations that take place over this dedicated line. A few more seconds and she plugs the phone cord back in and is on her feet and walking out of the bedroom just as the elevator door opens and Kate appears holding two crystal champagne flutes filled almost to the top with a pale orange liquid.

"This place is something," Lucy says.

"Your place must be something," Kate says, handing her a glass.

You should know, Lucy thinks. You spy on it enough.

"You'll have to give me a tour sometime," Kate says.

"Anytime. But I travel a lot." The pungent smell of champagne assaults Lucy's senses. She doesn't drink anymore. She learned the hard way about drinking and no longer touches the stuff.

Kate's eyes are brighter and she is looser than she was not even fifteen minutes earlier. She has left the station and is halfway to drunk. While she was downstairs, she probably threw back several flutes of whatever she concocted, and Lucy suspects that while there may be champagne in the glass she holds, Kate probably has vodka in hers. The elixir in Kate's glass is more diluted, and she is quite limber and lubricated.

"I looked out your gym windows," Lucy says, holding the flute while Kate sips. "You could have gotten a good look at anybody who might have come on my property."

" 'Could' is the operative word, hon. The operative word." She stretches her words the way people do when they've left the station and are happily on their way to drunk. "I don't make it a habit to be snoopy. Have way too much else for that, can't even keep up with my own life."

"Mind if I use your ladies' room?" Lucy asks.

"Help your little self. Right down there." She points to the north wing, swaying a little on her widely planted feet.

Lucy walks into a bathroom that includes a steam shower, a huge tub, his and her toilets and bidets, and a view. She pours half the drink down the toilet and flushes. She waits a few seconds and walks back out to the landing at the top of the stairs, where Kate stands, swaying slightly, sipping.

"What's your favorite champagne?" Lucy asks, thinking of the empty bottle by the bed.

"Is there more than one, hon?" She laughs.

"Yes, there are quite a few, depending on how much you want to spend."

"No kidding. Did I tell you about the time Jeff and I went crazy at the Ritz in Paris? No, of course I didn't tell you. I don't know you, really, now do I? But I feel we're becoming friends fast," she spits as she leans into Lucy and clutches her arm, then starts rubbing it as she spits some more. "We were . . . no, wait." She takes another sip, rubbing Lucy's arm, holding on to her. "It was the Hôtel de Paris in Monte Carlo, of course. You've been there?"

"Drove my Enzo there once," Lucy says untruthfully.

"Now which one is that. The silver or the black one?"

"The Enzo is red. It's not here." Lucy almost tells the truth. The Enzo isn't here because she doesn't own an Enzo.

"Then you have been to Monte Carlo. To the Hôtel de Paris," Kate says, rubbing Lucy's arm. "Well, Jeff and I were in the casino."

Lucy nods, lifting her flute as if she might have a sip, but she won't.

"And I was just knocking around on the two Euro slot machines and got lucky, boy did I get lucky." She drains her glass and rubs Lucy's arm. "You are very strong, you know. So I said to Jeff, we should celebrate, honey, back then when I called him honey instead of asshole." She laughs and glances at her empty crystal glass. "So we tottered back to our suite, the Winston Churchill Suite, I still re-member. And guess what we ordered?"

Lucy is trying to decide whether she should extricate herself now or wait until Kate does something worse than what she is already doing. Her cool, bony fingers are digging into Lucy's arm and she is pulling Lucy's arm into her thin, pickled body. "Dom?" Lucy asks.

"Oh honey. Not Dom Pérignon. *Mais non!* That's soda pop, just a rich man's soda pop, not that I don't love it, mind you. But we were feeling very naughty and ordered the Cristal Rosé at five hundred and sixty-something euros. Of course, that was Hôtel de Paris prices. You've had it?"

"I don't remember."

"Oh honey, you'd remember, trust me. Once you've had the rosé there's nothing else. There's only one champagne after that. Then, as if that wasn't bad enough, we moved on from Cristal to the most di-vine Rouge du Château Margaux," she says, pronouncing her French extremely well for one almost at her destination of drunk.

"Would you like the rest of mine?" Lucy holds out her flute as Kate rubs and pulls on her. "Here, I'll trade." She exchanges her half-full glass for Kate's empty one.

17.

|||HE REMEMBERS that time she came down to talk to his boss, meaning whatever she had on her mind was important enough for her to ride the freight elevator, and what a ghastly contraption that was.

It was iron and rusty and the doors shut not from the sides like a normal elevator but from top and bottom, meeting in the middle like a closed jaw. Of course, there were stairs. Fire codes meant there were always stairs in state buildings, but no one took the stairs to the Anatomical Division, certainly not Edgar Allan Pogue. When he needed to go up and down between the morgue and where he worked below ground, he felt eaten alive like Jonah when he slammed shut those iron elevator doors with a yank of the long iron lever inside. Its floor was corrugated steel and covered with dust, the dust of human ashes and bones, and usually there was a gurney parked inside that claustrophobic old iron elevator because who cared what Pogue left in there?

Well, she did. Unfortunately, she did.

So on the particular morning that Pogue has in mind as he sits in his lawn chair in his Hollywood apartment, polishing his tee ball bat with a handkerchief, she came off the service elevator, a long white lab coat over her teal green scrubs, and he'll never forget how quietly she moved across the brown tile floor in the subterranean windowless world where he spent his days and later some of his nights. She wore rubber-soled shoes, probably because they didn't slip and were easy on her back when she stood long hours in the autopsy suite cutting up people. Funny how her cutting up people is respectable because she is a doctor and Pogue isn't anything. He didn't finish high school, although his résumé states he did, and that lie among others has never been questioned.

"We need to stop leaving the gurney in the elevator," she said to Pogue's supervisor, Dave, a strange, slouching man with bruised smudges under his dark eyes, his dyed black hair wild and stiff with cowlicks. "Apparently the body tray is one you're using in the crematorium, which is why the elevator is filled with dust, and that just isn't good form. Probably not healthy, either."

"Yes, ma'am," Dave replied, and he was working the overhead chains and pulleys, hoisting the naked pink body out of a floor vat of pink formalin, a big sturdy iron hook in each of her ears because that was the way they lifted people out of the vats when Edgar Allan Pogue worked there. "But it's not in the elevator." Dave made a point of looking at the gurney. Scratched and dented, and rusting at the joints, it was parked in the middle of the floor, a translucent plastic shroud balled up on top of it.

"I'm just reminding you while I think about it. The elevator may not be used by most people in this building, but we still need to keep it clean and inoffensive," said she.

Right then Pogue knew she thought his job was offensive. How else was he supposed to interpret a comment like that? Yet the irony is, without those bodies donated to science, medical students wouldn't have cadavers to dissect, and without a cadaver, where would Kay Scarpetta be? Just where might she be without one of Edgar Allan Pogue's bodies, although she literally didn't become acquainted with one of his bodies when she was in medical school. That was before his time and not in Virginia. She went to medical school in Baltimore, not Virginia, and is older than Pogue by about ten years.

She did not speak to him on that occasion, although he can't accuse of her being uppity. She did make a point of saying hello Edgar Allan and good morning Edgar Allan and where is Dave, Edgar Allan, whenever she dropped by the Anatomical Division with one purpose or another on her mind. But she didn't speak to him on this occasion when she walked fast across the brown floor, her hands in the pockets of her lab coat, and maybe she didn't speak to Pogue because she didn't see him. She didn't look for him, either. Had she looked, she would have found him back by his hearth like Cinderella, sweeping up ashes and bits of bone he had just crushed with his favorite tee ball bat.

But what matters is she did not look. No, she did not. He, on the other hand, had the advantage of the dim concrete alcove where the oven was, and had a direct view into the main room where Dave had the pink old woman on hooks, and the motorized pulleys and chain were bumping along smoothly, and she was moving pinkly through the air, her arms and knees hitched up as if she were still sitting in the vat, and the overhead fluorescent lights flashed on the steel identification tag dangling from her left ear.

Pogue watched her progress and couldn't help but feel a touch of pride until Scarpetta said, "In the new building we're not going to do it like this anymore, Dave. We're going to stack them on trays in a cooler just like we do the other bodies. This is an indignity, something from the Dark Ages. It isn't right."

"Yes, ma'am. A cooler would be fine. We can fit more in the vats, though," Dave said, and he hit a switch and the chain came to a dead halt, and the pink old woman swayed as if she were riding a chair lift that suddenly came to a dead halt.

"Assuming I can finagle the space. You know how that goes, and they're taking every square foot away from me that they can. Everything depends on space," Scarpetta said, touching a finger to her chin, looking around, surveying her kingdom.

Edgar Allan Pogue remembers thinking at the time, All right then, this brown floor with the vats, the oven, and the embalming room are your kingdom at this minute. But when you aren't here, which is ninety-nine percent of the time, this kingdom is mine. And the people who roll in and are drained and sit in the vats and go up in flames and drift out the chimney are my subjects and friends.

"I was hoping for someone who hasn't been embalmed," Scarpetta said to Dave as the drawn-up pink old woman swayed from the chain overhead. "Maybe I should cancel the demo."

"Edgar Allan was too quick. Embalmed her and put her in the vat before I had a chance to tell him you needed one this morning," Dave said. "Don't have anyone fresh at the moment."

"She unclaimed?" Scarpetta looks at the body pinkly swaying.

"Edgar Allan?" Dave called out. "This one's unclaimed, isn't she?"

Edgar lied and said she was, knowing Scarpetta wouldn't use a claimed body because that wouldn't be in the spirit of what the person wanted when he donated his body to science. But Pogue knew this pink old woman wouldn't have cared. Not a bit. All she wanted was to pay God back for a few injustices, that was it.

"I guess it will be all right," Scarpetta decided. "I hate to cancel. So it will work out."

"I sure am sorry," Dave said. "I know it's not ideal to do a demo autopsy with an embalmed one."

"Don't worry about it." Scarpetta patted Dave's arm. "Wouldn't you know there aren't any cases today. The one day we don't have any, I happen to have the police academy coming through. Well, send her up."

"You betcha. I'm doing you a favor," Dave said with a wink, and sometimes he flirted with Scarpetta. "Donations are on the lean side."

"Just be grateful the general public doesn't see where they'd end up or you wouldn't get any donations at all," she replied, heading back to the elevator. "We got to work on those specs for the new building, Dave. Soon."

So Pogue helped Dave unhook their most recent donation, and they placed her on the same dusty gurney Scarpetta had been complaining about minutes earlier. Pogue wheeled the pink old lady across brown tile and onto the rusting service elevator and they rode up together and he pushed her out on the first floor, thinking that this was a ride the old woman never planned to take. No, she certainly didn't envision this detour, now did she? And he should know. He talked to her enough, didn't he? Even before she was dead, didn't he? The plastic shroud he had draped over her rustled as he rolled her through the heavy, deodorized air, and wheels clattered along white tile as he guided her toward the open double doors that led into the autopsy suite.

"And that, Mother Dear, is what happened to Mrs. Arnette," Edgar Allan Pogue says, sitting up on the lawn chair, photographs of the blue-haired Mrs. Arnette spread out on the yellow and white webbing between his naked, hairy thighs. "Oh I know, it sounds unfair and dreadful, doesn't it? But it really wasn't. I knew she'd rather have an audience of young policemen than to be carved on by some ungrateful medical student. It's a nice story, isn't it, Mother? A very nice story."

||| THE BEDROOM is big enough to hold a single bed and a small table to the left of the headboard, and a dresser next to the closet. The furniture is oak, not antique but not new, and it is nice enough, and taped to the paneled wall around the bed are scenic posters.

Gilly Paulsson slept at the steps of Siena's Duomo and woke up beneath the ancient Palace of Domitian on Rome's Palatine Hill. She may have dressed and brushed her long blond hair in the full-length mirror near Florence's Piazza Santa Croce with its statue of Dante. She probably did not know who Dante was. She may not have been able to find Italy on a map.

Marino is standing next to a window that overlooks the back-yard. He does not have to explain what he is seeing because it is obvious. The window is no more than four feet from the ground and locks by two thumb latches that when pressed allow the window to be slid up easily.

"They don't catch," Marino says. He is wearing white cotton gloves and pushes in the thumb latches, demonstrating how effortlessly one can raise the window.

"Detective Browning should know about this," Scarpetta says, getting out gloves, too, a white cotton pair that are slightly soiled because they permanently reside in a side pocket of her handbag. "But there is nothing in any of the reports I've seen that mentions the window lock is broken. Forced?"

"Naw," Marino replies, sliding the window back down. "Just old and worn out. I wonder if she ever opened her window. Hard to believe someone just happened to notice she was home from school and Mom's on a quick errand, and Hey, I'll break in, and Hey, aren't I lucky the window lock is busted."

"More likely someone already knew the window doesn't lock," Scarpetta says.

"My guess."

"Then someone familiar with this house or able to watch it and gather intelligence."

"Huh," Marino says, walking over to the dresser and opening the top drawer. "We need to know something about the neighbors. The one with the best view of her bedroom's going to be that house." He nods toward the window with its worn-out lock, indicating the house behind the back fence, the one with the mossy slate roof. "I'll find out if the cops questioned whoever lives back there." It sounds odd when he refers to police as cops, as if he never was one. "Maybe whoever lives there has noticed someone hanging around the house. I thought you might find this interesting."

Marino reaches inside the drawer and lifts out a man's black leather wallet. It is curved and smooth the way wallets are when they are habitually kept in a back pocket. He opens it and inside is the expired Virginia driver's license of Franklin Adam Paulsson, born August 14, 1966, in Charleston, South Carolina. There are no credit cards, no cash, nothing else inside the wallet.

"Dad," Scarpetta says, giving thoughtful attention to the photograph on the license, to the smiling blond man with a hard jaw and light gray-blue eyes the color of winter. He is handsome but she isn't sure what she thinks of him, assuming one can judge a person by the way he looks on a driver's license. Maybe he is cold, she thinks. He is something, but she doesn't know what and feels uneasy.

"See, I think this is weird," Marino says. "This top drawer's like a shrine to him. These t-shirts?" He holds up a thin stack of neatly folded white undershirts. "Size large, men's, maybe Dad's, and some are stained and have holes in them. And letters." He hands her a dozen or so envelopes, several of them greeting cards, it appears, and all with a Charleston return address. "And then there's this." His thick white cottony fingers pull out a dead long-stem red rose. "You notice the same thing I do?" he asks.

"It doesn't look very old."

"Exactly." He carefully sets it back inside the drawer. "Two weeks, three weeks? You grow roses," he adds as if that makes her an expert in wilted ones.

"I don't know. But it doesn't look months old. It isn't completely dried out. What do you want to do in here, Marino? Dust for prints? It should already have been done. What the hell did they do in here?"

"Make assumptions," he says. "That's what they did. I'll get my case out of the car, take pictures. I can dust for prints. The window, window frame, this dresser, especially the top drawer. That's about it."

"May as well. We can't mess up this crime scene now. Too many people got to it first." She realizes she has just referred to the bedroom as a crime scene and it is the first time she has called it that.

"Then I guess I'll wander out in the yard," he says. "Two weeks, though. Unlikely any of little Sweetie's poop would be out there unless it never rained once, and we know it has. So kind of hard to know if there's really a missing dog. Browning said nothing about it."

Scarpetta returns to the kitchen where Mrs. Paulsson sits at the table. It does not appear she has moved, but is in the same position in the same chair, staring off. She doesn't really believe her daughter died of the flu. How could she possibly believe such a thing?

"Has anybody explained to you why the FBI is interested in Gilly's death?" Scarpetta asks, sitting across the small table from her. "What have the police said to you?"

"I don't know. I don't watch that sort of thing on TV," she mutters, her voice trailing off.

"What sort of thing?"

"Police shows. FBI shows. Crime shows. Never have watched things like that."

"But you know the FBI is involved," Scarpetta says as her concerns about Mrs. Paulsson's mental health gather more darkly. "Have you talked to the FBI?"

"This woman came to see me, I already told you. She said she just had routine questions and was mighty sorry to bother me because I was upset. That's what she said, I was upset. She sat right here, right where we are, and she asked me things about Gilly and Frank and anybody suspicious I might have noticed. You know, did Gilly talk to strangers, did she talk to her father. What are the neighbors like. She asked about Frank, a lot about him."

"Why do you think that is? What kinds of questions about Frank?" Scarpetta probes, envisioning the blond man with the hard jaw and pale blue eyes.

Mrs. Paulsson stares at the wall to the left of the stove as if something is on the white-painted wall that captures her interest, but nothing is there. "I don't know why she asked about him except that women often do." She stiffens and her voice gets brittle. "Oh boy, do they ever."

"And he's where now? Right this minute, I mean."

"Charleston. We may as well have been divorced forever." She begins to pick at a hangnail, her eyes riveted to the wall, as if something on it seizes her attention, but there is nothing on it, nothing at all.

"Were he and Gilly close?"

"She worships him." Mrs. Paulsson takes a deep, quiet breath, her eyes wide, and her head begins to move, suddenly unsteady on her thin neck. "He can do no wrong. The couch in the living room below the window, it's just a plaid couch, nothing special about that couch except it was his spot. Where he watched TV, read the paper." She takes a deep, heavy breath. "After he left she used to go in there and lie down on it. I could hardly get her off it." She sighs. "He's not a good father. Isn't that the way it goes? We love what we can't have."

Marino's boots sound from the direction of Gilly's bedroom. This time his big, heavy feet are louder.

"We love what doesn't love us back," Mrs. Paulsson says.

Scarpetta has made no notes since returning to the kitchen. Her wrist rests on top of the notebook, the ballpoint pen ready but still. "What is the FBI agent's name?" she asks.

"Oh dear. Karen. Let me see." She shuts her eyes and touches her trembling fingers to her forehead. "I just don't remember things anymore. Let me see. Weber. Karen Weber."

"From the Richmond field office?"

Marino walks into the kitchen, a black plastic fishing tackle box gripped in one hand, the other hand holding his baseball cap. He has taken the cap off finally, perhaps out of respect for Mrs. Paulsson, the mother of a young girl who was murdered.

"Oh dear. I guess she was. I have her card somewhere. Where did I put it?"

"You know anything about Gilly having a red rose?" Marino asks from the doorway. "There's a red rose in her bedroom."

"What?" Mrs. Paulsson says.

"Why don't we show you," Scarpetta says, getting up from the table. She hesitates, hoping Mrs. Paulsson can handle what is about to happen. "I'd like to explain a few things."

"Oh. I guess we can." She stands and is shaky on her feet. "A red rose?"

"When did Gilly see her father last?" Scarpetta asks, and they head back to the bedroom, Marino leading the way.

"Thanksgiving."

"Did she go see him? Did he come here?" Scarpetta asks in her most nonaggressive voice, and it strikes her that the hallway seems tighter and darker than it was a few minutes ago.

"I don't know anything about a rose," Mrs. Paulsson says.

"I had to look in her drawers," Marino says. "You understand we have to do things like that."

"Is this what happens when children die of the flu?"

"I'm sure the police looked in her drawers already," Marino says. "Or maybe you weren't in the room when they were looking around and taking pictures."

He steps aside and lets Mrs. Paulsson enter her dead daughter's bedroom. She walks in as far as the dresser to the left of the doorway, against the wall. Marino digs in a pocket and pulls out his cotton gloves. He works his huge hands into them and opens the top dresser drawer. He picks up the drooping rose, one of those roses that was furled and never opened, the sort Scarpetta has seen wrapped in transparent plastic and sold in convenience stores, usually at the counter for a dollar and a half.

"I don't know what that is." Mrs. Paulsson stares at the rose, her face turning red, almost the same crimson red as the wilted rose. "I don't have any idea where she got that."

Marino doesn't react visibly.

"When you came back from the drugstore," Scarpetta says, "you didn't see the rose in her bedroom? Possible someone brought it to Gilly because she was sick? What about a boyfriend?"

"I don't understand," Mrs. Paulsson replies.

"Okay," Marino says, placing the rose on top of the dresser, in plain view. "You walked in here when you came home from the drugstore. Let's go back to that. Let's start with your parking the car. Where did you park when you got home?"

"In front. Right by the sidewalk."

"That's where you always park?"

She nods yes, her attention drifting to the bed. It is neatly made and covered with a quilt that is the same dusky blue as her estranged husband's eyes.

"Mrs. Paulsson, would you like to sit down?" Scarpetta says, giving Marino a quick look.

"Let me get you a chair," Marino offers.

He walks out, leaving Mrs. Paulsson and Scarpetta alone with a dead red rose and the perfectly smooth bed.

"I'm Italian," Scarpetta says, looking at the posters on the wall. "Not born there, but my grandparents were, in Verona. Have you been to Italy?"

"Frank's been to Italy." That's all Mrs. Paulsson has to say about the posters.

Scarpetta looks at her. "I know this is hard," she says gently. "But the more you can tell us, the more we can help."

"Gilly died of the flu."

"No, Mrs. Paulsson. She didn't die of the flu. I've looked at her. I've looked at her slides. Your daughter had pneumonia, but she was almost over it. You daughter has some bruising on the tops of her hands and on her back."

Her face is stricken.

"Do you have any idea how she might have gotten bruises?"

"No. How could that have happened?" She stares at the bed, her eyes flooded with tears.

"Did she bump into something? Did she fall down, perhaps fall out of the bed?"

"I can't imagine."

"Let's go step by step," Scarpetta says. "When you left for the pharmacy, did you lock the front door?"

"I always do."

"It was locked when you returned home?"

Marino is taking his time so Scarpetta can begin her approach. Theirs is a dance and they do it easily and with little premeditation.

"I thought so. I used my key. I called out her name to tell her I was home. And she didn't answer, so I thought . . . I thought, She's asleep. Oh good, she needs to sleep," she says, crying. "I thought she was asleep with Sweetie. So I called out, I hope you don't have Sweetie in the bed with you, Gilly."

19.

|||SHE DROPPED HER KEYS in their usual spot on the table beneath the coatrack. Sunlight seeping through the transom over the front door lit up the darkly paneled foyer, and white specks of dust moved in the bright light as she took off her coat and hung it on a peg.

"I kept calling out, Gilly, honey?" she tells the woman doctor. "I'm home. Is Sweetie with you? Sweetie? Where's Sweetie? Now you know if you have Sweetie in the bed loving up on him, and I know you are, he's going to come to expect it. And a little ol' basset hound with his little short legs can't be getting up and down off that bed by himself."

She walked into the kitchen and set several plastic bags on the table. While she was out, she stopped at the grocery store, figuring she may as well while she was right there at the shopping center on West Cary Street. She took two cans of chicken broth out of a bag and set them near the stove. Opening the freezer, she took out a package of chicken thighs and set it in the sink to thaw. The house was quiet. She could hear the wall clock tick-tock in the kitchen, a monotonous, chronic tick-tock she usually did not notice because she had too much else to notice.

In a drawer she found a spoon. In a cabinet she found a glass, and she filled the glass with cold tap water and carried the glass of water, the spoon, and the new bottle of cough syrup down the hallway toward Gilly's room.

"When I got to her room," she hears herself tell the woman doctor, "I said, Gilly? What on earth? Because what I was seeing . . . It didn't make sense. Gilly? Where are your pajamas? Are you that hot? Oh Lord, where's the thermometer? Don't tell me your fever's gone up again."

Gilly on top of the bed, facedown, naked, her slender back, buttocks, and legs bare. Her silky golden hair spilled over the pillow. Her arms stretched out straight above her head on the bed. Her legs bent like frog legs.

Oh Lord oh Lord oh Lord. Without warning, her hands began to shake violently.

The patchwork quilt and sheet and blanket beneath it were pulled down and hanging off the foot of the mattress, flowing off and pooled on the floor. Sweetie wasn't on the bed, and that got caught in her thoughts. Sweetie wasn't under the covers, because there were no covers, not on the bed. The covers were on the floor, pulled off and on the floor, and Sweetie was caught in her thoughts, and she wasn't startled, hardly even aware, when the bottle of cough syrup, the glass of water, and the spoon hit the floor. She wasn't conscious of letting go of them, and then they were bouncing, splashing, rolling on the floor, water spreading over old wood planks, and she was screaming, and her hands didn't seem to belong to her as they grabbed Gilly's shoulders, her warm shoulders, and shook her and turned her over, and shook her and screamed.

20.

|||RUDY HAS BEEN GONE from the house for a while, and in the kitchen Lucy picks up a copy of a Broward County Sheriff's Office offense report. It doesn't say much. A prowler was reported and it might be connected to an alleged breaking and entering that happened at the same residence.

Next to the report is a large manila envelope, and inside it is the pencil drawing of the eye that was taped to the door. The cop didn't take it. Good job, Rudy. She can do destructive testing on the drawing, and she looks out the window at her neighbor's house and wonders if Kate has begun her return trip from drunk, believing that going around the bend will somehow make her less drunk, or whatever it is that people believe when they are drunk. The remembered smell of champagne makes Lucy queasy and fills her with dread. She knows all about champagne and rubbing up on strangers who look better the more the alcohol flows. She knows all about it and never wants to make that trip again, and when she is reminded, she cringes and feels a deep, sick remorse.

She is grateful that Rudy has gone off somewhere. If he knew what just happened, he would be reminded, and both of them would fall silent, and the silences would only get deeper and more impenetrable until they finally have a fight and get beyond one more bad memory. When she was drunk she took what she thought she wanted, only to find out later that she didn't want what she had taken and was repulsed by it or simply indifferent. This is assuming she could always remember what she did or took, and after a while, she rarely remembered. For someone still in her twenties, Lucy has forgotten a lot in life. The last time she forgot, she began to remember when she was standing out on an apartment balcony some thirty stories up, dressed in nothing but a pair of running shorts in the dead of a very cold night in New York, a January night after a day of partying in Greenwich Village, just where in Greenwich Village she still has no idea and doesn't want to know.

Why she was out on the balcony she still isn't sure, but she might have thought she was going to the bathroom and took a wrong turn and opened the wrong door, and had she decided to step over the balcony, assuming it was the tub or who knows what, she would have fallen thirty stories to her death. Her aunt would have gotten the autopsy reports and determined along with the rest of the forensic profession that Lucy committed suicide while drunk. No test on earth would have revealed that all Lucy did was stumble out of bed to use the bathroom inside a strange apartment that belonged to a stranger she met somewhere in the Village. But that is another story and one she does not care to dwell on.

After those stories there are no others. She turned on alcohol to pay it back for all the times it turned on her, and now she doesn't drink. Now the smell of drink reminds her of the sour odor of lovers she did not love and would not have touched sober. She looks out at her neighbor's house, then walks out of the kitchen and upstairs to the second floor. At least she can be grateful that Henri was a decision that drinking did not make. At least Lucy can be grateful for that.

Inside her office, Lucy turns on a light and snaps open a black briefcase that is no bigger than a regular briefcase, but it is a rugged hard shell and inside is a Global Remote Surveillance Command Center that allows her to access covert remote wireless receivers from anywhere in the world. She checks to make sure the battery is charged and operational, and that the four channel repeaters are repeating and that the dual tape decks are dually capable of recording. She plugs in the command center to a telephone line, turns on the receiver, and slips on headphones to see if Kate might be talking to anyone from inside the gym or her bedroom, but she isn't and nothing has been recorded yet. Lucy sits at a table inside her office, looking out at the sun playing on the water and the palm trees playing in the wind, and she listens. Adjusting the sensitivity level, she waits.

A few minutes of silence pass, and she slips off the headphones and places them on the table. She gets up and moves the command center to the table where she has set up the Krimesite imager. The light in the room changes as clouds touch the sun and move on, and then more clouds drift past the sun and the light dims and brightens inside the office. Lucy pulls on white cotton gloves. She removes the drawing of the eye from its envelope and places it on a large sheet of clean black paper, and she sits down again, puts on the headphones again, and removes a can of ninhydrin from a fingerprint kit. She takes the top off the can and begins to spray the drawing, moistening it, but not too much. Though the spray contains no chlorofluorocarbons and is environment friendly, she has never found it especially human friendly. The mist bites her lungs and she coughs.

She takes off the headphones again and gets up again, carrying the chemical-smelling damp paper over to a countertop where a steam iron is plugged in and resting upright on top of a heat-resistant pad. She turns on the iron and it heats up fast, and she pushes the steam button to test it and steam hisses out. Placing the drawing of the eye on the heat-resistant pad, she holds the iron no less than four inches above the paper and starts the steam. Within seconds, areas of the paper begin to turn purple, and right away she can see purple marks from fingers, marks that she didn't leave because she knows where she touched the paper when she removed it from the door, and she didn't touch it with her bare hands, and the cop from Broward didn't touch the drawing because Rudy wouldn't have allowed that. She is careful not to steam the piece of tape, which is nonporous and will not react to ninhydrin, and the heat will melt the adhesive and any possible ridge detail on it.

Back at her work table, she seats herself, puts on the headphones and a pair of glasses, and slides the purple-spotted drawing under the lens of the imager scope. She turns it on, then turns on the UV lamp and looks into the eyepiece at a field of bright green, and she smells the unpleasant odor of the cooked chemical and paper. The pencil marks of the eye are thin white lines, and then there is pale ridge detail in a finger mark near the iris of the eye. She adjusts the focus, making the image as sharp as possible, and the ridge detail shows several characteristics and is more than enough to run in the FBI's Integrated Automated Fingerprint Identification System. When she ran the latent prints she lifted from the bedroom after Henri was almost murdered, the search produced nothing because the beast has no ten-print card on file. This time, she'll do a latent-to-latent search against more than two billion prints in the IAFIS database, and she'll also make sure her office does a manual comparison of the latents from the bedroom and the ones from the drawing. She mounts a digital camera on top of the scope's eyepiece and begins taking photographs.

Not five minutes later, when she is taking more pictures of another finger mark, this one a smudge with partial ridge detail, the first human sound comes through her headphones, and she turns up the volume and tinkers with the sensitivity level and makes sure one of the recorders is capturing what she is hearing live.

"What are you doing?" Kate's drunk voice sounds clearly in Lucy's headphones, and she leans forward in her chair and checks to make sure everything in the command center is up and running fine. "I can't play tennis today," Kate slurs, and her one-sided conversation is picked up clearly by the transmitter hidden in the adapter Lucy plugged into the wall socket near the window that overlooks the back of Lucy's house.

Kate is in the gym and there is no background noise of the treadmill or elliptical machine, not that Lucy expects her neighbor to be working out when she is drunk. But Kate isn't too drunk to spy. She is looking out the window at Lucy's house and has nothing better to do than spy, and she probably never has had anything better to do than spy and get drunk.

"No, you know I think I'm getting a cold. You hear it too. You should have heard me earlier. I'm so stopped up and you should have heard me when I got up."

Lucy stares at the red light on the tape recorder. Her eyes wander to the sheet of paper beneath the lens of the mounted crime scope. The paper is curled from the heat, and the purple smudges on it are large, large enough to be a man's maybe, but she knows better than to make assumptions. What matters is there are prints, assuming they are the prints of the beast who taped his beastly drawing to Lucy's door, assuming it is the one who came into her house and tried to kill Henri. Lucy stares at the purple remnants of him, his tracks, his amino acids from his perspiring oily skin.

"Well, I have a movie star next door, how 'bout them apples?" Kate's voice violates the inside of Lucy's head. "Heck no, honey, not surprised in the least. Let me tell you, I thought so all along. People in and out, all those fancy cars and pretty people in a house that cost what? Eight, nine, ten million? And a gaudy house, you ask me. Just like you expect with gaudy people."

He doesn't care if he leaves prints. He doesn't care, and Lucy's heart feels hollow, because if he cared she would be better off. If he cared, it would indicate that he very likely has a criminal record. He has no ten-print card in IAFIS or anywhere. He isn't worried, damn him. He doesn't care because he believes a match isn't going to happen. We'll see about that, Lucy thinks, and she feels his beastly presence as she looks at the purple smudges on the heat-curled drawing of the eye. She feels him watching and she feels Kate watching, and anger seethes inside Lucy, deep inside where her anger crawls and hides and sleeps until something pokes it.

". . . Tina . . . Now do you believe it? Her last name's flown right out of my head. If she ever told me. Of course she would have. She told me all about it, and her boyfriend and that girl that was attacked and moved back to Hollywood . . ."

Lucy turns up the volume and the purple on the paper blurs as she stares hard and listens closely to her neighbor talk about Henri. How did she know Henri was attacked? It wasn't in the news. All Lucy told Kate was that there was a stalker. Lucy never said a word about anyone being attacked.

"A cute thing, very cute. Blonde, nice face and nice figure, nice and thin. They're all like that, those Hollywood types. Now that part I'm not sure of. But my feeling is he's the other one's boyfriend, Tina's boyfriend. Why? Well now that's pretty obvious, hon. If he was the blonde's beau, don't you think he would have left when she did, and she's not been here since the house got broken into and all those police cars and the ambulance showed up."

The ambulance, damn it. Kate saw the ambulance, saw a stretcher being carried out, and she assumes this means Henri was assaulted. I'm not thinking straight, Lucy thinks. I'm not making the connections, she thinks angrily and in growing frustration and panic. What's wrong with you, she says to herself as she listens and stares at the tape recorder inside the briefcase on top of the table near the Krimesite imager. What the hell is wrong with you, she says to herself, and she thinks of her stupidity in the Ferrari when the Latino was following her.

"I wondered the same thing, why not a word in the news. I looked for it, believe you me," Kate talks on, her words chewy and distorted because she is around the bend and more drunk than before. "Yes, you would think so," she says with emphasis, the slurring more emphatic. "Movie stars and nothing in the news. But that's what I'm getting at. They're here in secret, so the media doesn't know. Well, it does too make sense. It does if you think about it, you silly goose . . ."

"Oh for God's sake, say something important," Lucy mutters to the room.

I've got to get a grip, she thinks. Lucy, get a grip. Think, think, think!

The long curly dark hairs on the bed. Oh dammit, she thinks. Dammit, I didn't ask her.

She pulls off the headphones and places them on the table. She stares around the room as the tape recorder continues to capture her neighbor's one-sided conversation. "Shit," she says out loud, realizing she doesn't have Kate's phone number or even know her last name, and she doesn't feel like spending the time and energy to find out either. Not that Kate will answer the phone if Lucy calls her.

Moving to a different desk, Lucy seats herself before a computer and creates a simple document from a template. She fabricates two VIP tickets to the premiere of her movie, *Jump Out,* which will be shown June 6 in Los Angeles, with a private party for the cast and special friends to follow. She prints out the tickets on glossy photographic paper and cuts them to size, and tucks them inside an envelope with a note that reads, "Dear Kate, loved our chat! Here's a movie trivia quiz: Who's the one with the long dark curly hair? (Can you figure it out?)," and she includes a cell phone number.

Lucy hurries outside and back to Kate's house, but Kate isn't answering the door or even the intercom. She is around the bend, past drunk and on her way to unconscious, if she isn't already unconscious, and Lucy places the envelope inside Kate's mailbox.

21.

||| SOMEHOW MRS. PAULSSON is now in the bathroom off the hallway. She doesn't know how she got there.

It is an old bathroom that hasn't been renovated since the early 1950s, the floor a checkerboard of blue and white tiles, and there are a plain white sink, a plain white toilet, and a plain white tub with a pink and purple floral shower curtain drawn across it. Gilly's toothbrush is in the toothbrush holder on top of the sink, the tube of toothpaste dented, half used up. She doesn't know how she got into the bathroom.

She looks at the toothbrush and toothpaste and cries harder. She splashes cold water on her face but it doesn't do any good. She is sorry she can't hold herself together as she leaves the bathroom and returns to Gilly's bedroom, where the Italian woman doctor from Miami waits for her. That big policeman is thoughtful enough to set a chair in the room, not far from the foot of the bed, and he is sweating. It is cool in the room and she realizes the window is open, but his face is flushed and glistens with sweat.

"Take a load off," the policeman dressed in black says to her with a smile that really doesn't make him look any friendlier, but she likes the way he looks. She likes him. She doesn't know why. She likes to look at him and she feels something when she looks at him or gets close to him. "Sit down, Mrs. Paulsson, and try to relax," he says.

"Did you open the window?" she asks, sitting in the chair and folding her hands in her lap.

"I was wondering if it might have been open when you came home from the drugstore," he replies. "When you walked in this bedroom, was the window open or shut?"

"It gets hot in here. The heat's hard to regulate in these old houses." She is looking up at the policeman and the woman doctor. It doesn't seem right to be sitting near the bed and looking up at them. She feels nervous and frightened and small as she sits looking up at them. "Gilly used to open that window all the time. It might have been open when I got home. I'm trying to remember." Curtains stir. The white gauzy curtains flutter like ghosts in the sharp cold air. "Yes," she says. "I think the window might have been open."

"Did you know the lock is broke?" the big policeman asks, standing perfectly still, his eyes on her. She can't remember his name. What was it? Marinara or something.

"No," she answers, and fear is cold around her heart.

The woman doctor walks over to the open window and shuts it with her white-gloved hands. She looks out at the backyard.

"It's not very pretty this time of year," Mrs. Paulsson says as her heart thuds. "Now in the spring, you should see it."

"I can tell," the woman doctor replies, and she has a way about her that Mrs. Paulsson finds fascinating but a little scary. Everything is scary now. "I love to garden. Do you?"

"Oh yes."

"Do you think someone came in the window?" Mrs. Paulsson asks, noticing black dust on the windowsill and around the window frame. She notices more black dust and what look like tape marks on the inside and outside of the glass.

"I lifted some prints," the big policeman says. "Don't know why the cops didn't bother, but I got some. We'll see if they're anything. I'm going to need to take yours for exclusionary purposes. I don't guess the cops took your prints?"

She shakes her head no as she stares at the window and the black dust everywhere.

"Who lives behind your house, Mrs. Paulsson?" asks the big policeman in black. "That old house behind the fence."

"A woman, an elderly woman. I haven't seen her in a while, a long while. Many years. In fact, I can't say she still lives back there. Last time I saw anyone back there was maybe six months ago. Yes, six months ago or so, because I was picking tomatoes. I have a little vegetable garden back there by the fence, and last summer I had more tomatoes than I could shake a stick at. Someone was on the other side of the fence, just walking back there, doing what I don't know. My impression was that whoever's back there isn't especially friendly. Well, I doubt it's the woman who used to live there, who lived there eight, nine, ten years ago. She was very old. I suppose she might be dead by now."

"Do you know if the police might have talked to her, assuming she ain't dead?" asks the big policeman.

"I thought you're the police."

"Not the same kind of police who've been here already. No, ma'am. We're not the same as them."

"I see," she says, although she doesn't see at all. "Well, I believe the detective, Detective Brown . . ."

"Browning," says the policeman in black, and she notices that his baseball cap is tucked into the back of his pants. His head is shaved and she imagines running her hand over his smooth, shaven head.

"He did ask me about the neighbors," she replies. "I said the old woman lived back there or used to. I'm not sure anybody lives there now. I guess I just said that. I never hear anybody back there, hardly ever, and you can see through the cracks in the fence that the grass is overgrown."

"You came home from the drugstore," the woman doctor gets back to that. "Then what? Please try to go step by step, Mrs. Paulsson."

"I carried things into the kitchen and then went to check on Gilly. I thought she was asleep."

After a pause, the lady doctor asks another question. She wants to know why Mrs. Paulsson thought her daughter was asleep, what position she was in, and the questions are confusing. Each one hurts like a cramp, like a spasm in a deep place. Why does it matter? What kind of doctor asks questions like this? She is an attractive woman in a powerful way, not a big woman but strong-looking in a midnight-blue pantsuit and midnight-blue blouse that sharpen her handsome features and set off her short blond hair. Her hands are strong but graceful and she wears no rings. Mrs. Paulsson stares at the doctor's hands and imagines them taking care of Gilly and starts to cry again.

"I moved her. I tried to wake her up." She hears herself saying the same thing again and again. Why are your pajamas on the floor, Gilly? What is this? Oh Lord oh Lord!

"Describe what you saw when you walked in," the doctor asks the same question in a different way. "I know this is hard. Marino? Would you please get her some tissues and a glass of water?"

Where's Sweetie? Oh Lord, where's Sweetie? Not in bed with you again!

"She just looked like she was asleep," Mrs. Paulsson hears herself say.

"On her back? On her front? What was her position on the bed? Please try to remember. I know this is terribly hard," the woman doctor says.

"She slept on her side."

"She was on her side when you walked into the room?" the woman doctor says.

Oh dear, Sweetie pee-peed in the bed. Sweetie? Where are you? Are you hiding under the bed, Sweetie? You were in the bed again, weren't you? You aren't supposed to do that! I'm going to give you away! Don't you try to hide things from me!

"No," Mrs. Paulsson says, crying.

Gilly, please wake up, oh please wake up. This can't be! This can't be!

The lady doctor is squatting by her chair, looking her in the eye. She is holding her hand. The lady doctor is holding her hand and saying something.

"No!" Mrs. Paulsson sobs uncontrollably. "She didn't have anything on. Oh dear God! Gilly wouldn't be lying there with nothing on. She wouldn't even get dressed without locking her door."

"It's all right," the lady doctor is saying, and her eyes and touch are kind. There is no fear in her eyes. "Take deep breaths. Come on. Breathe deeply. There. That's good. Slow, deep breaths."

"Oh Lord, am I having a heart attack?" Mrs. Paulsson blurts out in terror. "They took my little girl. She's gone. Oh, where's my little girl?"

The big cop in black is back the doorway, holding a handful of tissues and a glass of water. "Who's they?" he asks.

"Oh no, she didn't die of the flu, did she? Oh no. Oh no. My baby girl. She didn't die of the flu. They took her from me."

"Who's they?" he asks. "You think more than one person had something to do with this?" He steps into the room and the lady doctor takes the water from him.

She helps Mrs. Paulsson sip it slowly. "That's good. Drink slowly. Slow breaths. Try to calm down. Do you have someone who can come stay with you? I don't want you staying alone right now."

"Who's they?" Her voice rises as she repeats the policeman's question. "Who's they?" She tries to get up from the chair but her legs won't work. They don't seem to belong to her anymore. "I'll tell you who they are." Grief turns to rage, such a terrible rage that she is afraid of it. "Those people he invited over here. Them. You ask Frank who they are. He knows."

IIIIN THE TRACE EVIDENCE LAB, forensic scientist Junius Eise holds a tungsten filament in the flame of an alcohol lamp.

He prides himself that his favorite tool-making trick has been used by master microscopists for hundreds of years. That fact, among others, makes him a purist, a Renaissance man, a lover of science, history, beauty, and women. Gripping the short strand of stiff, fine wire with forceps, he watches the grayish metal quickly incandesce bright red and imagines that it is impassioned or enraged. He removes the wire from the flame and rolls the tip into sodium nitrite, oxidizing the tungsten and sharpening it. A dip in a petri dish of water, and the sharp-tipped wire cools with a quick hiss.

He screws the wire into a stainless-steel needle holder, knowing that taking time out to make a tool this time was procrastination. Taking time out to make a tool meant he could take himself out of service for a moment, focus on something else, briefly regain a sense of control. He peers into the binocular lenses of his microscope. Chaos and conundrums are right where he left them, only magnified fifty times.

"I don't understand this," he says to no one in particular.

Using his new tungsten tool, he manipulates paint and glass particles recovered from the body of a man who was crushed to death by his tractor a few hours ago. One would have to be brain damaged not to know that the chief medical examiner worries that the man's family is going to sue somebody, otherwise trace evidence would not be relevant in an accidental death, a careless one at that. The problem is, if you look, you might find something, and what Eise has found doesn't make sense. At times like this he remembers he is sixty-three, could have retired two years ago, and has repeatedly refused promotion to Trace Evidence Section Chief because there is no place he would rather be than inside a microscope. His idea of fulfillment is disconnected from wrestling with budgets and personnel problems, and his relationship with the chief medical examiner is the worst it has ever been.

In the polarized light of the microscope, he uses his new tungsten tool to manipulate paint and metal particles on a dry glass slide. They are mixed with other debris, some sort of dust that is gray-brown and strange, unlike anything he has seen before with one very significant exception. He saw this same sort of trace evidence two weeks ago in a completely unrelated case, and he assumes that the sudden, mysterious death of a fourteen-year-old girl is unrelated to the death of a tractor driver.

Eise scarcely blinks, his upper body tense. The chips of paint, about the size of dandruff, are red, white, and blue. They aren't automotive, not from a tractor, that's for sure, not that he would expect them to be automotive in the accidental death of a tractor driver named Theodore Whitby. The paint chips and the strange gray-brown dust were adhering to a gash on his face. Similar if not identical paint chips and a similar if not identical strange gray-brown dust were found on the inside of the fourteen-year-old girl's mouth, mainly on her tongue. The dust bothers Eise the most. It is a very odd dust. He has never seen dust like this dust. Its shape is irregular and crusty, like dried mud, but it isn't mud. This dust has fissures and blisters and smooth areas and thin transparent edges like the surface of a parched planet. Some particles have holes in them.

"What the hell is this?" he says. "I don't know what this is. How can this same weird stuff be in two cases? They can't be related. I don't know what's happened here."

He reaches for a pair of needle-tip tweezers and carefully removes several cotton fibers from the particles on the slide. Light passes through lenses and a congregation of magnified fibers look like snippets of bent white thread.

"You know how much I hate cotton swabs?" he asks the virtually empty laboratory. "You know what a pain in the ass cotton swabs are?" he asks the large angular area of black countertops, chemical hoods, work stations, and dozens of microscopes and all of the glass, metal, and chemical accoutrements that they demand.

Most of the lab's workers aren't at their work stations but are in other labs on this floor, preoccupied with atomic absorption, gas chromatography and mass spectroscopy, x-ray diffraction, the Fourier Transform Infrared Spectrophotometer, the scanning electron microscope or SEM/Energy Dispersive X-ray Spectrometer, and other instruments. In a world of endless backlogs and little money, scientists grab what they can, jumping onto instruments as if they are horses and riding the life out of them.

"Everybody knows how much you hate cotton swabs," remarks Kit Thompson, Eise's nearest neighbor at the moment.

"I could make a giant quilt out of all the cotton fibers I've collected in my short life," he says.

"I wish you would. I've been waiting to see one of your giant quilts," she replies.

Eise grips another fiber. They're not easy to catch. When he moves the tweezers or tungsten needle, just the slightest fan of air moves the fiber. He readjusts the focus and bumps down the magnification to 40X, sharpening his depth of focus. He barely breathes as he stares into the bright circle of light, trying to find the clues it holds. What law of physics dictates that when a disturbance of air dislodges a fiber, it moves away from you as if it is alive and on the lam? Why doesn't the fiber drift closer to captivity?

He backs off the objective lens several millimeters, and the tips of his needle-sharp tweezers hugely invade the field of view. The circle of light reminds him of a brightly lit circus ring, even after all he's been through. For an instant he sees trick elephants and clowns in a light so bright it hurts the eyes. He remembers sitting in wooden bleachers and watching big pink puffs of cotton candy float by. He gently grabs another cotton fiber and air-lifts it off the slide. He unceremoniously shakes it loose inside a small transparent plastic bag filled with other spidery cotton debris that most certainly is Q-tip-type contaminants and of no evidentiary value.

Dr. Marcus is the worst litterbug of all. What the hell is wrong with that man? Eise has sent him numerous memos insisting that his staff tape-lift trace evidence whenever possible, and please, please, don't use cotton-tipped swabs because they have zillions of fibers that are lighter than angel kisses and get all tangled up with the evidence.

Like white Angora cat hair on black velvet pants, he wrote Dr. Marcus several months back. Like picking pepper out of your mashed potatoes. Like spooning the creamer back out of your coffee. And other lame analogies and exaggerations.

"Last week I sent him two rolls of low-tack tape," Eise is saying. "And another package of Post-its, reminding him that low-tack adhesives are perfect for pulling hairs and fibers off things because they don't break or distort them or shed cotton fibers all over the ranch. Or, not to mention, interfere with x-ray diffraction and other results. So we're not just being finicky when we sit here picking them out of a sample all the livelong day."

Kit frowns at him as she unscrews the cap from a bottle of Permount. "Picking pepper out of mashed potatoes? You sent Post-Its to Dr. Marcus?"

When Eise gets impassioned, he says exactly what he thinks. He isn't always aware, and probably doesn't really care, that what is inside his head is also escaping from his lips and audible to all. "My point," he says, "is when Marcus or whoever checked the inside of that little girl's mouth, he swabbed it thoroughly with those cotton-tip swabs. Now, he didn't need to do that with the tongue. He cut the tongue out, now didn't he? Had it lying right there on the cutting board and could plainly see there's some sort of residue on it. He could have used a tape lift, but he kept on with the Q-tips, and all I do these days is pick out cotton fibers."

Once a person, particularly a child, has been reduced to a tongue on a cutting board, he becomes nameless. That's the way it goes, without exception. You don't say, we worked our hands into Gilly Paulsson's throat and reflected back tissue with a scalpel and finally removed the organs of Gilly's throat and Gilly's tongue, pulled them right out of that little girl's mouth, or we stuck a needle in little Timmy's left eye and drew vitreous fluid for toxicological testing, or we sawed off the top of Mrs. Jones's skull, removed her brain and discovered a ruptured berry aneurysm, or it took two doctors to sever the mastoid muscles in Mr. Ford's jaws because he was fully rigorous, very muscular, and we couldn't pry open his mouth.

This is one of those moments of awareness that passes over Eise's thoughts like the shadow of the Dark Bird. That's what he calls it. If he looks up, nothing is there, just an awareness. He won't go any further with truths of this sort because when people's lives become pieces and parts and eventually end up on his slides, it's best not to look too hard for the Dark Bird. The bird's shadow is awful enough.

"I thought Dr. Marcus was too busy and too important to do autopsies," Kit says. "In fact, I can count on one hand the number of times I've even laid eyes on him since he was hired."

"Doesn't matter. He's in charge and makes the policies. He's the one who authorizes all those orders for Q-tips or their generic and cheap equivalent. As far as I'm concerned, everything's his fault."

"Well, I don't think he did the autopsy on the girl. Not on the tractor driver who got killed at the old building either," Kit replies. "No way he would do either one. He'd rather be in charge and boss everybody around."

"How you doing for 'Eise Picks'?" Eise asks her, his slender hand agile and steady with the tungsten needle.

He's been known to go through obsessive-compulsive spells of handcrafting his tungsten needles, which somewhat magically appear on the desks of his colleagues.

"I can always use another Eise Pick," Kit dubiously replies, as if she really doesn't want one, but in his fantasies, she is reticent because she doesn't want to inconvenience him. "You know what? I'm not going to permanently mount this hair." She screws the cap back on the bottle of Permount.

"How many you got from the sick girl?"

"Three," Kit replies. "It'll be just my luck DNA will decide to do something with the hairs, although they didn't seem interested last week. So I'm not going to permanently mount this one or the others. Everybody's acting weird these days. Jessie was in a scraping room when I got here. They've got all the linens in there. Apparently DNA's looking for something they must not have found the first time, and Jessie about bit my head off and all I did was ask what was going on. Something strange is going on. They already had those linens in the scraping room more than a week ago, as you and I both know. Where do you think I got these hairs from? Strange. Maybe it's the holidays. I haven't even thought about Christmas shopping."

She dips needle-tipped forceps into a small transparent plastic evidence bag and gently lifts out another hair. It looks five or six inches long and black and curly from where Eise sits, and he watches Kit drape it over a slide and add a drop of xylene and a cover slip, mounting a weightless, barely visible piece of evidence that was recovered from the bed linens of the same dead girl who had paint chips and strange brown-gray particles of dust in her mouth.

"Well, Dr. Marcus certainly isn't Dr. Scarpetta," Kit then says.

"Only took you half a decade to realize they aren't one and the same? Let me see. You thought Dr. Scarpetta had a complete makeover and turned into that squirrelly little old maid Chief Bozo down there in the corner office, and now you've had an aha moment and realize they're two totally different people. And you figured it out without DNA, God bless you, girl. Why, you're so smart you should star in your own TV show."

"You're a crazy man," Kit says, laughing so hard she leans back from the microscope, worried her evidence will blow away on gusts of her breathy guffaws.

"Too many years of sniffing xylene, girl. I got cancer of the personality."

"Oh God," she says, taking a deep breath. "My point is, you wouldn't be picking cotton fibers off your slides if Dr. Scarpetta had done the case, any of the cases. She's here, you know. She was brought in because of the sick girl, the Paulsson girl. That's the buzz."

"You're fooling me." Eise can't believe it.

"If you didn't always leave before everybody else and weren't so antisocial, maybe you would be in on a few secrets," she says.

"Ho Ho Ho and a bottle of rum, girl." While it is true that Eise is not one to linger in the lab beyond five P.M., he is also the first scientist to arrive in the morning, rarely later than 6:15. "I would think Dr. Big Shot would be the last person called in for any reason," he says.

"Dr. Big Shot? Where'd that come from?"

"Peanut Gallery."

"You must not know her. People who do don't call her that." Kit places the slide on the microscope's stage. "Me? I'd call her in a heartbeat. And I wouldn't wait two weeks or even two minutes. This hair's dyed black as pitch, just like the other two. Shoot. Forget my doing anything with it. Can't see the pigment granules and might have some surface anti-frizz-type product on it, too. Bet they're going to decide on mitochondrial. Suddenly, DNA's going to send off my three precious hairs to the Almighty Bode Lab. You wait. Strange, strange. Maybe Dr. Scarpetta's figured out that poor little girl was murdered. Maybe that's what's going on."

"Don't mount the hairs," Eise says, and in the old days, DNA was just forensic science. Now DNA is the silver bullet, the platinum record, the superstar, and gets all the money and all the glory. Eise never offers his "Eise Picks" to anyone in DNA.

"Don't worry, I'm not mounting anything," Kit says, peering into her microscope. "No line of demarcation, now that's interesting. A little weird for a dyed hair. Means it didn't grow out any after it was dyed. Not even a micron."

She moves the slide around under the objective lens as Eise looks on, somewhat interested. "No root? Fall out or been pulled, broken, buckled, damaged by a curling iron, singed, tapered, or split distal tip? Or cut, squared, or angled? Come on girl, wake me up," he says.

"Definitely clean as a whistle, no root. Distal tip is cut at an angle. All three hairs are dyed black, no root, and that's weird. Both ends are cut in all three of them. Not just one hair but all three of them. Not pulled, broken, or pulled out by the root. The hairs didn't just fall out. They were cut. Now tell me why hair would be cut on both ends?"

"Maybe the person just came from the hairdresser and maybe some of the stray cut hair was on this person's clothing or still in his hair or had been on the rug or wherever for a while."

Kit is frowning. "If Dr. Scarpetta's in the building, I'd like to see her. Just say hi. I hated when she left. In my opinion, it was the second time this damn city lost the War. That damn fool Dr. Marcus. You know what? I'm not feeling too good. I woke up with a headache and my joints hurt."

"So maybe she's coming back to Richmond," Eise supposes. "Maybe that's really why she's here. At least when she used to send us samples, she never mislabeled them and we knew exactly where they came from. She didn't mind discussing cases, would come up here herself instead of treating us like robots at General Motors because we're not great and a mighty doctor-lawyer-Indian Chief. She didn't swab the hell out of everything if she could lift it with tape, Post-its, whatever we recommended. I guess you're right. Peanut Gallery's dead wrong."

"What the hell's a peanut gallery?"

"Don't know, really."

"Obscured cortical texture, totally," Kit says, peering at a magnified dyed black hair that looks as big as a dark winter tree in the circle of light. "Like someone dipped this hair in a pot of black ink. No line of demarcation, no sir, so either recently dyed or was cut off below the grown-out undyed roots."

She is making notes as she moves the slide around and adjusts the focus and magnification, doing her best to make a dyed hair speak.

It won't say much. The distinctive characteristics of the pigment in the cuticle have been obscured by dye, like an over-inked fingerprint that blots out ridge detail. Dyed, bleached, and gray hair are pretty worthless in microscopic comparison, and half the human population has dyed, bleached, gray, or permed hair. But these days in court, jurors expect a hair to announce who, what, when, where, why, and how.

Eise hates what the entertainment industry has done to his profession. People he meets say they want to be him, what an exciting profession he has, and it isn't true, it just isn't. He doesn't go to crime scenes or wear a gun. He never has. He doesn't get a special phone call and put on a special uniform or jumpsuit and rush out in a special all-terrain crime scene vehicle to look for fibers or fingerprints or DNA or Martians. Cops and crime scene technicians do that. Medical examiners and death investigators do that. In the old days when life was simpler and the public left forensic people alone, homicide detectives like Pete Marino drove their beat-up junkers to the scene, gathered the evidence themselves, and not only knew what to collect but what to leave.

Don't vacuum the whole goddamn parking lot. Don't stuff the poor woman's entire bedroom inside fifty-gallon plastic bags and bring all that shit in here. It's like someone panning for gold and bringing home the entire stream bed instead of carefully sifting through it first. A lot of the nonsense that goes on these days is laziness. But there are other problems, more insidious ones, and Eise keeps thinking that maybe he ought to retire. He has no time for research or just plain fun and is nagged by paperwork that must be perfect, just as his analysis must be perfect. He suffers from eyestrain and insomnia. Rarely is he thanked or given credit when a case is solved and the guilty person gets what he deserves. What kind of world do we live in? It has gotten worse. Yes it has.

"If you do run into Dr. Scarpetta," Eise remarks, "ask her about Marino. He and I used to pal around when he came down here, used to put away a few beers at the FOP lounge."

"He's here," Kit says. "He came with her. You know, I'm feeling a little weird, that tickle in my throat, and I'm aching. Hope I'm not getting the damn flu."

"He's here? Holy cow. I'm gonna call that boy right away. Well, hallelujah! So he's working on the Sick Girl too."

Gilly Paulsson now goes by that name, if she is referred to by a name at all. It's easier not to use a real name, assuming one can remember it. Victims become where they were found or what was done to them. The Suitcase Lady. The Sewer Lady. The Landfill Baby. The Rat Man. The Duct Tape Man. As for the real birth names of these dead people, most of the time Eise hasn't a clue. He prefers not to have a clue.

"If Scarpetta has any opinions about why Sick Girl has red, white, and blue paint and some other weirdo dust in her mouth, I'm listening," he says. "Apparently metal painted red, white, and blue. There's unpainted metal, too, bits of shiny metal. And something else. I don't know what the something else is." He manipulates the trace evidence on the slide, obsessively moving it around. "I'll run SEM/EDX next, see what kind of metal. Anything red, white, and blue at Sick Girl's house? Guess I'll be tracking down that boy Marino and buy him a few cool ones. Lord, I could use a few myself."

"Don't talk about cool ones right now," Kit says. "I'm feeling kind of sick. I know we can't catch things from swabs and tape lifts and all the rest. But sometimes I wonder when they send up all that crap from the morgue."

"Nope. All those little bacteria are as dead as doornails when they get to us," Eise says, looking up at her. "You look at 'em close enough, they all got on teeny-weeny toe tags. You look pale, girl." He hates to encourage her sudden bout of illness. It's lonely up here when Kit isn't around, but she doesn't feel good. It's obvious. It's not right of him to pretend otherwise. "Why don't you take a break, girl? Did you get a flu shot? They ran out by the time I got around to it."

"Me too. Couldn't get one anywhere," she says, getting up from her chair. "I think I'll go make some hot tea."

23.

||| LUCY DOES NOT LIKE to trust other people to do her work. As much as she relies on Rudy, she doesn't trust him with her work, not these days, because of Henri and the way he feels about her. Lucy looks at the printed results from the IAFIS search by herself while she sits in her office, headphones on, skipping through banal recordings of her neighbor Kate's banal telephone conversations. It is early Thursday morning.

Late yesterday, Kate called her back. She left a message on Lucy's cell phone. "Hugs and kisses for the tickets," and "Who is the pool lady? Someone famous?" Lucy does have a pool lady and she is nobody famous. She is a brunette in her fifties and looks much too small to use a skimmer, and she's not a movie star and she's not a beast. Lucy's bad luck holds strong with IAFIS, which returned no good candidates, meaning the automated search came up empty-handed. Matching latent prints to latent prints, especially when some of the prints are partial ones, is a crapshoot.

Each of a person's ten fingerprints is unique. For example, a person's left thumbprint does not match his right thumbprint. With no ten-print card on file, IAFIS could only get a hit on unknown latents if the perpetrator left a latent print of his right thumb at one crime scene and a latent of the same thumb at another crime scene, and both latents were entered into IAFIS, and both latents were either complete prints or just so happened to include the same friction ridge characteristics in each print.

A manual or visual comparison of the latent prints tells another story, however, and here Lucy's luck gets a little better. Latent partial prints she recovered from the drawing of the eye do match some of the partial prints she recovered from the bedroom after Henri was attacked. This doesn't surprise Lucy, but she is happy for the verification. The beast who entered her house is the same beast who left the drawing of the eye, and the same beast also scratched her black Ferrari, although no print was recovered from the car. But how many beasts go around drawing eyes? So he did it, although none of these matches tell Lucy who he is. All she knows is that the same beast is causing all this trouble, and he does not have a ten-print card on file in IAFIS or anywhere else, it seems, and he continues to stalk Henri and must not know that she is far away from here. Or maybe he assumes Henri is coming back or at least hears about his latest exploits.

In the beast's mind, if Henri at least knows he taped a drawing on the door, then Henri is frightened and upset again and maybe she will never come back. What matters to the beast is that he overpower her. That is what stalking is all about. It is an overpowering of another person. In a sense, the stalker takes his victim hostage without ever laying a finger on her or in some cases ever meeting her. As far as Lucy knows, the beast has never met Henri. As far as Lucy knows. What does she know, really? Not a hell of a lot.

She flips through a printout from a different computer search she ran last night, and she deliberates over whether to call her aunt. It has been a while since Lucy called Scarpetta, and there is no good excuse, although Lucy has made plenty of excuses. She and her aunt both spend much of their time in South Florida, not even an hour from each other. Scarpetta moved from Del Ray to Los Olas last summer, and Lucy has visited her new home only once, and that was months ago. The more time that has passed, the harder it is to call her. Unspoken questions will hover between them and it will be awkward, but Lucy decides it isn't right if she doesn't call her under the circumstances. So she does.

"This is your wake-up call," she says when her aunt picks up.

"If that's the best you can do, you won't fool anyone," Scarpetta replies.

"What's that supposed to mean?"

"You don't sound like the front desk and I didn't ask for a wake-up call. How are you? And where are you?"

"Still in Florida," Lucy says.

"Still? As in maybe you're leaving again?"

"I don't know. Probably."

"Where to?"

"I'm not sure," Lucy says.

"Okay. What are you working on?"

"A stalking case," Lucy replies.

"Those are very hard."

"No kidding. This one especially. But I can't talk about it."

"You never can."

"You don't talk about your cases," Lucy says.

"Usually not."

"So then what else is new?"

"Not a thing. When am I going to see you? I haven't seen you since September."

"I know. What have you been doing in the big bad city of Richmond?" Lucy asks. "What are they fighting over up there these days?
Any new monuments? Maybe the latest artwork on the flood wall?"

"I've been trying to figure out what's going on with the death of
this girl. Last night I was supposed to have dinner with Dr. Fielding. You remember him."

"Oh sure. How is he? I didn't know he was still there."

"Not so good," Scarpetta replies.

"Remember when he used to take me to his gym and we'd lift
weights together?"

"He doesn't go to the gym anymore."

"Damn. I'm shocked. Jack not go to the gym? That's like . . .
Well, I don't know what it's like. It's not like anything, I guess. I'm
shocked beyond words. See what happens when you leave? Everything and everybody fall apart."

"You won't be flattering me this morning. I'm not in a very good
mood," Scarpetta replies.

Lucy feels a twinge of guilt. It is her fault Scarpetta isn't in Aspen.

"Have you talked to Benton?" Lucy asks casually.

"He's busy working."

"That doesn't mean you can't call him." Guilt grips Lucy's stomach hard.

"Right now it does mean that."

"He told you not to call him?" Lucy imagines Henri in Benton's
town home. She would eavesdrop. Yes, she would, and Lucy feels sick
with guilt and anxiety.

"I got to Jack's house last night and he didn't answer the door."
Scarpetta changes the subject. "I have this funny feeling he was home.
But he didn't come to the door."

"What did you do?"

"I left. Maybe he forgot. Certainly, he's got his share of stress.
Definitely, he's preoccupied."

"That's not what this is about. He probably didn't want to see you. Maybe it's too late for him to see you. Maybe everything's too screwed up. I took it upon myself to do a little background check on Dr. Joel Marcus," Lucy then says. "I know you didn't ask me to. But you probably wouldn't have asked, am I right?"

Scarpetta doesn't answer.

"Look, he probably knows a hell of a lot about you, Aunt Kay. You may as well know something about him," she says, and she is stung. She can't help the way she feels, and she is angry and hurt.

"All right," Scarpetta says. "I don't feel this is necessarily the right thing to do, but you may as well tell me. I'd be the first to say I'm not having an easy time working with him."

"What interests me most," Lucy says, feeling a little better, "is how little there is on him. This guy's got no life. He was born in Charlottesville, father was a public school teacher, mother died in an automobile accident in 1965, went to University of Virginia for undergrad and medical school, so he's from Virginia and trained there but he never worked in the Virginia medical examiner system until he was appointed chief four months ago."

"I could tell you he never worked in the Virginia medical examiner system before last summer," Scarpetta replies. "You didn't need to launch some expensive background check or hack into the Pentagon or whatever you did for me to know that. I'm not sure I should be listening to this."

"His being appointed chief, by the way," Lucy says, "is totally bizarre, makes no sense. He was a private pathologist in some little hospital in Maryland for a while, and he didn't do a forensic fellowship or pass his boards until he was in his early forties and, by the way, he flunked his boards the first time he took them."

"Where did he do his fellowship?"

"Oklahoma City," Lucy replies.

"I'm not sure I should be listening to this."

"Was a forensic pathologist for a while in New Mexico, don't know what he did from 1993 to 1998 except get divorced from a nurse. No kids. In 1999 he moved to St. Louis and worked in that medical examiner's office until he moved to Richmond. He drives a twelve-year-old Volvo and he's never owned a house. You might be interested to know that the house he is renting now is in Henrico County, not too far from Willow Lawn Shopping Center."

"I don't need to hear this," Scarpetta says. "That's enough."

"He's never been arrested. Thought you'd want to know that. Only a few traffic violations, nothing dramatic."

"This isn't right," Scarpetta says. "I don't need to hear this."

"No problem," Lucy replies in the voice she gets when her aunt has just trampled her spirit and hurt her feelings. "That's about it anyway. I could find out a hell of a lot more, but preliminarily, that's it."

"Lucy, I know you're trying to help. You're amazing. I wouldn't want you after me. And he's not a nice man. And God knows what his agenda is, but unless we find out something that directly impacts his ethics or competence or something that might make him dangerous, then I don't need to know about his life. Do you understand? Please don't dig up anything else."

"He's dangerous all right," Lucy says in the voice she gets. "Put a loser like him in a position of power and he's dangerous. Good God. Who the hell hired him? And why? I can't imagine how much he must hate you."

"I don't want to talk about this."

"The governor's a woman," Lucy goes on. "Why the hell would a woman governor appoint a loser like him?"

"I don't want to talk about this."

"Of course, half the time, politicians don't do the picking. They just sign off on stuff, and she probably had bigger things to think about."

"Lucy, did you call me just to upset me? Why are you doing this? Please don't. I'm having a hard enough time."

Lucy is silent.

"Lucy? Are you there?" Scarpetta asks.

"I'm here."

"I hate the phone," Scarpetta says. "I haven't seen you since September. I think you're avoiding me."

24.

||| HE IS SITTING in his living room, the newspaper open in his lap, when he hears the garbage truck coming.

The engine has a deep diesel sound. The truck stops at the end of the driveway, and the whining of a hydraulic lift is added to the diesel throbbing, and trash cans thud against the metal sides of the huge garbage truck. Then the big men sloppily drop the empty cans at the end of the driveway and the truck rumbles on down the street.

Dr. Marcus sits in his big stuffed leather chair in his living room, dizzy and barely able to breathe, his heart thudding with terror as he waits. Garbage collection is on Mondays and Thursdays around eight-thirty in his upper-middle-class neighborhood of Westham Green, just west of the city in Henrico County. He is always late for staff meeting on the two days that the garbage collectors come, and not so long ago, he didn't go to work at all on the two days that the big truck and the big dark men on it came.

They call themselves sanitation engineers now, not garbage collectors, but it doesn't matter what they call themselves or what is politically correct or what anybody calls the big dark men in their big dark clothes and big leather gloves. Dr. Marcus is terrified of garbage collectors and their trucks, and his phobia has gotten worse since he moved here four months ago, and he will not go out of the house on garbage collection days until the truck and its men have come and gone. He is doing better since he began seeing the psychiatrist in Charlottesville.

Dr. Marcus sits in the chair and waits for his heart to slow down and the dizziness and nausea to subside and his nerves to stop firing, and then he gets up, still in his pajamas, robe, and slippers. There is no point in getting dressed until after garbage collection because he sweats so profusely as he anticipates the hideous guttural sound and heavy steel clanking of the big truck and its big dark men that by the time they are gone, he is soaking wet and shivering with cold, his fingernails blue. Dr. Marcus walks the length of the oak floor in his living room and looks out the window at the green Supercans sloppily left on the corner of his driveway, and he listens for the hideous noise to make sure the truck is nowhere near and not heading back this way, even though he knows the garbage route in his neighborhood.

By now, the truck and the men on it are stopping and starting, jumping off the truck and back on, and emptying Supercans several streets away, and they will keep on going until they turn off on Patterson Avenue, and where they go from there Dr. Marcus doesn't know or care, as long as they are gone. He stares out his window at his haphazardly placed Supercans and decides it is not safe to go out.

He doesn't feel up to going out yet, and he walks to his bedroom and checks again to make sure his burglar alarm is still armed, and he takes off his wet pajamas and robe and gets into the shower. He doesn't stay in the shower long, but when he is clean and warm, he dries off and gets dressed for the office, grateful that the attack has passed, and careful not to contemplate what might happen should an attack come on suddenly when he is in public. Well, it won't. As long as he is home or near his office, he can shut the door and safely wait out the storm.

In the kitchen, he takes an orange pill. He's already had one Klonopin and his antidepressant this morning, but he takes another .5 milligram of Klonopin. In the past few months he has gotten up to three milligrams a day, and he is not happy about being dependent on benzodiazepines. His psychiatrist in Charlottesville says not to worry. As long as Dr. Marcus doesn't abuse alcohol or other drugs, and he doesn't touch either, he is fine taking Klonopin. Better to take Klonopin than to be so crippled by panic attacks that he hides inside his house and loses his job or humiliates himself. He can't afford to lose his job or be humiliated. He isn't wealthy like Scarpetta and he could never endure the humiliations she seems to take in stride. Before he succeeded her as chief medical examiner of Virginia, he didn't need Klonopin or antidepressants, but now he has a comorbid disorder, according to his psychiatrist, meaning he has not one disorder but two. In St. Louis, he missed work sometimes and almost never traveled, but he managed. Life before Scarpetta was manageable.

In the living room, he looks out the window again at the big green Supercans and listens for the big truck and the men on it, but he does not hear them. Slipping on his old gray wool overcoat and an old pair of black pigskin gloves, he pauses by the front door to see how he is feeling. He seems to be fine, so he disarms the burglar alarm and opens the door. He walks briskly to the end of his driveway, checking up and down the street for the truck but not hearing or seeing it, and he feels fine as he rolls the Supercans to the side of the garage where they belong.

He returns to his house and takes off his coat and gloves, and he is much calmer now, even happy, and he thoroughly washes his hands and his thoughts return to Scarpetta and he feels relaxed and in good spirits because he is going to get his way about things. All these months he has heard Scarpetta-this and Scarpetta-that, and because he didn't know her, he could not complain. When the health commissioner said, "Her shoes will be hard to fill, probably impossible for you to fill, and there are still some people who won't respect you just because you aren't her," Dr. Marcus said not a word, because what could he say? He didn't know her.

When the new governor extended the courtesy of inviting Dr. Marcus to have coffee in her office after she appointed him, he had to decline because she set the time at eight-thirty on a Monday, which is the same day and time as garbage collection in Westham Green. Of course, he couldn't explain why he couldn't have coffee with her, but it was out of the question, just impossible, and he remembers sitting in his living room listening for the big truck and its big men and wondering how life was going to be for him in Virginia since he declined to have coffee with the governor, who is a woman and probably wouldn't respect him anyway because he's not a woman and he's not Scarpetta.

Dr. Marcus doesn't know for a fact that the new governor is an admirer of Scarpetta, but she probably is. He had no idea what he was up against when he accepted the job of chief and moved here from St. Louis, leaving behind an office full of women medical examiners and death investigators, all of whom knew about Scarpetta and told him what a lucky man he was to get her job because thanks to her, Virginia has the best ME system in the United States, and it was a shame she didn't get on with whoever the governor was back then, the one who fired her, and the women in his office encouraged him to take Scarpetta's job.

They wanted him gone. He knew that at the time. They couldn't figure out for the life of them why Virginia was interested in him, of all people, unless it was because he was nonconfrontational and nonpolitical and nonexistent. He knew what the women in his office were saying at the time. They whispered and worried that his opportunity was going to fall through and they would be stuck with him, and he knew exactly what was being said at the time.

So he moved to Virginia and not a month later found himself at odds with the governor, all because of garbage collection in Westham Green, and he blamed it on Scarpetta. He was cursed because of her. All he did was hear about her and complaints about him because he's not her. He was barely on the job when he came to hate her and everything she had accomplished, and he became masterful at showing his contempt in small ways, by neglecting whatever had been associated with Scarpetta way back when, whether it was a painting or a plant or a book or a pathologist or a dead patient who would have been better off were Scarpetta still chief. He became obsessed with proving that she is a myth and a fraud and a failure, but he couldn't destroy a perfect stranger. He couldn't even utter a negative word about her because he didn't know her.

Then Gilly Paulsson died and her father called the health commissioner, who in turn called the governor, who immediately called the director of the FBI, all because the governor heads a national terrorist committee and Frank Paulsson has connections with the Department of Homeland Security, and wouldn't it be awful if it turned out that little Gilly was killed by some enemy of the U.S. government?

The FBI was quick to agree that the matter merited checking into, and instantly the Bureau interfered with the local police and nobody knew what the other person was doing and some evidence went to the local labs and some evidence went to the FBI labs and other evidence wasn't collected at all, and Dr. Paulsson didn't want Gilly's body released from the morgue until all the facts were known. Mixed in with this mess was Dr. Paulsson's dysfunctional relationship with his estranged wife, and soon enough the death of this nobody little fourteen-year-old was so screwed up and politicized that Dr. Marcus had no choice but to ask the health commissioner what should be done.

"We need to bring in a big-gun consultant," the health commissioner replied. "Before things go really bad."

"They're already bad," Dr. Marcus replied. "The minute Richmond PD heard the FBI was involved, they backed off, ran for cover. And to make matters worse, we don't know what killed the girl. I think her death is suspicious, but we don't have a cause of death."

"We need a consultant. Immediately. Someone who's not from here. Someone who can take the brunt of it, if need be. If the governor gets a lot of shit from this case, national shit, heads will roll and mine won't be the only one, Joel."

"What about Dr. Scarpetta?" Dr. Marcus suggested, and it amazed him at the time that her name leaped to his tongue without premeditation. His response was that effortless and quick.

"Excellent idea. An inspired one," the health commissioner agreed. "Do you know her?"

"I will soon enough," Dr. Marcus said, and it amazed him that he was such a brilliant strategist.

He had never known just how brilliant a strategist he was before that moment, but since he had never criticized Scarpetta, because he didn't know her, he was justified in enthusiastically recommending her as a consultant. Because he had never uttered a negative word about her, he could call her himself, which is what he did that day, just day before yesterday. Soon he would know Scarpetta, oh yes he would, and then he could criticize her and humiliate her and do whatever he liked to her.

He would blame her for everything that went wrong with Gilly Paulsson and the OCME and anything else that might come up, and the governor would forget that Dr. Marcus had declined to have coffee with her. Should she ask him again and should she choose eight-thirty on a Monday or Thursday, Dr. Marcus will simply tell her scheduler that the OCME staff meeting is at eight-thirty, and could the governor do coffee later, because it is very important that he preside over staff meeting. Why he didn't think of that the first time he's not sure, but he'll know what to say next time.

Dr. Marcus picks up the phone in his living room and looks out at the empty street, relieved that garbage collection is of no concern for three more days, and he is feeling very good as he thumbs through a small black address book he has kept for so many years that half the names and numbers in it have been crossed out. He dials a number and looks out at his street and watches an old blue Chevrolet Impala drive by, and he remembers when his mother used to get her old white Impala stuck in the snow at the bottom of the hill, the same hill every winter, when he was growing up in Charlottesville.

"Scarpetta," she answers her cell phone.

"Dr. Marcus here," he says in his practiced, authoritative, but pleasant-enough voice, and he has many voices but at the moment he has chosen his pleasant-enough one.

"Yes," she replies. "Good morning. I hope Dr. Fielding briefed you on our reexamination of Gilly Paulsson."

"I'm afraid he did. He told me your opinion," he says, savoring the words "your opinion" and wishing he could see her reaction, because the words "your opinion" are ones a calculating defense attorney would say. A prosecutor, on the other hand, would say "your conclusion" because that is a validation of experience and expertise, whereas to say "your opinion" is a veiled insult.

"I'm wondering if you've heard about the trace evidence," he then says, thinking of the e-mail he got yesterday from the ever inappropriate Junius Eise.

"No," she says.

"It's quite extraordinary," he says ominously. "That's why we're having a meeting," Dr. Marcus says, and he set up the meeting yesterday but is telling her about it only now. "I'd like you to come by my office this morning at nine-thirty." He watches the old blue Impala pull into a driveway two houses down, and he wonders why it is stopping there and who it belongs to.

Scarpetta hesitates as if his last-minute suggestion doesn't suit her, then she replies, "Of course. I'll be there in half an hour."

"May I ask what you did yesterday afternoon? I didn't see you at my office," he inquires, watching an old black woman get out of the old blue Impala.

"Paperwork, a lot of phone calls. Why, did you need something?"

Dr. Marcus feels slightly giddy and dizzy as he watches the old black woman and the old blue Impala. The great Scarpetta is asking him if he needed something, as if she works for him. But she does work for him. Right now she does. This he finds hard to believe.

"I don't need anything from you at the moment," he says. "I'll see you at the meeting," and he hangs up, and it gives him great pleasure to hang up on Scarpetta.

The heels of his lace-up old-fashioned brown shoes click against the oak floors as he walks into the kitchen and puts on a second pot of decaffeinated coffee. Most of the first pot went to waste because he was too worried about the garbage truck and the men on it to remember the coffee, and it began to smell cooked and he poured it down the sink. So he puts on the coffee and walks back into the living room to check on the Impala.

Through the same window he usually looks out, the one across from his favorite big leather chair, he watches the old black woman pull bags of groceries from the back of the Impala. She must be the housekeeper, he thinks, and it irks him that a black housekeeper would drive the same car his mother did when he was growing up. That was a nice car once. Not everybody had a white Impala with a blue stripe down the side, and he was proud of that car except when it got stuck in the snow at the bottom of the hill. His mother wasn't a good driver. She shouldn't have been allowed to drive that Impala. An Impala is named for a male African antelope that can leap great distances and is easily startled, and his mother was nervous enough when she was just on her own two feet. She didn't need to be behind the wheel of anything named after a male African antelope that was powerful and easily spooked.

The old housekeeper moves slowly, gathering up plastic bags of groceries from the back of the Impala, and moving in an old tired waddle from the car to a side door of the house, then back to the car, gathering up more bags, then closing the car door with her hip. That was a fine car once, Dr. Marcus thinks, staring out his window. The housekeeper's Impala must be forty years old and it seems to be in good shape, and he can't remember the last time he's seen a '63 or '64 Impala. That he should see one today strikes him as significant but he doesn't know what the significance is, and he returns to the kitchen to get his coffee. If he waits another twenty minutes, his doctors will be busy with autopsies and he won't have to talk to anyone, and his pulse picks up speed again as he waits. His nerves start firing again.

At first he blames his racing heart and shakiness and twitching on the trace of caffeine in decaffeinated coffee, but he's had only a few sips, and he realizes something else is happening. He thinks of the Impala across the street and becomes more agitated and out of sorts, and he wishes the housekeeper had never driven up, today of all days, when he was home because of garbage collection. He returns to the living room and sits down in his big leather chair and leans back, trying to relax, and his heart is pounding so violently he can see the front of his white shirt moving, and he takes deep breaths and closes his eyes.

He's lived here four months and never seen that Impala before. He imagines the thin blue steering wheel that has no airbag, and the blue dash on the passenger's side that isn't padded and has no airbag, and old blue seat belts that go around the lap because there aren't shoulder harnesses. He imagines the interior of the Impala, and it isn't the Impala across the street he imagines, but the white one with the blue stripe down the side that his mother drove. His coffee is forgotten and cold on the table by his big leather chair, and he sits back with his eyes shut. Several times Dr. Marcus gets up and looks out the window, and when he doesn't see the blue Impala anymore, he sets the alarm, locks his house, and walks into the garage, and it occurs to him with a stab of fear that maybe the Impala doesn't exist and was never there at all, but it was. Of course it was.

A few minutes later he drives slowly down his street and stops in front of the house several doors down and stares at the empty driveway where he saw the blue Impala and the old black housekeeper carrying in groceries. He sits in his Volvo, which has the highest safety rating of just about any car made, and he stares at the empty driveway, then finally turns into it and gets out. He is old-fashioned but neat in the long gray coat and gray hat and black pigskin gloves that he has worn in cold weather since before he lived in St. Louis, and he knows he looks respectable enough as he rings the front doorbell. He pauses, then rings it again, and the door opens.

"May I help you?" says the woman who answers the door, a woman who might be in her fifties and is wearing a tennis warm-up suit and tennis shoes. She looks familiar and is gracious but not overly friendly.

"I'm Joel Marcus," he says in his pleasant-enough voice. "I live across the street and happened to notice a very old blue Impala in your driveway a little while ago." He is prepared to suggest that he might have her house mixed up with another one should she say she doesn't know anything about a very old blue Impala.

"Oh, Mrs. Walker. She's had that car forever. Wouldn't trade it for a brand new Cadillac," the somewhat familiar neighbor says with a smile, to his vast relief.

"I see," he says. "I was just curious. I collect old cars." He doesn't collect cars, old or otherwise, but he wasn't imagining things, thank the Lord. Of course not.

"Well, you won't be collecting that one," she says cheerfully. "Mrs. Walker sure does love that car. I don't believe we've formally met, but I do know who you are. You're the new coroner. You took the place of that famous woman coroner, oh what was her name? I was shocked and disappointed when she left Virginia. Whatever happened to her, anyway? Here you are, standing out in the cold. Where are my manners? Would you like to come in? She was such an attractive woman too. Oh, what was her name?"

"I really must be on my way," Dr. Marcus replies in a different voice, this one stiff and tight. "I'm afraid I'm quite late for a meeting with the governor," he lies rather coldly.

25.

||| THE SUN IS WEAK in the pale gray sky and the light is thin and cold. Scarpetta walks through the parking lot, her long dark coat flapping around her legs. She walks quickly and with purpose toward the front door of her former building and is annoyed that the number-one parking place, the parking place reserved for the chief medical examiner, is empty. Dr. Marcus isn't here yet. As usual, he is late.

"Good morning, Bruce," she says to the security officer at the desk.

He smiles at her and waves her on. "I'll sign you in," he says, pushing a button that unlocks the next door, the one that leads into the medical examiner's wing of the building.

"Has Marino gotten here?" she asks as she walks.

"Haven't seen him," Bruce replies.

When Fielding didn't answer his door last night, she stood on his front porch trying to call him on the phone, but the old home number she had for him didn't work anymore, and then she tried Marino and could barely hear him because of loud voices and laughter in the background. He might have been in a bar, but she didn't ask and simply told him that Fielding didn't seem to be home and if he didn't show up soon, she was going back to the hotel. All Marino had to say about it was, okay, Doc, and see you later, Doc, and call if you need me, Doc.

Then Scarpetta tried to open Fielding's front and back doors, but they were locked. She rang the bell and knocked, getting increasingly uneasy. Her former assistant chief and right-hand helper and friend had a car under a tarp in the carport, and she had little doubt that the car under the tarp was his beloved old red Mustang but she pulled up an edge of the tarp to make sure, and she was right. She had noticed the Mustang in the number 6 parking place behind the building that morning, so he was still driving it, but just because his Mustang was home under the tarp didn't mean he was inside the house and refusing to come to the door. He might have a second vehicle, perhaps an SUV. It would make sense for him to have a backup, more rugged vehicle, and he might be out somewhere in his SUV or whatever else he was driving these days, and was on his way and running a little late or had forgotten he had invited her to dinner.

She went through all these convolutions as she waited for him to come to the door, and then she began to worry that something had happened to Fielding. Maybe he had hurt himself. Maybe he was suffering a violent allergic reaction and had broken out in hives or was going into anaphylactic shock. Maybe he had committed suicide. Maybe he timed his suicide with her coming to his house because he would think she could handle it. If you kill yourself, somebody has to handle it. Everybody always assumes she can handle anything, so it would be her terrible lot in life to be the one to find him in bed with a bullet in his head or a stomach full of pills and handle the situation. Only Lucy seems to know that Scarpetta has her limitations, and Lucy rarely tells her anything. She hasn't seen Lucy since September. Something is going on, and Lucy doesn't think Scarpetta can handle it.

"Well, I can't seem to find Marino," Scarpetta says to Bruce. "So if you hear from him, please tell him I'm looking for him, that there's a meeting."

"Junius Eise may know where he is," Bruce replies. "You know, from Trace? Eise was going to hook up with him last night. Maybe go to the FOP lounge."

Scarpetta thinks of what Dr. Marcus said when he called her barely an hour ago, something about the trace evidence, which apparently is the reason for this meeting, and she can't find Marino. He was at his old Fraternal Order of Police watering hole hangout last night, probably drinking with Mr. Trace Evidence himself, and she has no idea what is going on and Marino isn't answering the phone. She pushes open the opaque glass door and steps inside her former waiting area.

She is shocked to see Mrs. Paulsson sitting on the couch, staring vacantly, her hands clutching the pocketbook in her lap. "Mrs. Paulsson?" Scarpetta says with concern, walking over to her. "Is someone helping you?"

"They told me to be here when they opened," Mrs. Paulsson says. "Then I was told to wait because the chief hasn't gotten here yet."

Scarpetta was not informed that Mrs. Paulsson would be present at the meeting with Dr. Marcus. "Come on," she says to her. "I'll take you inside. You're meeting with Dr. Marcus?"

"I think so."

"I'm meeting with him too," Scarpetta says. "I guess we're going to the same meeting. Come on. You can come with me."

Mrs. Paulsson slowly gets up from the couch, as if she is tired and in pain. Scarpetta wishes there were real plants in the waiting area, just a few real plants to add warmth and life. Real plants make people feel less alone and there is no lonelier place on earth than a morgue, and no one should ever have to visit a morgue, much less wait to visit one. She presses a buzzer next to a window. On the other side of the glass is a countertop, then a stretch of gray-blue carpet, then a doorway leading to the administrative offices.

"May I help you?" a woman's voice blares over the intercom.

"Dr. Scarpetta," she announces herself.

"Come in," the voice says, and the glass door to the right of the window clicks open.

Scarpetta holds the door for Mrs. Paulsson. "I hope you haven't been waiting long," Scarpetta says to her. "I'm so sorry you had to wait. I wish I'd known you were coming. I would have met you or made sure you had a comfortable place to sit and some coffee."

"They told me to get here early if I wanted a parking place," she replies, looking around as they walk into the outer office where the clerks file and work on their computers.

Scarpetta can tell that Mrs. Paulsson has never visited the OCME before. She isn't surprised. Dr. Marcus isn't the type to spend much time having sit-down visits with families, and Dr. Fielding is too used up to have sit-down emotionally wrenching meetings with families. She is suspicious that the reason for summoning Mrs. Paulsson to a meeting is political and is probably going to make Scarpetta angry and disgusted. From her cubicle a clerk tells them that they can go on back to the conference room, that Dr. Marcus is running a little late. It strikes Scarpetta that the clerks never seem to leave their cubicles. When she walks into the front office, it is as if cubicles work here, not people.

"Come on," Scarpetta says, touching Mrs. Paulsson's back. "Would you like coffee? Let's get you some and we'll go sit down."

"Gilly's still here," she says, walking woodenly and looking around with frightened eyes. "They won't let me take her." She begins to cry, twisting the strap of her pocketbook. "It's not right that she's still here."

"What reason are they giving you?" Scarpetta asks as they walk slowly toward the conference room.

"It's all because of Frank. She was so attached to him, and he said she could come live with him. She wanted to." She cries harder as Scarpetta stops at the coffee machine and begins pouring coffee into styrofoam cups. "Gilly told the judge she wanted to move to Charleston after she finishes this school year. He wants her there, in Charleston."

Scarpetta carries their coffees into the conference room and this time sits at the middle of the long polished table. She and Mrs. Paulsson are alone in the big empty room and Mrs. Paulsson stares numbly at the Guts Man, then at the anatomical skeleton hanging from his rack in a corner. Her hand trembles as she lifts the coffee to her lips.

"Frank's family's buried in Charleston, you see," she says. "Generations of them. My family's buried here in Hollywood Cemetery, and I have a plot there too. Why does this have to be so hard? It's already so hard. He just wants Gilly so he can spite me, so he can pay me back, so he can make me look bad. He always said he'd drive me mad and they'd end up locking me in some hospital. Well, he's about done it this time."

"Are you two talking to each other?" Scarpetta asks.

"He doesn't talk. He tells me things, gives me orders. He wants everyone to think he's a wonderful father. But he doesn't care about her the way I do. It's his fault she's dead."

"You've said that before. How is it his fault?"

"I just know he did something. He wants to destroy me. First it was take Gilly away to live with him. Now it's take Gilly away forever. He wants me to go crazy. Then nobody sees what a bad husband and father he really is. Nobody sees the truth, and there's a truth all right. They just see that I'm crazy and feel sorry for him. But there's a truth all right."

They turn around as the conference room door opens and a well-dressed woman walks in. She appears to be in her late thirties or early forties and has the fresh look of someone who finds plenty of time for sleep, a proper diet and exercise, and regular touch-ups to her highlighted blond hair. The woman sets a leather briefcase on top of the table and smiles and nods at Mrs. Paulsson as if they have met before. The clasps of her briefcase spring free in loud snaps and she gets out a file folder and a legal pad and sits down.

"I'm FBI Special Agent Weber. Karen Weber." She looks at Scarpetta. "You must be Dr. Scarpetta. I was told you'd be here. Mrs. Paulsson, how are you today? I wasn't expecting to see you."

Mrs. Paulsson finds a tissue in her pocketbook and wipes her eyes. "Good morning," she replies.

Scarpetta has to control her impulse to bluntly ask Special Agent Weber why the FBI has inserted itself or has been inserted into the case. But Gilly's mother is sitting at the table. There is very little Scarpetta can bluntly ask. She tries an indirect approach.

"Are you from the Richmond Field Office?" she says to Special Agent Weber.

"From Quantico," she replies. "The Behavioral Science Unit. Perhaps you've seen our new forensic labs at Quantico?"

"No, I'm afraid not."

"They're something. Really something."

"I'm sure they are."

"Mrs. Paulsson, what brings you here today?" Special Agent Weber asks.

"I don't know," she replies. "I came for the report. They're supposed to give me Gilly's jewelry. She has a pair of earrings she was wearing and a bracelet, a little leather bracelet she never took off. They said the chief wanted to say hello to me."

"You're here for this meeting?" the FBI agent asks with a puzzled look on her attractive, well-maintained face.

"I don't know."

"You're here for Gilly's reports and belongings?" Scarpetta asks as it begins to enter her mind that a mistake has been made.

"Yes. I was told I could come by for them at nine. I haven't been able to come here before now, I just couldn't. I have a check written because there's a fee," Mrs. Paulsson says with the same scared look in her eyes. "Maybe I'm not supposed to be in here. Nobody said anything about a meeting."

"Yes, well, while you're here," says Special Agent Weber, "let me ask you a question, Mrs. Paulsson. You remember when we talked the other day? You said your husband, your former husband, is a pilot? Is that correct?"

"No. He's not a pilot. I said he wasn't."

"Oh. Okay. Because I couldn't find any record of his ever having a pilot's license of any type," Special Agent Weber replies. "So I was a little confused." She smiles.

"A lot of people assume he's a pilot," Mrs. Paulsson says.

"Understandably."

"He likes to spend time with pilots, especially military ones. He especially likes women pilots. I've always known what he's about," Mrs. Paulsson says dully. "You'd have to be blind, deaf, and dumb not to know what he's about."

"Could you elaborate on that?" Special Agent Weber asks.

"Oh, he gives the pilots physicals. You can imagine," she says. "That's what floats his boat. A woman comes in wearing a flight suit. You can just imagine."

"You've heard stories about him sexually harassing female pilots?" Special Agent Weber asks somberly.

"He always denies it and gets away with it," she adds. "You know he has a sister in the Air Force. I've always wondered if it has to do with that. She's quite a lot older than him."

It is at this precise moment that Dr. Marcus walks into the conference room. He wears another white cotton shirt, a sleeveless undershirt showing through it, and his tie is dark blue and narrow. His eyes drift past Scarpetta and fix on Mrs. Paulsson.

"I don't believe we've met," he says to her in an authoritative but cordial tone.

"Mrs. Paulsson," Dr. Scarpetta says, "this is the chief medical examiner, Dr. Marcus."

"Did one of you invite Mrs. Paulsson?" He looks at Scarpetta, then at Special Agent Weber. "I'm afraid I'm confused."

Mrs. Paulsson gets up from the table, her movements slow and muddled as if her limbs are communicating different messages to each other. "I don't know what's happened. I just came for the paperwork and her little gold heart earrings and the bracelet."

"I'm afraid it's my fault," Scarpetta says, getting up too. "I saw her waiting and made an assumption. I apologize."

"That's right," Dr. Marcus says to Mrs. Paulsson. "I heard you might come by this morning. Please let me express my sympathy." He smiles his condescending smile. "Your daughter is a very high priority here."

"Oh," Mrs. Paulsson replies.

"I'll walk you out." Scarpetta opens the door for her. "I'm truly sorry," she says as they walk along the gray-blue carpet, past the coffee machine, and into the main corridor. "I hope I haven't embarrassed or upset you."

"Tell me where Gilly is," she says, stopping in the middle of the corridor. "I have to know. Please tell me exactly where she is."

Scarpetta hesitates. Such questions are not unusual for her but they are never simple to answer. "Gilly is on the other side of those doors." She turns around and points down the length of the corridor to a set of doors. Beyond them is another set of doors, then the morgue and its coolers and freezers.

"I suppose she's in a coffin. I've heard about the pine boxes places like this have," Mrs. Paulsson says, her eyes filling with tears.

"No, she's not in a coffin. There are no pine boxes here. Your daughter's body is in a cooler."

"My poor baby must be so cold," she cries.

"Gilly doesn't feel the cold, Mrs. Paulsson," Scarpetta says kindly. "She's not feeling any discomfort or pain. I promise."

"You've seen her?"

"Yes, I have," Scarpetta replies. "I examined her."

"Tell me she didn't suffer. Please tell me she didn't."

But Scarpetta can't tell her that. To tell her that would be a lie. "There are a lot of tests still to be done," she replies. "The labs will be doing tests for quite some time. Everybody's working very hard to find out exactly what happened to Gilly."

Mrs. Paulsson cries quietly as Scarpetta leads her down the corridor, back to the administrative offices, and asks one of the clerks to leave her cubicle to give Mrs. Paulsson copies of the reports she has requested and to release Gilly's personal effects, which are a pair of gold heart earrings and a leather bracelet, nothing more. Her pajamas and bedding and whatever else the police gathered are considered evidence and aren't going anywhere right now. Scarpetta is just walking back to the conference room when Marino appears, walking quickly along the corridor, his head bent and face flushed.

"Not a good morning so far," she comments when he walks up. "Not for you either, it appears. I've been trying to get hold of you. I guess you got my message."

"What's she doing here?" he blurts out, referring to Mrs. Paulsson and visibly upset.

"Picking up Gilly's personal effects, copies of reports."

"She can do that when they can't even decide who gets her body?"

"She's next of kin. I'm not sure what reports they're releasing to her. I'm not sure of anything that goes on around here," she says. "The FBI's shown up for the meeting. I don't know who else has or will. The latest twist is that Frank Paulsson allegedly sexually harasses female pilots."

"Huh." Marino is in a hurry and acting perfectly bizarre, and he smells like booze and looks like hell.

"Are you all right?" she asks. "What am I saying? Of course you're not."

"It's no big deal," he says.

26.

||| MARINO HEAPS SUGAR into his coffee. He must be in very bad shape to take refined white sugar, because it is off-limits in his diet, absolutely the worst thing he can put into his mouth right now.

"You sure you want to do that to yourself?" Scarpetta asks. "You're going to be sorry."

"What the hell was she doing here?" He stirs in another spoonful of sugar. "I walk in the morgue and there's the kid's mother walking down the hallway. Don't tell me she was viewing Gilly, because I know she isn't viewable. So what in the hell was she doing here?"

Marino is dressed in the same black cargo pants and windbreaker and LAPD baseball cap, and he hasn't shaved and his eyes are exhausted and wild. Maybe after the FOP lounge, he went out to see one of his women, one of those lowlife women he used to meet in the bowling alley and get drunk with and sleep with.

"If you're going to be in a mood, maybe it's better you don't go into the meeting with me," Scarpetta says. "They didn't invite you. So I don't need to make matters worse by showing up with you when you're in a mood. You know how you get when you eat sugar these days."

"Huh," he says, looking at the closed conference room door. "Yeah, well, I'll show those assholes a mood."

"What's happened?"

"There's talk going around," he says in a low, angry voice. "About you."

"Talk going around where?" She hates the kind of talk he means and usually pays little attention to it.

"Talk about you moving back here, and that's really why you're here." He looks accusingly at her, sipping his poisonously sweet coffee. "What the hell are you holding back from me, huh?"

"I wouldn't move back here," she says. "I'm surprised you would listen to baseless, idle talk."

"I ain't coming back here," he says, as if the talk is about him and not her. "No way. Don't even think about it."

"I wouldn't think about it. Let's don't think about it at all right now." She walks on to the conference room and opens the dark wooden door.

Marino can follow her if he wants, or he can stand out by the coffee machine, eating sugar all day. She isn't going to coax or cajole him. She'll have to find out more about what's bothering him, but not now. Now she has a meeting with Dr. Marcus, the FBI, and Jack Fielding, who stood her up last night, and whose skin is more inflamed than when she saw him last. No one speaks to her as she finds a chair. No one speaks to Marino as he follows her and pulls out a chair next to hers. Well, this is an inquisition, she thinks.

"Let's get started," Dr. Marcus begins. "I guess you've been introduced to Special Agent Weber from the FBI Profiling Unit," he says to Scarpetta, calling the unit by the wrong name. It is the Behavioral Science Unit, not the Profiling Unit. "We have a real problem on our hands, as if we didn't have enough problems." His face is grim, his small eyes glittering coldly behind his glasses. "Dr. Scarpetta," he says loudly. "You reautopsied Gilly Paulsson. But you also examined Mr. Whitby, the tractor driver, did you not?"

Fielding stares down at a file folder and says nothing, his face raw and red.

"I wouldn't say I examined him," she replies, giving Fielding a look. "Nor do I have any idea what this is about."

"Did you touch him?" asks Special Agent Karen Weber.

"I'm sorry. But is the FBI also involved in the tractor driver's death?" Scarpetta asks.

"Possibly. We'll hope not, but quite possibly," says Special Agent Weber, who seems to enjoy questioning Scarpetta, the former chief.

"Did you touch him?" It is Dr. Marcus who asks this time.

"Yes," Scarpetta replies. "I did touch him."

"And of course you did," Dr. Marcus says to Fielding. "You did the external examination and began the autopsy, and then at some point joined her in the decomp room to reexamine the Paulsson girl."

"Oh yeah," Fielding mutters, glancing up from his case file, but not looking at anyone in particular. "This is bullshit."

"What did you say?" Dr. Marcus asks.

"You heard me. This is bullshit," Fielding says. "I told you that yesterday when this came up. This morning I'll tell you the same damn thing. It's bullshit. I'm not going to be hung on some cross in front of the FBI or anyone else."

"I'm afraid it isn't bullshit, Dr. Fielding. We have a major problem with the evidence. The trace evidence recovered from Gilly Paulsson's body seems identical to trace evidence recovered from the tractor driver, Mr. Whitby. Now, I just don't see how that's possible unless there's been some sort of cross-contamination. And by the way, I also don't understand why you were looking for trace evidence in the Whitby case to begin with. He's an accident. Not a homicide. Correct me if I'm wrong."

"I'm not prepared to swear to anything," Fielding replies, his face and hands so raw it is painful to look at them. "He was crushed to death, but how that happened remains to be proven. I didn't witness his death. I swabbed a wound on his face to see if there might have been any grease, for example, in the event someone comes forward and says he was assaulted, hit in the face with something as opposed to being just run over."

"What's this about? What trace?" asks Marino, and he is surprisingly calm for a man who has just shocked his system with a dangerous dose of sugar.

"Frankly, I don't consider this any of your business," Dr. Marcus says to him. "But since your colleague insists on having you in tow wherever she goes, I must accept that you're here. I must in turn insist that what is said in this room stays in the room."

"Insist away," Marino says, smiling at Special Agent Weber. "And to what do we owe the pleasure?" he asks her. "I used to know the unit chief up there in Marine Corps Land. Funny how everyone forgets that Quantico is more about the Marines than it is the FBI. Ever heard of Benton Wesley?"

"Of course."

"Ever read all the shit he's written about profiling?"

"I'm very familiar with his work," she says, her fingers laced on top of a legal pad, her long nails flawlessly manicured and painted deep red.

"Good. Then you probably know he thinks profiling's about as reliable as fortune cookies," Marino says.

"I didn't come here to be abused," Special Agent Weber says to Dr. Marcus.

"Gee, I sure am sorry," Marino says to Dr. Marcus. "It's not my intention to run her off. I'm sure we could use an expert from the FBI Profiler Unit to tell us all about trace evidence."

"That's quite enough," Dr. Marcus says angrily. "If you can't behave as a professional, then I must ask you to leave."

"No, no. Don't mind me," Marino says. "I'll sit here nice and pretty and listen. Go right ahead."

Jack Fielding is slowly shaking his head, staring down at the file folder.

"I'll go ahead," Scarpetta says, and she no longer cares about being nice or even diplomatic. "Dr. Marcus, this is the first you've mentioned trace evidence in Gilly Paulsson's case. You call me to Richmond to help with her case and then fail to tell me about trace evidence?" She looks at him, then at Fielding.

"Don't ask me," Fielding tells her. "I did the swabs. I didn't get the report back from the labs, not even a phone call. Not that I usually do anymore. At least not directly. I only heard about this late yesterday when he"—he means Dr. Marcus—"mentioned it to me as I was getting into my car."

"I didn't find out until late in the day," Dr. Marcus snaps. "One of those inane little notes that what's-his-name Ice or Eise is always sending me about the way we do things, as if he could do them better. There was nothing especially helpful about what the labs have found so far. A few hairs and other debris, including possible paint chips that I suppose could have come from anywhere, including an automobile, I suppose, or something inside the Paulsson house. Perhaps even a bicycle or a toy."

"They should know if the paint is automotive," Scarpetta replies. "Certainly, they should be able to match it back to anything inside the house."

"I think my point is that there is no DNA. The swabs were negative for that. And of course, if we're thinking homicide, DNA on a vaginal or oral swab would have been very significant. I was more focused on whether there was DNA than on these alleged paint chips until I get this e-mail late yesterday from trace evidence and come to find out the astonishing fact that the swabs you took on the tractor driver apparently have this same debris on them." Dr. Marcus stares at Fielding.

"And this so-called cross-contamination would have happened how, exactly?" Scarpetta asks.

Dr. Marcus raises his hands in a slow, exaggerated shrug. "You tell me."

"I don't see how," she replies. "We changed our gloves, not that it matters, because we didn't swab Gilly Paulsson's body again. That would have been an exercise in futility after she's been washed, autopsied, swabbed, washed again, and reautopsied after being stored inside a pouch for two weeks."

"Of course you wouldn't have swabbed her again," Dr. Marcus says as if he is very big and she is very small. "But I'm assuming you weren't finished autopsying Mr. Whitby and perhaps returned to him after reexamining the Paulsson girl."

"I swabbed Mr. Whitby, then worked on the Paulsson girl," Fielding says. "I did not swab her. That's clear. And there couldn't have been any trace left on her to transfer to him or anyone else."

"This isn't for me to explain," Dr. Marcus decides. "I don't know what the hell happened, but something did. We have to consider every possible scenario because you can rest assured that attorneys will, should either case ever go to court."

"Gilly's death will go to court," Special Agent Weber says as if she knows this for a fact and is personally connected to the dead fourteen-year-old. "Maybe there's been some kind of mix-up in the lab," she then considers. "Some sample mislabeled or one sample contaminated another sample. Did the same forensic scientist do both analyses?"

"Eise, I guess that's his name, did them both," Dr. Marcus answers. "He did the trace or is doing the trace, but not the hair."

"You've mentioned hair twice. What hair?" Scarpetta asks. "Now you're telling me hair was recovered."

"Several hairs from the Gilly Paulsson scene," he replies. "I think from the bed linens."

"Let's hope like hell it ain't the tractor driver's hair," Marino remarks. "Or maybe you should hope it is. He kills the girl then can't take the guilt and runs over himself with his tractor. Case exceptionally cleared."

No one thinks he is funny.

"I asked that her bed linens be checked for ciliated respiratory epithelium," Scarpetta says to Fielding.

"The pillowcase," he says. "The answer's yes."

She should be relieved. The presence of that biological evidence suggests that Gilly was asphyxiated, but the truth hurts her deeply. "An awful way to die," she says. "Perfectly awful."

"I'm sorry," Special Agent Weber says. "Am I missing something?"

"The kid was murdered," Marino replies. "Other than that, I don't know what the hell you're missing."

"You know, I really don't have to put up with this," she says to Dr. Marcus.

"Yeah, she really does," Marino says to him. "Unless you want to pry me out of this room yourself. Otherwise, I'm just gonna sit here nice and pretty and say whatever the hell I want."

"While we're having this open, honest conversation," Scarpetta says to the special agent, "I'd like to hear directly from you why the FBI is involved in Gilly Paulsson's case."

"Very simply, the Richmond police asked for our assistance," Special Agent Weber replies.

"Why?"

"I suppose you should ask them that."

"I'm asking you," Scarpetta tells her. "Someone's going to shoot straight with me or I'm walking out of this office and not coming back."

"It's not quite that simple." Dr. Marcus looks at her long and steady with heavy-lidded eyes, reminding her of a lizard. "You've involved yourself. You examined the tractor driver, and now we have possible cross-contamination of evidence. I'm afraid it's not as easy as your just walking out and not coming back. The choice is no longer yours to make."

"This is such bullshit," Fielding mutters again, staring down at his raw, scaly hands in his lap.

"I'll tell you why the FBI's involved." It is Marino who offers this. "At least I'll tell you what the Richmond PD has to say about it, if you really want to know. It might hurt your feelings," he says to Special Agent Weber. "And by the way, did I mention how much I like your suit? And your red shoes. Love 'em, but what happens if you get into a foot pursuit in those things?"

"I've had enough," she says in a smoldering tone.

"No! I've had enough!" Jack Fielding suddenly slams his fist on the table and is on his feet. He steps back from the table and looks around it with flashing, enraged eyes. "Fuck all of this. I quit. Do you hear me, you little numb-nut asshole," he says to Dr. Marcus. "I quit. And fuck you too." He jabs a finger in the air, poking his index finger at Special Agent Weber. "You stupid fucking Feds, coming in here like God and you don't know shit. You couldn't work a fucking homicide if it happened right in your own fucking bed! I quit!" He backs toward the door. "Go ahead, Pete. I know you know," he says, staring at Marino. "Tell Dr. Scarpetta the truth. Go on. Someone should."

He strides out the door and shuts it loudly.

After a stunned silence, Dr. Marcus says, "Well, that was quite something. I apologize," he says to Special Agent Weber.

"Is he having a nervous breakdown?" she asks.

"Is there something you need to say?" Scarpetta looks at Marino, and she is more than a little unhappy that he might have information he hasn't bothered to pass on to her. She wonders if he stayed out all night drinking, and didn't bother to let her know information that could make a difference.

"From the way I hear it," he replies, "the Feds are interested in little Gilly because her dad's a snitch, you might say, for Homeland Security. He's down there in Charleston supposedly snitching on pilots who might have terrorist inclinations, and that's a big worry down there since they've got the biggest fleet of C-17 cargo planes in the country, each one about one hundred and eighty-five million a pop. Wouldn't be a good thing if some terrorist pilot suddenly crashed a plane into that fleet, now would it?"

"It probably would be a good idea for you to shut up right about now," Special Agent Weber says to him, her fingers still laced on top of her legal pad, but her knuckles are white. "You don't want to be getting into this."

"Oh, I'm in it," he replies, taking off his baseball cap and rubbing the sandy stubble sprinkled over his otherwise perfectly bald head. "Sorry. I was up kind of late and didn't have time to shave this morning." He rubs his stubbly jaw and it scratches like sandpaper. "Me and Forensic Scientist Eise and Detective Browning had a bonding moment at the FOP, and then I had a few other chats I won't go into for confidentiality reasons."

"You can stop right now," FBI Special Agent Weber warns him, as if she might just arrest him for talking, as if talking is a new federal crime. Maybe in her mind he is about to commit treason.

"I'd rather you didn't stop," Scarpetta says.

"The FBI and Homeland Security don't like each other much," Marino says. "See, a big chunk of Justice's budget has been forked over to Homeland Security, and we all know how much the FBI likes a big fat budget. What is it last I heard?" He looks coolly at Special Agent Weber. "About seventy lobbyists on Capitol Hill, every one of them there to beg for money while all you empty suits run around trying to take over everybody's jurisdiction, take over the goddamn world?"

"Why are we sitting here listening to this?" Special Agent Weber asks Dr. Marcus.

"The story is," Marino says to Scarpetta, "the Bureau's been sniffing around Frank Paulsson for a while. And you're right. There's rumors about him, all right. Seems he supposedly abuses his privileges as a flight surgeon, which is especially scary in light of him being a snitch for Homeland Security. Sure would hate for him to sign off on a pilot—especially a military pilot—because maybe he's getting favors. And nothing the Bureau would like better than to nail Homeland Security and make them look like idiots, so when the governor got a little worried about things and called the FBI, that opened the gate, now didn't it." He looks at the special agent. "Now I doubt the governor knows just what kind of help she asked for. Didn't realize the Bureau's idea of help was to make another federal agency look like shit. In other words, this is all about power and money. But then, ain't everything?"

"No, not everything," Scarpetta replies in a hard voice, and she has had as much of this as she intends to take. "This is about a fourteen-year-old girl who died a painful, terrifying death. It's about Gilly Paulsson's murder." She gets up from her chair and snaps shut her briefcase and picks it up by its leather handles and looks at Dr. Marcus, then at Special Agent Weber. "That's what this is supposed to be about."

27.

|||BY THE TIME they reach Broad Street, Scarpetta is ready to get the truth out of him. It doesn't matter what he wants. He is going to tell her.

"You did something last night," she says, "and I'm not just talking about your hanging out at the FOP with whoever you were drinking with."

"I don't know what you're getting at." Marino is big and gloomy in the passenger's seat, his cap pulled low over his sullen face.

"Oh yes you do. You went to see her."

"Now I sure as hell don't know what you're talking about." He stares out his side window.

"Oh yes you do." She cuts across Broad at a vigorous rate of speed, driving because she insisted on it, because there was no way she was going to allow Marino or anyone else to be in the driver's seat right this minute. "I know you. Damn it, Marino. You've done this before. If you did it again, just tell me. I saw the way she looked at you when we were at her house. You saw it, you damn well did, and were happy about it. I'm not stupid."

He doesn't answer her, staring out his window, his face shadowed by the cap and averted from her.

"Tell me, Marino. Did you go see Mrs. Paulsson? Did you meet up with her somewhere? Tell me the truth. I'm going to get it out of you eventually. You know I will," Scarpetta says, stopping abruptly at a yellow light turning red. She looks over at him. "Okay. Your silence speaks volumes. That's why you acted so strange when you ran into her at the office this morning, isn't it? You were with her last night and maybe things didn't go quite the way you hoped, so you got surprised this morning when you saw her at the office."

"That's not it."

"Then tell me."

"Suz just needed someone to talk to and I needed information. So we helped each other out," he says to the window.

"Suz?"

"She helped out, now didn't she?" he goes on. "I got some insight about all this Homeland Security, about what a dickhead her ex-husband is, about what a sleaze he is and why the FBI might be after him."

"Might be?" She swings left on Franklin Street, heading to her first office in Richmond, her former building that is being torn down. "You seemed pretty sure of yourself in the meeting, if what just happened can be called a meeting. This was guessing on your part? Might be? What are you saying, exactly?"

"She called my cell phone last night," Marino replies. "They've torn down a lot since we got here. A lot's been torn down in more ways than one." He looks out at the demolition ahead.

The precast building is smaller and more pitiful than when they first saw it. Or maybe they are no longer surprised by the destruction, and it only seems smaller and more pitiful. Scarpetta slows as she approaches 14th Street and looks for a place to park the car.

"We're going to have to go up Cary," she decides. "There's a pay lot just a block or two up Cary, or at least there used to be."

"The hell with it. Drive right up to the building and off the road," Marino says. "I've got us covered." He reaches down and unzips his black cloth briefcase, and pulls out a red Chief Medical Examiner plate. He slides it between the windshield and dash.

"Now how did you manage that?" She can't believe it. "How the hell did you do that?"

"Things happen when you take time to chat with the girls in the front office."

"You're very bad," she says, shaking her head. "I've missed having one of those," she adds, because once upon a time, parking was not the problem or inconvenience that it has become. She could roll up on any crime scene and park anywhere she wanted. She could show up for court during rush hour and tuck her car in some illegal spot, easily, because she had a little red plate with CHIEF MEDICAL EXAMINER stamped on it in big white letters. "Why did Mrs. Paulsson call you last night?" She can't quite bring herself to call her Suz.

"She wanted to talk," he says, opening his door. "Come on, let's get this over with. You should have worn boots."

 28.

||| ALL THE TIME since last night Marino has been thinking about Suz. He likes the way she wears her hair just long enough to brush her shoulders, and he likes it blond. Blond is his favorite, it always has been.

When he met her at her house for the first time, he liked the curve of her cheek and the fullness of her lips. He liked the way she looked at him. She made him feel big and important and strong, and in her eyes he saw that she believed he knew what to do about problems, even though her problems are beyond fixing, no matter who she might look at. She would have to look at God Himself to get her problems fixed, and that isn't going to happen because God probably isn't moved in the same way men like Marino are.

Her looking at Marino the way she did was probably what got to him most, and when she moved close to him as they were searching

Gilly's bedroom, he felt her closeness. He knew trouble was on its way. He knew if Scarpetta sensed the truth, he would hear an earful.

He and Scarpetta are walking through thick red mud, and it always amazes him that she can walk through anything in the damndest shoes and she just keeps on going and doesn't complain. Wet red mud sucks at Marino's black boots, and his feet slip as he picks his steps carefully, and she doesn't even seem to notice that she doesn't have boots. She's wearing low-heeled black lace-up shoes that make sense and look good with her suit, or did. Now she may as well be walking on clods of red mud, and the red mud is spattering the hem of her pants and her long coat as she and Marino make their way toward their beat-up and half-ruined old building.

The demolition crew stops working as Marino and Scarpetta walk like fools through rubble and mud, heading straight into all the violence, and a big man in a hard hat stares at them. He is holding a clipboard, talking to another man in a hard hat. The man with the clipboard starts walking toward them and waving his hand, as if shooing them away like tourists. Marino starts motioning for the man to keep coming because they need to have a conversation. When the man with the clipboard gets to them and notices Marino's black LAPD baseball cap, he pays more attention. That cap is turning out to be a damn good thing, Marino thinks. He doesn't need to identify himself falsely or identify himself at all because the cap takes care of introductions. It takes care of other things, too.

"I'm Investigator Marino," he says to the man with the clipboard. "This is Dr. Scarpetta, the medical examiner."

"Oh," the man with the clipboard says. "You're here about Ted Whitby." He starts shaking his head. "I couldn't believe it. You probably heard about his family."

"Tell me," Marino says.

"Wife's pregnant with their first baby. Second marriage for Ted. Anyway, see that guy over there?" He turns back toward the busted-up building and points at a man in gray climbing out of the cab of a crane. "That's Sam Stiles, and he and Ted had their problems, let's just put it that way. She—that's Ted's wife—is saying that Sam swung the wrecking ball too close to Ted's tractor and that's why he fell off and got run over."

"What makes you think he fell off?" asks Scarpetta.

She's wondering about what she saw, Marino thinks. She still believes she saw Ted Whitby right before he got run over, that when she saw him he was standing on his own two feet doing something to the engine. Maybe what she saw is exactly right. Knowing her, it probably is.

"Don't think that necessarily, ma'am," the man with the clipboard replies, and he is about Marino's age but with plenty of hair and wrinkles. His skin is tanned and weathered like a cowboy's, and his eyes are bright blue. "All I'm telling you is what the wife, the widow I guess, is going around mouthing off to everybody. Of course she wants money. Isn't that always the way? Not that I don't feel sorry for her. But it ain't right to be blaming people for somebody getting killed."

"Were you here when it happened?" the Doc asks.

"Right there, not more than a couple hundred feet from where it happened." He points to the front right corner of the building, or what is left of it.

"You saw it?"

"No, ma'am. Nobody I know saw it, exactly. He was in the back parking lot working on the engine because it was stalling. So he jumped it, is my guess, and the rest's history. Next thing I saw or anybody else saw for that matter was the tractor rolling off with nobody on it, and it hit that yellow pole near the bay door and got hung. But Ted was on the ground, hurt bad. He was bleeding bad. I mean, it was bad."

"Was he conscious when you got to him?" the Doc asks, and as usual, she's writing notes in her black notebook, and slung over her shoulder is a black nylon scene case that has a long strap.

"I didn't hear him say nothing." The man with the clipboard makes a painful face and looks away from them. He swallows hard and clears his throat. "His eyes were open and he was trying to breathe. That's mainly what sticks in my mind and probably always will. Is him trying to breathe and his face turning blue. Then he was gone, just that quick. The police got here, of course, and an ambulance, but nobody could do a thing."

Marino is just standing here in the mud, listening, and he decides he better ask a thing or two, because it makes him uneasy when he stands too long with his mouth shut, like he's stupid. Scarpetta makes him feel stupid. She doesn't try to and would never try to, and that's worse.

"This Sam Stiles guy," Marino says, nodding his black LAPD cap toward the motionless crane and its wrecking ball that is swaying slightly from the cable attached to the boom. "Where was he when Ted got run over? Anywhere near him?"

"Naw. That's just ridiculous. The idea that Ted somehow got knocked off his tractor by the wrecking ball is so ridiculous it would be funny if any of this was funny. You got any idea what a wrecking ball would do to a man?"

"Wouldn't be pretty," Marino comments.

"Knock his brains right out of his head. Wouldn't need no tractor to run him over after that."

Scarpetta is writing all this down. Now and then she looks around thoughtfully and writes something else. One time Marino happened across her notes in plain view on her desk while she was out of the office. Curious about what goes on in her head, he took the opportunity to take a good look. He couldn't make out more than one word, and that one word happened to be his name, Marino. Not only is her writing that bad, but when she makes notes she has her own secret language, her own weird shorthand that no one but her secretary Rose can decipher.

Now she is asking the man with the clipboard his name, and he is telling her it is Bud Light, which is easy enough for Marino to remember, even if he doesn't believe in Bud Lite or Miller Lite or Michelob Lite or anything lite. She is explaining that she needs to know exactly where the body was found because she needs to take soil samples. Bud doesn't seem the least bit curious. Maybe he assumes good-looking women medical examiners and big cops in LAPD caps always take soil samples when some construction worker is run over by a tractor. So they start walking through the thick wet mud again, getting closer to the building, and all the while this is going on, Marino is thinking about Suz.

Last night he was just starting another round of whisky at the FOP lounge, having a nice honest conversation with Junius Eise, or Eise-Ass, as Marino has called him for years. Browning had already gone home and Marino was talking away when his cell phone rang. By this point, he was feeling pretty good and probably shouldn't have answered his cell phone. Probably it should have been turned off, but he hadn't turned it off because Scarpetta had called earlier when Fielding wouldn't come to the door, and Marino told her to call back if she needed him. That's the real reason he answered his cell phone when it rang, although it is also true that when he's enjoying another round he is, at that moment more than any other, most likely to answer the door or the phone or talk to a stranger.

"Marino," he said above the din inside the FOP lounge.

"This is Suzanna Paulsson. I'm so sorry to bother you." She began to cry.

It doesn't matter what she said after that, and some of it he can't remember as he's picking his way through thick red mud while Scarpetta digs into her shoulder bag for packets of sterile wooden tongue depressors and plastic freezer bags. The most important part of what happened last night Marino can't remember and probably never will, because Suz had whisky at her house, sour-mash bourbon, and lots of it. She was wearing jeans and a soft pink sweater when she led him into the living room and drew the drapes across the windows, then sat next to him on the couch and told him about her scumbag ex-husband and Homeland Security and women pilots and other couples he used to invite to the house. She kept referring to these other couples as if it were important, and Marino asked her if these couples were who she meant when she said "them" several times while he and Scarpetta were here. Suz wouldn't answer him directly. She said the same thing. She said, Ask Frank.

I'm asking you, Marino replied.

Ask Frank, she kept saying. He had all kinds in here. Ask him.

Had them here for what reason?

You'll find out, she said.

Marino stands back watching Scarpetta as she pulls on latex gloves and rips open a white paper packet. There is nothing left of the tractor driver's death scene but muddy asphalt in front of a back door that is next to the huge bay door. He watches her get down and look around the muddy pavement, and he remembers yesterday morning, when they were cruising by in the rental car, talking about the past, and if he could go back to yesterday morning, he would. If only he could go back. His stomach is sour and stabbed by nausea. His head throbs in rapid rhythm with his racing heart. He breathes in the cold air and tastes the dirt and the concrete of the building that is falling down around them.

"So what you looking for exactly, you don't mind me asking?" Bud is saying, looking on.

She carefully scrapes a wooden tongue depressor over a small area of dirt and sand that is stained, maybe with blood. "Just checking on what's here," she explains.

"You know, I watch some of those TV shows. At least I catch a bit here and there when the wife is watching."

"Don't believe everything you see." Scarpetta drops more dirt in the bag, then drops in the tongue depressor after it. She seals the bag and marks it with more of that writing of hers that Marino can't make out. She gently tucks the bag inside the nylon scene kit, which is upright on the pavement.

"So you ain't gonna take this dirt back and put it inside some magic machine," Bud jokes.

"No magic involved," she says, opening another white packet as she squats in the parking lot near the door she used to unlock and walk in every morning when she was chief.

Several times this morning Marino has had flashes in the throbbing darkness of his soul. They are electrical, like a picture blinking in and out of a TV that is seriously malfunctioning, severely damaged, and blinking in and out so fast that he can't see what's there, but is given only fuzzy impressions of what might be there. Lips and tongue. Fragments of hands and shut eyes. And his mouth going on her. What he knows for a fact is that he woke up naked in her bed at seven minutes past five this morning.

Scarpetta works like an archaeologist, as much as Marino knows about an archaeologist's methods. She carefully scrapes the top of a muddy area where he thinks he might see dark spots of blood. Her coat drapes around her and drags along the filthy blacktop and she doesn't care. If only all women cared as little as she does about things that don't matter. If only all women cared as much as she does about things that do matter. Marino imagines Scarpetta would understand a bad night. She would make coffee and hang around long enough to talk about it. She wouldn't lock herself in the bathroom and cry and holler and order him to get the hell out of her house.

Marino walks off quickly from the parking lot and back through the red mud, his big boots slipping. He slips and catches himself with a grunt that turns into a heave as he vomits, bending over deeply in loud heaves, a bitter brown liquid splashing on his boots. He is trembling and gagging and believing he will die when he feels her hand on his elbow. He would know that hand anywhere, that strong, sure hand.

"Come on," she says quietly, gripping his arm. "Let's get you back into the car. It's all right. Put your hand on my shoulder and for God's sake watch where you step or both of us are going down."

He wipes his mouth on his coat sleeve. Tears flood his eyes as he wills one foot at a time to move, holding on to her and holding himself up as he squishes through the muddy bloody-red battlefield around the ruined building where they first met.

"What if I raped her, Doc?" he says, so sick he might die. "What if I did?"

29.

||||IT IS VERY HOT inside the hotel room and Scarpetta has given up adjusting the thermostat. She sits in a chair by the window and watches Marino on the bed. He is stretched out in his black pants and black shirt, the baseball cap lonely on the dresser, his black boots lonely on the floor.

"You need to get some food in you," she says from her chair near the window.

Nearby on the carpet is her mud-spotted black nylon crime scene kit, and draped over another chair is her mud-spattered coat. Wherever she has walked in the room she has tracked red mud, and when her eyes fall on the trail she has made, she is reminded of a crime scene, and then she thinks about Suzanna Paulsson's bedroom and what crime may or may not have occurred there within the past twelve hours.

"I can't eat nothing right now," Marino says from his supine position. "What if she goes to the police?"

Scarpetta has no intention of giving him false hope. She can't give him anything because she doesn't know anything. "Can you sit up, Marino? It would be better if you sit up. I'm going to order something."

She gets up from the chair and leaves behind her more bits and flakes of drying mud as she walks to the phone by the bed. She finds a pair of reading glasses in a pocket of her suit jacket and puts them on the tip of her nose, and she studies the phone. Unable to figure out the number for room service, she dials zero for the operator and is transferred to room service.

"Three large bottles of water," she orders. "Two pots of hot Earl Grey tea, a toasted bagel, and a bowl of oatmeal. No thank you. That will do it."

Marino works himself up to a sitting position and shoves pillows behind his back. She can feel him watching her as she returns to her chair and sits down, tired because she is overwhelmed, her brain a herd of wild horses galloping in fifty different directions. She is thinking about paint chips and other trace evidence, about the soil samples in her nylon bag, about Gilly and the tractor driver, about what Lucy is doing, about what Benton might be doing, and trying to imagine Marino as a rapist. He has been foolish, no, stupid, with women before. He has mixed business with the personal, specifically he has gotten sexually involved with witnesses and victims in the past, more than once, and it has cost him but never more than he can afford. Never before has he been accused of rape or worried that he might have committed rape.

"We have to do the best we can to sort through this," she begins. "For the record, I don't believe you raped Suzanna Paulsson. The obvious problem is whether she believes you did or wants to believe you did. If it's the latter, then we will have to get to motive. But let's start with what you remember, the last thing you remember.

And Marino?" She looks at him. "If you did rape her, then we'll deal with that."

Marino just stares at her from his upright position on the bed. His face is flushed, his eyes glassy with fear and pain, and a vein has popped out on his right temple. Now and then, he touches the vein.

"I know you probably have no burning desire to give me every detail of what you did last night, but I can't help you if you don't. I'm not squeamish," she adds, and after all they've been through, such a comment should be funny. But nothing is going to be funny for a while.

"I don't know if I can." He looks away from her.

"What I'm capable of imagining is worse than anything you may have done," she tells him in a quiet but objective tone.

"That's right. You probably wasn't born yesterday."

"Not hardly," she says. "If it makes you feel any better, I've done a thing or two myself." She smiles a little. "As hard as that might be for you to imagine."

30.

||||IT ISN'T HARD for him to imagine. All these years, he has pre-
ferred not to imagine what she has done with other men, especially
with Benton.

Marino stares past her head out the window. His plain single
room is on the third floor, and he can't see the street, just the gray
sky beyond her head. He feels very small inside and has a childish
urge to hide under the covers, to sleep and hope when he wakes up
he'll discover that nothing has happened. He wants to wake up and
discover he is here in Richmond with the Doc, working a case, and
nothing has happened. Funny how many times he has opened his eyes
in a hotel room and wished he would find her there looking at him.
Now here she is in his hotel room looking at him. He tries to think
where to begin, then the childish urge clutches him again and he

loses his voice. His voice dies somewhere between his heart and his mouth, like a firefly going out in the dark.

His thoughts about her have been long and drawn out, for years they have been, ever since they first met, if he is honest about it. His erotic imaginings are the most skillful, creative, incredible sex he's ever had, and he would never want her to know, he could never let her know, and he has not stopped hoping something might happen with her, but if he starts talking about what he remembers, then she might get an idea of what it would be like to be with him. That would ruin any chance. No matter how remote the chance, it would be killed. To confess in detail what little he does remember would be to show her what it would be like to be with him. That would ruin it. His fantasies wouldn't survive, either, and then he wouldn't even have them, never again. He considers lying.

"Let's go back to when you arrived at the FOP lounge," Scarpetta says, her eyes steady on him. "What time did you go there?"

Good. He can talk about the FOP lounge. "Around seven," Marino says. "I met Eise there and then Browning got there and we had something to eat."

"Details," she tells him without moving in the chair, her eyes directly on his. "What did you eat and what had you eaten during the day?"

"I thought we were starting with the FOP, not what I ate earlier."

"Did you eat breakfast yesterday?" she persists with the same steadiness and patience she has when she talks to those left behind after someone is annihilated by randomness or by an Act of God or by a murderer.

"Had coffee in my room," he replies.

"Snacks? Lunch?"

"Nope."

"I'll lecture you about that another time," she says. "No food all day, just coffee, and then you went to the FOP lounge at seven. Did you drink on an empty stomach?"

"I started with a couple beers. Then I had a steak and a salad."

"No potato or bread? No carbs? You were on your diet."

"Huh. About the only good habit I stuck to last night, that's for sure."

She doesn't answer, and he senses she is thinking that his low-carb habit isn't exactly a good habit, but she isn't going to lecture him about nutrition right now when he's sitting on a bed, miserable with a hangover and in pain and panicky because he might have committed a felony or is about to be accused of committing one, assuming he hasn't already been accused. He looks at the gray sky out the window and imagines a Richmond police unmarked Crown Victoria prowling the streets, looking for him. Hell, it could be Detective Browning himself out there ready to serve a warrant on him.

"Then what?" Scarpetta asks.

Marino imagines himself in the backseat of the Crown Vic and wonders if Browning would handcuff him. Out of professional respect he could let Marino sit in the back unrestrained, or he could forget respect and snap handcuffs on him. He would have to handcuff him, Marino decides.

"You drank a few beers and ate a steak and a salad starting at seven," Scarpetta prods him in that easygoing but unstoppable way of hers. "How many beers, exactly?"

"Four, I think."

"Not think. How many, exactly."

"Six," he replies.

"Glasses or bottles or cans? Tall ones? Regulars? What size, in other words?"

"Six bottles of Budweiser, regular size. That ain't all that much for me, by the way. I can hold it. Six beers for me is like half a beer for you."

"Unlikely," she replies. "We'll talk about your math later."

"Well, I don't need a lecture," he mutters, glancing at her, then staring steadily at her in sullen silence.

"Six beers, one steak, a salad at the FOP with Junius Eise and Detective Browning, and about when did you hear the rumor that I'm moving back to Richmond? Might this have been while you were eating with Eise and Browning?"

"Now you're really putting two and two together," he says crabbily.

Eise and Browning were sitting across from him in the booth, a candle moving in the red glass globe, all three of them drinking beer. Eise asks Marino what he thinks of Scarpetta, what he really thinks. Is she a big-shot doctor-chief, what is she really like. She's a big shot but don't act like one, were Marino's exact words. He does remember that much, and he remembers the way he felt when Eise and Browning started talking about her, about her getting reappointed as chief and moving back to Richmond. She hadn't said a word to Marino about any such thing, not even given him a hint, and he was humiliated and furious. That's when he switched from beer to bourbon.

I always thought she was hot, that idiot Eise had the balls to say, and then he switched to bourbon. Quite a set that one's got, he added a few minutes later, cupping his hands at his chest, grinning. Wouldn't mind getting into the lab coat of that one. Well, you've worked with her forever, haven't you, so maybe when you've been around her enough, you don't notice her looks anymore. Browning said he's never seen her, but he'd heard about her, and he was grinning too.

Marino didn't know what to say, so he drank the first bourbon and ordered another one. The thought of Eise looking at her body put him in a mood to punch him. Of course he didn't. He just sat in the booth and drank and tried not to think about the way she looks when she takes off her lab coat, when she drapes it over her chair or hangs it on the hook behind her door. He did his best to block out images of her taking off her suit jacket at a scene, unbuttoning the sleeves of her blouse, doing and undoing whatever is needed when a dead body is waiting for her. She has always been easy about herself, not showing it, not conscious of what she's got and whether anyone might be looking at it when she's unbuttoning and taking off and reaching and moving, because she has work and because the dead don't care about seeing it. They're dead. It's just Marino who isn't dead. Maybe she thinks he's dead.

"I'll say it again, I have no plans for moving back to Richmond," Scarpetta says from her chair, her legs crossed, the hem of her dark blue pants speckled with mud, her shoes so smeared with mud it's hard to remember they were shiny black earlier today. "Besides, you don't really think I would make plans like that and not tell you, do you?"

"You never know," he replies.

"You do know."

"I ain't moving back here. Especially not now."

Someone knocks on the door and Marino's heart jumps and he thinks of the police and of jail and court. He shuts his eyes in relief when a voice on the other side of the door says, "Room service."

"I'll get it," Scarpetta says.

Marino sits still on the bed, and his eyes follow her as she moves across the small room and opens the door. If she were alone, were he not sitting right here, she would probably ask who is there and look through the peephole. But she isn't worried because Marino is right here and wears a Colt .280 semiautomatic in an ankle holster, not that it would be necessary to shoot anyone. He wouldn't mind beating the hell out of someone, though. Right now he would be happy to slam his big fists into someone's jaw and solar plexus, like he used to do when he boxed.

"How you folks today?" the pimply-faced young man in a uniform asks as he rolls in the cart.

"Fine, just fine," she says, digging in a pocket of her pants and pulling out a ten-dollar bill that is neatly folded. "You can leave it right there. Thank you." She hands him the folded bill.

"Thank you, ma'am. You all have a really nice day now." And he leaves. And the door shuts softly.

Marino doesn't move on the bed, only his eyes do as he watches her. He watches her loosen plastic wrap from the bagel and the oatmeal. He watches her open a pat of butter and mix the butter into the oatmeal, then sprinkle it with salt. She opens another pat of butter and spreads it on the bagel, then she pours two cups of tea. She does not put sugar in the tea. In fact, there is no sugar, none at all, on the cart.

"Here," she says, setting the oatmeal and a cup of strong tea on the table by the bed. "Eat." She walks back to the cart and carries the bagel to him. "The more you eat, the better. Maybe when you start feeling better, your memory will have a miraculous recovery."

The vision of the oatmeal causes a protest that rocks his gut, but he picks up the bowl and slowly dips in the spoon, and the spoon digging into the congealing oatmeal makes him think of Scarpetta digging the tongue depressor into the mud on the pavement, and then he imagines something else similar to oatmeal that causes another wave of disgust and remorse. If only he had been too drunk to do it. But he's done it. Seeing the oatmeal makes him certain he did it last night, finished what he started.

"I can't eat this," he says.

"Eat it," she replies, sitting back in the same chair like a judge, sitting up straight, looking right at him.

He tastes the oatmeal and is surprised that it's pretty good. It feels good going down. Before he knows it, he's eaten the entire bowl and is working on the bagel, and while he's doing this, he can feel her watching him. She isn't talking and he knows damn well why she's not saying anything and is watching him. He hasn't told her the truth yet. He is holding back the details that he is certain will kill the fantasy. Once she knows, he'll have no chance, and the bagel is suddenly dry in his throat and he can't swallow it.

"Feel a little bit better? Drink some of the tea," she suggests, and now she really is a judge dressed in dark clothes, sitting upright in the chair beneath the gray window. "Eat all of the bagel and drink at least one cup of the tea. You need food and you're dehydrated. I've got Advil."

"Yeah, Advil might be good," he says, chewing.

She reaches down into her nylon bag, and pills rattle as she pulls out a small bottle of Advil. He chews and gulps tea, suddenly very hungry, and he watches her walk back to him again, all the way to where he is propped against the pillows, and she removes the child-proof cap easily because anything childproof may as well not exist when it gets into her hands. She shakes out two pills and places them in his palm. Her fingers are agile and strong and seem small against his huge palm, and they lightly brush his skin, and her touch feels better to him than most things he has felt in life.

"Thanks," he says as she returns to her chair.

She'll sit in that chair for a month if she has to, he thinks. Maybe I should just let her sit there for a month. She's not going anywhere until I tell her. I wish she'd quit looking at me like that.

"How's our memory doing?" she asks.

"Some things are lost for good, you know. It happens," he replies, draining the cup of tea and concentrating on the pills to make sure they haven't gotten stuck somewhere in his throat.

"Some things never do come back," she agrees. "Or were never completely gone. Other things are just hard to talk about. You were drinking bourbon with Eise and Browning, then what? About what time was it when you started on the bourbon?"

"Maybe eight-thirty, nine. My cell phone rings and it was Suz. She was upset and said she needed to talk to me, asked me if I could come by her house." He pauses, waiting for Scarpetta's reaction. She doesn't have to say it. She is thinking it.

"Please continue," she says.

"I know what you're thinking. You're thinking I shouldn't have gone over there after drinking a few."

"You have no idea what I'm thinking," she replies from her chair.

"I was feeling all right."

"Define few," she adds.

"The beer, a couple bourbons."

"A couple?"

"No more than three."

"Six beers equals six ounces of alcohol. Three bourbons is another four or five ounces, depending on how well you know the bartender," she calculates. "Let's say over a three-hour period. That equals approximately ten ounces, I'm being conservative. Let's say you metabolized one ounce per hour, that's the norm. You still had at least seven ounces on board when you headed out of the FOP lounge."

"Shit," he says. "I sure could do without the math. I was feeling all right. I'm telling you I was."

"You hold it well. But you were legally drunk, more than legally drunk," the doctor-lawyer says. "By my calculations, more than point one-oh. You got to her house safe and sound, I presume. And by now it is what time?"

"Ten-thirty, maybe. I mean, I wasn't looking at my watch every damn minute." He stares at her and feels dark and sluggish slumped against pillows on the bed. What happened next heaves darkly inside him and he doesn't want to step into that darkness.

"I'm listening," Scarpetta says. "How are you feeling? Do you need some more tea? More food?"

He shakes his head no and feels again for the pills, worried they might be stuck somewhere and burning holes inside his throat. He burns in so many places, two more little burns might be hard to detect, but he doesn't need them.

"The headache better?"

"You ever been to a shrink?" he suddenly asks. " 'Cause that's what I'm feeling like. Like I'm sitting in a room with a shrink. But since I ain't never been to a shrink, I don't know if it feels like this. I thought you would know." He isn't sure why he said it, but it came out. He looks at her, helpless and angry and desperate to do anything that keeps him out of the heaving darkness.

"Let's not talk about me," she replies. "I'm not a shrink, and you know that better than anyone. This isn't about why you did what you did or why you didn't. This is about what. What is where trouble lies or doesn't. Psychiatrists don't care much about what."

"I know. What is it. What sure as hell is the problem, all right. I don't know what, Doc. That's the God's truth," he lies.

"We'll back up a little. You got to her house. How? You didn't have the rental car."

"Taxi."

"You have the receipt?"

"Probably in my coat pocket."

"It would be good if you still have it," she suggests.

"It should be in a pocket."

"You can look later. What happened next?"

"I got out and walked to the door. I rang the bell, she came to the door and let me in." The heaving darkness is right in front of his face now, like a storm about to break open on top of him. He takes a deep breath and his head throbs.

"Marino, it's all right," she says quietly. "You can tell me. Let's find out what. Exactly what. That's all we're trying to do."

"She . . . uh, she was wearing boots, like paratrooper boots, like steel-toed black leather boots. Military boots. And she had on a big camouflage t-shirt." The darkness swallows him, seems to swallow him whole, swallows more of him than he knew he had. "Nothing else, just that, and I was just sort of shocked, and didn't know why she was dressed like that. I didn't think nothing of it, not the way you might think. Then she shut the door behind me and put her hands on me."

"Where did she put her hands on you?"

"She said she'd wanted me the minute we walked in that morning," he says, embellishing a little, but not a lot, because whatever her exact words were, the message he got was just that. She wanted him. She had wanted him the first instant she saw him, when he and Scarpetta showed up at her house to ask about Gilly.

"You said she put her hands on you. Where? What part of your body?"

"My pockets. In my pockets."

"Front or back pockets?"

"Front." His eyes drop to his lap and he blinks as he looks at the deep front pockets of his black cargo pants.

"The same pants you have on now?" Scarpetta asks, her eyes never leaving him.

"Yeah. These pants. I didn't exactly get around to changing my clothes. I didn't exactly get back to my room this morning. I got a cab and went straight to the morgue."

"We'll get to that," she replies. "After she put her hands in your pockets, then what?"

"Why do you want to know all this?"

"You know why. You know exactly why," she says in that same calm, steady tone, her eyes on him.

He remembers Suz's hands digging deep into his pockets and her pulling him into her house, laughing, saying how good he looked as she pushed the door shut with her foot. A fog swirls in his thoughts like fog swirling in the headlights as the taxi drove him to her house, and he knew he was heading into the unknown, but he went, and then she had her hands in his pockets and was pulling him into the living room, laughing, dressed in nothing but a camouflage t-shirt and combat boots. She pressed against him and he knew she could feel him and she knew he could feel her soft and tight against him.

"She got a bottle of bourbon out of the kitchen," he says, and he listens to his voice but he isn't seeing anything inside the hotel room as he tells Scarpetta. He's in a trance as he tells her. "She poured us drinks and I said I shouldn't have any more. Maybe I didn't say that. I don't know. She had me going. What can I tell you? She had me going. I asked her what's the thing with the camouflage, and she said he was into that, Frank was. Uniforms. He used to get her to dress up for him and they would play."

"Was Gilly around when he would ask Suz to wear uniforms and play?"

"What?"

"Maybe we'll get to Gilly later. What did Frank and Suz play?"

"Games."

"Did she want you to play games last night?" Scarpetta asks.

The room is dark and he feels the darkness, and he can't see what he did because it is unbearable, and all he can think about as he tries to be truthful is how the fantasy will die forever. She will imagine him and it will never happen, never, and there will be no point in his ever hoping again, remotely hoping, because she will know what it might be like with him.

"This is important, Marino," she says quietly. "Tell me about the game."

He swallows and imagines he feels the pills in his throat, deep inside it and burning. He wants more tea but can't move and he can't bear to ask her to get him tea or anything else. She is sitting straight in the chair but not tensely, her strong, capable hands on the armrests. She is erect but relaxed in her mud-spattered suit. Her eyes are keen as she listens.

"She told me to chase her," he begins. "I was drinking. And I said what do you mean by chase. And she told me to go into the bedroom, her bedroom, and hide behind the door and to time it. She said for me to wait five minutes, exactly five minutes, and then start looking for her like . . . Like I was going to kill her. And I told her it wasn't right. Well, I didn't really tell her." He takes another deep breath. "I probably didn't tell her, because she had me going."

"What time was it by now?"

"I'd been there maybe an hour."

"She puts her hands in your pants the minute you walked through the front door at approximately ten-thirty and then an hour passes? Nothing happened during that hour?"

"We were drinking. In the living room, on the couch." He won't look at her now. He will never look at her again.

"Lights on? Curtains open or closed?"

"She'd built a fire. The lights were off. I don't remember if the curtains were open." He thinks about it. "They were closed."

"What did you do on the couch?"

"Talked. And made out, I guess."

"Don't guess. And I don't know what that means. What does it mean when you say you made out?" Scarpetta replies. "Kissing, fondling? Did you take your clothes off? Did you have intercourse? Oral sex?"

He feels his face turn hot. "No. I mean, the first part we did. Kissing, mostly. You know, making out. Like people do. Making out. We were on the couch and talked about the game." His face burns. He knows she can see how hot his face is and he refuses to look at her.

The lights were out and the light from the fire moved over her flesh, her pale flesh, and when she grabbed him, it hurt and excited him, and then it simply hurt. He told her to be careful because it hurt, and she laughed and said she liked it rough, liked it very rough, and would he bite her, and he said no, he didn't want to bite her, not hard. You'll like it, she promised, you'll like biting hard. You don't know what you're missing if you've never done it rough, and all the while she talked her flesh caught the light of the fire as she moved, and he tried to keep his tongue in her mouth and please her while he crossed his legs and maneuvered himself so she wouldn't hurt him. Don't be such a sissy, she kept saying as she tried to shove him down hard on the couch and force his zipper, but he managed to keep her from getting to him. He was thinking about her teeth showing white in the firelight and what it would be like if she got those white teeth on him.

"The game began on the couch?" Scarpetta asks from her distant chair.

"That's where we talked about it. Then I got up and she took me into the bedroom and told me to step behind the door and wait five minutes, like I said."

"Were you still drinking?"

"She'd poured me another drink, I guess."

"Don't guess. Big drinks? Little drinks? How many by now?"

"Nothing that woman does is in a small way. Big drinks. Three at least by the time she told me to go behind the door. It starts getting really fuzzy now," he says. "After the game started, it all starts to fade. Maybe it's a damn good thing."

"It's not a good thing. Try to remember. We need to know the what. The what. Not the why. I don't care about the why, Marino. Trust me. There's nothing you can tell me that I haven't heard before. Or seen. I don't shock easily."

"No, Doc. I'm sure you don't. But maybe I do. Maybe I didn't think so, but maybe I do. I remember looking at my watch and having a real hard time seeing the time. My eyesight ain't what it used to be anyway, but it was blurring bad and I was keyed up, real keyed up, not in a real good way. I don't know why I went along with it, to tell you the truth."

He was sweating profusely behind the door, trying to read his watch, then he starting counting silently, counting up to sixty and losing his place and starting again until he was sure five minutes had passed. His excitement was not the sort that he had ever felt with a woman, no woman or encounter with a woman he could recall, not ever. He stepped out from behind the door and realized the entire house was dark. He couldn't see his own hands unless he held them very close to his face, and he felt along the walls and realized she could hear him, and this was when he realized in his drunken obtuseness, somehow as drunk as he was he realized his heart was pounding and he was breathing hard because he was excited and scared, and he doesn't want Scarpetta to know he was scared. He reached down to his ankle and lost his balance and found himself on the hallway floor, feeling for his gun, but his gun wasn't in its holster. He doesn't know how long he sat there. It's possible he fell asleep, briefly.

When he came to, he didn't have his gun and his heart was pounding in his neck as he sat without moving, barely breathing, on the wooden floor, sweat streaming into his eyes, listening, trying to hear where the son of a bitch was. The darkness was so complete it was thick and airless and it wrapped around him like black cloth as he tried to get to his feet without making noise and giving away his position. The bastard was in here somewhere, and Marino didn't have his gun. With his arms out like oars, he barely brushed the walls as he moved himself forward, listening, ready to pounce, knowing he was going to get shot if he didn't catch the piece of shit by surprise.

He moved slowly like a cat, his brain focused on the enemy, and the thought that kept coming to him was how did he get into the house and what house and what son of a bitch and where was his backup? Where the fuck was everybody? Oh Christ, maybe they were down. Maybe he was the only one left and now he was going down because he didn't have his gun and somehow he had lost his radio, and he didn't know where he was. And then he felt something hit him. And then he passed in and out of a heaving darkness, a hot darkness that drove the air out of him as it moved and he became aware of pain, of burning pain as the darkness moved and grabbed at him and made terrible wet noises.

"I don't know what happened," he hears himself say, and it surprises him that his voice sounds sane because inside he feels crazy. "I just don't know. I woke up in her bed."

"Clothed?"

"No."

"Where were your clothes, your belongings?"

"In a chair."

"In a chair? Neatly in a chair?"

"Yeah, pretty neatly. My clothes and my pistol was on top of them. I sat up in bed and nobody else was there," he says.

"Was her side of the bed unmade? Did it look slept in?"

"The covers were pulled down and messed up, real messed up. But nobody was there. I looked around and didn't know where the hell I was and then I remembered I'd taken a taxi to her house, and I remembered her coming to the door dressed the way she was, you know, the night before. I looked around and saw a glass of bourbon on the table on my side of the bed, and a towel. The towel had blood on it and it scared the shit out of me. I tried to get up and couldn't. I just sat there. I couldn't get up."

He realizes his teacup is full, and it terrifies him that he has no recollection of Scarpetta getting up from her chair and refilling his tea or if maybe he did, but he doubts he did. He has a sense that he is in the same position on the bed that he has been in, and he notices the clock and more than three hours have passed since he and Scarpetta started talking in his hotel room.

"Do you think it's possible she drugged you?" Scarpetta asks him. "Unfortunately, I don't think a drug test would be helpful at this point. Too much time has passed. It depends on the drug."

"Oh, that would be great. If I go get a drug test, then I may as well call the police myself, assuming she ain't already done it."

"Tell me about the bloody towel," she says.

"I don't know whose blood it was. Maybe it was mine. My mouth hurt." He touches it. "I hurt like shit. I guess that's what she's into, hurting, but all I can say is . . . Well, I don't know what I did because I didn't see her. She was in the bathroom and when I started calling out her name to see where the hell she was, she started screaming at me, screaming for me to leave her house and saying I . . . She was saying all these things."

"I don't guess you thought to take the bloody towel with you."

"I don't even know how I managed to call a taxi to get out of there. In fact, I don't remember doing it. Obviously I did. No, I didn't take the towel, goddamn it."

"You came straight to the morgue." She frowns a little, as if this part doesn't make sense.

"I stopped for coffee. A Seven-Eleven. Finally, I got the cabdriver to drop me off several blocks from the office so I could walk, hoping I could clear my head. It helped a little. I felt half human again, and then I walked in the office and damn if she's not there."

"Before you got to the OCME, did you listen to your phone messages?"

"Oh. Maybe I did."

"Otherwise you couldn't have known about the meeting."

"No. I knew about the meeting," Marino says. "Eise told me at the FOP lounge that he'd passed on some information to Marcus. An e-mail, that's what he said." He tries to remember. "Oh yeah, now I know. Marcus was on the phone as soon as he opened the e-mail and said he was going to have to call a meeting for the next morning and he told Eise to make sure he was in the building in case he needed him to come down and explain things."

"So you knew about the meeting last night," Scarpetta says.

"Yeah, last night was the first I heard about it, and it seemed like Eise said something to make me think you was going to be there, so I knew I had to be there."

"You knew the meeting was to be at nine-thirty?"

"I must have. I'm sorry I'm so foggy, Doc. But I knew about the meeting." He looks at her and can't figure out what's going through her mind. "Why? What's the big deal about the meeting?"

"He didn't tell me about it until eight-thirty this morning," she replies.

"He's shooting bullets at your feet, making you dance," Marino says, and he hates Dr. Marcus. "Let's get us a plane and go back to Florida. Fuck him."

"When you saw Mrs. Paulsson at the office this morning, did she speak to you?"

"She looked at me and walked off. Like she didn't know me. I don't understand nothing about this, Doc. I just know something happened and it's bad, and I'm scared shitless I did something really bad and now I'm going to get it. After all the shit I've done, now this is going to do it. This is it."

Scarpetta slowly gets up from her chair, and she looks tired, but she is alert, and he can see the worry in her eyes but he can also see that she is thinking, she is making connections he sure as hell isn't making. Her eyes are full of thoughts as she looks out the window and walks over to the service cart and drains the last little bit of tea into her cup.

"She injured you, didn't she?" she says, standing near the bed, looking down at him. "Show me what she did to you."

"Hell no! Hell no, I can't," he says in a whine that makes him sound ten years old. "I can't do that. No way."

"Do you want me to help you or not? You think you have something I've never seen before?"

He covers his face with his hands. "I can't do it."

"You can call the police and they'll get you down to the station and photograph your injuries. Then you've just started a case. Maybe that's what you want. Not a bad plan, assuming she's already called the police. But I suspect she hasn't."

He lowers his hands and looks up at her. "Why?"

"Why do I suspect that? Very simple. People know we're staying here. Doesn't Detective Browning know you're staying here? Doesn't he have your phone numbers? So why haven't the police shown up to arrest you? You think they wouldn't be all over you if Gilly Paulsson's mother called nine-one-one and said you raped her? And why didn't she scream when she saw you at the office? You just raped her and she doesn't make a scene or call the police right then?"

"Ain't no way I'm calling the police," he says.

"Then I'm all you've got." She walks back to her chair and picks up her nylon scene kit. She unzips it and pulls out a digital camera.

"Holy shit," he says, staring at the camera as if it is a gun pointed at him.

"Sounds like the victim here is you," she says. "Sounds like she wants you to think you did something to her. Why?"

"Shit if I know. I can't do it."

"You're hungover but not stupid, Marino."

He looks at her. He looks at the camera down by her side. He looks at Scarpetta standing in the middle of his room in her dark, mud-spattered suit.

"We're here working the death of her daughter, Marino. Mama clearly wants some kind of leverage or money or attention or some kind of something, and I intend to find out what it is she wants. Oh yes. I will find out. Take your shirt off, your pants off, take off whatever you need to take off to show me what that woman did to you during her sick little game last night."

"Now what are you gonna think of me?" he says, pulling his black Polo shirt over his head, carefully, the fabric hurting him where it rubs the bite and suck marks all over his chest.

"God. Sit still. God damn it, why didn't you show me this earlier? We've got to take care of this or you're going to get infections. And you're worried about her calling the police? Are you out of your mind?" All this while she takes photographs, moving over him, getting close-ups of each wound.

"Thing is, I ain't seen what I did to her," he says, a little calmer, realizing that getting checked out by the Doc might not be as bad as he thought.

"You did even half of this to her, your teeth should hurt."

He pays very close attention to his teeth and feels nothing at all, just his usual teeth and the usual way they feel. Thank God his teeth don't hurt.

"What about your back?" she asks, standing over him.

"It don't hurt."

"Lean forward. Let me look."

He bends over and feels her carefully move the pillows away from his back. He feels her warm fingers between his shoulder blades, her hands lightly touching his bare skin and pushing him farther forward as she examines his back, and he tries to remember whether she's ever touched his bare back before. She hasn't. He would remember.

"What about your genitals?" she asks as if it is nothing. When he doesn't respond, she says, "Marino, did she injure your genitals? Is there something there I should photograph, not to mention treat, or are we going to pretend that I somehow don't know that you have male genitalia like half the rest of the human race? Well, obviously she hurt your genitals, or else you would simply tell me no. Correct?"

"Correct," he mutters, covering his crotch with his hands. "Yeah, I'm hurting, okay? But maybe you got enough already to prove your point, to prove she hurt me, no matter what I did to her, assuming I did something."

She sits on the edge of the bed not more than two feet from him and looks at him. "How about a verbal description. Then we'll decide if you need to take your pants off."

"She bit me. All over. And I got bruises."

"I'm a doctor," Scarpetta says.

"I know that all right. But you ain't my doctor."

"I would be if you died. If she'd killed you, who do you think would want to see you and know every damn thing about it? But you're not dead, for which I'm extremely grateful, but you got attacked and have the same sort of injuries you might have were you dead. And this all sounds perfectly ridiculous, even to me, even as I'm saying it. Will you please let me take a look and see if you need medical treatment and if we need to take photographs?"

"What kind of medical treatment?"

"Probably nothing that a little Betadine won't cure. I'll pick some up at the drugstore."

He tries to imagine what will happen if she sees him. She has never seen him. She doesn't know what he has, and he might not be above average or below average, and ordinarily just being ordinary will get one by, but he doesn't know what to expect because he has no idea what she likes or is accustomed to. So it's probably not smart to take off his pants. Then he thinks of riding in the back of an unmarked car and being photographed in lockup and going to court, and he unbuttons his pants and pulls down the zipper.

"If you laugh I'll hate you the rest of your life," he says, and his face burns hot and he is sweating, and the sweat stings whatever it touches.

"You poor boy," she says. "That crazy bitch," she says.

31.

| | | It is raining a cold hard rain when Scarpetta pulls off to the side of the street and parks in front of Suzanna Paulsson's house. For a few minutes she sits with the engine running and the wiper blades sweeping back and forth, and she looks out at the uneven brick sidewalk that leads to the sloping porch and imagines Marino's path last night. She doesn't have to imagine much else.

What he told her was more than he thinks. What she saw was worse than he knows. He may not believe he told her every detail, but he told her plenty. She turns off the wipers and watches the rain spatter the glass and run down it, and then it is raining so hard all she can hear is a steady wet splashing, and the water on the windshield looks like rippled ice. Suzanna Paulsson is home. Her minivan is parked near the sidewalk and the lights are on in the house. She didn't walk anywhere in this weather.

Scarpetta's rental car has no umbrella and she doesn't have a hat. She gets out and the smacking of water is suddenly louder and rain dashes her face as she hurries along the slippery old bricks that lead to the house of a girl who is dead and a mother who is sexually insane. Perhaps it is overly dramatic to consider her sexually insane. Scarpetta reconsiders, but she is much angrier than Marino knows. He may not realize she is angry at all, but she is quite angry and Mrs. Paulsson is about to see what it is like when Scarpetta is angry. She firmly taps the brass pineapple against the front door and contemplates what to do if the woman refuses to open it, if she pretends she isn't home like Fielding did. She taps the pineapple again, slower and harder.

Night is coming quickly like a cloud of black ink because of the storm, and she can see her breath as she stands on the porch, surrounded by splashing water, and she raps again and again. I'll just keep standing here, she thinks. You're not getting out of this, don't think there's a chance I'll turn around and leave. She pulls her cell phone and a scrap of paper out of her coat pocket and looks at a number she jotted down when she was here yesterday, when she was quiet and gentle with this woman, when she felt sorry for her. She dials and can hear the phone ring inside the house, and she raps the pineapple again as loud as she can. If the door knocker breaks she doesn't care.

Another minute passes and she redials the number and the phone rings and rings inside and she hangs up before the answering machine begins. You're home, she thinks. Don't pretend you're not. You probably know it's me out here. Scarpetta steps back from the door and looks at the lighted windows along the front of the small brick house. Filmy white curtains are drawn across them, and they are full of soft, warm light, and she sees a shadow pass before the window on her right. She can see the outline of a person as it drifts past the window, pauses, then turns around and vanishes.

She raps on the door again and redials. This time when the answering machine picks up, Scarpetta stays on the line and says, "Mrs. Paulsson, it's Dr. Kay Scarpetta. Please answer your door. It's very important. I'm standing outside your front door. I know you're home." She ends the call and raps some more, and the shadow moves again, this time past the window to the left of the door, and then the door opens.

"Good heavens," Mrs. Paulsson says in feigned surprise that is unconvincing. "I didn't know who it was. What a storm. Come in out of the rain. I don't answer the door when I don't know who it is."

Scarpetta drips into the living room and takes off her long, dark, soaking-wet coat. Cold water drips from her hair and she pushes it off her face, realizing her hair is as wet as it would be had she just stepped out of the shower.

"God knows you're going to get pneumonia," Mrs. Paulsson says to her. "Here I am telling you. You're the doctor. Come on in the kitchen and let me get you something warm to drink."

Scarpetta looks around the tiny living room, at the cold ashes and chunks of burned wood in the fireplace, at the plaid couch beneath the windows, at the doorways on either side of the living room that lead into other parts of the house. Mrs. Paulsson catches Scarpetta looking and a tightness comes over her face, a face that is almost pretty but cheap and rough.

"Why are you here?" Mrs. Paulsson says in a different voice. "What are you doing here? I thought you might be here for Gilly, but I can see that's not it."

"I'm not sure anybody was here for Gilly," Scarpetta replies, standing in the middle of the living room, dripping on the hardwood floor and looking around, making it obvious that she is looking around.

"You have no right to say that," Mrs. Paulsson snaps. "I think you should leave right now. I don't need the likes of you in my house."

"I'm not leaving. Call the police if you want. But I'm not going anywhere until we've had a conversation about what happened last night."

"I should call the police all right. After what that monster did. After all I've been through, and then he comes over here and takes advantage like that. Going after someone who's hurting the way I am. I should have known. He looks the type."

"Go on," Scarpetta says. "Call the police. I have a story too. Quite a story. If you don't mind, I believe I'll look around. I know where the kitchen is. I know where Gilly's room is. I presume if I head through this doorway and turn left instead of right, I might just find your bedroom," she says as she walks that way.

"You can't just walk around my house," Mrs. Paulsson exclaims. "You get out of my house this minute. You have no cause to be snooping around."

The bedroom is bigger than Gilly's but not much. In it are a double bed, a small antique walnut nightstand on either side, and two dressers crammed against a wall. A doorway leads into a small bathroom, and another doorway opens into a closet, and there in plain view on the closet floor is a pair of black leather combat boots. Scarpetta digs inside a pocket of her suit jacket and pulls out a pair of cotton gloves. She puts them on as she stands in the closet door-way, looking down at the boots. She scans the clothes hanging from the rod and abruptly turns around and walks into the bathroom. Draped over the side of the tub is a camouflage t-shirt.

"He told you a story, didn't he?" Mrs. Paulsson says from the foot of the bed. "And you believe it. We'll see what the police believe. I don't think they'll believe him or you."

"How often did you play soldier when your daughter was around to see it?" Scarpetta asks, looking right at her. "Apparently Frank liked to play soldier? Is that where you learned the game, from him? Or are you the creator of this vile little charade of yours? How much did you do in front of Gilly, and who played the game with you when Gilly was here? Group sex? Is that who 'them' is? Other people who played the game with you and Frank?"

"How dare you accuse me of such a thing!" she exclaims, and her face is twisted by contempt and rage. "I don't know a thing about any game."

"Oh, there's plenty of accusing to go around, and there will probably be more," Scarpetta says, moving closer to the bed and with a gloved hand pulling back the covers. "It doesn't look like you changed the linens. That's good. See the blood spots on this sheet right here? How much do you want to bet that comes back as Marino's blood. Not yours." She gives her a long look. "He's bleeding and you aren't. Now that's curious. I believe there's a bloody towel around here somewhere too." She looks around. "Maybe you've washed it, but it doesn't matter. We can still get what we need from something that's been washed."

"I have this happen to me and you're worse than he is," Mrs. Paulsson says, but her expression has changed. "I would think another woman would have at least a little compassion."

"For someone who mauls another person and then accuses him of assault? I don't believe you'll find a decent woman on this planet who would have compassion for that, Mrs. Paulsson." Scarpetta starts pulling the cover off the bed.

"What are you doing? You can't do that."

"I'm going to do that and more. Just watch." She strips off the sheets and rolls them and the pillows into the quilt.

"You can't do that. You're not a cop."

"Oh, I'm worse than any cop. Trust me." Scarpetta picks up the bundle of linens and places it on top of the bare mattress. "What next?" She looks around. "You may not have noticed when you ran into Marino at the medical examiner's office this morning, but he had on the same pants that he had on last night. And the same underwear. All day, as a matter of fact. You probably know that when a man has sex he is likely to leave at least a little something in his underwear and possibly even in his pants. But he didn't. He didn't leave a trace of anything in his underwear or pants, except blood from where you hurt him. You also may not know that people can see through your curtains, see if you're with someone, if you're fighting or having a romantic encounter, assuming you're still on your feet. No telling what the neighbors across the street have seen when your lights are on or you've got a fire going."

"Maybe it started out all right between the two of us and got out of hand," Mrs. Paulsson says, and she seems to have made a decision. "It was innocent enough, just a man and a woman enjoying each other. Maybe I got a little carried away because he frustrated me. Got me all dressed up with no place to go. He couldn't do it. A big man like him, and he couldn't do it."

"I guess not when you kept filling his glass with bourbon," Scarpetta says, and she is pretty sure Marino didn't do it. She doesn't see how he could. The problem is, he still worries that he did it and he worries that he couldn't, so there isn't much room for discussion with him.

Scarpetta squats inside the closet and retrieves the boots. She places them on the bed, and they look very sinister and large against the bare mattress.

"Those are Frank's boots," Mrs. Paulsson tells her.

"If you've worn them, your DNA will be inside them."

"They're way too big for me."

"You heard what I said. DNA will tell us a lot." She walks into the bathroom and picks up the camouflage t-shirt. "I suppose this is Frank's, as well."

Mrs. Paulsson has nothing to say.

"We can go into the kitchen now if you want," Scarpetta says. "Something warm to drink would be nice. Maybe some coffee. What kind of bourbon were you drinking last night? You shouldn't feel very good right now either, unless you spent more time filling his glass than your own. Marino's in pretty bad shape today. Pretty bad. He required medical treatment." All this as Scarpetta walks briskly toward the back of the house, toward the kitchen.

"What do you mean?"

"I mean he needed a doctor."

"He went to the doctor?"

"He was examined and photographed. Every inch of him. He's not in good shape," Scarpetta says, walking into the kitchen and spotting the coffeemaker near the sink, very close to where the bottle of cough syrup was the other day. The bottle isn't there now. It is nowhere in sight. She takes off her cotton gloves and tucks them in her suit pocket.

"He ought to be after what he did."

"You can stop that story now," Scarpetta says, filling the glass coffeepot with tap water. "That story is a lie and you may as well give it up. If you have injuries, let's see them."

"If I show them to anybody, it will be the police."

"Where do you keep the coffee?"

"I don't know what you're thinking, but it isn't the truth," Mrs. Paulsson says, opening the freezer and setting a bag of coffee by the pot. She opens a cupboard and finds a box of filters, letting Scarpetta help herself.

"Truth seems hard to find these days," Scarpetta replies, opening the coffee and placing a filter in the coffeemaker, then measuring coffee with a small scoop she found in the bag. "I wonder why that is. We can't seem to find the truth about what happened to Gilly. Now the truth about what happened last night seems to elude us. I'd like to hear what you have to say about truth, Mrs. Paulsson. That's why I decided to drop by tonight."

"I wasn't going to say anything about Pete," she says bitterly. "If I was going to, don't you think I would have? Truth is, I thought he had a good time."

"A good time?" Scarpetta leans against the counter and crosses her arms at her waist. Coffee drips and the aroma of it seeps around the edges of the kitchen. "If you looked like he does today, I'm wondering if you'd think you had a good time."

"You don't know what I look like."

"I can tell by the way you move that he didn't hurt you. In fact, he didn't do much of anything, not after all that bourbon. You just told me that yourself."

"You got something with him? Is that why you're here?" She looks slyly at Scarpetta, and interest glints in her eyes.

"I have something with him. But it isn't something you're likely to understand. Did I mention to you that I'm also a lawyer? Would you like to hear what happens to people who falsely accuse someone of assault or rape? Have you ever been to jail?"

"You're jealous. I see what this is about." She smiles smugly.

"Think what you want. But think about jail, Mrs. Paulsson. Think about crying rape and the evidence proving you to be a liar."

"I won't be crying rape, don't you worry," she says, her face turning harder. "Nobody rapes me anyway. Let them try. What a big baby. That's what I have to say about him. A baby. I thought he would be fun. Well, I thought wrong. You can have him, Miss Doctor or Lawyer or whatever you are."

The coffee is ready and Scarpetta asks about cups, and Mrs. Paulsson finds two in a cupboard and then two spoons. They sip coffee standing up, and then Mrs. Paulsson begins to cry. She bites her lower lip and tears spill out and stream down her face and she starts shaking her head.

"I'm not going to jail," she says.

"That would be what I prefer. I'd rather you didn't go to jail," Scarpetta says, sipping her coffee. "Why did you do it?"

"It's personal what people do with each other." She won't look at her.

"When you draw blood and bruise someone, it's not personal. It's a crime. Is rough sex a habit of yours?"

"You must be some kind of Puritan," she says, wandering to the table and sitting down. "I guess there must be a lot you've never heard of."

"You might be right. Tell me about the game."

"Get him to."

"I know what Marino has to say about your game, at least the one you played last night." Scarpetta sips her coffee. "You've played your games for a while, haven't you? Did they start with your ex-husband, with Frank?"

"I don't have to talk to you," she says from the table. "I don't see why I should."

"The rose we found in Gilly's dresser. You said Frank might know something about it. What did you mean?"

She will not answer, and she looks angry and full of hate as she sits at the table and cradles the coffee cup in both hands.

"Mrs. Paulsson, do you think Frank might have done something to Gilly?"

"I don't know who left the rose," she says, staring at the same spot on the wall she stared at when Scarpetta was here yesterday. "I know I didn't. I know it wasn't there before, not out in her room, not where I could see it. And I'd been in her drawers. I went in them the day before, putting away laundry and things. Gilly was bad about putting things away. I was always picking up after her. I never saw anything like it. She couldn't put something back to save her." She catches herself and falls silent, staring at the wall.

Scarpetta waits to see if she will say more. What must be a minute passes, and the silence is heavy.

"The worst thing was the kitchen," Mrs. Paulsson finally says. "Taking out food and just leaving it on the counter. Even ice cream. Can't tell you how much food I threw out." Her face collapses into grief. "And milk. Always pouring milk down the sink because she left it out half the day." Her voice rises and falls and shakes. "Do you know what it's like to pick up after somebody all the damn time?"

"Yes," Scarpetta says. "That's one reason I'm divorced."

"Well, he's not much better," she says, staring off. "Between the two of them that's all I did, pick up."

"If Frank did something to Gilly, what do you think it might have been?" Scarpetta asks, and she is careful not to ask questions that can be answered with a simple yes or no.

Mrs. Paulsson stares at the wall, not blinking. "In his own way he did something."

"I'm talking physically. Gilly is dead."

Her eyes fill with tears and she roughly wipes them with a hand as she stares at the wall. "He wasn't here when it happened. Not in this house, not that I know of."

"When what happened?"

"While I was gone to the drugstore. Whatever it was happened then." She wipes her eyes again. "The window was open when I came home. It wasn't when I left. I don't know if she opened it. I'm not saying Frank did it. I'm saying he has something to do with it. Everything he got near died or was ruined. Kind of funny to think that about someone who's a doctor. You should know."

"I'm going to go now, Mrs. Paulsson. I know this hasn't been an easy conversation, none of it has. You've got my cell phone number. If you think of anything that is important, I want you to call me."

She nods, staring and crying.

"Maybe someone's been in this house before whom we ought to know about. Someone besides Frank. Maybe someone Frank had over, someone he knew. Maybe someone who played the game."

She doesn't get up from her chair as Scarpetta moves to the doorway.

"Anyone at all who might come to your mind," Scarpetta says. "Gilly didn't die of the flu," she repeats. "We need to know what happened, exactly what happened to her. We will know. Sooner or later. I believe you'd rather have it sooner, wouldn't you?"

She just stares at the wall.

"You can call me anytime," Scarpetta says. "I'm going to go now. If you need something, you can call me. I could use a couple of large trash bags if you have them."

"Under the sink. If they're for what I think, you don't need them," she mutters.

Scarpetta opens the cupboard under the sink and pulls four large plastic trash bags out of a box. "I'll take them anyway," she replies. "Hopefully I won't need them."

She stops by the bedroom and collects the balled-up linens, the boots, and the t-shirt, and places them inside the plastic bags. In the living room she puts on her coat and steps back out into the rain, carrying four bags, two heavy with linens, the other two having nothing in them but a t-shirt and a pair of boots. Puddles on the brick walk splash over her shoes and cold water soaks her feet, and the rain is half frozen as it slaps down all around her.

3 2.

||| INSIDE THE Other Way Lounge it is very dark, and the women who work here have stopped giving Edgar Allan Pogue sidelong looks that at first were curious, then disdainful, and finally indifferent before stopping altogether. He picks at the stem of a maraschino cherry and takes his time tying it in a knot.

He drinks Bleeding Sunsets in the Other Way, a specialty of the house that is a mixture of vodka and Other Stuff, as he thinks of it, Other Stuff that is orange and red and drifts unevenly to the bottom of the glass. A Bleeding Sunset looks like a sunset until a few tilts of the glass mix the liquids and syrups and Other Stuff together, and then the drink is simply orangish. When the ice melts, whatever is left in his glass looks like those orange drinks he used to get as a kid. They were in plastic oranges and he drank them out of green straws that were supposed to look like stems, and the orange drink was diluted and boring, but the plastic orange it came in always promised that the drink would be fresh and delicious. He would beg his mother to buy him one of the plastic oranges every time they came to South Florida, and every time he got disappointed again.

People are like those plastic oranges and what's in them. People are one thing to look at and another thing to taste. He lifts his glass and swirls the orangish swill that is left in the bottom. He thinks about ordering another Bleeding Sunset as he calculates how much cash he has left and also takes into account his sobriety. He isn't a drunk. He has never been drunk in his life. He worries excessively about being drunk and can't drink a Bleeding Sunset or any other concoction without analyzing every ounce he swallows, worrying about the effect. He also worries about being fat, and alcohol is fattening. His mother was fat. She got fatter in time, and it was a shame because she had been pretty once. It runs in the family, she used to say. You keep eating like that and you'll see what I mean, she used to say. That's the way it starts, right around the middle, she used to say.

"I'll have one more," Edgar Allan Pogue says to whoever might be listening.

The Other Way is like a very small clubroom scattered with wooden tables covered with black cloths. There are candles on the tables, but they have never been lit when he's here. In a corner is a pool table, but no one has played pool when he's here, and he suspects that the clients here are not interested in pool and the scarred table with its red felt cloth might be left over from an earlier incarnation. Quite likely the Other Way was something else once. Everything was something else once.

"I believe I'll have one more," he says.

The women who work here are hostesses, not waitresses, and they expect to be treated like hostesses. Gentlemen drift in and out of the Other Way and do not snap their fingers at the ladies because they are hostesses and demand respect, so much respect that Pogue feels they are doing him a favor to let him come in and spend his money on their runny, bloody Bleeding Sunsets. His eyes move in the dark and he sees the redhead. She wears a skimpy, short black jumper that should have a blouse under it but doesn't. The jumper barely covers what she needs to cover, and he has never seen her bend over unless it is for reasons other than brushing off a tablecloth or setting down a drink. She bends over to give special men something to see, those special men who tip well and know how to talk the talk. The jumper has a bib that is nothing more than a square of black cloth smaller than a sheet of typing paper and held up by two black straps. The bib is loose. When she leans into a conversation or to pick up an empty glass, she jiggles inside the bib and may even spill out of it, but it is dark, very dark, and she has not bent over his table and probably won't and he cannot see well from where he sits.

He gets up from his table near the door because he has no desire to yell out that he wants another Bleeding Sunset, and he's no longer sure he wants one. He keeps thinking of the bright plastic orange with the green straw, and the more he sees it and remembers his disappointment, the more unfair it is. He stands by the table and reaches into a pocket and pulls out a twenty. Money in the Other Way is what it takes, like steak to a dog, he thinks. The redhead clicks over in her little stilt-high pointed shoes, jiggling inside her bib, pumping inside her tight little skirt. Up close, she is old. She is fifty-seven or fifty-eight, maybe sixty.

"You heading out, hon?" She plucks the twenty off the table and doesn't look at him.

There is a mole on her right cheek and it is drawn on, probably with eyeliner. He could have done a much better job. "I wanted another one," he says.

"Don't we all, hon." Her laughter reminds him of a cat in pain. "Hold the phone and I'll bring ya one."

"It's too late," he says.

"Bessie girl, where's my whisky?" a quiet man asks from a nearby table.

Pogue saw him earlier, saw him drive up in a big new Cadillac, a silver one. He is very old, at least eighty or eighty-one or eighty-two, and dressed in a pale blue seersucker suit and pale blue tie. Bessie shakes and bounces over to him and suddenly Pogue is gone even though he hasn't left yet. So he leaves. He may as well leave since he is already gone. He walks out the heavy dark door, out into the gravel parking lot, out into the dark, out to the black olive trees and palms along the sidewalk. He stands in the dense shadows of the trees and looks at the Shell station across North 26th Avenue, at the big seashell lit up bright yellow in the night, and he feels the warm breeze and is content to just stand for a few minutes, looking.

The lit-up shell makes him think of the plastic oranges again. He doesn't know why, unless his mother used to buy the drinks for him at gas stations, and maybe she did. That would make sense if she bought them now and then, probably for a dime apiece when they were driving from Virginia to Florida, to Vero Beach every summer to visit her mother, who had money, a lot of it. He and his mother always stayed in a place called the Driftwood Inn, and he doesn't re- member much about it except it looked like it was built of driftwood and at night he slept on the same inflated plastic raft that he floated on during the day.

The raft was not very big and his arms and legs hung off it the same way they did when he was paddling around in the waves, and that was what he slept on in the living room while his mother stayed inside the bedroom with the door locked, the only air conditioner rat- tling from the window inside her closed-up and locked bedroom. He remembers how hot and sweaty he got, how his sunburned skin stuck to the plastic raft and every time he moved it felt like a Band-Aid being ripped off, all night long, all week long. That was their vacation. It was the only one they took each year, in the summer, always in August.

Pogue watches headlights coming and taillights going, bright white and red eyes flying by in the night, and he looks up ahead to his left and waits for the traffic light to change. When it does, the traffic slows, and then he trots across the clear lane of eastbound traffic and darts between cars in the westbound lane. At the Shell station, he looks up at the bright yellow shell floating high above him in the dark and he watches an old man in baggy shorts pumping gas at one pump and another old man in a rumpled suit pumping gas at a different pump. Pogue stays in the shadows and moves silently to the glass door and a bell jingles as he walks inside and heads straight back to the drink machines. The lady at the counter is ringing up a bag of chips, a six-pack of beer, and gas, and doesn't look at him.

Near the coffee machine is the soda machine, and he takes five of the biggest plastic cups and lids and walks up to the counter with them. The cups are bright with cartoon designs and the lids he picks out are white with a little spout for drinking. He sets the cups and lids on the counter.

"Do you have any plastic oranges with green straws? Orange drinks?" he asks the lady behind the counter.

"What?" She frowns and picks up one of the cups. "There's nothing in these. You buying Big Slurps or not?"

"Not," he says. "I just want the cups and the lids."

"We don't sell just cups."

"That's all I want," he says.

She peers over her glasses to look at his face, and he wonders what she sees when she looks at his face like that. "We don't sell just the cups, I'm telling you."

"I'd rather buy the orange drinks if you've got them," he replies.

"What orange drinks?" Her impatience flares. "See that big cooler back there? What's in there is what we got."

"They're in plastic oranges that look just like oranges and come with a green straw."

Her frown dissolves into a look of amazement and her brightly painted lips part in a gaping smile that reminds him of a jack-o'-lantern. "Well, I'll be damned, now I know exactly what you're talking about. Those damn orange drinks. Darling, they haven't been sold in years. Damn, I haven't thought about those forever."

"Then I'll just take the cups and lids," he insists.

"Lord, I give up. Good thing my shift's about to end, tell you that."

"A long night," he says.

"Just got longer." She laughs. "Those damn oranges with the straws." She looks toward the door as the old man in baggy shorts comes in to pay for his gas.

Pogue doesn't pay any attention to him. Pogue stares at her, at her dyed hair as platinum as fishing line and her powdered skin that looks like a soft, wrinkled cloth. If he touched her skin, it would feel like butterfly wings. If he touched her skin, the powder would come off, just like butterfly wings. Her name tag says EDITH.

"Tell you what," Edith is speaking to him. "I'm gonna charge you fifty cents per empty cup and throw in the lids for nothing. Now I got other customers." Her fingers peck on the register and the drawer slides open.

Pogue hands Edith a five-dollar bill and his fingers touch her fingers as he takes his change, and her fingers are cool and quick and soft, and he knows the skin on them is loose, the loose skin that women her age have. Outside in the humid night, he waits for traffic and crosses the street the same way he did minutes earlier. He lingers beneath the same black olive trees and palms, watching the front door of the Other Way Lounge. When no one comes or goes, he walks rapidly to his car and gets in.

33.

||| "YOU SHOULD TELL HIM," Marino says. "Even if it don't turn out the way you think, he ought to know what's going on."

"That's how people head off down the wrong path," Scarpetta replies.

"It's also how they get a head start."

"Not this time," she says.

"You're the boss, Doc."

Marino is stretched out on his bed inside the Marriott on Broad Street, and Scarpetta is sitting in the same chair she was sitting in earlier, but she has pulled it closer to him. He looks very big but less threatening in loose white cotton pajamas she found for him at a department store south of the river. Beneath the light, soft fabric his wounds are dark orange with Betadine. He claims his injuries aren't hurting as much, not nearly as much. She has changed out of her mud-spattered midnight blue suit and is wearing tan corduroys and a dark blue turtleneck sweater and loafers. They are in his room because she did not want him in her room, so she decided his room was safe enough, and they have eaten sandwiches sent up by room service and now they are just talking.

"But I still don't see why you can't just bounce it off him," Marino says, and he is fishing. His curiosity about her relationship with Benton is as pervasive as dust. She notices it constantly and it gets on her nerves, and there is no use trying to get rid of it.

"I'll take the soil samples to the labs first thing in the morning," she tells him. "We'll know in a hurry whether a mistake has been made. If one has, there is no point in my telling Benton about it. A mistake is not germane to the case. It would simply be a mistake. A bad one."

"You don't believe it, though." He looks at her from clouds of pillows she plumped behind him. His color is better. His eyes are brighter.

"I don't know what I believe," she says. "It makes no sense either way. If the trace evidence found on the tractor driver isn't a mistake, then how do you explain it? How could the same type of evidence turn up in Gilly Paulsson's case? Perhaps you have a theory."

Marino thinks hard, his eyes fixing on the window filled with blackness and the lights of downtown. "I can't think how," he says. "I swear to God, I can't come up with anything except what I said in the meeting. And that was just being a smartass."

"Who? You?" she asks dryly.

"Seriously. How could what's-his-name Whitby have the same trace on him that she did? In the first place, she died two weeks before he did. So why would he have it on him at all, especially two weeks after she got it on her? It don't look good," he decides.

Her spirit recoils and she feels a sickness that she has learned to recognize as fear. The only logical explanation at the moment is cross-contamination or mislabeling. Either can happen more easily than people might think. All it takes is for one evidence bag or test tube to be placed in the wrong envelope or rack or the wrong label to be stuck on a sample. This can happen in five seconds of inattention or confusion and then the evidence suddenly came from a source that either makes no sense or, worse, answers a question that could set a suspect free or send him to court, to prison, to the death chamber. She thinks of dentures. She envisions the Fort Lee soldier trying to force the wrong dentures into the dead obese woman's mouth. That's all it takes, one lax moment like that.

"I still don't see why you don't bounce it off Benton," Marino says, reaching for a glass of water by the bed. "What would be wrong with my having a few beers? A few hairs of the dog?"

"What would be right with it?" She has file folders in her lap and is idly flipping through copies of reports, seeing if anything she already knows about Gilly and the tractor driver might suddenly tell her something new. "Alcohol interferes with healing," she says. "It's not been much of a friend to you anyway, has it?"

"Last night it wasn't."

"Order what you want. I'm not going to tell you what to do."

He hesitates and she senses that he wants her to tell him what to do, but she won't. She's done it before and it is a waste, and she doesn't want to be his co-pilot as he flies like a crazed mad bomber through life. Marino looks at the phone, his hands in his lap, and he reaches for the water.

"How are you feeling?" she asks, turning a page. "Need more Advil?"

"I'm okay. Nothing a few beers wouldn't fix."

"That's up to you." She turns another page, scanning the long list of Mr. Whitby's ruptured and lacerated organs.

"You sure she's not going to call the cops?" Marino asks.

She feels his eyes on her. They shine on her like the soft heat from a lamp and she doesn't blame him for feeling scared. The accusations alone would ruin him, that is the truth of the matter. He would be destroyed in law enforcement, and it is quite possible that a Richmond jury would find him guilty just because he is a man, a very big man, and Mrs. Paulsson is skilled at acting pitiful and helpless. The thought of her sharpens Scarpetta's anger.

"She won't," she says. "I called her bluff. Tonight she'll dream about all the magical evidence I carried out of her house. Most of all, she'll dream about the game. She doesn't want the cops or anyone else knowing about the little game or games that go on in her historic little house. Let me ask you something." She looks up from the papers in her lap. "Had Gilly been alive and home, do you think Suz, as you call her, would have done what she did last night? Conjecture, granted. But what's your instinct?"

"I think she does whatever the hell she wants," he replies in a dead tone, the flat tone of resentment and outrage restrained by shame.

"Do you remember if she was drunk?"

"She was high," he replies. "High as a kite."

"On alcohol or maybe something else in addition?"

"I didn't see her pop any pills or smoke nothing or shoot up. But there's probably a lot I didn't see."

"Someone is going to have to talk to Frank Paulsson," Scarpetta says, looking at another report. "Depending on what we find out tomorrow, we might see if Lucy would help."

Marino gets a look on his face and smiles for the first time in hours. "Holy shit. What an idea. She's a pilot. Let her loose on the pervert."

"Exactly." Scarpetta turns a page and takes a deep, quiet breath. "Nothing," she says. "Absolutely nothing that tells me anything more about Gilly. She was asphyxiated and had chips of paint and metal in her mouth. Mr. Whitby's injuries are consistent with his being run over by the tractor. For the hell of it, we should find out if there is any possibility he has some connection to the Paulssons."

"She would know," Marino says.

"You're not calling her." She does tell him what to do in this situation. He is not to call Suzanna Paulsson. "Don't push your luck." She looks up at him.

"I wasn't saying I would. Maybe she knew the tractor driver. Hell, maybe he was into the game. Maybe they have a perverts' club."

"Well, they aren't neighbors." Scarpetta looks at paperwork in Whitby's folder. "He lived over near the airport, not that it matters, necessarily. Tomorrow while I'm in the labs, maybe you can see what you can find out."

Marino doesn't answer her. He doesn't want to talk to any Richmond cops.

"You've got to walk into it," she says, closing the file folder.

"Walk into what?" He looks at the phone by the bed, probably thinking about beer again.

"You know what."

"I hate it when you talk like that," he says, getting crabby. "Like I'm supposed to figure out something from a word or two. I guess some guys would be grateful to know a woman who only talks in a few words."

She folds her hands on top of the file folder in her lap and is somewhat amused. Whenever she's right, he gets cranky. She waits to see what he'll say next.

"All right," he says, unable to stand the silence for long. "Walk into what? Just tell me what the hell I need to walk into besides the loony bin, because right about now I'm feeling half crazy."

"You need to walk into what you fear. And you fear the police because you're still afraid that Mrs. Paulsson has called them. She hasn't. She won't. Get it over with and then the fear will be gone."

"It ain't about fear. It's about being stupid," he retorts.

"Good. Then you'll call Detective Browning or someone, because if you don't, you're being stupid. I'm going back to my room now," she adds, getting up from the chair and moving it back near the window. "I'll see you in the lobby at eight."

34.

||| SHE DRINKS a glass of wine in bed, and it is not a very good wine, a Cabernet that has a sharp aftertaste. But she drinks every drop in the glass as she sits alone inside her hotel room. It is two hours earlier in Aspen and maybe Benton is out to dinner or in a meeting, busy with his case, his secret case that he will not discuss with her.

Scarpetta rearranges the pillows behind her back, propped up in bed, and sets the empty wineglass on the bedside table, next to the phone. She looks at the phone, then looks at the TV wondering if she should turn it on. Deciding not to turn on the TV, she looks at the phone again and picks up the receiver. She dials Benton's cell phone number because he said not to call his town home, and he meant it when he told her that. He was clear about it. Don't call the condo, he told her. I won't be answering the land line, he said.

That doesn't make sense, she replied what now seems months ago. Why won't you answer the phone in your condo?

I don't want distractions, he replied. I won't be answering the land line. If you really have to reach me, Kay, call my cell phone. Please don't take it personally. It's just the way it is. You know how it is.

Benton's cell phone rings twice and he answers.

"What are you doing?" she asks, staring at the blank TV screen opposite the bed.

"Hi," he says softly but distantly. "I'm in my office."

She imagines the third-floor bedroom he has turned into an office inside his Aspen condo. She imagines him sitting at his desk, a document opened on his computer screen. He is working on his case, and she feels better knowing he is home, working.

"It was a pretty rough day," she says. "How about you?"

"Tell me what's going on."

She starts to tell him about Dr. Marcus but doesn't want to get into it. Then she starts to tell him about Marino, but the words won't come out. Her brain is sluggish and for some reason she feels stingy toward Benton. She longs for him and feels stingy toward him and doesn't want to tell him much of anything.

"Why don't you tell me about yours," she says instead. "Did you ski or snowshoe?"

"No."

"Is it snowing?"

"This very minute, yes," he says. "And where you are?"

"Where I am?" She is getting annoyed. It doesn't matter what he told her days ago or what she knows. She is hurt and annoyed. "Are you asking me generically because you can't remember where I am? I'm in Richmond."

"Of course. That's not what I meant."

"Is someone there? Are you in the middle of a meeting or something?" she asks.

"Very much so," he says.

He can't talk, and she is sorry she called. She knows what he is like when he doesn't feel it is safe to talk, and she wishes she hadn't called him. She imagines him in his office and wonders what else he might be doing. Maybe he worries that he is under electronic surveillance. She shouldn't have called. Maybe he simply is preoccupied, but she would rather believe he is cautious than so preoccupied that he can't focus on her. She shouldn't have called.

"Okay," she says. "I'm sorry I called. We haven't talked in two days. But I understand you're in the middle of whatever it is you're doing, and I'm tired."

"You called because you're tired?"

He is teasing her, very subtly kidding her and at the same time maybe a little stung. He doesn't want to think she called him because she is tired, she considers, and she smiles, pressing the phone against her ear. "You know how I get when I'm tired," she jokes. "I can't control myself when I'm tired." She hears a noise in the background, perhaps a voice, a woman's voice. "Is someone there?" she asks again, no longer joking.

A long pause, and she detects the muffled voice again. Maybe he has the radio or TV on. Then she hears nothing.

"Benton?" she says. "Are you there? Benton? Damn it," she mutters. "Damn it," she says, hanging up.

35.

||| THE PUBLIX at Hollywood Plaza is busy. Edgar Allan Pogue walks through the parking lot with his plastic grocery bags, his eyes moving in all directions as he scans for anybody noticing him. No one does. If someone did, it wouldn't matter. No one will remember him or think of him. No one ever does. Besides, he is only doing what is right. A favor to the world, he thinks as he passes along the edges of the light shining down from tall lamps in the parking lot. He keeps to the shadows and walks briskly but not anxiously.

His white car is like about twenty thousand other white cars in South Florida, and he has parked it in a far corner of the lot between two other white cars. One of the white cars, the Lincoln that was parked to the left of him earlier, is no longer there, but as destiny dictated, another white car, this one a Chrysler, took its place. At magical, pure times like this, Pogue knows he is being watched and guided. The eye watches. He is guided by the eye, by the higher power, the god of all gods, the god who sits on top of Mount Olympus, the biggest god of all gods, who is incomprehensibly more immense than any movie star or person who has an attitude and thinks she is an almighty herself. Like her. Like the Big Fish.

Using the remote to unlock his car, he opens the trunk and lifts out another bag, this one from All Season Pools. In the front seat of his white car, he sits in the warm darkness, debating whether he can see well enough for the task at hand. Lights from the lamps in the parking lot barely reach the outer limits where he sits, and he waits for his eyes to adjust, and they do. Inserting the key into the ignition, he turns on the battery so he can listen to music, and he pushes a button on the side of his seat to move it as far back as it will go. He needs plenty of room to work, and his heart trips into gear as he opens the plastic bag and pulls out a pair of thick rubber gloves, a box of granulated sugar, a bottle of generic soda pop, rolls of aluminum foil and duct tape, several large permanent markers, and a package of peppermint chewing gum. The inside of his mouth has tasted like stale cigars ever since he left his apartment at six P.M. He can't smoke now. Smoking another cigar gets rid of the stale, dirty tobacco taste, but he can't smoke now. Peeling the wrapper off a stick of gum, he curls the gum into a tight roll and places it inside his mouth and then opens two more sticks and does the same thing, making himself wait before he lets his teeth sink into the three rolls of gum, and his salivary glands explode painfully, like needles shooting through his jaws, and he begins to chew, in big, hard chews.

He sits in the dark, chewing. Soon annoyed with rap music, he seeks other channels until he finds what is called adult rock these days, and he opens the glove box and pulls out a Ziploc plastic pouch. Coils of black human hair press against the clear plastic as if he has a human scalp inside. He carefully withdraws the soft curly wig and pets it as he looks at the ingredients of his alchemy on the passenger's seat. He starts the car.

The pastels of downtown Hollywood float past like a dream, and the tiny white lights strung in the palms are galaxies as he moves through space and feels the energy of what's next to him on the passenger's seat. He turns east on Hollywood Boulevard and drives exactly two miles per hour below the speed limit toward the A1A highway. Up the road the Hollywood Beach Resort is massive and pale pink and terra-cotta, and on the other side of it is the sea.

3 6 .

| | | DAWN IS on the ocean and tangerine and rose spread along the
dusky blue horizon as if the sun is a broken egg. Rudy Musil pulls
his combat green Hummer into Lucy's driveway and pushes the remote to open her electric gate, and instinctively he looks around,
looks everywhere and listens. He doesn't know why, but he is so un-
settled this morning that he jumped out of bed and decided he would
check on Lucy's house.

The black bars of the metal gate slowly roll open, shuddering at
intervals along the track because it curves, and although the gate is
curved too, it doesn't like curves, it seems. Just one of many design
flaws, Rudy often thinks when he comes to Lucy's salmon-color mansion. The biggest design flaw of all was the one she made when she
bought this damn house, he thinks. Living like a filthy-rich damn
drug dealer, he thinks. The Ferraris are one thing. He can understand

wanting the best cars and the best helicopter. He likes his Hummer, for that matter, but it's one thing to want a rocket or a tank and another thing to want an anchor, a huge gaudy anchor.

He noticed it when he pulled into the driveway but he doesn't take a second look or think anything about it until he pulls past the open gate and gets out of the Hummer. Then he backtracks to pick up the newspaper and sees the flag is up on the mailbox. Lucy doesn't get mail at her house and she isn't home to put the flag up. She wouldn't put the flag up even if she were home. All deliveries and outgoing mail are handled at the training camp and office a half hour south in Hollywood.

This is weird, he thinks, and he walks over to the mailbox and stands near it, the newspaper in one hand, the other hand pushing his sun-streaked hair down because it is in cowlicks this early morning. He hasn't shaved or showered either, and he needs to. All night he thrashed about, sweating in bed, unable to get comfortable no matter what he did. He looks around, thinking. No one is out. No one is jogging or walking the dog. One thing he certainly has noticed about this neighborhood is that people keep to themselves and don't enjoy their rich homes or even their modest ones. Rarely does anyone sit on the patio or use the pool, and those who have boats rarely go out in them. What a weird place, he thinks. What an unfriendly, peculiar, nasty place, he thinks, angrily.

Of all places to move, he thinks. Why here? Why the hell here? Why the hell do you want to be around assholes? You've broken all your rules, Lucy, every one of them, Lucy, he thinks as he yanks open the mailbox door and looks inside and instantly jumps to one side. He backs up ten feet without thinking and his adrenaline kicks in before what he's seeing registers.

"Shit!" he says. "Holy shit!"

37.

||| DOWNTOWN TRAFFIC is bad, as usual, and Scarpetta is driving because Marino is moving slowly. The injuries to places best not discussed seem to be his greatest source of pain, and he is walking slightly bowlegged and was awkward when he climbed into the SUV a few minutes earlier. She knows what she saw, but the outraged reddish-purple hue of fragile tissue was nothing more than a silent scream compared with the loud noise pain must be making now. Marino will not be himself for a while.

"How are you feeling?" she asks him again. "I'm trusting you to tell me." What she means is implicit. She's not going to ask him to take off his clothes one more time. She will look at him if he asks, but she hopes it won't be necessary. Besides, he won't ask.

"I think I'm better," he replies, staring out at the old police department on 9th Street. The building has looked bad for years, paint peeling and tiles around the top border missing. Now it looks worse because it is silent and empty. "I can't believe how many years I wasted in that joint," he adds.

"Oh come on." She flips up the blinker and it click-clicks like a loud watch. "That's no way to talk. Let's don't start the day with that kind of talk. I'm trusting you to tell me if the swelling gets worse. It's very important you tell me the truth."

"It's better."

"Good."

"I put the iodine stuff on myself this morning."

"Good," she says. "Keep applying it every time you get out of the shower."

"It doesn't sting as much anymore. Really not at all. What if she's got some kind of disease like AIDS? I've been thinking about it. What if she does? How do I know she doesn't?"

"You don't know, unfortunately," Scarpetta says, moving slowly along Clay Street, the huge brown Coliseum crouching in the midst of empty parking lots off to their left. "If it makes you feel any better, when I looked around her house, I didn't see any prescription medicines that would indicate she has AIDS or any other sexually transmitted disease or any infection of any sort. That doesn't mean she isn't HIV-positive. She might be and not know it. The same could be said for anyone you've been intimate with. So if you want to worry yourself sick, you can."

"Believe me, I don't want to worry," he replies. "But it's not like you can wear a rubber if someone's biting you. It's not like you can protect yourself. You can't exactly have safe sex if someone's biting you."

"The understatement of the year," she replies as she turns onto 4th Street. Her cell phone rings, and it worries her when she recognizes Rudy's number. Rarely does he call her, and when he does, it is either to wish her a happy birthday or to pass along bad news.

"Hi, Rudy," she says, slowly winding around the back parking lot of the building. "What's up?"

"I can't get hold of Lucy," his stressed voice sounds in her ear. "She's either out of range or has her cell phone off. She headed out in the helicopter this morning for Charleston," he says.

Scarpetta glances over at Marino. He must have called Lucy after Scarpetta left his room last night.

"It's a damn good thing," Rudy says. "A damn good thing."

"Rudy, what's going on?" Scarpetta asks, and she is getting more unnerved by the second.

"Someone put a bomb in her mailbox," he says, talking fast. "It's too much to go into. Some of it she needs to tell you."

Scarpetta creeps almost to a halt inside the parking lot, heading in the direction of the visitors' slots. "When and what?" she asks.

"I just found it. Not even an hour ago. Came by to check on the place and saw the flag up on the mailbox, which didn't make sense. I opened it and this big plastic cup's inside, the whole thing colored orange with marker, and the lid's colored green with a piece of duct tape around the lid and over the opening, you know, the little spout you drink out of, and I couldn't see what was in it so I got one of those long poles out of the garage, what do you call it. Has the grippers on the end for changing light bulbs that are high up. I picked the damn thing up with it, carried it out back, and took care of it."

She takes her time parking, the car barely moving while she listens. "How did you manage that? I hate to ask."

"Shot it. Don't worry. With snake shot. It was a chemical bomb, a bottle bomb, you know the type. With little pieces of tinfoil balled up inside."

"Metal to accelerate the reaction." Scarpetta starts going through the differential diagnosis of the bomb. "Typical in bottle bombs made out of household cleaners that contain hydrochloric acid like the Works for toilet bowls that you can get from Wal-Mart, the grocery store, a hardware store. Unfortunately, the recipes are available on the Internet."

"It had an acid odor, more like chlorine, but since I shot it by the pool, maybe that's what I was smelling."

"Possibly granulated pool chlorine and some type of sugary soda pop. That's also popular. A chemical analysis will tell."

"Don't worry. One will be done."

"Anything left of the cup?" she asks.

"We'll check for prints and get anything we find right into IAFIS."

"Theoretically, you can get DNA from prints, if they're fresh. It's worth a try."

"We'll swab the cup and the duct tape. Don't worry."

The more he says don't worry, the more she will.

"I haven't called the police," he adds.

"It's not my place to advise you about that." She has given up advising him or anyone associated with him. The rules of Lucy and her people are different and creative and risky, and quite often they are inconsistent with what is legal. Scarpetta has ceased demanding to know details that will keep her awake at night.

"This may be related to some other things," Rudy says. "Lucy needs to tell you. If you talk to her before I do, she needs to call me ASAP."

"Rudy, you'll do what you want. But let me just say I hope there aren't any other devices out there, that whoever did this didn't leave more than one, didn't have more than one target," she says. "I've had cases of people who died when these chemicals exploded in their faces or were thrown in their faces and it got into the airway and lungs. The acids are so strong the reaction doesn't even need to go to completion before the thing blows."

"I know, I know."

"Please find some way to make sure there aren't other victims or potential victims out there. That's what concerns me if you handle things on your own." It is her way of saying that if he doesn't intend to call the police, he should at least be responsible enough to do what he can to protect the public.

"I know what to do. Don't worry," he says.

"Jesus," Scarpetta says, ending the call and looking over at Marino. "What in God's name is going on down there? You must have called Lucy last night. Did she tell you what's going on down there? I haven't seen her since September. I don't know what's going on."

"An acid bomb?" He is sitting up straighter in his seat, always ready to pounce if anyone is after Lucy.

"A chemical-reaction bomb. The kind of bottle bombs we had trouble with out of Fairfax. Remember all those bombs in northern Virginia some years ago? A bunch of kids with too much time on their hands who thought it was funny blowing up mailboxes and a woman died?"

"Dammit," he says.

"Easily accessible and terribly dangerous. A pH of one or less, so acidic it's off the scale. It could have blown up in Lucy's face. I hope to God she wouldn't have pulled it out of the mailbox herself. I never know with her."

"At her house?" Marino asks, getting angrier. "The bomb was at that mansion of hers down in Florida?"

"What did she say to you last night?"

"I just told her about Frank Paulsson, what was going on up here. That was it. She said she'd take care of it. At that huge house of hers with all the cameras and shit? The bomb was at her house?"

"Come on," Scarpetta says, opening her car door. "I'll tell you as we go in."

| | |Close to the window, the morning light warms the desk where Rudy sits typing on the computer. He hits keys and waits, then rapidly types and waits some more, pressing arrows and scrolling, searching the Internet for what he believes is there. Something is there. The psycho saw something that set him off. Rudy now knows the bomb isn't random.

He's been at the training camp office for the past two hours doing nothing but maneuver through the Internet while one of the forensic scientists in the nearby private lab has scanned prints and partial prints into IAFIS, and already there is news. Rudy's nerves are screaming like one of Lucy's Ferraris in sixth gear. He dials the phone and tucks the receiver under his chin as he types and stares at the flat video screen.

"Hey Phil," he says. "Big plastic cup with the Cat in the Hat on it. Big Gulp type of cup. Lid originally white. Yeah, yeah, the type of big cup you get in a convenience store, a gas station, and fill it up yourself. The Cat in the Hat, though. How unusual? Can we track it? No, I'm not kidding. That's a proprietary thing, right? But the movie, it's not recent. Last year, Christmastime, right? No, I didn't go see it and quit being funny. Seriously, what place would still have Cat in the Hat cups left after all this time? Worst case, he's had 'em for a while. But we gotta try. Yeah, we got prints on it. This guy's not even trying. I mean, he doesn't give a rat's ass about leaving his prints all the hell over the place. On the drawing he taped to the boss's door. Inside the bedroom where Henri was attacked. Now on a bomb. And now we got a hit in IAFIS. Yeah, can you believe it? No, don't have a name yet. Might not, either. The hit's on a latent-to-latent search, matching up with partials from some other case. We're checking. That's all I've got right now."

He hangs up and turns back to the computer. Lucy has more search engines in the Internet than Pratt & Whitney has jet turbines, but she has never worried that information on the World Wide Web might have to do with her. Not so long ago, she had no reason to worry. Special operatives don't usually court publicity unless they're inactive and hungry for Hollywood, but then Lucy got hooked into Hollywood, and then she got hooked into Henri, and then life changed dramatically and for the worse. Damn Henri, he thinks as he types. Damn her. Damn failed actress Henri who decided to be a cop. Damn Lucy for recruiting her.

He starts a new search, typing in the key words "Kay Scarpetta" and "niece." Now this is interesting. He picks up a pencil and starts twirling it between his fingers like a baton as he reads an article that ran last September on the AP. It is a very short article and simply states that Virginia has appointed a new chief medical examiner, Dr. Joel Marcus from St. Louis, and it mentions his taking Scarpetta's place after years of limbo and chaos and so on. But Lucy's name appears in the brief article. Since leaving Virginia, the article says, Dr. Scarpetta has worked as a consultant for the private investigation firm The Last Precinct, founded by her niece, former FBI agent Lucy Farinelli.

Not quite true, Rudy thinks. Scarpetta doesn't exactly work for Lucy, but that doesn't mean they don't find themselves involved in the same cases now and then. There is no way Scarpetta would ever work for Lucy, and he can't blame her, and he's not sure how he works for Lucy. He had forgotten all about the article, and now he remembers getting angry with Lucy about it and demanding to know how the hell her name and the name of The Last Precinct ended up in a damn story about Dr. Joel Marcus. The last thing TLP needs is publicity, and there never used to be publicity until Lucy got involved with the entertainment industry, and then all sorts of gossip started leaking into the newspapers and onto television magazine shows.

He executes another search, squinting his eyes, trying to come up with something he hasn't thought of, and then his fingers seem to type on without the rest of him and he types in the key words "Henrietta Walden." A waste of time, he thinks. Her name when she was a B-list out-of-work actress was Jen Thomas or something forgettable like that. He reaches for his Pepsi without looking at it and can't believe his good fortune. The search returns three results.

"Come on, be something," he says to the empty office as he clicks on the first entry.

A Henrietta Taft Walden died a hundred years ago, was some sort of wealthy abolitionist from Lynchburg, Virginia. Whoa, that must have gone over like a lead balloon. He can't imagine being an abolitionist in Virginia around the time of the Civil War. Gutsy lady, he'll give her that. He clicks on the second entry. This Henrietta Walden is alive but ancient and lives on a farm, also in Virginia, raises show horses and recently gave a million dollars to the NAACP. Probably a descendant of the first Henrietta Walden, he thinks, and he wonders if Jen Thomas borrowed the name Henrietta Walden from these somewhat noteworthy female abolitionist types, one dead, one barely alive. If so, why? He envisions Henri's striking blond looks and uppity ball-busting attitude. Why would she be inspired by women who were passionate about the plight of blacks? Probably because it was the liberal Hollywood thing to do, he cynically decides, clicking on the third entry.

This one is a short article from *The Hollywood Reporter*. It was published in mid-October:

THIS ROLE'S FOR REAL

Former actress-turned-LAPD-cop Henri Walden has signed on with the prestigious international private protection agency The Last Precinct, owned and directed by a former special ops helicopter-flying, Ferrari-driving Lucy Farinelli, who just so happens to be the niece of the famed real-life Quincy Dr. Kay Scarpetta. TLP, which is headquartered in a lesser Hollywood, the one in Florida, recently opened an office in Los Angeles and has expanded its cloak-and-dagger activities to protecting stars. Although its clients are top-secret, the *Reporter* has learned that some of them are the biggest names on the A list and in the music industry and include such mega-luminaries as actor Gloria Rustic and rapper Rat Riddly.

"My most exciting, daring role yet," Walden said of her newest escapade. "Who better to protect stars than someone who once worked in the industry?"

"Work" may be a bit of an exaggeration, since the blond beauty had a lot of leisure time during her stint as an actress. Not that she needs the money. It is well known that her family has plenty of it. Walden is best known for playing small roles in big-budget films such as *Quick Death* and *Don't Be There*. Keep your eye out for Walden. She's the one with a gun.

Rudy prints the article and sits in the chair, his fingers lightly resting on the keyboard as he stares at the screen and contemplates whether Lucy knows about the article. How could she not be furious, if she knew, and if she does know, why didn't she fire Henri months ago? Why didn't Lucy tell him? Such a breach of protocol is hard to imagine. It shocks him that Lucy would allow it, assuming she did. He can't think of a single instance when someone who works for TLP gave an interview to the media or even indulged in loose talk unless it was part of a highly planned operation. There is only one way to find out, he thinks, reaching for the phone.

"Hey," he says when Lucy answers. "Where are you?"

"In St. Augustine. On a fuel stop." Her voice is wary. "I already know about the fucking bomb."

"Not what I'm calling about. I guess you talked to your aunt."

"Marino called. I don't have time to chat about it," she says angrily. "Something else going on?"

"Did you know your friend gave an interview about coming on board with us?"

"None of this is about her being my friend."

"We'll argue about that later," Rudy says, acting far calmer than he feels, and he is seething. "Just answer me. Did you know?"

"I know nothing about an article. What article?"

Rudy reads it to her over the phone, and after he's finished, he waits to see how she'll react, and he knows she will react and that makes him feel a little better. All along this hasn't been fair. Now, maybe Lucy will be forced to admit it. When Lucy doesn't respond, Rudy asks, "Are you there?"

"Yes," she answers him abruptly and testily. "I didn't know."

"Well, now you do. Now we have another whole solar system to take a look at. Like her rich family and whether there's any connection between it and the so-called Waldens and who the hell knows what else. But bottom line, did the psycho see this article, and if so, why and what the hell is that about? Not to mention, her acting name is this abolitionist's name and she's from Virginia. So are you, sort of. Maybe when you got hooked up with her it wasn't exactly coincidental."

"That's ridiculous. Now you're really going off," Lucy says hotly. "She was on a list of LAPD cops who worked security . . ."

"Oh bullshit," Rudy replies, and his anger is showing too. "Fuck the list. You interviewed local police and there she was. You knew damn well how inexperienced she was in private protection, but you hired her anyway."

"I don't want to talk about this on a cell phone. Not even on our cell phones."

"I don't either. Talk to the shrink." That's his code name for Benton Wesley. "Why don't you call him, I'm serious. Maybe he'll have some ideas. Tell him I'm e-mailing the article to him. We've got prints. Same psycho who did your pretty little sketch also left the little gift in your mailbox."

"Big surprise. Like I said, who wants two of them? I've talked to the shrink," she then says. "He'll be monitoring what I do here."

"Good thinking. Oh, I almost forgot. I found a hair sticking to the duct tape. The duct tape on the chemical bomb."

"Describe it."

"About six inches long, curly, dark. Looks like head hair, obviously. More later, call me from a land line. I got a lot of work to do," he says. "Maybe your friend knows something, if you can get her to tell the truth for once."

"Don't call her my friend," Lucy says. "Let's don't fight about this anymore."

39.

|| AFTER KAY SCARPETTA entered the OCME with Marino slowly following her, doing his best to walk normally, Bruce at the security desk sat up straighter and got a look of dread on his face.

"Uh, I've been given instructions," Bruce says, refusing to meet her eyes. "The chief says no visitors. Maybe he doesn't mean you? Is he expecting you?"

"He isn't," Scarpetta says with ease. Nothing surprises her at this point. "He probably does mean me."

"Gee, I sure am sorry." Bruce is acutely embarrassed, his cheeks burning pink. "How'ya doing, Pete?"

Marino leans against the desk, his feet spread, his pants hanging lower than usual. If he got in a foot pursuit, he might lose his pants. "Been better," Marino says. "So Chief Little Thinks He's Big Man ain't letting us in. That what you're telling us, Bruce?"

"That guy," Bruce says, catching himself. Like most people, Bruce would like to keep his job. He wears a nice Prussian blue uniform, carries a gun, and works in a beautiful building. Better to hold on to what he's got, even if he can't stand Dr. Marcus.

"Huh," Marino says, stepping back from the console. "Well, hate to disappoint the Chief Little, but we ain't here to see him, anyway. Got evidence to drop off at the labs, at Trace. But I'm curious, what order did you get, exactly? I'm just curious about the wording."

"That guy," Bruce says, and he starts to shake his head but catches himself. He likes his job.

"It's all right," Scarpetta says. "I get the message loud and clear. Thanks for letting me know. Glad someone did."

"He should have told you." Bruce stops himself again, looking around. "Just so you know, everybody's been mighty happy to see you, Dr. Scarpetta."

"Almost everybody." She smiles. "It's not a problem. Can you let Mr. Eise know we're here? He is expecting us," she adds, emphasizing the word "is."

"Yes, ma'am," Bruce says, cheering up a little. He picks up the phone and dials the extension and passes on the message.

For a minute or two, Scarpetta and Marino stand before the elevator, waiting for it. One can push the button all day and it won't do any good unless the person has a magic magnetic swipe card or the elevator is sent by someone who does. The doors open and they step aboard, and Scarpetta presses the button for the third floor, her black crime scene bag slung over her shoulder.

"I guess the son of a bitch canned you," Marino comments, the elevator car lurching slightly as it begins its short ascent.

"I guess he did."

"So? What are you gonna do about it? You can't just let him get away with this. He begs you to come to Richmond and then treats you like shit. I'd get him fired."

"He'll get himself fired one of these days. I have better things to do," she replies as the stainless-steel doors open onto Junius Eise, who is waiting for them in a white corridor.

"Junius, thank you," Scarpetta says, offering her hand. "Nice to see you again."

"Oh, I'm happy to do it," he says, slightly flustered.

He is a strange man with pale eyes. The middle of his upper lip fades into a fine scar that reaches to his nose, a typical poor mending job that she has seen many times before in people who were born with cleft palates. Appearance aside, he is odd, and Scarpetta thought so years ago when she used to encounter him now and then in the labs. She never talked to him much back then, but occasionally she consulted him on certain cases. When she was chief, she was pleasant and made it a practice to show the respect she honestly felt for all of the lab workers, but she was never overly friendly. As she accompanies Eise along the maze of white corridors and big glass windows that allow glimpses of the scientists at work in the labs, she is aware that the perception when she was here was that she was cold and intimidating. As chief she got respect but rarely affection. That was hard, extremely hard, but she lived with it because it went with the position. Now she doesn't have to live with it.

"How have you been doing, Junius?" she asks. "Understand you and Marino have been keeping the lights burning late at the FOP. I hope you aren't stressing yourself out too much about this recent trace evidence curiosity. If anyone can figure it out, you can."

Eise glances at her, a look of disbelief on his face. "Let's hope so," he says, flustered. "Well, I have to say, I know I didn't mix anything up. I don't care what anyone says. I damn well know I didn't."

"You're the last person who would mix something up," she says.

"Well, thank you. That means a lot coming from you." He lifts the swipe card from the lanyard around his neck and waves it past the sensor on the wall, and a lock clicks free. He opens the door. "It's not for me to say what anything means," he adds as they walk into the Trace Evidence section. "But I know I didn't mislabel a sample. I never have. Not once. At least not once when I didn't catch it right away and the courts were none the wiser."

"I understand."

"Do you remember Kit?" Eise asks, as if Kit is nearby, but she isn't in sight. "She's not here, is out sick, as a matter of fact. I tell you, half the world has the flu. But I know she wanted to say hello. She'll be sorry she missed you."

"Tell her I'm sorry too," Scarpetta says as they reach a long black countertop in Eise's work area.

"Tell you what," Marino says. "You got a quiet place with a phone?"

"You bet. The section chief's office around the corner. She's in court today. Help yourself, I know she wouldn't mind."

"I'll leave you guys to play in the mud," Marino says, walking off slowly, slightly bowlegged, like a cowboy who just came in from a long, rough ride.

Eise covers a section of countertop with clean white paper and Scarpetta opens her black bag and pulls out the soil samples. He pulls up another chair so she can sit next to him at the compound microscope and hands her a pair of examination gloves. The first stage of the many in this process is the simplest. Eise takes a tiny steel spatula, dips it into one of the bags, wipes a minute residue of red clay and sandy dirt on a clean slide, and places it on the stage of the microscope. Peering into the lenses, he adjusts the focus and slowly moves the slide around while Scarpetta looks on, unable to see anything except the swipe of damp reddish dirt on the glass. Removing the slide and setting it on a white paper towel, he uses the same method to prepare several more slides.

It is not until they are working on a second bag of the soil Scarpetta collected from the demolition site that Eise finds something.

"If I wasn't seeing this, I wouldn't believe it," he says, looking up from the binocular eyepiece. "Help yourself." He rolls back his chair, giving her room.

She moves closer to the microscope and looks through the lenses at a microscopic landfill of sand and other minerals, fragments of plant and insect pieces, and parts and bits of tobacco—all typical for a dirty parking lot—and she sees several flecks of metal that are partially a dull silver. This is not typical. She looks for a needle-pointed tool and finds several within reach. She carefully manipulates the metallic chips, isolating them, and sees that there are exactly three of them on this slide, all slightly bigger than the largest grain of silica or rock or other debris. Two are red and one is white. Moving the tungsten tip around a little more, she unearths one more find that captivates her interest. This one she recognizes quickly, but she takes her time saying so. She wants to be sure.

It is about the size of the smallest paint chip and grayish-yellow and a peculiar shape that is neither mineral nor man-made. In fact, the particle looks like a prehistoric bird with a hammer-shaped head, an eye, a narrow neck, and a bulbous body.

"The flat plates of the lamellae. They look like concentric circles and are the layers of bone like the rings of a tree," she says, moving the particle a little. "And the grooves and channels of the canaliculi. That's the holes we're seeing, the haversian canals or canaliculi, where tiny blood vessels run through. You put this under the PolScope and you should see an undulating, wavy fanlike extension. My guess is when you get around to the XRD it's going to come up as calcium phosphate. Bone dust, in other words. I can't say I'm surprised, considering the context. That old building certainly would have had plenty of bone dust in it."

"I'll be darned," Eise says happily. "I've been making myself crazy over it. The same damn thing I found in the Sick Girl case, the Paulsson case, if we're on the same sheet of music. Mind if I look?"

She rolls back her chair, relieved but just as perplexed as she was before. Paint chips and bone dust might make sense in the tractor driver's case, but not in Gilly Paulsson's death. How can it be that the same type of microscopic trace evidence was recovered from inside her mouth?

"Same damn stuff," Eise says with certainty. "Let me get Sick Girl's slides and show you. You won't believe it." He picks up a thick envelope from a pile on his desk and peels tape off the flap and pulls out a cardboard file of slides. "Been keeping her stuff handy because I've looked at it so many times, believe you me." He places a slide on the stage. "Red, white, and blue paint particles, some adhering to metal chips, some not." He moves the slide around and gets it into focus. "Paint's single-layer, at least an epoxy enamel, and it may have been modified. Meaning, whatever the object is, it might have started out white and had additional paint added, specifically the red, white, and blue added. Take a look."

Eise has painstakingly removed all particles from whatever was submitted to him in the Paulsson case, and only red, white, and blue paint chips are on the slide. They look big and bright, like a child's building blocks but irregularly shaped. Some of them adhere to dull silver metal and some seem to be just paint. The color and texture of the paint seems identical to what she just saw when she looked at her soil sample, and her growing disbelief is well on its way to numbness. She can't think. Her brain is slowing down like a computer running out of memory. She simply can't find the logical connections.

"Here's the other particles you're calling bone dust." He pulls away the side and replaces it with another one.

"And this was on her swabs?" She wants to make sure because it is hard to believe.

"No question about it. You're looking at it."

"The same damn dust."

"Think how much of that would be down there. More dust than

there are stars in the universe if you started scraping up all the dirt down there," Eise says.

"A few of these particles look like they're old and the product of natural flaking or exfoliation as the periosteum begins to break down," Scarpetta says. "See how rounded and gradually thinned the edges are? I expect dust like that with skeletal remains, bones dug up or carried in from the woods and so on. Untraumatized bones will have untraumatized dust. But a few of these"—she isolates a particle of bone dust that is jagged and fractured and several shades lighter in color—"look pulverized to me."

He leans in to see for himself, and then moves out of her way, and she peers into the lenses.

"In fact, I'm thinking this particle here is burned. Did you notice how fine it is? I'm seeing a little blackish margin. It looks carbonized, burned. Bet if I put my finger on this particle it would probably stick to the oil on my skin, and regular flaked bone won't," she says, intrigued. "I think some of what we're looking at is from cremains." She peers at the bluish-white ragged particle with its carbonized margin in the bright circle of light. "It looks chalky and fractured but not necessarily heat fractured. I don't know. I've never had a reason to pay attention to bone dust, certainly not burned bone dust. An elemental analysis will tell you. With burned bone you should get different levels of calcium, higher levels of phosphorus," she explains without moving her eyes from the binocular lenses. "And by the way, I might expect dust from cremains in the rubble and dirt at the old building since there was a crematorium oven. God knows how many bodies were cremated in that place over the decades. But I'm a little perplexed that the debris from this soil I brought in would have bone dust in it. I scraped that soil from the pavement near the back door. They haven't started knocking down the back of the building and digging up the back parking lot yet. The Anatomical Division should still be completely intact. Remember the back door of the old building?"

"Sure I do."

"That's where it was. Why would dust from cremains be in the parking lot, right there on top of the parking lot? Unless it was tracked outside the building?"

"You mean someone stepped in it down there in the Anatomical Division and then tracked it out into the parking lot?"

"I don't know, possibly, but it appears Mr. Whitby's bloody face must have been against the pavement, the muddy dirty pavement, and this trace evidence adhered to his wound and the blood on his face."

"Take me back to the part about bone dust getting fractured," Eise says, mystified. "So you got burned bone and then how does it get fractured if not by heat?"

"As I said, I don't know for a fact, but dust from cremains mixed in with dirt on pavement and perhaps run over by a tractor and cars and even people stepping on it. Could bone dust exposed to that sort of traffic look traumatized? I just don't know the answer."

"But why the hell would there be cremated bone dust in Sick Girl's case?" Eise asks.

"That's right." She tries to clear her head and organize her thoughts. "That's right. This isn't from the Whitby case. This burned-looking fractured dust isn't from his case. I'm looking at her trace."

"Dust from cremains inside Sick Girl's mouth? Holy Mother of God! I can't explain that. Sure as heck can't. Can you?"

"I don't have a clue why bone dust has turned up in her case to begin with," Scarpetta replies. "What else have you found? I understand they brought in a number of things from Gilly Paulsson's house."

"Just stuff from her bed. Kit and I were back there in the Scraping Room for ten hours, and then I spend half my life picking out cotton fibers because Dr. Marcus has a thing about cotton swabs. Must have stock in Q-tips," Eise complains. "Course, DNA had a crack at the linens too."

"I know about it," Scarpetta says. "They were looking for respiratory epithelium and found it."

"We also found hairs, dyed black hairs, on the sheets. I know Kit's been aggravated over those."

"Human, I presume. DNA?"

"Yes, human. They've been sent to Bode for mito."

"What about pet hairs? What about canine hair?"

"No," he says.

"Not from her bed linens or pajamas, not from anything they carried in from her house?"

"No. How about dust from an autopsy saw?" he says, obsessing over the bone dust. "That could be at your old building too."

"Nothing I'm seeing looks like that." She sits back in the chair and looks at him. "Dust from a saw would be fine granules mixed with chunks, and you might also find particles of metal from the blade."

"Okay. Can we talk about something I do know before I rupture something in my head?"

"Please," she says.

"Thank you, Lord. Now you're the bone expert, I'll grant you that." He returns several slides to Gilly Paulsson's folder. "But I do know about paint. In both the Sick Girl and the Tractor Man cases, there's not a sign of topcoat, not a trace of primer, so we know it isn't automotive. And the bits of metal underneath aren't attracted to a magnet, so they're not ferrous. I tried that out day one, and to cut to the chase, we're talking aluminum."

"Something aluminum painted with red, white, and blue enamel paint," Scarpetta thinks out loud. "Mixed with bone dust."

"I give up," Eise says.

"For the moment, so do I," she replies.

"Human bone dust?"

"Unless it's fresh, we're not going to know."

"How fresh is fresh?"

"Several years at most as opposed to decades," she replies. "We can swab fingerprints and get STR and mito, so it doesn't take much, assuming the sample isn't too old or in bad shape. With DNA it's quality versus quantity, but if I had to bet, I think we're out of luck. In the first place, with cremains you can forget DNA entirely. As for the unburned bone dust I'm seeing, I don't know why exactly, but it strikes me as old. It just looks eroded and old. Now, you can send some of this unburned dust off to Bode Laboratories for mito or even let them try STR, but with a sample this small it's going to be consumed. Do we want it consumed knowing we may not get anything anyway?"

"DNA ain't my department. If it was, my budget would be a hell of a lot bigger."

"Well, it's not my decision anyway," she says, getting up from the chair. "I suppose if it were, I would vote for preserving the integrity of the evidence in case we need it later. What matters is that bone dust has shown up in two cases that should not be even remotely related."

"That definitely matters."

"I'll let you pass on the happy news to Dr. Marcus," she says.

"He loves my e-mails. I'll send him another one," Eise replies. "Wish I had happy news for you, Dr. Scarpetta. But the fact is, all these bags of dirt are going to take me a while. Days. I'll spread all of it out on watch glasses, dry it good, then sieve it to separate the particles, and that's a pain in the neck because you have to bang the damn sieves on the counter every other minute to get them to drain into the receiver pan, and I've given up begging for particle separators that have automatic shakers because they can cost up to six grand, so forgetez-vous that. The drying and the sieving will take a few days, then it's just me, myself, and I and the microscope, and then SEM and whatever else we try. By the way, did I ever give you one of my handmade tools? Around here, they're affectionately known as 'Eise Picks.' "

He finds several on his desk and decides on one, turning it slowly this way and that to make sure the tungsten isn't bent and doesn't need sharpening. Holding it up proudly, he presents it to her with a flourish as if he is giving her a long-stem rose.

"That's very nice of you, Junius," she says. "Thank you very much. And no. You never did give me one."

40.

| | | UNABLE TO LOOK at the problem from any angle that introduces clarity, Scarpetta stops thinking about the painted aluminum and bone dust. She decides she will soon drive herself into complete exhaustion if she continues to obsess about red, white, and blue chips of paint and particles of probable human bone that are smaller than cat dander.

The early afternoon is gray and the air is so heavy it threatens to collapse like a rain-soaked ceiling. She and Marino get out of the SUV and the doors sound muffled when they close them. She begins to lose faith when she sees no lights on in the brick house with the mossy slate roof that is on the other side of the Paulssons' backyard fence.

"You sure he'll be here?" Scarpetta asks.

"He said he would. I know where the key is. He told me, so obviously he doesn't care if we know."

"We're not going to break in, if that's what you're suggesting," she says, looking down the cracked walkway to the aluminum storm door and the wooden door behind it and the dark windows on either side. The house is small and old and has the sad face of neglect. It is overwhelmed by bold magnolias, prickly shrubs that haven't been pruned in years, and pines that are so tall and full of themselves they have littered their needles and cones in layers that clog gutters and smother what is left of the lawn.

"Wasn't suggesting nothing," Marino replies, looking up and down the quiet street. "Just letting you know he told me where the key is and said there's no alarm system. You tell me why he told me that."

"It doesn't matter," she says, but she knows it does. Already she can see what is in store for them.

The real-estate agent can't be bothered to show up or doesn't want to be involved, so he has made it possible for them to wander in and around the house unattended. She digs her hands in the pockets of her coat, her scene kit over her shoulder and noticeably lighter without the bags of soil that are now being dried at the trace evidence lab.

"I'm at least looking in the windows." He starts off down the walkway, moving slowly, legs spread a little wide, watching where he steps. "You coming or hanging out by the car?" he asks without turning around.

What little they know began with the city directory, which was enough for Marino to track down the real-estate agent, who apparently hasn't shown the house in more than a year and doesn't give a damn about it. The owner is a woman named Bernice Towle. She lives in South Carolina and refuses to spend a penny to fix up the place or lower the price enough to make its sale remotely possible. According to the real-estate agent, the only time the house is used is when Mrs. Towle lets guests stay in it, and no one knows how often that is—or if they ever do. The Richmond police did not check out the house or its history because for all practical purposes it is not lived in and therefore not relevant to the Gilly Paulsson case. The FBI have no interest in the dilapidated Towle residence for the same reason. Marino and Scarpetta are interested in the house because in a violent death everything should be of interest.

Scarpetta walks toward the house. The concrete beneath her feet is slick with a film of green slime from the rain, and were it her walkway she would scrub it with bleach, she thinks as she gets closer to Marino. He is on the small, sloping porch, hands cupped around his eyes, peering through a window.

"If we're going to be prowlers we may as well commit the next crime," she says. "Where's the key?"

"That flowerpot under the bush there." He looks at a huge, unkempt boxwood and a muddy flowerpot barely visible beneath it. "The key's under it."

She steps off the porch and works her hands between branches, and sees that the pot is filled with several inches of green rainwater that smells like swamp water. She moves the pot and finds a flat square of aluminum foil covered with dirt and cobwebs. Folded inside it is a copper key as tarnished as an old penny. No one has touched this key in some time, months at least, maybe longer, she thinks, and on the porch she gives it to Marino because she doesn't want to be the one to unlock the house.

The door creaks open to a musty odor. It is cold inside, and then she thinks she smells cigars. Marino feels for a light switch, but when he finds one and flips it up and down, nothing happens.

"Here." Scarpetta hands him a pair of cotton gloves. "I just happened to have your size."

"Huh." He works his huge hands into the gloves while she puts on a pair too.

On a table against a wall is a lamp, and she tries that with success. "At least the electricity is on," she says. "I wonder if the phone is." She picks up the receiver of an old black Princess phone and holds it up to her ear and hears nothing. "No phone," she says. "I keep thinking I smell old cigar smoke."

"Well, you gotta keep power or your pipes will freeze," Marino says, sniffing and looking around, and the living room seems small with him in it. "I don't smell cigars, just dust and mildew. But you've always been able to smell shit I can't smell."

Scarpetta stands in the glow of the lamp, staring across the small, dim room at the floral upholstered couch beneath the windows and a blue Queen Anne chair in a corner. Piled on the dark wooden coffee table are stacks of magazines, and she heads that way and begins to pick them up to see what they are. "Now this I wouldn't have expected," she says, looking at a copy of *Variety*.

"What?" Marino steps closer and stares at the black-and-white weekly.

"A trade publication for the entertainment industry," Scarpetta says. "Strange. A year ago last November," she reads the date on it. "But still very strange. I wonder if Mrs. Towle, whoever she is, has ties with the movie business."

"Maybe she's just starstruck like half the rest of the world." Marino isn't very interested.

"Half the rest of the world reads *People, Entertainment Weekly,* that sort of thing. Not *Variety.* This is hard-core," she says, picking up more magazines. "*Hollywood Reporter, Variety, Variety, Hollywood Reporter,* going back some two years. The last six months aren't here. Maybe the subscription expired. Mailing label is Mrs. Edith Arnette, this address. That name mean anything to you?"

"Nope."

"Did the real-estate agent say who used to live here? Was it Mrs. Towle?"

"He didn't say. I got the impression it was Mrs. Towle."

"Maybe we should do better than an impression. How about calling him." She unzips her black scene kit and pulls out a heavy plastic trash bag, and she loudly shakes it open and drops in the copies of *Variety* and *The Hollywood Reporter.*

"You taking those?" Marino stands in a doorway, his back to her. "Why?"

"Can't hurt to check them for prints."

"Stealing," he says, opening a piece of paper and reading the number on it.

"Trespassing, breaking and entering. May as well steal," she says.

"If it turns out to be something, we don't have a warrant." He is playing with her a little.

"Do you want me to put them back?" she asks.

Marino stands in the doorway and shrugs. "We find something, I know where the key is. I'll sneak 'em back inside and get a warrant after the fact. I've done it before."

"I wouldn't admit that in public," she comments, leaving the bag of magazines on the dusty hardwood floor and moving to a small table to the left of the couch and thinking she smells cigars again.

"A lot of things I don't admit in public," he replies, entering a number in his cell phone.

"Besides, this isn't your jurisdiction. You can't get a warrant."

"Don't worry. Me and Browning are tight." He stares off as he waits and she can tell by his tone that he's gotten voice mail when he says, "Hey, Jim. Marino here. Was wondering who lived in this house last? What about an Edith Arnette? Please call me ASAP." He leaves his number. "Huh," he says to Scarpetta. "Ol' Jimbo had no intention of meeting us here. Do you blame him? What a dump."

"It's a dump all right," Scarpetta says as she opens a drawer in a small table to the left of the couch. It is full of coins. "But I'm not sure that's why he didn't come. So you and Detective Browning are tight. The other day you were afraid he might arrest you."

"That was the other day." Marino steps inside the dark hallway. "He's an okay guy. Don't worry. I need a warrant, I'll get a warrant. Enjoy reading about Hollywood. Where the hell are the lights around here?"

"Must be fifty dollars in quarters." Coins lightly clink as Scarpetta pushes her fingers through them inside the drawer. "Just quarters. No pennies, nickels, or dimes. What do you pay for in quarters around here? Newspapers?"

"Fifty cents for the Garbage-Patch," he snidely refers to the local *Times-Dispatch*. "Got one just yesterday out of the machine in front of the hotel and it cost me two quarters. Twice what *The Washington Post* is."

"It's unusual to leave money in a place where no one lives," Scarpetta says, shutting the drawer.

The hallway light is out, but she follows Marino into the kitchen. Right away it strikes her as odd that the sink is full of dirty dishes and the water is disgusting with congealed fat and mold. She opens the refrigerator and is increasingly convinced that someone has been staying in the house, and not long ago at all. On the shelves are cartons of orange juice and soy milk that have expiration dates for the end of this month, and dates on meat in the freezer show it was purchased some three weeks ago. The more food she discovers in cabinets and the pantry, the more anxious she becomes as her intuition reacts before her brain does. When she moves to the end of the hallway and begins to explore the bedroom at the back of the house, and smells cigars, she's sure of it, and her adrenaline is rushing.

The double bed is covered with a cheap dark blue spread, and when she pulls it back she sees that the linens beneath it are wrinkled and soiled and scattered with short hairs, some of them red hairs, probably head hairs, and others darker and curlier and probably pubic hairs, and she sees the stains that have dried stiff and she suspects she knows what those stains are. The bed faces a window, and from it she can see over the wooden fence, she can see the Paulsson house, she can see the dark window that was Gilly's. On a table by the bed is a black and yellow ceramic Cohiba ashtray that is quite clean. There is more dust on the furniture than there is in the ashtray.

Scarpetta does what she needs to do and has little awareness of time passing or shadows changing or the sound of rain hitting the roof as she goes through the closet and every dresser drawer in that room and finds a withered red rose still in its plastic wrapper; men's coats, jackets, and suits, all out of style and grim and buttoned up and primly arranged on wire hangers; stacks of neatly folded men's pants and shirts in somber colors; men's underwear and socks, old and cheap; and dozens of dingy white handkerchiefs, all folded into perfect squares.

Then she is sitting on the floor, pulling cardboard boxes out from under the bed and opening them and going through stacks of old trade publications for mortuary science and funeral home directors, a variety of monthly magazines with photographs of caskets and burial clothes and cremation urns and embalming equipment. The magazines are at least eight years old. On every one she has looked at so far, the mailing label has been peeled off and all that is left are only a few letters and part of a zip code here and there but nothing more, not enough to tell her what she wants to know.

She goes through one box after another, looking at every magazine, hoping for a complete mailing label and finally there are a few, just a few, at the very bottom of a box. She reads the label and sits on the floor staring at it, wondering if she's confused or if there might be a logical explanation, and all the while she is yelling for

Marino. She calls out his name as she gets to her feet and stares at a magazine that has a casket shaped like a race car on the cover.

"Marino! Where are you?" She steps into the hallway, looking and listening. She is breathing hard and her heart is beating hard. "Damn it," she mutters as she walks quickly along the hallway. "Where the hell did you go? Marino?"

He is on the front porch, talking on his cell phone, and when his eyes meet hers, he knows something too, and she holds up the magazine, holds it close to him. "Yeah. We'll be here," he says into the phone. "I have a feeling we'll be here all night."

He ends the call, and his eyes have that flat look in them that she's seen before when he smells his quarry and has to find him. No matter what, he has to. He takes the magazine from her and studies it in silence. "Browning's on his way," he then says to her. "He's at the magistrate's right now, getting a warrant." He turns the magazine over and looks at the mailing label on the back cover. "Shit," he says. "Jesus Christ," he says. "Your old office. Jesus Christ."

"I don't know what it means," she replies, as a soft cold rain pats the old slate roof. "Unless it's someone who used to work for me."

"Or someone who knows someone who used to work for you. The address is the OCME." He checks again. "Yeah, it is. Not the labs. June 1996. Definitely when you were there, all right. So your office had a subscription to this." He steps back into the living room, moving close to the lamp on the table, and flips through the magazine. "Then you must know who was getting it."

"I never authorized a subscription to that magazine or anything like it," she replies. "Not a funeral home magazine. Never. Someone either didn't have my permission or got it on his own."

"Got any idea who?" Marino places the magazine beneath the lamp on the dusty table.

She thinks of the quiet young man who worked in the Anatomical Division, the shy young man with red hair who retired on disability. She hasn't thought of him since he left, probably not once. There would be no reason to think of him.

"I have an idea," she replies unhappily. "His name is Edgar Allan Pogue."

41.

||| No one is home inside the salmon-colored mansion, and he realizes the disappointing truth that somehow his plans were spoiled. They had to be, or he would notice some sort of activity around the mansion or evidence of earlier activity, such as crime scene tape, or he would have heard about it in the news, but when he drives slowly past where the Big Fish lives, the mailbox looks fine. The little metal flag is down and there is no sign that anyone is home.

He drives around the block back out to A1A and can't resist looping around again as he thinks about the mailbox flag. It was up when he placed the Big Orange in the mailbox, he's quite sure of that. But it does enter his racing mind that the chlorine bomb might still be inside the mailbox, all swollen with gases and ready to explode. What if it is? He has to know. He won't sleep or eat unless he knows, and anger writhes in its deep place, an anger as familiar and present as the short breaths he breathes. Just off A1A on Bay Drive is a row of one-story apartments that are painted white, and he pulls into the parking lot and gets out of his white car. He begins to walk, and the kinky long tresses of his black wig stray in front of his eyes and he pushes them back and heads down the street in the low sun.

He can smell the wig at times, usually when he is thinking about something else or busy, and then the odor touches the inside of his nose and is hard to describe. The odor of plastic is about the best he can come up with, and he is puzzled because the wig is human hair, not synthetic, and it shouldn't smell like plastic, new plastic, unless what he is really detecting is some chemical it was treated with when it was put together. Palm fronds flutter against the dusky sky, and fragile ribbons of clouds are lit up pale orange around the edges as the sun settles in. He follows the sidewalk, noticing the cracks and the grass sprouting up between them. He is careful not to look at the fine houses he passes, because people in neighborhoods like this are fearful about crime and keenly aware of strangers.

Just before he reaches the salmon-colored mansion he passes a big white house that rises squarely against the sunset, and he wonders about the lady inside. He has seen her three times and she deserves to be ruined. Once late at night when he was on the seawall behind the salmon-colored mansion, he saw her in the third-floor bedroom window. The shades were up and he could see the bed and other furniture and a huge flat-screen TV that was on, and pictures of people running and then a high-speed motorcycle chase flashed on the screen. She was naked in front of the window, pressed up against it, her breasts grotesquely flattened against the glass, and she touched the glass with her tongue and moved in disgustingly immoral ways. At first he worried that she might see him out on the seawall, but she seemed half asleep as she put on her act for boaters out at night and the Coast Guardsmen across the inlet. Pogue would like to know her name.

He wonders if she leaves her back door unlocked and the alarm off when she goes out by the pool, if she forgets when she comes back in. She might not go out by the pool, he considers. He's never seen her outside her house, never seen her on the patio or out by the boat, not once. If she never leaves her house, that would make it hard for him. He fingers the white handkerchief in his pocket, pulling it out and wiping his face with it, glancing around him, moving to the driveway and mailbox next door. He acts relaxed, as if he belongs here, but he knows his long dark tangled tresses don't belong here, not hair that came from a black or a Jamaican, not in this white-bread neighborhood.

He has been on this street before. He was wearing the wig then, and he has always worried that it would call attention to him, but better to have on the wig than to look like himself. Opening the Big Fish's mailbox, he is neither disappointed nor relieved that it is empty. He smells no chemicals and sees no damage, not even a discoloring of the black paint on the inside of the mailbox, and he has to accept the fact that most likely his bomb had no effect, none whatsoever. It does please him slightly that the bomb is gone, that someone found it. Then she knows about it, at least, and that is better than nothing, he supposes.

It is six P.M. and the naked lady's house begins to glow against the encroaching dark, and he steals a glance up her pink concrete walkway, through the wrought-iron screen to the courtyard and the massive glass front doors. Pogue moves on at a relaxed pace and thinks of her against the window and hates her for pressing herself against that huge window, hates her for being ugly and disgusting and flaunting her ugly, disgusting body. People like her think they rule the world and are doing people like him a favor when they stingily share their flesh or favors, and the naked lady is stingy. She is all show, that is all.

A tease, that's what Pogue's mother used to call women like the naked lady. His mother was a tease, a terrible tease, which is why his father finally drank himself into believing it was a fine idea to hang himself from a rafter in the garage. Pogue knows all about teases, and should a man in a tool belt and work boots knock on the naked lady's door and ask her to finish what she started, she would scream furious and terrified obscenities and call the police. That's what people like the naked lady do. They do it daily and think nothing of it.

He has gone many days now and has not finished what he started. That is too long. Before days it was weeks, and then three months, but that's assuming he counts digging up someone who is already finished. That's assuming he also counts carrying out all those other finished people in their leaky, dusty boxes from belowground in the Anatomical Division, from his private space down there, and struggling with scores of boxes, carrying up the stairs two or three finished people at a time, his stiff lungs on fire and hardly able to breathe, and getting the boxes into the parking lot and setting them down, then going back for more, then putting all of them into his car and eventually into big trash bags, and this was back in September when he heard the news, the terrible, outrageous news that his building was going to be torn down.

But dug-up bones and dusty boxes aren't the same thing, they just aren't. All those people are already finished, and that certainly isn't the same thing as finishing the person himself. Pogue has felt the power and the glory and was vindicated briefly when he felt it, and he slips the faint-plastic-smelling wig off his red head as he closes himself inside his car. He drives out of the white apartment parking lot, reentering the dark early-night streets of South Florida, and his thoughts carry him in the direction of the Other Way Lounge.

42.

||| LIGHTS FROM flashlights poke like long yellow pencils in the black backyard. Scarpetta stands by the window, looking out, hopeful the police will have some luck at this hour, but she is pricked by doubt. What she suggested seems remote if not paranoid, perhaps because she is very tired.

"So you don't remember him living with Mrs. Arnette?" Detective Browning asks, tapping a pen on top of a notepad and chewing gum as he sits in a simple wooden chair inside the bedroom.

"I didn't know him," she replies, watching the long lights moving in the dark and feeling cold air seep in around the window. Chances are, they won't find anything, but she worries that they will. She thinks about the bone dust in Gilly's mouth and on the tractor driver and worries the police will find something. "I wouldn't have any way of knowing who he lived with, assuming he lived with anybody. I can't remember ever having a real conversation with him."

"Not sure what you'd talk about with a squirrel like that."

"Unfortunately, those who worked in the Anatomical Division were viewed as rather odd by everybody else. What they did was off-putting to the rest of my staff. They were always invited to parties, picnics, the Fourth of July cook-out I always had at my home. But you never knew if they'd show up or not," she says.

"He ever show up?" Browning is chewing gum. She can hear him working the gum vigorously between his teeth as she stands looking out the window.

"I honestly don't remember. Edgar Allan could come and go without anyone noticing. It may sound unkind, but he was the most non-existent person who ever worked for me. I hardly remember what he looked like."

"Looked is operative here. We got no clue what he looks like now," Browning supposes, flipping a page in his notepad. "You said he was a little guy with red hair back then. What? Five-eight, five-nine? One-fifty?"

"More like five-foot-six, maybe a hundred and thirty pounds," she recalls. "I can't remember the color of his eyes."

"According to DMV, brown. But maybe not, 'cause he lied about his height and weight. On his license he's got himself five-foot-ten, one-eighty."

"Then why did you ask me?" She turns around and looks at him.

"To give you a chance to remember before I jinxed you with what is probably false information." He winks at her, chewing gum. "He's also got himself as having brown hair." He taps the notepad with his pen. "So back then, what was a guy like him making embalming bodies and doing whatever he did down there in the Anatomical Division?"

"Eight, ten years ago?" She looks out the window again, at the night, at the lights burning in Gilly Paulsson's house on the other side of the fence. The police are in her yard too. They're in her bedroom. She can see shadows moving behind the curtained window in her bedroom, the same window Edgar Allan Pogue probably peeped into whenever he could, looking and fantasizing and maybe watching the games that went on in that house while he left stains on his sheets. "I would say he wasn't making more than twenty-two thousand a year back then."

"And then all of a sudden he quit. Saying he was disabled for one reason or another. Ain't that a common story."

"Exposure to formaldehyde. He wasn't faking. I had to review his medical reports and probably did talk to him then. I must have. He had respiratory disease from formaldehyde, had fibrosis in his lungs that showed up on x-ray and biopsy. As I recall, tests showed the oxygen concentrations in his blood were off, significantly off, and spirometry clearly demonstrated diminished respiratory function."

"Spir-what?"

"A machine, a device. You breathe in and out, and it measures respiratory function."

"Gotcha. When I used to smoke, I probably would've flunked that one."

"If you kept smoking, eventually you would have."

"Alrighty. So Edgar Allan really had a problem. Am I to assume he still would?"

"Well, once he was no longer exposed to formaldehyde or any other irritant, his disease shouldn't have progressed. But that doesn't mean it reversed itself, because he's going to have scarring. Scarring is permanent. So yes, he still has a problem. How serious a problem, I don't know."

"He should have a doctor. You think we could find out the name of his doctor from old personnel files?"

"They'd be in state archives, assuming they still exist. Actually, Dr. Marcus is the one to ask. I don't have the authority."

"Uh huh. In your medical opinion, Dr. Scarpetta, I guess what I'm really wanting to know is how sick this guy is. Is he so sick he might still be going to the doctor or a clinic or be on prescription drugs?"

"Certainly he could be on prescription drugs. But he might not be. As long as he's taken reasonable care of his health, his biggest concern is probably going to be avoiding sick people, staying away from people who have colds or the flu and are contagious. He doesn't want to get an upper respiratory infection because he doesn't have much healthy lung in reserve, not like you and I do. So he can get seriously ill. He can get pneumonia. If he is susceptible to asthma, then he's going to avoid whatever sets that off. He might have prescription drugs, steroids for example. He might take allergy shots. He might use over-the-counter remedies. He might do all kinds of things. He might do nothing."

"Right, right, right," he says, tapping his pen and chewing hard. "He'd probably get really out of breath if he struggled with someone, then."

"Probably." This has been going on for more than an hour and Scarpetta is very tired. She has eaten little all day and her energy is used up. "I mean, he could be strong but his physical activity is going to be limited. He's not running sprints or playing tennis. If he's been on steroids on and off for years, he might be fat. His endurance isn't good." The long bright probes of the flashlights slash over the front of the wooden shed behind the house, and the lights focus on the doorway, and a uniformed cop is illuminated as he lifts bolt cutters to a lock on the door.

"Strike you as odd he might have done something to Gilly Paulsson when she was sick with the flu? Wouldn't he be worried he'd catch it?" Browning asks.

"No," she says, looking out at the cop with the bolt cutters, and seeing the door suddenly open wide and the beams of light stab into the darkness inside the shed.

"How come?" he asks as her cell phone vibrates.

"Drug addicts don't think about hepatitis and AIDS when they're suffering withdrawal. Serial rapists and killers aren't thinking about sexually transmitted diseases when they're in a mood to rape and murder," she says, sliding the phone out of her pocket. "No, I wouldn't expect Edgar Allan to be thinking about the flu if he were seized by the urge to kill a young girl. Excuse me." She answers her phone.

"It's me," Rudy says. "Something's come up, something you need to know about. The case you're on in Richmond, well, latents from it match latents from a case we're working in Florida. IAFIS matched up latents. Unknown latents."

"Who's we?"

"One of our cases. A case Lucy and I are working. You don't know about it. It's too much to go into right now. Lucy didn't want you to know about it."

Scarpetta listens and disbelief thaws her numbness, and through the window she watches a big figure in dark clothing walk away from the woodshed behind the house, his flashlight moving as he moves. Marino is heading toward the house. "What kind of case?" she asks Rudy.

"I'm not supposed to be talking about it." He pauses and takes a breath. "But I can't get Lucy. Her damn phone, I don't know what she's doing but she's not answering it again, hasn't for the past two hours, dammit. An attempted murder of one of our rookies, a female. She was inside Lucy's house when it happened."

"Oh God." Scarpetta briefly shuts her eyes.

"Weird as shit. I thought at first she was faking for attention or something. But prints on the bottle bomb are the same as ones we lifted in the bedroom. Same as prints from your case in Richmond, the girl's case you got called in to work."

"The woman in your case. What happened to her, exactly?" Scarpetta asks while Marino's heavy footsteps sound in the hallway, and Browning gets up and goes to the doorway.

"Was in bed, sick with the flu. We aren't sure after that, except he got in an unlocked door and must have gotten scared off when Lucy came home. The victim was unconscious, in shock, had a seizure, hell if I know. Doesn't remember what happened, but was nude, facedown in the bed, covers off the bed."

"Injuries?" She can hear Marino and Browning talking just outside the bedroom. She hears the word "bones."

"Nothing except bruises. Benton says bruises on her hands, chest, back."

"So Benton knows about this. Everybody does except me," she says, getting angry. "Lucy kept this from me. Why didn't she tell me?"

Rudy hesitates, and it seems hard for him to say, "Personal reasons, I think."

"I see."

"I'm sorry. Don't get me started. But I'm really sorry. I shouldn't even be telling you, but you need to know since it now looks like your case is connected. Don't ask me how, Jesus, I've never seen anything as creepy-weird as this. What the hell are we dealing with? Some freak?"

Marino walks into the bedroom, his eyes intense on Scarpetta. "A freak, yes," she says to Rudy and looks at Marino. "Very possibly a white male named Edgar Allan Pogue, in his thirties, mid-thirties. There are databases for pharmacies," she says. "He might be in a pharmaceutical database, maybe different ones, might be on steroids for respiratory disease. That's all I'm going to say."

"That's all you need to say," he says, sounding encouraged.

Scarpetta ends the call and keeps looking at Marino while she thinks, only fleetingly, of how her view of rules has changed as light changes with the weather and the season, and things that looked one way in the past look another way now and will look different in days and years to come. There are few databases on earth that TLP can't hack into. At this moment, it is all about tracking monsters. The hell with rules. The hell with the doubt and guilt she feels as she stands in the bedroom and tucks the phone back into her pocket.

"From his bedroom window he could see into hers," Scarpetta says to Marino and Browning. "If Mrs. Paulsson's games, so-called games, went on in the house, he might have seen them through the windows. And God forbid, if something went on in Gilly's room, he could have seen that, too."

"Doc?" Marino starts to say, his eyes intense and angry.

"My point is, human nature, damaged human nature, is a strange thing," she adds. "Seeing someone victimized can make someone want to victimize that person again. Watching sexual violence through a window could be very provocative to someone who is marginal . . ."

"What games?" Browning interrupts her.

"Doc?" Marino says, and his eyes are hot and hard with the fury that goes with the hunt. "Looks like there's quite a crowd out there in the shed, a lot of dead people. Think you might want to take a look."

"You were saying something about another case?" Browning asks as they follow the narrow, dim, cold hallway. The smell of dust and mildew suddenly seems choking to Scarpetta, and she tries not to think about Lucy, about what she deems personal and off-limits. Scarpetta tells Browning and Marino what Rudy just told her. Browning gets excited. Marino gets quiet.

"Then Pogue is probably in Florida," Browning says. "I'm on that like a flea on a dog." He looks confused by a host of thoughts that flicker in his eyes, and in the kitchen he stops and adds, "I'll be out in a minute," and he unclips his phone from his belt.

A crime scene technician in a navy blue jumpsuit and a baseball cap is dusting the plate around a light switch in the kitchen, and Scarpetta hears other cops on the other side of the small depressing house, in the living room. By the back door are big black trash bags tied and tagged as evidence, and Junius Eise enters her mind. He is going to be busy sorting through the demented trash of Edgar Allan Pogue's demented life.

"This guy ever work for a funeral home?" Marino asks Scarpetta, and beyond the back door the yard is overgrown and dead and thick with soggy leaves. "The shed back here is piled, I mean piled, with boxes of what looks like human ashes. They've been around for a while, but I don't think they've been here long. Like maybe he just moved them out there in the shed."

She doesn't say anything until they get to the shed. Then she borrows a flashlight from one of the cops, and she directs the strong beam inside the shed. The light picks out big plastic garbage bags that the cops have opened. Spilling out of them are white ashes, bits of chalky bone, and cheap metal boxes and cigar boxes that are coated with white dust. Some of them are dented. A cop stands to one side of the open door and reaches inside it with a retractable tactical baton that he has opened. He pokes into an open bag of ashes.

"You think he burned up these people himself?" the cop asks Scarpetta. Her light moves through the blackness inside the shed, stopping on long bones and a skull the color of old parchment.

"No," she replies. "Not unless he has his own crematorium somewhere. These are typical for cremains." She moves the light to a dusty, dented box half buried in ashes inside a trash bag. "When the ashes of your person are returned to you, it's in a plain cheap box like this. You want something fancier, you buy it." She moves the light back to the unburned long bones and skull, and the skull stares at them with black empty eyes and a gap-toothed grimace. "To reduce a human body to ash requires temperatures as high as eighteen hundred degrees or two thousand degrees."

"What about the bones that aren't burned?" He points his baton at the long bones and skull, and the baton is steady in his hand but she can tell that he is unnerved.

"I'd check to see if there have been any grave robberies around here in recent memory," she replies. "These bones look pretty old to me. Certainly, they aren't fresh. And I don't smell any odor, not like we'd smell if bodies have been decomposing out here." She stares at the skull and it stares back at her.

"Necrophilia," Marino comments, flashing his light around the inside of the shed, at the white dust of what must be scores and scores of people that has been accumulating somewhere for years and years and then recently was dumped inside the shed.

"I don't know," Scarpetta replies, turning off her light and stepping back from the shed. "But I'd say it's very possible he has a scam going, taking cremains for a fee, ostensibly to fulfill some poor person's wish to have his ashes scattered over a mountain, over the sea, in a garden, in his favorite fishing hole. You take the money and dump the ashes somewhere. I guess eventually in this shed. No one knows. It's happened before. He may have started doing it while he worked for me. I'd check with local crematoriums too, see if he hung around any of them, looking for business. Of course, they probably won't admit to it." She walks off through the wet dead leaves.

"So this is all about money?" the cop with the baton follows her, incredulity in his voice.

"Maybe he got so attracted to death, he starting causing it," she replies, walking through the yard. The rain has stopped. The wind is quiet, and the moon has come out of the clouds and is thin and pale like a shard of glass high above the mossy slate roof of the house where Edgar Allan Pogue lived.

4 3.

||| OUT ON THE foggy street, the light from the nearest lamp reaches Scarpetta just enough to cast her shadow on the asphalt as she stares across the soggy, dark yard at the lighted windows on either side of the front door.

Whoever lives in this neighborhood or drives through it should have noticed lights on and a man with red hair coming and going. Maybe he has a car, but Browning told her a minute ago that if Pogue has a vehicle of any description, there is no record of it. Of course, that is peculiar. It means that if he has a car, the plates on it are not registered to him. Either the car isn't his or the plates are stolen. It is possible he has no car, she thinks.

Her cell phone feels awkward and heavy although it is small and doesn't weigh much, but she is burdened by thoughts of Lucy and halfway dreads calling her under the circumstances. Whatever Lucy's personal situation is, Scarpetta dreads knowing the details. Lucy's personal situations are rarely good, and the part of Scarpetta that seems to have nothing better to do than worry and doubt spends a considerable amount of time blaming herself for Lucy's failure at relationships. Benton is in Aspen, and Lucy must know it. She must know that Scarpetta and Benton are not in a good place and haven't been since they got back together again.

Scarpetta dials Lucy's number as the front door opens and Marino steps out onto the deeply shadowed porch. Scarpetta is struck by the oddity of seeing him emerge empty-handed from a crime scene. When he was a detective in Richmond, he never left a crime scene without hauling off as many bags of evidence as he could fit in his trunk, but now he carries nothing because Richmond is no longer his jurisdiction. So it is wise to let the cops collect evidence and label it and receipt to the labs. Perhaps these cops will do an adequate job and not leave out anything important or include too much that isn't, but as Scarpetta watches Marino slowly follow the brick walk, she feels powerless, and she ends her call to Lucy before voice mail answers.

"What do you want to do?" she asks Marino when he gets to her.

"I wish I had a cigarette," he says, looking up and down the unevenly lit street. "Jimbo the fearless real-estate agent called me back. He got hold of Bernice Towle. She's the daughter."

"The daughter of whoever Mrs. Arnette was?"

"Right. So Mrs. Towle knows nothing about anybody living in the house. According to her, the house has been empty for several years. There's some weirdo shit about a will. I don't know. The family's not allowed to sell the house for less than a certain amount of money, and Jim says no way in hell he'll ever get that price. I don't know. I sure could use a cigarette. Maybe I did pick up on cigar smoke in there and it's got me craving a cigarette."

"What about guests? Did Mrs. Towle allow guests to stay in the house?"

"Nobody seems to remember the last time this dump had guests. I guess he could do like the hobos who lived in abandoned buildings. Have free run of the place and if you see someone coming, you scram. Then when the coast is clear, you come back. Who the hell knows. So what do you want to do?"

"I guess we should go back to the hotel." She unlocks the SUV and looks again at the lighted house. "I don't think there's much else we can do tonight."

"I wonder how late the hotel bar stays open," he says, opening the passenger door and hiking up his pants leg as he steps on the running board and carefully climbs up into the SUV. "Now I'm wide awake. That's what happens, dammit. I don't guess it would hurt me if I had a cigarette, just one, and a few beers. Then maybe I'll sleep."

She shuts her door and starts the engine. "Hopefully the bar is closed," she replies. "If I drink anything, it will only make matters worse because I can't think. What has happened, Marino?" She pulls away from the curb, the lights from Edgar Allan Pogue's house moving behind her. "He's been living in this house. Didn't anybody know? He's got a woodshed full of human remains and nobody ever saw him in the backyard going into the shed, nobody ever did? You telling me Mrs. Paulsson never saw him moving around back there? Maybe Gilly did."

"Why don't we just swing around to her house and ask her?" Marino says, looking out his window, his huge hands in his lap, as if he is protecting his injury.

"It's almost midnight."

Marino laughs sarcastically. "Right. Let's be polite."

"Okay." She turns left on Grace Street. "Just be prepared. No telling what she'll say when she sees you."

"She ought to be worried about what I say, not the other way around."

Scarpetta does a U-turn and parks on the same side of the street as the small brick house, behind the dark blue minivan. Only the living room light is on, glowing through the filmy curtains. She tries to think of a foolproof way to get Mrs. Paulsson to come to the door and decides it would be wise to call her first. She scrolls through a list of recently made calls on her cell phone, hoping the Paulsson number is still there, but it isn't. She digs inside her bag until she finds the scrap of paper she's had since her first encounter with Suzanna Paulsson, and she enters it in her phone and sends it along the airways or wherever calls go, and imagines the phone ringing beside Mrs. Paulsson's bed.

"Hello?" Mrs. Paulsson's voice sounds uneasy and groggy.

"This is Kay Scarpetta. I'm outside your house and something has happened. I need to talk to you. Please come to the door."

"What time is it?" she asks, confused and frightened.

"Please come to the door," Scarpetta says, getting out of the SUV. "I'm outside your door."

"All right. All right." She hangs up.

"Sit in the car," Scarpetta says into the SUV. "Wait until she opens the door, then come out. If she sees you through the window, she's not going to let us in."

She shuts her door and Marino sits quietly in the dark as she walks to the porch. Lights go on as Mrs. Paulsson passes through the house, heading to the door. Scarpetta waits, and a shadow floats across the living room curtain. It moves as Mrs. Paulsson peeks out, then the curtain flutters shut and sways as the door opens. She is dressed in a zip-up red flannel robe, her hair flat where it was pressed against the pillow, her eyes puffy.

"Lord, what is it?" she asks, letting Scarpetta in the house. "Why are you here? What's happened?"

"The man living in the house behind your fence," Scarpetta says. "Did you know him?"

"What man?" She looks baffled and scared. "What fence?"

"The house back there." Scarpetta points, waiting for Marino to show up at the door any second. "A man has been living there. Come on. You must know someone's been living back there, Mrs. Paulsson."

Marino knocks on the door and Mrs. Paulsson jumps and grabs at her heart. "Lord! What now?"

Scarpetta opens the door and Marino walks in. His face is red and he won't look at Mrs. Paulsson, but shuts the door behind him and steps inside the living room.

"Oh shit," Mrs. Paulsson says, suddenly angry. "I don't want him here," she says to Scarpetta. "Make him leave!"

"Tell us about the man behind your fence," Scarpetta says. "You must have seen lights on back there."

"He call himself Edgar Allan or Al or go by some other name?" Marino says to her, his face red and hard. "Don't be giving us a bunch of crap, Suz. We ain't in the mood. What did he call himself? I bet the two of you were chummy."

"I'm telling you, I don't know about any man back there," she says. "Why? Did he . . . ? You think . . . ? Oh God." Her eyes shine with fear and tears, and she seems to be telling the truth as much as any good liar seems to, but Scarpetta doesn't believe her.

"He ever come to this house?" Marino demands to know.

"No!" She shakes her head side to side, clasping her hands at her waist.

"Oh really?" Marino says. "How do you know if you don't even know who we're talking about, huh? Maybe he's the milkman. Maybe he dropped in to play one of your games. You don't know who we're talking about, then how can you say he's never once been to your house?"

"I'm not going to be talked to like this," she says to Scarpetta.

"Answer the question," Scarpetta replies, looking at her.

"I'm telling you . . ."

"And I'm telling you that his damn fingerprints were in Gilly's bedroom," Marino replies aggressively, stepping closer to her. "You let that little redheaded bastard in here for one of your games? Is that it, Suz?"

"No!" Tears spill down her face. "No! Nobody lives back there! Just the old woman, and she's been gone for years! And maybe somebody's in there now and then, but nobody lives there, I swear! His fingerprints? Oh God! My little baby. My little baby." She sobs, hugging herself, crying so hard her bottom teeth are bared, and she presses her hands against her cheeks, and her hands are trembling. "What did he do to my little baby?"

"He killed her, that's what," Marino says. "Tell us about him, Suz."

"Oh no," she wails. "Oh Gilly."

"Sit down, Suz."

She stands there and cries into her hands.

"Sit down!" Marino orders her angrily, and Scarpetta knows his act.

She lets him do what he does so well, even if it is hard to watch.

"Sit down!" He points at the couch. "For once in your goddamn life tell the goddamn truth. Do it for Gilly."

Mrs. Paulsson collapses on the plaid couch beneath the windows, her face in her hands, tears running down her neck and spotting the front of her robe. Scarpetta moves in front of the cold fireplace, across from Mrs. Paulsson.

"Tell me about Edgar Allan Pogue," Marino says, loudly and slowly. "You listening, Suz? Hell-o? You listening, Suz? He killed your little girl. Or maybe you don't care about that. She was such a pain in the ass, Gilly was. I heard about what a slob she was. All you did was pick up after her spoiled little ass . . ."

"Stop it!" she shrieks, her eyes wide and red and glaring as she stares hate at him. "Stop it! Stop it! You fucking . . . You . . ." She sobs and wipes her nose with a trembling hand. "My Gilly."

Marino sits in the wing chair, and neither of them seems aware that Scarpetta is in the room, but he knows. He knows the act. "You want us to get him, Suz?" he asks, suddenly quieter and calmer. He leans forward and rests his thick forearms on his big knees. "What do you want? Tell me."

"Yes." She nods, crying. "Yes."

"Help us."

She shakes her head and cries.

"You aren't gonna help us?" He leans back in the chair and looks over at Scarpetta in front of the fireplace. "She isn't gonna help us, Doc. She don't want to catch him."

"No," Mrs. Paulsson sobs. "I . . . I don't know. I only saw him, I guess it was . . . One night I went out, you know. I . . . I went over to the fence. I went over to the fence to get Sweetie, and a man was in the yard back there."

"The yard behind his house," Marino says. "On the other side of your back fence."

"He was behind the fence, and there's cracks between the boards, and he had his fingers through, petting Sweetie through the fence. I said, Good evening. That's what I said to him . . . Oh shit." She can hardly catch her breath. "Oh shit. He did it. He was petting Sweetie."

"What did he say to you?" Marino asks, his voice quiet. "He say something?"

"He said . . ." Her voice goes up and vanishes. "He . . . he said, I like Sweetie."

"How'd he know your puppy's name?"

"I like Sweetie, he said."

"How'd he know your puppy's name was Sweetie?" Marino asks.

She breathes hard, not crying as much, staring down at the floor.

Marino says, "Well, I guess he might have taken your puppy too. Since he liked her. You haven't seen Sweetie, have you?"

"So he took Sweetie." She clenches her hands in her lap, and her knuckles blanch. "He took everything."

"That night when he was petting Sweetie through the fence, what did you think? What did you think about some man being back there?"

"He had a low voice, you know, not a loud voice, kind of a slow voice that wasn't friendly or unfriendly. I don't know."

"You didn't say nothing else to him?"

She stares at the floor, her hands clenched in fists in her lap. "I think I said to him, 'I'm Suz. You live in the neighborhood?' He said he was visiting. That was all. So I picked up Sweetie and headed into the house. And when I was walking in, in through the kitchen door, I saw Gilly. She was in her bedroom, looking out the window. Watching me get Sweetie. As soon as I was at the door, she ran from the window to meet me and to get Sweetie. She loved that dog." Her lips twitch as she stares at the floor. "She would be so upset."

"The curtains was open when Gilly was looking out the window?" Marino asks.

Mrs. Paulsson stares at the floor, unblinking, fists clenched so hard her nails are digging into her palms.

Marino glances at Scarpetta and she says from the fireplace, "It's all right, Mrs. Paulsson. Try to calm down. Try to relax a little bit. When he was petting Sweetie through the fence, how long was this before Gilly died?"

Mrs. Paulsson wipes her eyes and shuts them.

"Days? Weeks? Months?"

She raises her eyes and looks at her. "I don't know why you came back here. I told you not to."

"This is about Gilly," Scarpetta says, trying to get Mrs. Paulsson to focus on what she doesn't want to think about. "We need to know about the man you saw through the fence, the man you said was pet-ting Sweetie."

"You can't just come back here when I told you not to."

"I'm sorry you don't want me here," Scarpetta replies, standing quietly in front of the fireplace. "You may not think so, but I'm try-ing to help. All of us want to find out what happened to your daugh-ter. And what happened to Sweetie."

"No," she says with dry eyes that stare weirdly at Scarpetta. "I want you to leave." She doesn't indicate that Marino should leave. She doesn't even seem aware of him sitting in the chair to the left of the couch, not even two feet from where she sits. "If you don't get out, I'm calling someone. The police. I'll call them."

You want to be alone with him, Scarpetta thinks. You want more of the game because games are easier than what is real. "Remember when the police took things out of Gilly's bedroom?" she asks. "Re-member they took the linens off her bed. There were a lot of things taken to the labs."

"I don't want you here," she says, motionless on the couch, her harshly pretty face staring coldly at her.

"Scientists look for evidence. Everything on Gilly's bed linens, everything on her pajamas, everything the police took from your house was looked at. And she was looked at. I looked at her," Scar-petta goes on, staring back at Mrs. Paulsson's cheap, pretty face. "The scientists didn't find any dog hairs. Not one."

Mrs. Paulsson stares at her and a thought moves in her eyes like a minnow moving in shallow brown water.

"Not one dog hair. Not one hair from a basset hound," Scarpetta says in the same quiet, firm voice from the higher ground of the fire-place where she stands, looking down at Mrs. Paulsson on the couch. "Sweetie's gone, all right. Because she never existed. There is no puppy. There never was."

"Tell her to leave," Mrs. Paulsson says to Marino without looking at him. "Make her get out of my house," she says as if he is her ally or her man. "You doctors do what you want to people," she says to Scarpetta. "You doctors do exactly what you want to people."

"Why'd you lie about the puppy?" Marino asks.

"Sweetie's gone," she replies. "Gone."

"We would know if there'd been a dog in your house," he says.

"Gilly started looking out her window a lot. Because of Sweetie, looking out at Sweetie. Opening her window and calling out to Sweetie," Mrs. Paulsson says, staring down at her clenched hands.

"There never has been a puppy, now has there, Suz?" Marino asks.

"She put her window up and down because of Sweetie. When Sweetie was in the yard, Gilly would open her window and laugh and call out. The lock broke." Mrs. Paulsson slowly opens her palms and stares down at them, looking at the crescent wounds from her nails, looking at the crescents of blood. "I should have gotten it fixed," she says.

44.

| | | TEN O'CLOCK the next morning, Lucy walks around the room, picking up magazines and acting impatient and bored. She hopes that the helicopter pilot sitting near the television will hurry up and go in for his appointment or get an urgent call and leave. She walks around the living room of the house near the hospital complex, and pauses in front of a window with old wavy glass and looks out at Barre Street and the historic homes on it. The tourists won't flock to Charleston until spring, and she doesn't see many people out.

Lucy rang the bell some fifteen minutes ago, and a chubby older woman let her in and showed her to the waiting room, which is just off the front door and was probably a small formal parlor back in the glory days of the house. The woman gave her a blank Federal Aviation Administration form to fill out, the same form Lucy has filled out every two years for the past decade, and then the woman went up a long flight of polished wooden stairs. Lucy's form is on the coffee table. She started filling it out and then stopped. She plucks another magazine off a table, glances at it and places it back on the stack as the helicopter pilot works on his form and now and then looks up at her.

"Don't mind me telling you what to do," he says in a friendly tone, "but Dr. Paulsson doesn't like it if your form's not filled out when he gets to you."

"So you know the ropes," Lucy says, sitting down. "These damn forms. I'm not good with forms. I flunked forms in high school."

"I hate them," the helicopter pilot agrees with her. He is young and fit with closely shorn dark hair and closely spaced dark eyes, and when he introduced himself a few minutes ago, he said he flies Black Hawks for the National Guard and Jet Rangers for a charter company. "Last time I did it, I forgot to check off the box for allergies because I've been taking allergy shots. My wife has a cat and I had to start taking shots. They worked so well I forgot I have allergies and the computer kicked out my application."

"It stinks," Lucy says. "One inconsistency and a computer screws up your life for months."

"This time I brought a copy of an old form," he says, holding up a folded piece of yellow paper. "Now my answers are all the same. That's the trick. But I'd fill out your form, if I were you. He won't like it when you go in, if you haven't done it."

"I made a mistake," Lucy replies, reaching for her form. "Put the city in the wrong blank. I have to do it again."

"Uh oh."

"If that lady comes back, I need another form."

"She's been here forever," the helicopter pilot says.

"How do you know?" Lucy inquires. "You're too young to know if anybody's been around forever."

He grins and is beginning to flirt with her a little. "You'd be surprised how much I've been around. Where do you fly out of? I've never seen you around here. You didn't tell me. Your flight suit doesn't look military, not any military I've ever seen."

Her flight suit is black with the patch of an American flag on one shoulder and an unusual patch on her other shoulder, a blue and gold patch of her own design with an eagle surrounded by stars. Her leather name tag today reads "P. W. Winston." It attaches with Velcro and she can change her name whenever she wants, depending on what she is doing and where she's doing it. Because her biological father was Cuban, Lucy can pass for Hispanic, Italian, or Portuguese without resorting to makeup. Today she is in Charleston, South Carolina, and is simply a pretty white woman with a passable southern inflection, a very sweet lilt to her otherwise General American accent.

"Part Ninety-one," she says. "The guy I fly for owns a Four-thirty."

"Lucky him," the pilot says, impressed. "Must be some rich guy, is all I gotta say. That's one hell of a bird, the Four-thirty. How do you like the sight picture? Did it take a while to get used to it?"

"Love it," she replies, wishing he would shut up. She can talk helicopters all day but is more interested in figuring out where she should plant covert transmitters in Frank Paulsson's house and how she is going to do it.

The plump woman who showed Lucy into the waiting room reappears and tells the other pilot he can come with her, that Dr. Paulsson is ready for him and has he finished filling out his form and is he satisfied that his answers are correct.

"If you're ever around Mercury Air, we've got an office in the hangar, you'll see it off the parking lot. I've got a soft-tail Harley parked back there," he says to Lucy.

"A man with my taste," she replies from her chair. "I need a new form," she tells the woman. "I messed this one up."

The woman gives her a suspicious look. "Well, let me see what I can do. Don't throw that one away. You'll mess up the sequence numbers."

"Yes, ma'am. I have it right here on the table." To the pilot, Lucy says, "I just traded my Sportster in for a V-Rod. It's not even broken in yet."

"Damn! A Four-thirty and a V-Rod. You're living my life," he says admiringly.

"Maybe we'll ride sometime. Good luck with the cat."

He laughs. She hears him go up the stairs while he explains to the unsmiling, chunky woman that when he met his wife she wouldn't give up her cat and it slept in her bed and he used to break out in hives at the most inopportune times. Lucy has the downstairs to herself for at least a minute, at least long enough for the woman to get another blank form and come back down to the waiting area. Lucy slips on a pair of cotton gloves and moves quickly around the room, wiping off every magazine she touched.

The first bug she plants is the size of a cigarette butt, a wireless microphone-audio transmitter she custom-mounts in a waterproof plant-green plastic tube that looks like nothing. Most bugs should be disguised to look like something, but now and then a bug should simply look like nothing. She places the green tube inside the bright ceramic pot of the lush green silk plant on the coffee table. She quickly walks to the back of the house and plants another nothing-looking green bug in another green silk plant that is on a table inside the eat-in kitchen, and she hears the woman's feet on the stairs.

45.

| | |INSIDE BENTON'S town home, in the third-floor bedroom that he uses as an office, he sits at the desk in front of his laptop computer and waits for Lucy to activate her hidden video camera that is disguised as a pen and connected to a cellular interface that looks like a pager. He waits for her to activate the high-sensitivity audio transmitter disguised as a mechanical pencil. On the desk to the right of his laptop is a modular audio intelligence monitoring system built into a briefcase. The briefcase is open, the tape recorder and receivers inside on standby.

It is twenty-eight minutes past ten A.M. in Charleston and two hours earlier than that here in Aspen. He stares at the black screen of his laptop, sitting patiently at his desk and wearing headphones, as he waits. He has been waiting for almost an hour. Lucy called him when she landed in Charleston late yesterday her time and told him she had the appointment. Dr. Paulsson is overbooked, she added. She told the lady who answered the phone that it was urgent. Lucy had to get a flight physical right away because her medical certificate expired in two days. Why had she waited until the last minute? the woman at Dr. Paulsson's office wanted to know.

Lucy described her theatrics to Benton, proud of them. She said she faltered and sounded scared. She stammered a bit and replied that she just hadn't been able to get around to it, that the helicopter owner she worked for had been flying her all over the place and she just hadn't been able to get around to the flight physical. And, well, she'd been having personal problems, she told the woman, and if she didn't get her physical, she wouldn't be legal to fly and she might lose her job, and the last thing she needed on top of everything else was to lose her job. The woman put Lucy on hold. When she got back to her, she said Dr. Paulsson would fit her in at ten A.M. the next morning, which is now this morning, and he was doing her quite a favor because he was cancelling his weekly doubles match because of her predicament. Lucy had better not change the appointment and she had better show up, because of the huge favor the important, busy Dr. Paulsson was doing for her.

So far, all is well and according to plan. Lucy has an appointment. She is at the flight surgeon's house now. Benton waits at his desk and looks out the window at a snow sky that is lower and denser than it was not even half an hour ago. It is supposed to start snowing again by dark and snow all night. He is getting tired of snow. He is getting tired of his town home. He is getting tired of Aspen. Ever since Henri invaded his life, he has been getting tired of just about everything.

Henri Walden is a sociopath, a narcissist, a stalker. She is a waste of his time. His post-incident stress counseling is a joke to her, and he might feel sorry for Lucy were he not angry with her for allowing Henri to do so much damage. Henri lured her and used her. Henri

got what she wanted. Maybe she didn't plan on being attacked inside Lucy's Florida home, maybe there are a lot of things she didn't
plan on, but in the end Henri looked for Lucy and found her and took
what she wanted from her, and now she is making a mockery of him.
He has sacrificed his Aspen vacation with Scarpetta so some socio-
pathic failed-actress-failed-investigative-agent named Henri can
mock and infuriate him. He gave up his time with Scarpetta, and he
could not afford to give up that time. He couldn't. Already things
were bad. Maybe now they will be over. He wouldn't blame her. The
thought is unbearable, but he wouldn't blame her.

Benton picks up a transmitter that looks like a small police radio.
"Are you up?" he says to Lucy.

If she's not, she won't pick up the transmission through the tiny
wireless receiver inside her ear canal. The earpiece is invisible but
she'll have to be clever about wearing it. Certainly, she can't have it
on when Dr. Paulsson checks inside her ears, so Lucy will have to be
very quick and shrewd. Benton warned her that the one-way receiver
would be helpful but risky. I'd like to be able to talk to you, he told
her. It would be extremely helpful if I could cue you. But you know
the risks. At some point during the examination, he's going to discover it. She said she would rather not be cued. He said he would
rather she was.

"Lucy? Are you up?" he broadcasts again. "I'm not hearing or seeing you, so I'm checking."

The video is suddenly activated and he watches images fill the
screen of his laptop, and he hears Lucy's footsteps. A picture of
wooden stairs in front of her bobs up and down as she climbs the
stairs, and in the headphones he hears her feet. He hears her breathe.

"I got you loud and clear," he says into the transmitter, holding
it close to his lips. The voice and video and recorder lights have
switched from standby to active.

Lucy's fist intrudes into the picture and is very clear and loud as she knocks on a door. Benton sits at his desk, watching, and the door opens and a lab coat fills the screen, and he sees a male neck, then the face of Dr. Paulsson sternly greeting Lucy, backing away from her, telling her to have a seat, and as she moves, the pen camera sweeps around the small, stark examination room and the white-paper-covered examination table comes into view.

"Here's the old form. And the second one I filled out," Lucy says, handing forms to him. "I'm sorry. I hope I didn't mess up your system. I'm not good with forms. Flunked forms, you know, in high school." She laughs nervously as Dr. Paulsson seriously scans the forms, both of them.

"Loud and clear," Benton says into the transmitter.

Her hand passes over his computer screen as she passes her hand in front of the pen, acknowledging that she hears him through the tiny receiver in her ear.

"Did you go to college?" Dr. Paulsson asks her.

"No, sir. I wanted to, but . . ."

"That's too bad," he replies, unsmiling, and he wears small rimless glasses and is a very attractive man. Some people might call him handsome. He is taller than Lucy but not much, maybe several inches taller, maybe around five-foot-ten or -eleven, and he is slender and looks strong based on what Benton is able to see. He is able to see only what the pen camera picks up from the breast pocket of Lucy's flight suit.

"Well, I don't need to go to college to fly a helicopter," Lucy says with uncertainty. She is doing an excellent job of acting insecure and intimidated and basically invalidated by life.

"My secretary mentioned you've been going through personal problems," Dr. Paulsson says, still looking over her forms.

"A little bit."

"Tell me what's been going on," he says.

"Uh, just the usual boyfriend stuff," she says nervously, sheepishly.

"I was supposed to get married and it didn't work out. You know, with my schedule. I've been gone the last five months out of six if you added it up, I bet."

"So your boyfriend couldn't handle your absenteeism and bolted," Dr. Paulsson says, placing her paperwork on a countertop where there is a computer. Lucy is doing a fine job of turning her body to capture him on the video camera concealed as a pen.

"Good," Benton transmits, glancing at his closed, locked door. Henri went out for a walk, but he has locked his door because he isn't sure that she won't just walk in. She hasn't learned about boundaries because to her nothing is out of bounds.

"We broke up," Lucy replies. "I'm all right. But that and everything else . . . It's been stressful, but I'm fine."

"That's why you waited until the last minute to come in for a physical?" Dr. Paulsson asks, moving closer to her.

"I guess so."

"That's not very smart. You can't fly without your medical. There are flight surgeons all over the country, you should have taken care of it. What if I couldn't have seen you today? I had one emergency appointment this morning for the son of a friend of mine and the rest of the day off, but I made an exception for you. What if I'd said no? Your medical expires tomorrow, assuming the date you put down is correct."

"Yes, sir. I know it was stupid to wait. I can't tell you how much I appreciate . . ."

"I'm very pressed for time. So let's move along and get you out of here." He retrieves a blood pressure cuff from the counter and tells her to roll up her right sleeve, and he wraps the cuff around her upper arm and begins to pump. "You're very strong. Do you work out a lot?"

"I try to," she replies in a shaky voice as he brushes a hand against her breast, and Benton feels the violation as he watches it on his laptop more than a thousand miles away in Aspen, Colorado. No one looking at Benton would see a reaction, not even a spark in his eyes or a tightening of his lips. But he feels the violation as much as Lucy does.

"He's touching you," Benton transmits, for the taped record. "He's begun touching you now."

"Yes," Lucy seems to be answering Dr. Paulsson but she is answering Benton, and she moves her hand across the camera lens, verifying her affirmative response. "Yes, I work out a lot," she says.

46.

| | | "ONE-THIRTY over eighty," Dr. Paulsson says, touching her again as Velcro rips and he removes the cuff. "Is it usually that high?"

"No, not at all," Lucy says, acting shocked. "It is? I mean, you would know. But it's usually about one-ten over seventy. Almost too low, usually."

"You nervous?"

"I never have liked going to doctors," she says, and since she is sitting on the table and lower than he is, she leans back a little. She wants Benton to see Dr. Paulsson's face as he talks to her and tries to intimidate and manipulate her. "Maybe I'm a little nervous."

He places his hands on her neck, high under her jaw. His skin is warm and dry as he palpates the soft areas under her ears, and her hair is over her ears. He couldn't possibly see the hidden receiver. He tells her to swallow, feeling her lymph nodes and taking his time as she sits upright and continues to will herself into a state of anxiety, knowing he can feel her pulse beating hard in her neck.

"Swallow," he says again, feeling for her thyroid, checking to see if her trachea is midline, and it flits through her thoughts that she knows all about physical examinations. Whenever she had one as a child she asked her Aunt Kay questions and wasn't satisfied until she knew the reason for the examining doctor's every touch and remark.

He begins palpating her lymph nodes again, pressing in closer to her, and his breath is light on the top of her head.

"Getting nothing but the lab coat," Benton's voice sounds clearly in her left ear.

Nothing I can do about it, she thinks.

"Have you been feeling tired lately, feeling not so great?" Dr. Paulsson asks in his matter-of-fact, intimidating way.

"No. Well, I mean, I've been working so hard, traveling so much. Maybe just a little tired," she stumbles, pretending she is as frightened as she sounds while he presses up against her knees, and she feels him. He is hard against one knee then the other, and the camera can't capture what she feels, unfortunately.

"I need to go to the ladies' room," she says. "I'm sorry. I'll be quick."

He backs off and suddenly the room is there again. It is as if the cover has been removed from a hole in the earth and she is allowed to climb out. She slips down from the table and walks quickly to the doorway while he steps over to the computer and picks up her form, the one she filled in correctly. "There's a cup in a plastic bag on the sink," he says as she leaves the room.

"Yes, sir."

"Just leave it on top of the toilet when you're finished."

But she doesn't use his toilet, merely flushes it and says "Sorry" for Benton's benefit. That's all she says as she removes the receiver from her ear and tucks it into a pocket. She doesn't leave her urine in a cup on top of the toilet, because she has no intention of leaving any part of her biological self. Although it is unlikely that her DNA is on a database, she never assumes that it isn't. Over the years, she has employed stringent measures to make sure her DNA and fingerprints aren't on any database in this country or abroad, but she is programmed to live with worst-case scenarios foremost in her mind, so she doesn't leave urine for this doctor, who soon enough will be quite motivated to go after P. W. Winston. Since entering his house, she has wiped off the surfaces she has touched, leaving no prints that might identify Lucy Farinelli, former FBI, former ATF.

She returns to the examination room, willing herself to anticipate the worst. Her pulse reacts accordingly.

"Your lymph nodes seem slightly enlarged," Dr. Paulsson says, and she knows he is lying. "When is the last time . . . Well, you said you don't like going to the doctor, so you probably haven't had a thorough physical in quite a while. Not bloodwork, either, I am to assume?"

"They're enlarged?" Lucy says, reacting with the expected panic.

"You've been feeling okay of late? No extreme fatigue? No fever? Nothing like that?" He steps close to her again and sticks the otoscope in her left ear, his face very close to her cheek.

"I haven't felt sick," she replies, and he moves the scope to her other ear and looks.

He sets down the otoscope and picks up the ophthalmoscope. He peers into her eyes, his face inches from hers, then he gets the stethoscope. Lucy lets herself be afraid even though she is more angry than afraid. In fact, she isn't afraid at all, she realizes as she sits on the edge of the examination table, and paper crinkles softly whenever her weight shifts even slightly.

"If you'll just unzip your flight suit and pull it down to your waist," he says in the same matter-of-fact tone.

Lucy just looks at him. Then she says, "I think I need to use the ladies' room again. I'm sorry."

"Go ahead," he says rather impatiently. "But I'm running late."

She hurries to the bathroom and is in and out in less than a minute, the toilet flushing in her wake, the receiver back in her ear.

"Sorry," she says again. "I drank a big Diet Coke right before I got here. Mistake."

"Pull down your flight suit," he orders her.

She hesitates. Now the challenge comes, but she knows what to do. Unzipping her flight suit, she pulls it down to her waist, manipulating the position of the pen so it is angled just right, the wire connected to the cellular interface taped on the inside of the flight suit and not visible.

"Not quite so vertical," Benton's voice is in her ear. "Angled down maybe ten degrees."

She subtly adjusts the top of the flight suit that is around her waist, and Dr. Paulsson says, "Your sports bra, too."

"I have to take it off?" she asks timidly, scared. "I never have before . . ."

"Miss Winston. I really am in a hurry. Please." He tucks the stethoscope earpieces into his ears, his face stern as he moves close, waiting to listen to her heart and lungs, and she pulls her sports bra over her head and sits very still, frozen on top of the white-paper-lined table.

He presses the stethoscope under one breast, then the other, touching her as she sits very still. She is breathing rapidly, her heart racing, registering her anger, not fear, but she knows he thinks she is afraid, and she wonders what images Benton is picking up. Subtly, she adjusts the flight suit around her waist, touching the pen camera as Dr. Paulsson touches her and pretends he has no interest in what he is seeing and feeling.

"Ten degrees down, to the right," Benton instructs her.

Subtly, she adjusts the pen, and Dr. Paulsson leans her forward and moves over her back with the stethoscope. "Deep breaths," he is saying, and he is quite skilled at doing his job while he manages to touch and brush against and even cup his hands around, as he presses against her, hard. "Do you have any scars or birthmarks? I'm not seeing any." He runs his hands over her, looking.

"No sir," she says.

"You must have something. From an appendectomy, maybe? Anything?"

"No."

"That's enough," Benton says in Lucy's ear, and she detects anger in his calm tone.

But it's not enough.

"I need you to get up now and stand on one foot," Dr. Paulsson says.

"Can I dress?"

"Not yet."

"That's enough," Benton's voice sounds in her ear.

"Stand up," Dr. Paulsson orders her.

Lucy sits on the table and pulls up her flight suit, working her arms into the sleeves and zipping it up, but not bothering with her bra because she doesn't have time. She stares at him, and suddenly she is no longer acting nervous or afraid and he sees the change in her and his eyes react. She gets off the table and steps close to him.

"Sit down," she tells him.

"What are you doing?" His eyes widen.

"Sit down!"

He doesn't move, staring at her. As is typical of every bully she's ever met, he looks scared. She moves in to frighten him more, pulling the pen out of her breast pocket, lifting it up so he can see the attached wire. "Freq test," she says to Benton, because he can check the concealed transmitters she planted in the waiting area and the kitchen downstairs.

"Clear," he comes back.

Good, she thinks. He isn't picking up on any sounds downstairs.

"You don't even want to know how much trouble you're in," Lucy says to Dr. Paulsson. "You don't even want to know who's watching and listening to all of this in real time, live. Sit down. Sit down!" She returns the pen to her pocket, its hidden lens looking right at him.

He moves unsteadily, fumbles with a chair, rolls it out from the counter, and sits, looking at her, his face white. "Who are you? What are you doing?"

"I'm your destiny, motherfucker," Lucy says to him, and she tries to will her rage back into its cage, but it is easier for her to will herself to seem scared than it is for her to will her rage into submission. "You do this sort of shit with your daughter? With Gilly? You molest her too, you son of a bitch?"

He stares at her, his eyes wild.

"You heard me. You heard me loud and clear, asshole. The FAA's going to hear you soon enough too."

"Get out of my office." He is thinking of grabbing her, she can see it in the tensed muscles of his body, in his eyes.

"Don't try it," Lucy warns him. "Don't think of moving out of that chair until I tell you to. When was the last time you saw Gilly?"

"What is this about?"

"The rose," Benton cues her.

"I'm the one asking questions," Lucy tells Dr. Paulsson, and a part of her wants to tell Benton the same thing. "Your ex-wife is spreading stories around. Did you know that, Dr. Homeland Security Snitch?"

He wets his lips, his eyes wide and frantic.

"She's making a pretty good case for you being the reason Gilly's dead. Did you know that?"

"The rose," Benton sounds in her ear.

"She says you came to see Gilly not long before she suddenly died. You brought her a rose. Oh, we know about it. Everything in that poor little girl's room has been gone through, trust me."

"A rose was in her room?"

"Get him to describe it," Benton says.

"You tell me," Lucy says to Dr. Paulsson. "Where'd you get the rose?"

"I didn't. I don't know what you're talking about."

"Don't waste my time."

"You're not going to the FAA . . ."

Lucy laughs and shakes her head. "Oh, assholes like you are cut out with a cookie cutter. You really think you'll get away with your shit, you really think it. Talk to me about Gilly. Then we'll talk about the FAA."

"Turn it off." He indicates the camera pen.

"You tell me about Gilly, I'll turn it off."

He nods.

She touches the pen and pretends she's turning it off. His eyes are scared and don't trust her.

"The rose," she repeats.

"I swear to God, I don't know anything about a rose," he replies. "I would never hurt Gilly. What is she saying? What is that bitch saying?"

"Yes, Suzanna." Lucy stares at him. "She has a lot to say. The way she tells it, you're the reason Gilly's dead. Murdered."

"No! Good God, no!"

"You play soldier with Gilly, too? You dress her up in camouflage and boots, asshole? You let perverts in your house to play your sick little games?"

"Oh God," he groans, shutting his eyes. "That bitch. It was between us."

"Us?"

"Suz and me. Couples do things."

"And who else? You have other people over playing your games?"

"It was my private home."

"What a pig you are," Lucy says menacingly. "Doing shit like that in front of a little girl."

"Are you FBI?" He opens his eyes, and they look dead with hate, like shark eyes. "You are, aren't you. I knew it would happen. I should have known. As if my life has to do with anything. I knew it. I've been set up."

"I see. The FBI forced you to make me take my clothes off for a routine flight physical."

"It has nothing to do with anything. It doesn't matter."

"I beg to differ," she replies sarcastically. "It matters all right. You're going to find out just how much it matters. I'm not the FBI. You aren't that lucky."

"This is all about Gilly?" He is more relaxed in the chair, defeated and barely moving. "I loved my daughter. I haven't seen her since Thanksgiving and that's the God's truth."

"The puppy," Benton cues her, and Lucy considers ripping the receiver out of her ear.

"You think someone killed your daughter because you're a snitch for Homeland Security?" Lucy knows better, but she is going to get him. "Come on, Frank. Tell the truth! Don't make it worse for yourself!"

"Someone killed her," he repeats. "I don't believe it."

"Believe it."

"That can't be."

"Who came to your house to play the game? You know Edgar Allan Pogue? The guy living behind your house? Living where Mrs. Arnette used to live?"

"I knew her," he says. "She was a patient of mine. Hypochondriac. Damn pain in the ass, really."

"This is important," Benton says, as if Lucy doesn't know. "He's confiding. Be his friend."

"Your patient in Richmond?" Lucy asks Dr. Paulsson, and the last thing she wants is to be his friend, but she softens, acts interested. "When?"

"When? Oh God. Forever ago. Actually, I bought our Richmond house from her. She owned a number of houses in Richmond. At the turn of the century, her family owned the whole damn block, was one big estate, got divided up for members of her family, eventually for sale. I bought our house from her, for a bargain. Some bargain."

"Sounds like you didn't like her much," Lucy says, as if she and Dr. Paulsson get along fine, as if he wasn't molesting her a few minutes ago.

"She'd come by the house, my office, whenever she wanted. Pain in the ass. Always complaining."

"What happened to her?"

"Died. Eight, ten years ago. Long time ago."

"Of what?" Lucy asks. "What did she die of?"

"She'd been sick, had cancer. She died at home."

"Details," Benton says.

"What do you know about it?" Lucy asks. "She alone when she died? She have a big funeral?"

"Why are you asking all this?" Dr. Paulsson sits in the chair, looking at her. But he is feeling better because she is friendly. It's obvious.

"It might be related to Gilly. I know things you don't. Let me ask the questions."

"Careful," Benton warns her. "Keep him close."

"Well, ask me then," Dr. Paulsson says snidely.

"Did you go to her funeral?"

"I don't remember her having one."

"She must have had a funeral," Lucy says.

"She hated God, blamed him for all her aches and pains, for nobody wanting to be around her, which was understandable if you knew her. What a disgusting old lady. Just intolerable. Doctors don't get paid enough to treat people like her."

"She died at home? She was that sick with cancer and died all alone at home?" Lucy asks. "She was in hospice?"

"No."

"She's a wealthy woman and dies all alone at home, no medical care, nothing?"

"More or less. Why does all this matter?" His eyes move around the examination room, and he is alert and more confident.

"It matters. You're making things better for yourself. A lot better," Lucy assures him and threatens him at the same time. "I want to see Mrs. Arnette's medical records. Show them to me. Pull her up on your computer."

"I would have purged her record. She's dead." His eyes mock her. "Funny thing about Dear Mrs. Arnette is she donated her body to science because she didn't want a funeral, because she hated God, and that was that. I guess some poor med student had to work on the old bitch. I used to think about that from time to time and feel sorry for the poor med student whose luck of the draw was to get her withered, ugly old body." He is calmer and more sure of himself, and the more confident he gets, the more Lucy's hatred rises like bile.

"The puppy," Benton says in her ear. "Ask him."

"What happened to Gilly's puppy?" Lucy asks Dr. Paulsson. "Your wife says their puppy disappeared and you had something to do with it."

"She's no longer my wife," he says, his eyes hard and cold. "And she's never had a dog."

"Sweetie," Lucy says.

He looks at her, and something glints in his eyes.

"Where's Sweetie?" Lucy asks.

"The only Sweetie I know is me and Gilly," he says, a smirk on his face.

"Don't be funny," Lucy warns him. "There's nothing funny about any of this."

"Suz calls me Sweetie. She always has. And I called Gilly Sweetie."

"That's the answer," Benton says. "That's enough. Get out."

"There's no puppy," Dr. Paulsson says. "That's a lot of shit." He leans into the conversation more, and she sees what is coming. "Who are you?" he asks. "Give me the pen." He gets up from the chair. "You're just some stupid little girl sent in to sue me, aren't you? Think you're getting money. You see how foolish this is, don't you? Give me the pen."

Lucy stands with her arms by her sides, her hands ready.

"Move out," Benton says. "Now."

"So a couple of you Whirly-Girls get together, think you're going to get a few bucks?" He stands before her, and she knows what is about to happen.

"Move out," Benton says emphatically. "It's over."

"You want the camera?" Lucy asks Dr. Paulsson. "You want the micro-recorder?" She has no recorder. Benton does. "You really want them?"

"We can just pretend this never happened," Dr. Paulsson says, smiling. "Give them to me. You got the information you wanted, now didn't you? So we'll just forget everything else. Let me have them."

She taps the cellular interface that is clipped to a belt loop, the wire connected to it running through a tiny hole inside her flight suit. She pushes a switch, turning off the interface. Benton's screen just went blank. He can hear and talk but he can't see.

"Don't," Benton says in her ear. "Get out. Now."

"Sweetie," Lucy mocks Dr. Paulsson. "What a joke. Can't imagine anybody calling you Sweetie. That's sickening. You want the camera, the recorder, come and get them."

He rushes at her and runs right into her fist, and then his legs go out from under him and he is on the floor with a grunt and a cry and she is on his back, a knee pinning his right arm, her left hand pinning his left arm. His arms are wrenched and trapped painfully behind his back.

"Let me go!" he yells. "You're hurting me!"

"Lucy! No!" Benton is talking but she isn't listening.

She grips the back of Dr. Paulsson's hair, and she is breathing hard and tastes her rage, and she lifts his head by his hair. "Hope you had a nice time today, Sweetie," Lucy says, jerking his head by the hair. "I should beat your fucking brains out. You molest your own daughter? You let other perverts do it when they came to your house for sex games? You molest her in her own bedroom right before you moved out last summer?" She presses his head against the floor and holds it hard as if she is drowning him in the white tile floor. His cheek is squashed against the floor. "How many lives have you ruined, you motherfucker?" She bangs his head on the floor, hard enough to remind him she could smash his brains out. He grunts and cries out.

"Lucy! Stop!" Benton's voice pierces her eardrum. "Move out!"

She blinks, suddenly aware of what she is doing. She can't kill him. She must not kill him. She gets off him. She starts to kick him in the head, but stops her foot. She breathes hard, sweating, backing off, wanting to kick him, wanting to beat him to death, and she could, easily. "Don't move," she snarls, backing away from him, her heart flying as she realizes just how much she wants to kill him. "Lie right there and don't move. Don't move!"

She reaches toward the countertop and snatches up her bogus FAA forms, then backs up to the door and opens it. He stays down and doesn't move, his face against the floor. Blood drips from his nose and is bright red against the white tile.

"You're finished," she says to him from the doorway, wondering where the plump woman is, the secretary, glancing out toward the stairs and seeing no one. The house is perfectly quiet and she is alone inside it with Dr. Paulsson, just the way he planned. "You're finished. You're lucky you're not dead," she says, shutting the door behind her.

47.

||| ALONG THE narrow streets inside the training camp, five agents armed with Beretta Storm nine-millimeter rifles with Bushnell scopes and tactical lights move in from different directions on a small stucco house with a cement roof.

The house is old and in poor repair, and the small overgrown yard is gaudy with inflated Santas, snowmen, and candy canes. Palm trees are sloppily strung with multicolored lights. Inside the house, a dog barks nonstop. The agents wear their Storms on tactical slings that angle across their bodies and hold the muzzles down at a forty-degree angle. Dressed in black, they are not wearing body armor, which is unusual on a raid.

Rudy Musil waits calmly inside the stucco house behind a high barricade of turned-over tables and upended chairs that block the narrow doorway leading into the kitchen. He is dressed in camouflage pants and tennis shoes and armed with an AR-15 that is not a light-weight search weapon like the Storm but a high-power combat weapon with a twenty-inch barrel that can take out the enemy up to three hundred yards away. He doesn't need a weapon to clear the house because he is in the house. He moves from the doorway to the broken window over the sink, looking out. He sees movement behind a Dumpster about fifty yards from the house.

He props the AR-15 on the edge of the sink and rests the barrel on the rotting windowsill. Through the scope he finds his first prey crouching behind the Dumpster, just a sliver of his black-clothed body exposed. Rudy squeezes the trigger and the rifle cracks and the agent screams, and then another agent darts out of nowhere and hits the dirt behind a palm tree and Rudy shoots him too. That agent doesn't scream or make any sound that Rudy can hear, and he moves from the window to the barricade in the doorway, angrily kicking and tossing tables and chairs out of his way. He breaks through his own barricade and rushes to the front of the house and smashes out the living room window and begins firing. Within five minutes, all five agents have been slammed with rubber bullets, but they keep on coming until Rudy orders them over the radio to halt.

"You guys are worthless," he says into his radio as he sweats inside the raid house that the training camp uses for simulated combat. "You're dead. Every one of you. Fall in."

He steps outside the front door as the agents in black walk toward the yard festively decorated for Christmas, and Rudy has to give them credit. At least they are not showing their pain, and he knows they hurt like hell where the rubber bullets slammed into their unprotected bodies. You get hit enough times with rubber bullets and you want to break down and cry like a baby, but at least this batch of new recruits is hard-faced and able to take the pain. Rudy presses a small remote control and the CD of the barking dog inside the house stops.

Rudy stands in the doorway and looks at the agents. They are breathing hard and sweating and angry with themselves. "What happened?" Rudy asks. "The answer's easy."

"We fucked up," an agent replies.

"Why?" Rudy asks, the AR-15 down by his side. Sweat streams down his muscular bare chest, and veins rope along his tanned, chiseled arms. "I'm looking for one answer. You did one thing and that's why you're dead."

"We didn't anticipate you having a combat rifle. Maybe assumed you had a handgun," an agent offers, wiping her dripping face on her sleeve and breathing hard from nerves and physical exertion.

"Never assume," Rudy replies loudly to the group. "I might have a fully automatic machine gun in here. I might be firing fifty-caliber rounds in here. But you made one fatal mistake. Come on. You know what it is. We've talked about it."

"We faced off with the boss," someone says, and everybody laughs.

"Communication," Rudy says slowly. "You, Andrews." He looks at an agent whose black fatigues are covered with dirt. "As soon as you took a round in your left shoulder, you should have alerted your comrades that I was firing from the kitchen window behind the house. Did you?"

"No, sir."

"Why not?"

"I guess I've never been shot before, sir."

"Hurts, don't it?"

"Like hell, sir."

"That's right. And you weren't expecting it."

"No, sir. Nobody said we'd get shot with live rounds."

"And that's why we do it down here at Camp Pain and Misery," Rudy says. "When something bad happens in real life, we usually haven't been briefed first, now have we? So you got hit and it hurt like hell and scared the shit out of you, and as a result you didn't get on the radio and warn your comrades. And everybody got killed. Who heard the dog?"

"I did," several agents say.

"You got a fucking dog barking like holy hell," Rudy replies impatiently. "Did you get on the radio and let everybody know? The damn dog is barking, so the guy in the house knows you're coming. A clue, maybe?"

"Yes, sir."

"The end," Rudy dismisses them. "Get out of here. I gotta get cleaned up for your funerals."

He steps back into the house and shuts the door. His two-way radio-phone vibrated twice from his belt while he was talking to the recruits, and he checks to see who is trying to get hold of him. Both calls are from his computer geek, and Rudy calls him back.

"What's up?" Rudy asks.

"Looks like your guy's about to run out of prednisone. Last filled a prescription twenty-six days ago at a CVS," and he gives Rudy the address and phone number.

"Problem is," Rudy replies, "I don't think he's in Richmond. So now we've got to figure out where the hell he might get his drugs next. Assuming he'll bother."

"He's been filling his prescription every month at the same Richmond pharmacy. So it looks like he needs the stuff or thinks he does."

"His doc?"

"Dr. Stanley Philpott." He gives Rudy that phone number.

"No record of him filling a prescription anywhere else? Not in South Florida?"

"Just Richmond, and I looked nationally. Like I said, he's got five days left of the most recent prescription, and then he's out of luck. Or should be, unless he's got some other source."

"Good job," Rudy says, opening the refrigerator in the kitchen and grabbing a bottle of water. "I'll follow up."

48.

|||PRIVATE JETS look like toys against giant white mountains that soar around wet black pavement. The linesman in a jumpsuit and earplugs waves orange cones, directing a Beachjet as it taxies slowly, its turbine engines whining. From inside the private terminal, Benton can hear Lucy's plane arrive.

It is Sunday afternoon in Aspen, and rich people with the fur coats and baggage of the rich move around behind him, drinking coffee and hot cider near the huge fireplace. They are heading home and complain about delays because they have forgotten the days of commercial travel, if they ever knew about those days. They flash gold watches and large diamonds, and they are tan and beautiful. Some travel with their dogs, which, like their owners' private planes, come in all shapes and sizes and are the best money can buy. Benton watches the Beechjet's door open and the steps lower. Lucy skips down them carrying her own bags, moving with athletic grace and confidence and without hesitation, always knowing where she's going even if she has no right to know.

She has no right to be here. He told her no. He said when she called, No, Lucy. Don't come here. Not now. This isn't the time.

They didn't argue. They could have for hours but neither of them has a temperament suited for long, loopy dissents filled with illogical outbursts and redundancies, not anymore they don't, so they tend to fire quick, rapid rounds and put an end to it. Benton isn't sure it pleases him that as time passes he and Lucy have more traits in common, but apparently they do. It is becoming more apparent all the time, and the analytical part of his brain that sorts and stacks and dispatches without pause has already considered or maybe concluded that the similarities between Lucy and him could explain his relationship with Kay as much as it can be explained. She loves her niece intensely and unconditionally. He has never quite understood why Kay loves him intensely and unconditionally. Now maybe he's beginning to know.

Lucy shoves the door open with a shoulder and walks in, a duffel bag in each hand. She is surprised to see him.

"Here. Let me help you." He takes a bag from her.

"I didn't expect to see you here," she says.

"Well, I'm here. Obviously, you are. We'll make the best of it."

The rich in their animal pelts and animal hides probably think Benton and Lucy are an unhappy couple, he the wealthy older man, she the beautiful young girlfriend or wife. It crosses his mind that some people might think she is his daughter, but he doesn't act like her father. He doesn't act like her lover, either, but if he had to wage a bet, he would bet that observers assume they are a typical rich couple. He wears neither furs nor gold and he doesn't look conspicuously rich, but the rich know other rich, and he has a rich air about him because he is rich, very rich. Benton had many years of living quietly and invisibly. He had many years to accumulate nothing but fantasies and schemes and money.

"I have a rental car," Lucy says as they walk through the terminal, which looks very much like a small rustic lodge of wood, stone, leather furniture, and Western art. Out front is a huge bronze sculpture of a rampant eagle.

"Pick up your rental car then," Benton tells her, his breath a pale smoke drifting on the bright, sharp air. "I'll meet you at Maroon Bells."

"What?" She stops on the circular drive out front, ignoring the valets in their long coats and cowboy hats.

Benton's hard, tan, handsome face looks at her. His eyes smile first, then his lips smile a little as if he is amused. He stands on the drive near the huge eagle and looks her up and down. She is dressed in boots, cargo pants, and a ski jacket.

"I've got snowshoes in the car," he says.

His eyes are fixed on hers, and the wind lifts her hair, which is longer than when he saw her last and a deep brown touched by red as if it has been touched by fire. The cold stings color into her cheeks, and he has always thought that looking into her eyes must be something like looking into the core of a nuclear reactor or inside an active volcano or seeing what Icarus saw as he flew toward the sun. Her eyes change with the light and her volatile moods. Right now they are bright green. Kay's are blue. Kay's are just as intense but in different ways. Their varying shades are more subtle and can be as soft as haze or as hard as metal. Right now, he misses her more than he knew he did. Right now Lucy has brought back his pain with a fresh cruelty.

"I thought we'd walk and talk," he tells Lucy, walking toward the parking lot as he announces intentions that are not negotiable. "We need to do that first. So I'll meet you at Maroon Bells, up there where they rent the snowmobiles, where the road's closed off. Can you handle the altitude? The air's thin."

"I know about the air," she says to his back as he walks away from her.

49.

|||On either side of the pass are snow-covered mountains, and the late-afternoon shadows are settling low and wide, and in the high ridges to the right of them it is snowing. There's no use skiing or shoeing past three-thirty, because darkness comes early in the Rockies and by now the road they are on is freezing over and the air is biting.

"We should have headed back sooner," Benton says, stabbing a ski pole ahead of his leading snowshoe. "The two of us are dangerous together. We never know when to quit."

Not content to turn back after the fourth avalanche marker where Benton had suggested they stop, they kept shoeing steadily uphill toward Maroon Lake, only to turn back not even half a mile before they could see it. As it is, they'll barely make it to their cars before it is too dark to see, and they are cold and hungry. Even Lucy is worn out. She won't admit it, but Benton can tell the altitude is getting to her; she has slowed down considerably and is having a hard time talking.

For a few minutes their snowshoes scrape over the crusting snow on Maroon Creek Road, and the only sound is their scraping and crunching and their poles puncturing the glazing rutted snow. Their breathing is quite smoky now but quiet enough, and it is only now and then that Lucy takes in a lot of air and blows it out. The more they talked about Henri, the more they walked, and they've gone too far for their own good.

"I'm sorry," Benton says, the aluminum frame of his shoe clanking ice. "I should have turned us around sooner. I don't have any more protein bars or water."

"I'll make it," says Lucy, who under ordinary conditions can keep up with him just fine, can more than keep up with him. "Those little planes. I didn't eat. I've been running and biking. Doing a lot. I didn't think this would bother me."

"Every time I come here I forget," he replies, looking around at the snowstorm to their right as it sinks lower over the white peaks, slowly moving toward them like fog. It is maybe a mile off and a thousand feet above them, if that. He hopes they make it back to their cars before the snow moves in. The road is easy to follow and there is no way to go except down. They won't die.

"I won't forget," Lucy says, breathing hard. "Next time I'll eat. Maybe not shoe the first hour I get here either."

"Sorry," he says again. "Sometimes I forget you have limitations. It's easy to forget that."

"I seem to have a lot of them lately."

"If you had asked me, I would have told you it would happen." He reaches his pole ahead and steps. "But you wouldn't have believed me."

"I listen to you."

"I didn't say you don't listen. I said you don't believe. In this case you wouldn't have."

"Maybe so. How much farther? What marker are we on?"

"I hate to tell you, but only three. We've got a few miles to go," Benton replies. He looks up at the thick, smoky storm. In just a few minutes it has moved lower and the top half of the mountains has vanished into it and the wind has picked up. "It's been like this since I got here," he says. "Snows almost every day, usually late in the day, five or six inches. When you become the target you can't be objective. As warriors, we tend to objectify those we pursue the same way they objectify their victims. It's different when we are the ones objectified, when we are the victims, and to Henri you are an object. As much as you hate the word, you are a victim. She objectified you before you even met her. You fascinated her and she wanted to possess you. In a different way, Pogue has objectified you too. But for his own reasons, different ones from Henri's reasons. He didn't want to sleep with you or live your life or be you. He just wants you to hurt."

"You really believe he's after me and not Henri?"

"Yes, I do. You are the intended victim. You are the object." His words are punctuated with stabs of the ski poles and clanks of the shoes. "You mind if we rest for a minute?" He doesn't need to, but he's sure she does.

They stop and lean forward in their snowshoes, leaning on their poles, breathing in big puffs of white air and watching the snowstorm suffocate the mountains to their right about a mile off and close to their own altitude now.

"I give it less than half an hour," Benton says, taking off his sunglasses and tucking them into a pocket of his ski jacket.

"Trouble coming," Lucy says. "Kind of symbolic."

"One of the good things about coming out here or to the ocean.

Nature puts things in perspective and has a few things to say," he replies as he watches the gray foggy storm smothering the mountains, knowing that inside the clouds it is snowing hard and soon enough it will be doing that where they are. "Trouble is coming. I'm afraid you're right. He's going to do something else if he isn't stopped."

"I hope he tries it with me."

"Don't hope that, Lucy."

"I hope it," she says, and she starts walking again. "The nicest thing he could do for me is try it on me. It will be the last thing he tries."

"Henri's pretty capable of taking care of herself," he reminds her as he takes big, sure steps, planting one shoe then the other into the crusting snow.

"Not as capable as I am. Not close. Did she tell you what she did at the training camp?"

"I don't think so."

"Using the Gavin de Becker style of simulated combat, we're pretty savage," she replies. "None of the trainees are told what to expect, appropriately, because in real life we don't know what to expect. So after about the third time of siccing the K-9's on them, they get a little surprise. The dogs come and lunge for them, only this time they don't have the muzzles on. Of course, Henri had on the padding but when she realized the dog wasn't muzzled, she totally freaked out. Screamed, started running, got knocked down. She was crying and half crazy and said she was quitting."

"I'm sorry she didn't. There's the second marker." He holds up a ski pole, pointing at an avalanche marker painted with a large 2.

"She got over it," Lucy says as she steps in tracks made earlier, because it is easier. "She got over the rubber bullets too. But she didn't like that sim com much either."

"You'd have to be crazy to like it."

"I've had a few crazies come through who did. Maybe I'm one of them. They hurt like hell, but it's a rush. Why are you sorry she didn't quit? Do you think she should? I mean, well, I know I should fire her."

"Fire her for being attacked in your house?"

"I know. I can't fire her. She'll sue me."

"Yes," he says. "I think she should quit. Hell yes." He looks at her as he poles ahead. "When you hired her away from LAPD your vision was as covered up as the mountains over there." He indicates the storm. "Maybe she was a good enough cop, but she's not cut out for your level of operation and I hope to hell she quits before something really bad happens."

"Right," she says ruefully in a puff of frozen breath. "Really bad."

"No one got killed."

"So far," Lucy replies. "God, this is getting to me. You do this every day?"

"Just about. Time permitting."

"Running half-marathons is easier."

"If you run where there's oxygen in the air," Benton says. "There's the number-one marker. One and two are close together, you'll be happy to know."

"Pogue doesn't have a criminal record. He's just some loser. I can't believe it," Lucy says. "Some loser who worked for my aunt. Why? Why me? Maybe it's her he's really after. Maybe he blames Aunt Kay for his health problems and God knows what."

"No," Benton replies. "He blames you."

"Why? That's crazy."

"Yes, more or less, it's crazy. You fit into his delusional thinking, that's all I can tell you, Lucy. He's punishing you. He was probably punishing you when he went after Henri. We can't know what goes through a mind like his. His logic is all his own, nothing like ours. I can tell you he's psychotic, not psychopathic, impulse-driven, not calculating. Delusional with magical thinking. That's about all I can tell you. Here it comes," he says, and tiny flakes of snow suddenly are swirling around them.

Lucy lowers her goggles as gusts of wind rock aspen trees finely stenciled in dark shades of gray against the white mountains. The snow hits fast and is a small dry snow, and the wind is a crosswind that shoves them sideways as they move one snowshoe in front of another, picking their way along the frozen road.

 50.

||| OUTSIDE, THE SNOW is piled high in the branches of the black spruce and in the crooks of the aspen trees. From her third-story window Lucy hears the crunch of ski boots on the crusty sidewalk below. The St. Regis is a sprawling red brick hotel that reminds her of a dragon crouched at the base of Ajax Mountain. The gondolas have not come to life yet at this early hour but people have. The mountains block the sun, and dawn is a blue-gray shadow with no sound except the cold, crunching steps of skiers on their way to the slopes and the buses.

After their crazy trek up Maroon Creek Road yesterday afternoon, Benton and Lucy got into their separate vehicles and went their separate ways. He did not want her to come to Aspen to begin with, and he certainly never intended for Henri, whom he scarcely knew, to end up here, but that is life. Life brings with it strangeness and surprises and upsets. Henri is here. Now Lucy is here. Benton said Lucy could not stay with him, understandably. He does not want her to cripple the progress he might be making with Henri, what little he might be making, if he has made any progress with her. But today Lucy will see Henri when it suits Henri. Two weeks have passed and Lucy can't stand it anymore, can't stand the guilt and the unanswered questions. Whatever Henri is, Lucy needs to see it for herself.

As the morning becomes lighter, everything Benton did and said is clear. First he wore Lucy out in thin air, where it was hard for her to say too much too soon or give vent to her fear-driven fury. Then, for all practical purposes, he sent her to bed. She isn't a child, even if he seemed to treat her like one yesterday, and she knows he cares. She's always known. He has always been good to her, even when she hated him.

She digs inside a duffel bag for a pair of stretch ski pants, a sweater, long silk underwear, and socks, and lays them on the bed next to her nine-millimeter Glock pistol with tritium sights and magazines that hold seventeen rounds, a gun she chooses when routine indoor self-protection is on her mind, when she wants a close contact gun with firepower, not knockdown power, because she wouldn't want to shoot a .40 or .45 caliber bullet or a high-power rifle round inside a hotel room. She hasn't figured out what she'll say to Henri or how she'll feel at the sight of her.

Don't expect anything good, she thinks. Don't expect her to be happy to see you or to be nice or polite. Lucy sits on the bed and pulls off her sweatpants and grabs her t-shirt, snatching it off over her head. She pauses in front of the full-length mirror, looking at herself and making sure she isn't allowing age and gravity to get the best of her. They haven't and they shouldn't, because she isn't quite thirty.

Her body is muscular and lean but not boyish, and she really has no complaint about her physical self but experiences an odd sensation whenever she studies her reflection. Then her body becomes a stranger, different on the outside from what she is inside. Not less or more attractive, just different from how she feels. And it drifts through her thoughts that no matter how many times she makes love, she will never know how her body feels, how her touch feels to her lover. She wishes she knew and is glad she doesn't.

You look all right, she thinks, walking away from the mirror. You look good enough to get by, she thinks as she steps into the shower. The way you look isn't going to matter today, not one bit. You aren't going to be touching anyone today, she tells herself as she turns on the water. Or tomorrow. Or the next day. God, what am I going to do? she says out loud as hot water blasts against marble and splashes the glass door and drives down hard on her flesh. What have I done, Rudy? What have I done? Please don't quit on me. I promise I'll change. She has secretly cried in showers for almost half her life. When she started out in the FBI she was a teenager who got summer jobs and internships because of her influential aunt, and she had no business living in a dormitory at Quantico and shooting guns and running obstacle courses with agents who did not panic or cry, or at least she never saw them panic or cry. She assumed they never did. She believed many myths back then because she was young and gullible and in awe, and now she may know better but her early programming twisted her in a way that can't be straightened. If she cries, and she rarely does, she cries alone. When she hurts, she hides it.

She is almost dressed when she becomes aware of the silence. Quietly swearing and suddenly frantic, she digs in a pocket of her ski jacket and finds her cell phone. The battery is dead. Last night she was too tired and unhappy to think about her phone and she forgot it and left it in her pocket, and that isn't like her, that is so unlike her. Rudy doesn't know where she is staying. Neither does her aunt. Neither of them knows the alias she is using, so even if they tried the St. Regis, they wouldn't find her. Only Benton knows where and who she is, and for her to cut Rudy off like this is unthinkable and unprofessional and he will be furious. Of all times, now was not the time to push him farther away. If he quits, what then? She trusts no one else she works with the way she trusts him. Finding the charger, she plugs in the phone and turns it on, and she has eleven messages, most of them left since six A.M. Eastern Standard Time, most of them from him.

"I thought you'd dropped off the map," Rudy says the instant he answers. "I've been trying to get you for three hours. What are you doing? Since when don't you answer the phone? Don't tell me it's not working. I don't believe it. That phone works anywhere, and I've been trying you on the radio too. You've had the damn thing turned off, haven't you?"

"Calm down, Rudy," she says. "My battery went dead. The phone, the radio don't work when the battery's dead. I'm sorry."

"You didn't bring a charger?"

"I said I'm sorry, Rudy."

"Well, we have a little bit of intelligence. It would be good if you could get back here ASAP."

"What's going on?" Lucy sits down on the floor near the socket where her phone is plugged in.

"Unfortunately, you're not the only one who got a little present from him. Some poor old woman got one of Pogue's chemical bombs, only she wasn't so lucky."

"Jesus," Lucy says, shutting her eyes.

"A waitress at a sleazy bar in Hollywood that's right across the street from a Shell station where guess what? They sell Big Gulps in Cat in the Hat cups. The victim's burned pretty bad but is going to make it. Apparently he's been coming into the place she works, the Other Way Lounge. Ever heard of it?"

"No," she says almost inaudibly, thinking of the burned woman. "Jesus," she mutters.

"So we're canvassing the area. I've got some of our people out. Not the recruits. They ain't the sharpest knives in the drawer, these ones aren't."

"Jesus," is all she can think to say about it. "Can anything go right?"

"They're going more right than they were. Two other things. Your aunt says Pogue might be wearing a wig. A long black curly wig. A dyed black human-hair wig. I guess the mitochondrial DNA was going to be pretty funny, right? Probably come back to some hooker who sold her hair to a wig company so she could buy crack."

"You just telling me this now? A wig?"

"Edgar Allan Pogue has red hair. Your aunt saw the red hairs in the bed in his house, in the house where he was staying. A wig could explain the long wavy dyed black hairs recovered from Gilly Paulsson's bed linens and from your bedroom and also the duct tape on the chemical bomb left in your mailbox. A wig would explain a lot of things, according to your aunt. We're also looking for his car. Turns out the old woman who died in the house where he's been staying, Mrs. Arnette, had a white 1991 Buick, and no one knows what happened to it after she died. The family never gave it a thought. Sounds like they never gave her a thought either. We think Pogue might be driving the Buick. It's still registered to Mrs. Arnette. It would be good if you come on back here ASAP. Probably not a good idea for you to stay in your house, though."

"Don't worry," she says. "I won't ever stay in that house again."

51.

|||EDGAR ALLAN POGUE closes his eyes. He sits in his white Buick in a parking lot off A1A, listening to what people call adult rock these days. He keeps his eyes shut and tries not to cough. Whenever he coughs, his lungs burn and he feels dizzy and cold. He doesn't know where the weekend went, but it went all right. The adult rock station says it's rush hour, Monday morning. Pogue coughs, and tears fill his eyes as he tries to breathe deeply.

He has caught a cold. He is certain he caught it from the red-haired waitress at the Other Way Lounge. She came close to his table when he was leaving Friday night. She came close, wiping her nose on a tissue, and she got much too close to him because she wanted to make sure he paid. As usual, he had to push back his chair and stand up before she bothered to check on him. The truth was, he would have liked another Bleeding Sunset and would have ordered one, but the redhaired waitress couldn't be bothered. None of them can be bothered. So she got a Big Orange and that's what she deserved.

The sun comes through the front windshield and is warm on Pogue's face as he sits behind the steering wheel, the seat pushed back, his eyes shut. He hopes the sun will cure his cold. His mother always said that sunlight has vitamins in it and cures just about everything, which was why when people get old they move to Florida. That's what she told him. Someday, Edgar Allan, you'll move to Florida. You're young now, Edgar Allan, but someday you'll be old and worn-out like I am, like most people are, and you'll want to move to Florida. If only you had a respectable job, Edgar Allan. I doubt you'll be able to afford Florida the rate you're going.

His mother nagged him about money. She worried him to death about it. Then she died and left him enough to move to Florida someday if he wanted, and then he retired and started getting a check in the mail every two weeks, and the last check must be sitting in his post office box because he isn't in Richmond to pick it up. He has a little money even without his checks. For now, he has enough. He can still afford his expensive cigars, so he has enough, and if his mother were here she would nag him about smoking with a cold, but he's going to smoke. He thinks about the flu shot he missed, all because he heard that his old building was being torn down and that the Big Fish had opened an office in Hollywood. In Florida.

Virginia hired a new chief medical examiner, and next thing Pogue knew, they were going to tear the old building down so the city could build a parking deck, and Lucy was in Florida, and if Scarpetta hadn't abandoned Pogue and Richmond, there would have been no need for a new chief and therefore the old building would be fine because everything would have stayed the same, and he would not have been late for his flu shot and would have gotten one. Tearing down his old building wasn't right or fair and no one bothered to ask him how he felt about it. It was his building. He still gets a paycheck every two weeks and he still has his key to the back door and he still works in the Anatomical Division, usually at night.

He worked there all he wanted until he heard the building was coming down. He was the only one using the building. No one else cared about it in the least, and now he suddenly had to get his things out of there. All those people he had down there in little dented boxes had to be moved late at night, when no one could see him do it. What an ordeal, going up and down the stairs, in and out of the parking lot, his lungs burning as ashes leaked everywhere. One box slid off the stack he was carrying and spilled on the parking lot, and it was very hard to pick up ashes that seemed lighter than air and blew everywhere. What an awful ordeal. It wasn't fair, and next thing he knew, a month had passed and he was late for his flu shot and there was no more vaccine. He coughs and his chest burns and his eyes tear up, and he sits very still in the sun, soaking in the vitamins, and he thinks of the Big Fish.

He feels depressed and angry when he thinks of her. She knows nothing about him and never even said hello to him, and now he has stiff lungs because of her. He has nothing because of her. She has a mansion and cars that cost more than any house he's ever lived in, and she couldn't bother to say she was sorry the day it happened. In fact, she laughed. She thought it was funny when he jumped and gave out a little yelp like a little dog as he was walking out of the embalming room and she rattled past, riding a gurney. She was standing on a rung of the gurney, rattling past, laughing, and her aunt was standing by an open vat, talking to Dave about something going on with the General Assembly, some problem.

Scarpetta never came down unless there was a problem. This particular day, and it was this same time of year, Christmastime, she brought the spoiled know-it-all Lucy with her, and he already knew about Scarpetta's niece. Everybody there did. He knew that she was from Florida. She lived in Florida, in Miami, with Scarpetta's sister. Pogue doesn't know all the details, but he knows enough, and he knew enough back then to realize that Lucy could soak in vitamins and not have anyone nag and complain that she would never do well enough to live in Florida.

She already lived there, was born there and did nothing to earn it, and then she laughed at Pogue. She rode by on the gurney and almost hit him when he was walking past, pushing an empty fifty-gallon drum of formaldehyde on a dolly, and because of Lucy, he jumped and came to an abrupt halt and the dolly tipped and the drum toppled over and rolled, and Lucy clattered by on the gurney like a bratty kid riding a shopping cart in the grocery store, only she wasn't a kid, she was a teenager, a very bratty pretty prideful seventeen-year-old, and Pogue remembers her age exactly. He knows her birthday. For years he has sent her anonymous sympathy cards on her birthday, in care of Scarpetta at the OCME at the old 9 North 14th Street address, even after the building was abandoned. He doubts Lucy ever got them.

That day, that fateful day, Scarpetta stood by the open vat, and she was wearing a lab coat over a very smart dark suit because she had a meeting with a legislator, she told Dave, and was going to address whatever the problem was. She was going to talk to the legislator about some proposed cockeyed bill, and Pogue can't remember what it was because at the time the bill wasn't the point of anything. He takes a breath and it rattles in his stiff lungs as he sits in the sun. Scarpetta was a very good-looking woman when she was dressed smartly like she was that morning, and it always pained Pogue to look at her when she wasn't looking at him, and he would feel a deep twinge that he couldn't define when he watched her from a distance. He felt something for Lucy but it was different, what he felt for her. He sensed the intensity of what Scarpetta felt for her, and that made him feel something for Lucy. But it was different.

The empty drum made the most god-awful racket as it rolled across the tile, and Pogue rushed to grab it as it rolled right toward Lucy on the gurney, and it was never possible to get every drop of formaldehyde out of a fifty-gallon metal drum, and the swill in the bottom was spilling and splashing as the drum rolled. Several drops hit his face as he grabbed the drum, and one drop went into his mouth and he inhaled it. Then he was coughing and vomiting in the bathroom and no one came to check on him. Scarpetta didn't. Lucy certainly didn't. He could hear Lucy through the closed bathroom door. She was riding the gurney again, laughing. No one knew that Pogue's life was broken at that precise moment, broken for good.

Are you all right? Are you all right, Edgar Allan? Scarpetta asked through the shut door, but she didn't come in.

He has replayed what she said, replayed it so many times he is no longer certain he has her voice right, that he has remembered it right, exactly right.

Are you all right, Edgar Allan?

Yes, ma'am. I'm just washing up.

When Pogue finally emerged from the bathroom, Lucy's gurney go-cart was abandoned in the middle of the floor and she was gone and Scarpetta was gone. Dave was gone. Only Pogue was there, and he was going to die because of a single drop of formaldehyde that he could feel exploding and burning into his lungs like red-hot sparks, and nobody was there but him.

So you see, I know all about it, he later explained to Mrs. Arnette when he was lining up six bottles of pink embalming fluid on the cart next to her stainless-steel table. Sometimes you have to suffer in order to feel the suffering of others, he told Mrs. Arnette as he cut off sections of string from a roll on the cart. I know you remember how much time I spent with you when we talked about your paperwork and your intentions and what would happen to you if you went to MCV or UVA. You said you love Charlottesville, and I promised you I'd make sure you went to UVA since you love Charlottesville. I listened to you for hours in your house, didn't I? I came by whenever you called, at first because of the paperwork, then because you needed someone to listen and were afraid your family would overrule you.

They can't, I told you. This paperwork is a legal document. It's your last wishes, Mrs. Arnette. If you want your body to go to science and later to be cremated by me, your family can't do a thing about it.

Pogue fingers six brass-and-lead .38 caliber cartridges deep in his pocket as he sits in the sun inside the white Buick, and he remembers feeling the most powerful he'd ever felt in his life when he was with Mrs. Arnette. He was God when he was with her. He was the law when he was with her.

I'm a miserable old woman and nothing works anymore, Edgar Allan, she said the last time they were together. My doctor lives on the other side of the fence, and he can't be bothered to check on me anymore, Edgar Allan. Don't ever get this old.

I won't, Pogue promised.

They're strange people on the other side of the fence, she told him with a wicked laugh, a laugh that implied something. His wife is such a trashy thing, that one. Have you met her?

No, ma'am. Don't believe I have.

Don't. She shook her head and her eyes implied something. Don't ever meet her.

I won't, Mrs. Arnette. That's terrible your doctor can't be bothered. He shouldn't get away with that.

People like him get what they deserve, she said from her pillow on the bed in the back room of the house. Take my word for it, Edgar Allan, people get what they dish out. I've known him for many a year and he can't be bothered. Don't count on him signing me out.

What do you mean? Pogue asked her, and she was so small and feeble in her bed, and covered up with many layers of sheets and quilts because she said she couldn't get warm anymore.

Well, I reckon when you go on, somebody has to sign you out, don't they?

Yes, they do. Your attending doctor signs your death certificate. One thing Pogue knew was how death worked.

He'll be too busy. You mark my words. Then what? God throws me back? She laughed harshly, a laugh that wasn't funny. He would, you know. Me and God don't get along.

I can certainly understand that, Pogue assured her. But don't you worry, he added, knowing fully that he was God at that moment. God wasn't God. Pogue was. If that doctor on the other side of your fence won't sign you out, Mrs. Arnette, you can trust I'll take care of it.

How.

There are ways.

You are the dearest boy I've ever known, she said from her pillow. Oh how lucky your mother was.

She didn't think so.

Then she was a wicked woman.

I'll sign you out myself, Pogue promised her. I see those certificates every day and half of them are signed by doctors who don't care.

Nobody cares, Edgar Allan.

I'll forge a signature if I have to. Don't you waste a minute worrying.

You are such a love. What would you like of mine? It's in my will, you know, that they can't sell this house. I fixed them but good. You can live in my house, just don't let them know, and you can just take my car, course I haven't driven it in so long, the battery's probably dead. The time is coming, you and I know it. What do you want? Just tell me. I wish I had a son like you.

Your magazines, he told her. Those Hollywood magazines.

Oh Lordy. Those things on my coffee table? I ever tell you about the times I spent at the Beverly Hills Hotel and all those movie stars I'd see in the Polo Lounge and out around the bungalows?

Tell me again. I love Hollywood more than anything.

That scoundrel husband of mine at least took me to Beverly Hills, I'll give him that, and we had us some real times out there. I love the movies, Edgar Allan. I hope you watch movies. There's nothing like a good movie.

Yes, ma'am. There's nothing like it. Someday I'm going to Hollywood.

Well, you should. If I weren't so old and worthless, I'd take you to Hollywood. Oh what fun.

You're not old and worthless, Mrs. Arnette. Would you like to meet my mother? I'll bring her over sometime.

We'll have us a little gin and tonic and some of those bite-size sausage quiches I make.

She's in a box, he told her.

Now that's a strange thing to say.

She passed on but I have her in a box.

Oh! Her ashes, you mean.

Yes, ma'am. I wouldn't part with them.

What a sweet thing. Nobody would give a damn about my ashes, I'll tell you. You know what I want done with my ashes, Edgar Allan?

No, ma'am.

Sprinkle them right over there on the other side of that goddamn fence. She laughed her harsh laugh. Let Dr. Paulsson put that in his pipe and smoke it! He couldn't be bothered and I'll fertilize his lawn.

Oh no, ma'am. I couldn't disrespect you like that.

You do it, I'll make it worth your while. Go in the living room and fetch my purse.

She wrote him a check for five hundred dollars, money in advance for carrying out her wishes. After he cashed the check, he bought her a rose and wiped his hands on his handkerchief and was sweet with her, talking and wiping his hands.

Why do you wipe your hands like that, Edgar Allan? she asked from the bed. We need to take the plastic off that lovely rose and put it in a vase. Now why are you putting it in a drawer? she asked.

So you can keep it forever, he replied. Now I need you to turn over for a minute.

What?

Just do it, he said. You'll see.

He helped her turn over and she couldn't have weighed anything, and he sat on her back and tucked his white handkerchief in her mouth so she would be quiet.

You talk too much, he said to her. Now is not the time to talk, he told her.

You should never have talked so much, he kept saying as he held her hands on the bed, and he can still feel her jerk her head and weakly struggle beneath his weight as he took her breath away. When she went still, he let go of her hands and gently took his white handkerchief out of her mouth, and he sat on top of her when she was all quiet like that, making sure she stayed quiet and didn't breathe while he talked to her the same way he did the girl, the doctor's daughter, the pretty little girl whose father did things in that house. Things Pogue should never have seen.

He jumps and gasps as something sharp raps on his window. His eyes fly open and he coughs dryly, strangling. A big grinning black man is on the other side of the car window, rapping the glass with his ring and holding up a big box of M&M's.

"Five dollars," the man says loudly through the glass. "It's for my church."

Pogue cranks the engine and shoves the white Buick into reverse.

5 2 .

| | | Dr. Stanley Philpott's office in the Fan is in a white brick row house on Main Street. He is a general practitioner and was very gracious when Scarpetta reached him on the phone late yesterday and asked if he would talk to her about Edgar Allan Pogue.

"You know I can't do that," he said at first.

"The police can get a warrant," she replied. "Would that make you more comfortable?"

"Not really."

"I need to talk to you about him. Could I come by your office first thing in the morning?" she said. "I'm afraid the police are going to talk to you about him one way or another."

Dr. Philpott doesn't want to see the police. He doesn't want their cars near his office and he doesn't want police showing up in his waiting room and scaring his patients. A gentle-looking man with bright white hair and a graceful way of carrying himself, he is quite polite when his secretary lets Scarpetta in through the back door and shows her into the tiny kitchen where he is waiting for her.

"I've heard you speak several times," Dr. Philpott says, pouring coffee from a drip coffeemaker on the counter. "Once at the Richmond Academy of Medicine, another time at the Commonwealth Club. You'd have no reason to remember me. What do you take?"

"Black, please. Thank you," she says from a table by a window that overlooks a cobblestone alleyway. "That was a long time ago, the Commonwealth Club."

He sets the coffees on the table and pulls out a chair, his back to the window. Light breaking through clouds shines on his neatly combed thick white hair and starchy white lab coat. The stethoscope is loosely forgotten around his neck, his hands big and steady. "You told some rather entertaining stories, as I recall," he says thoughtfully. "All in good taste. I remember thinking at the time that you were a brave woman. Back then not too many women were invited to the Commonwealth Club. Still aren't, really. You know, it actually crossed my mind that maybe I should sign up as a medical examiner. That's how inspirational you were."

"It's not too late," she replies with a smile. "I understand they have quite a shortage, more than a hundred short, which is a significant problem since they're the ones who sign out most deaths and respond to scenes and decide if a case needs to come in for an autopsy, especially out in the hinterlands. When I was here, we had about five hundred docs statewide who volunteered as medical examiners. The troops, I called them. I don't know what I would have done without them."

"Doctors don't want to volunteer their time for much of anything anymore," Dr. Philpott says, cradling the coffee mug in both hands.

"Especially the young ones. I'm afraid the world's become a very self-ish place."

"I try not to think that or I get depressed."

"That's probably a good philosophy. What can I help you with exactly?" His light blue eyes are touched by sadness. "I know you're not here to give me happy news. What has Edgar Allan done?"

"Murder, it appears. Attempted murder. Making bombs. Malicious wounding," Scarpetta replies. "The fourteen-year-old girl who died several weeks ago, not far from here. I'm sure you've heard about it on the news." She doesn't want to be any more specific.

"Oh God," he says, shaking his head, staring down into his coffee. "Dear God."

"How long has he been your patient, Dr. Philpott?"

"Forever," he says. "Since he was a boy. I saw his mother too."

"Is she still alive?"

"She died, I want to say ten years ago. A rather imperious woman, a difficult woman. Edgar Allan is the only child."

"What about his father?"

"An alcoholic who committed suicide quite a long time ago. Maybe twenty years ago. Let me tell you right off that I don't know Edgar Allan well. He's come in from time to time for routine problems, mainly for flu and pneumococcal pneumonia vaccines. The vaccines he's done as regular as clockwork every September."

"Including this past September?" Scarpetta asks.

"As a matter of fact, no. I went over his chart right before you got here. He came in on October fourteenth, got a pneumonia vaccine but not the flu shot. I'm afraid I was out of influenza vaccine. You know, there's been a shortage. I ran out. So he just got the one vaccine for pneumonia and left."

"What do you remember about that?"

"He came in, said hello. I asked how he was doing with his bad lungs. He has a pretty significant case of pulmonary interstitial fibrosis from chronic exposure to embalming fluid. Apparently he worked in a funeral home once."

"Not quite," she replies. "He worked for me."

"Well, I'll be darned," he says, surprised. "Now that I didn't know. I wonder why he . . . Well, he said he worked in a funeral home, was an assistant director or something."

"He didn't. He worked in the Anatomical Division, was there when I became chief back in the late eighties. Then he retired on disability in ninety-seven, right before we moved into our new building on East Fourth Street. What story did he give you about how he got his lung disease? Chronic exposure?"

"He said he got splashed one day and inhaled formaldehyde. It's in his chart. He had a rather grotesque story about it. Edgar Allan's a bit strange, I'll give you that. I've always known that. According to him, he was working in the funeral home and embalming a body and he forgot to stuff something in the mouth, this is according to him, and embalming fluid started bubbling out of the mouth because the rate of flow was too fast, or something grotesque like that, and a hose blew. He can be quite dramatic. Well, why am I telling you? If he worked for you, you know more than I do. I really don't need to repeat his fanciful tales."

"I've never heard that story before," she says. "All I remember is the chronic exposure part and that he did have fibrosis, or I should say he does have pulmonary fibrosis."

"There's no question about that. He has scarring of the interstitial tissue, significant damage to the lung tissue as evidenced by biopsy. He isn't faking."

"We're trying to find him," Scarpetta says. "Is there anything you can tell me that might give us a lead as to where to look?"

"I don't mean to state the obvious. But what about people he worked with?"

"The police are checking all of that. I'm not hopeful. When he worked for me he was a loner," she replies. "I know his prescription for prednisone is due to be renewed within days. Is he religious about doing that?"

"It's been my experience he goes through phases with his meds. He'll be fastidious for a year, then maybe he backs off from the stuff for months because it makes him gain weight."

"Is he overweight?"

"Last time I saw him, he was very overweight."

"How tall is he and how much did he weigh?"

"He's maybe five-eight. When I saw him in October, he looked like he weighed in excess of two hundred pounds and I told him that just put more of a strain on his breathing, not to mention his heart. I've gone back and forth with him about the corticosteroids because of the weight problem, and he can get very paranoid when he's on his meds."

"You worry about steroid psychosis?"

"Always worry about that with anyone. If you've ever seen steroid psychosis, you worry. But I've never decided if Edgar Allan is off when he's on his meds or just off. How did he do it, if you don't mind my asking? How did he kill the girl, the Paulsson girl?"

"You've heard of Burke and Hare? Early-nineteenth-century Scotland, the two men who killed people and sold their bodies for medical dissection? There was quite a scarcity of bodies for dissection and in fact the only way some medical students could learn anatomy was from robbing fresh graves or getting bodies in other illicit ways."

"Body snatching," Dr. Philpott says. "I know a little about burking, as it's called. Can't say I've ever heard of a modern case. The Resurrectionists, I believe those men were called back then, the ones who robbed graves and procured bodies for dissection."

"These days we're not talking about killing someone and selling the body. But Burking happens. It's so difficult to detect, we don't know just how often it happens."

"Suffocation or arsenic or what?"

"In forensic pathology, Burking refers to homicide by mechanical asphyxia. Burke's MO, legend has it, was to select someone feeble, usually an old person, a child, someone sick, and sit on the chest and cover the nose and mouth."

"That's what happened to that poor girl?" Dr. Philpott asks, his face deeply lined with distress. "That's what he did to the Paulsson girl?"

"As you know, sometimes a diagnosis is made based on the lack of a diagnosis. A process of elimination," Scarpetta replies. "She has no findings except what appear to be fresh bruises that certainly would be consistent with someone sitting on her chest, her hands pinned. She had a nosebleed." She doesn't want to say much more about it. "Obviously, this is extremely confidential."

"I have no idea where he might be," Dr. Philpott grimly says. "If he calls in for any reason, I'll tell you right away."

"Let me give you Pete Marino's number." She starts writing it down.

"Edgar Allan's really not someone I know much about. I never did like him, truth be told. He's a strange one, gave me a creepy feeling, and while his mother was alive, she always came with him to his appointments. I'm talking about when he was a grown man, right up until she died."

"What did she die of?"

"That worries me, now that we're talking about this," he says, his face grim. "She was obese and took terrible care of herself. One winter she got the flu and died at home. There was nothing suspicious about it at the time. Now I wonder."

"Might I look at his medical record? And hers, if you still have it?" Scarpetta asks.

"Now, I wouldn't have hers easily accessible since she died so long ago. But I can let you look at his. You can sit right here and do it. I have it out on my desk." He gets up from his chair and leaves the kitchen, and he moves more slowly and seems tireder than he did earlier.

Scarpetta looks out the window at a blue jay robbing the bird feeder dangling from the bare branch of an oak tree. The jay is a flurry of blue aggression, and seeds fly as it pillages the feeder, bounces off in a feathery blue spurt, and is gone. Edgar Allan Pogue may get away with it. Fingerprints don't prove much, and the cause and manner of death will be debated. There is no telling how many people he has killed, she thinks, and now she has to worry about what he was doing when he worked for her. What was he doing down there belowground? She sees him down there in scrubs. He was pale and thin back then, and she remembers his white face looking at her, stealing shy glances at her when she got off that awful service elevator and showed up to talk to Dave, who didn't like Edgar Allan much either and probably wouldn't have a clue where he is.

Scarpetta spent as little time in the Anatomical Division as she could. It was a depressing place, and there was so little state funding for it, so little paid by the medical colleges that needed the bodies, not enough money to allow the dead any dignity at all. And the crematorium was always breaking down. There were baseball bats propped in a corner because when cremains were removed from the oven, some chunks of bone needed to be pulverized or they would not fit in the cheap urns supplied by the state. A grinder was too expensive, and a baseball bat worked fine for reducing chunks of bone to a manageable size, to dust. She didn't want to be reminded of what went on down there, and she visited that division only when necessary and avoided the crematorium, avoided looking at the baseball bats. She knew about the baseball bats and kept away from them, pretending they weren't there.

I should have bought a grinder, she thinks as she sits looking at the empty bird feeder. I should have bought one with my own money. I should never have allowed baseball bats. I wouldn't allow them now.

"Here," Dr. Philpott says as he returns to the kitchen and hands her a thick file folder with Edgar Allan Pogue's name printed on it. "I've got to get back to my patients. But I'll check in to see if you need anything."

The truth is, she wasn't keen on the Anatomical Division. She is a forensic pathologist, a lawyer, and not a funeral home director or embalmer. She always assumed that those dead people had nothing to say to her because there was no mystery surrounding their deaths. If people can die peacefully, those people did. Her mission is people who don't die peacefully. Her mission is people who die violently and suddenly and suspiciously, and she did not want to talk to the people in the vats, so she avoided that subterranean part of her world back then. She avoided the people who worked in it and she avoided the people who were dead in it. She didn't want to spend time with Dave or Edgar Allan. No, she did not. When pink bodies were cranked up by pulleys and chains and with hooks, she didn't want to see it. No, she did not.

I should have paid more attention, she thinks, and her stomach is sour from the coffee. I didn't do as much as I could have. She slowly scans Pogue's medical records. I should have bought a grinder, she thinks, and she looks for the address Pogue gave Dr. Philpott. According to Pogue's records, he lived in Ginter Park, on the north side of the city, until 1996, then his address changed to a post office box. Nowhere in his record is there a mention of where he has lived since 1996, and she wonders if that is when he moved into the house behind the Paulssons' back fence, Mrs. Arnette's house. Maybe he killed her too and became a squatter.

A titmouse lands on the feeder outside the window, and she

watches it, her hands quiet on top of Pogue's medical records. Sunlight touches the left side of her face and is warm but not hot, just a winter warmth touching her as she watches the small gray bird peck at seeds, its eyes bright, its tail flicking. Scarpetta knows what some people say about her. Throughout her career she has run from the comments ignorant people make about doctors whose patients are dead. She is morbid. She is peculiar and can't get along with living people. Forensic pathologists are antisocial and odd and cold-blooded and utterly lacking in compassion. They choose this subspecialty in medicine because they are failed doctors, failed fathers, failed mothers, failed lovers, failed human beings.

Because of what ignorant people say, she has avoided the darker side of her profession, and she doesn't want to go to that dark side, but she could. She understands Edgar Allan Pogue. She does not feel what he does, but she knows what he feels. She sees his white face stealing furtive glances at her, and then she remembers the day she took Lucy down to where he worked because she was spending the Christmas holiday with her. Lucy loved to go to the office with her, and on this occasion, Scarpetta had business with Dave, so Lucy accompanied her belowground to the Anatomical Division and she was rowdy and irreverent and playful. She was Lucy. Something happened that day while Lucy was in that place, when she was there briefly. What was it?

The titmouse pecks at seeds and looks directly at Scarpetta through the glass. She lifts her coffee mug and the bird flutters off. Pale sunlight shines on the white mug, a white mug with the Medical College of Virginia crest on it. She gets up from Dr. Philpott's kitchen table and dials Marino's cell phone.

"Yo," he answers.

"He won't come back to Richmond," she says. "He's smart enough to know we're looking for him here. And Florida is a very good place for people with respiratory problems."

"I'd better head on down there. What about you?"

"I've got just one more thing, then I'm finished with this city," she replies.

"You need my help?"

"No, thanks," she says.

53.

|||THE CONSTRUCTION WORKERS are taking their lunch break, sitting on cinder blocks or on the seats of their big yellow machines, eating. Hard hats and weathered faces watch Scarpetta as she walks through thick red mud, holding up her long dark coat as if it is a long skirt.

She doesn't see the foreman she met the other day or anybody else who seems to be in charge, and the crew watches her and no one steps forward to see what she wants. Several men in dark, dusty clothing are gathered around a bulldozer, eating sandwiches and drinking sodas, and they stare at her as she picks her way in the mud, holding up her coat.

"I'm looking for the supervisor," she says when she gets close to them. "I need to get inside the building."

She glances at what is left of her former office. Half of the front area is now on the ground, but the back is still intact.

"No way," one of the men says with his mouth full. "Ain't nobody going inside." He resumes chewing and looks at her as if she is a crazy woman.

"The back of the building looks all right," she replies. "When I was chief medical examiner, this was my office. I came out here the other day after Mr. Whitby got killed."

"You can't go in there," the same man replies, and he gives his comrades a look as they stand around listening to the conversation. He gives them a look that says she is crazy.

"Where's your foreman?" she asks. "Let me talk to him."

The man removes a cell phone from his belt and calls the foreman. "Hey Joe," he says. "It's Bobby. Remember the lady who was down here the other day? The lady and the big cop from L.A.? Yeah, yeah, that's right. She's back and wants to talk to you. Okay." He ends the call and looks at her. "He went to get cigarettes and will be here in a minute," he says to her. "Why do you want to go in there anyway? I wouldn't think there's anything in there."

"Except ghosts," another man says, and his comrades laugh.

"When exactly did you start tearing this down?" she asks them.

"About a month ago. Right before Thanksgiving. Then we got weathered out for about a week because of the ice storm."

The men talk among themselves, arguing in a good-natured way about when exactly the wrecking ball struck the building the first time, and Scarpetta watches a man come around the side of the building. He is dressed in khaki work pants, a dark green jacket, and boots, his hard hat tucked under an arm as he heads toward them through the mud, smoking.

"That's Joe," the construction worker named Bobby says to her. "He's not gonna let you go in there, though. You don't want to go in there, ma'am. It ain't safe for a lot of reasons."

"When you started tearing this place down, did you have the power shut off or was it already off?" she asks.

"No way we'd start if the power was on."

"It hadn't been shut off long," another man says. "Remember before we started? People had to go through it. There were lights on then, weren't there?"

"Got no idea."

"Good afternoon," Joe the foreman says to Scarpetta. "What can I do for you?"

"I need to get inside the building. In the back door near the bay door," she replies.

"No way," he says adamantly, shaking his head and looking at the building.

"Could I talk to you for a minute?" Scarpetta says to him, and she moves away from the other workers.

"Hell no, I'm not letting you go in there. Why the hell would you want to?" Joe says, now that they are a good ten feet from the others and have a little privacy. "It isn't safe. Why do you want to?"

"Listen," she says, shifting her weight in the mud and no longer holding up the hem of her coat, "I helped examine Mr. Whitby. We found some strange evidence on his body, suffice it to say."

"You're kidding me."

She knew that would get his attention, and she adds, "There's something I need to check inside the building. Is it really unsafe or are we worried about lawsuits, Joe?"

He stares at the building and scratches his head, then rakes his fingers through his hair. "Well, it isn't going to fall down on us, not in the back there. I wouldn't go in the front."

"I don't want to go in the front," she replies. "The back is fine. We can go through that back door next to the bay door, and off to the right at the end of the hallway are stairs. We can take the stairs down one more level, to the lowest level. That's where I need to go."

"I know about the stairs. I've been in there before. You want to go down there to the first level? Good God. Now that's something."

"How long has the power been cut off?"

"I made sure of that before we started."

"Then it was on the first time you went through?" she says.

"There was lights. That would have been back in the summer, the first time I had to walk through the place. Be dark as pitch in there now. What evidence? I don't get it. You thinking something happened to him besides the tractor running him over? I mean, his wife's making a fuss, accusing all kinds of people of this and that. A lot of nonsense. I was here. Ain't nothing happened to him except he was in the wrong place at the wrong time and had to fool with the starter."

"I need to look," she says. "You can come with me. I'd appreciate it if you would. All I need to do is take a look. I imagine the back door is locked. I don't have a key."

"Well, that's not what's going to keep us out." He stares at the building, then looks back at his men. "Hey Bobby!" he calls out. "Can you drill out the lock in the back door? Do it now. All right then," he says to her. "All right. I'll take you in there as long as we don't go near the front and we don't stay but a minute."

54.

||| LIGHTS DANCE OVER cinder-block walls and beige-painted concrete steps, and their feet make scuffing sounds as they go down to where Edgar Allan Pogue worked when Scarpetta was chief. There are no windows in the first two levels of the building because the level they entered the building from was where the morgue used to be, and there shouldn't be windows in morgues and usually aren't, and there aren't windows belowground. The darkness in the stairwell is complete, and the air is sharp and damp and thick with dust.

"When they gave me a tour of this place," Joe is saying as he goes down the steps ahead of her, his flashlight bobbing with each step, "they didn't take me down here. All I did was do a walk-through up-stairs. I thought this was a basement. They didn't take me down here," he says, and he sounds uneasy.

"They should have," she replies, and dust tickles her throat and prickles her skin. "There are two floor vats down here, about twenty feet by twenty feet and ten feet deep. You wouldn't want to roll a tractor into one or fall in, for that matter."

"Now that really makes me mad," he says, and he sounds mad. "They should have at least showed me pictures. Twenty by twenty feet. Damn! Now that really pisses me off. This is the last step. Be careful." He sweeps his light around.

"We should be in a hallway. Turn left."

"Looks like that's the only way we can turn." He starts moving again, slowly. "Why the hell didn't they tell us about those vats?" He just can't believe it.

"I don't know. Depends on who showed you around."

"Some guy, oh hell, what was his name. All I remember is he was with General Services and didn't like being in here worth a damn. I'm not sure he even knew much about the building."

"Probably didn't," Scarpetta says, looking at the filthy white tile floor shining dully in her light. "They just wanted it torn down. The guy from GSA probably didn't even know about the floor vats. He may not ever have been down here in the Anatomical Division. Not many people have been down here. They're right over there." She points her light ahead of them, and the beam of light pushes back the dense darkness of a huge empty room and dimly illuminates the dark iron rectangular covers of the vats in the floor. "Well, the covers are on. I don't know if that's good or not," she says. "But this is a terrible biological hazard down here. Be sure you're aware of what you're dealing with when you start knocking down this part of the building."

"Oh don't you worry. I just can't believe it," he says angry and nervous as he shines his light around.

She moves away from the vats, back to an area of the Anatomical Division that's on the other side of the big space, passing the small room where the embalming used to be done, and she shines her light in it. A steel table attached to thick pipes in the floor gleams in her light, and a steel sink and cabinets flow by in her light. Parked against the wall in that room is a rusting gurney with a wadded plastic shroud on top. To the left of that room is an alcove, and she imagines the crematorium built into cinder block before she sees it. Then her light shines on the long dark iron door in the wall and she remembers seeing fire in the crack of the door, remembers the dusty steel trays that got shoved in with a body on them and pulled out when there was nothing much on them but ashes and chunks of chalky bone, and she thinks of the baseball bats used to pulverize the chunks. She feels shame when she thinks of the bats.

Her light moves over the floor. It is still white with dust and small bits of bone that look like chalk, and she can feel grit under her shoes as she moves. Joe hasn't come in here with her. He waits just beyond the alcove and helps from his distance by shining his light around the floor and in the corners, and the shape of her in the coat and hard hat are huge and black on the cinder-block wall. Then the light flashes over the eye. It is spray-painted in black on beige cinder block, a big black staring eye with eyelashes.

"What the hell is that?" Joe asks. He is looking at the eye on the wall, even though she can't see him looking. "Jesus Christ. What is it?"

Scarpetta doesn't answer him as her light moves around. The baseball bats are gone from the corner where they were propped when she was chief, but there is a lot of dust and bits of bone, quite a lot, she thinks. Her light finds a spray can of black paint, and two touch-up paint bottles, one red enamel paint and the other blue enamel paint, both empty, and she places them inside a plastic bag and the can of spray paint in a separate bag. She finds a few old cigar boxes that have a residue of ashes inside and she notices cigar butts on the floor and a crumpled brown paper bag. Her gloved hands enter her beam of light and pick up the bag. Paper crackles as she opens it, and she can tell the bag hasn't been down here eight years, not even one year.

She vaguely smells cigars as she opens the bag, and it isn't smoked cigars she thinks she smells but unburnt cigar tobacco, and she shines her light inside the bag and sees bits of tobacco and a receipt. Joe is watching her and has steadied his light on the bag in her hands. She looks at the receipt and feels a sense of disconnection and unreality as she reads the date of this past September fourteenth, when Edgar Allan Pogue, and she feels sure it was Pogue, spent more than a hundred dollars at a tobacco store just down the street at the James Center for ten Romeo y Julieta cigars.

55.

| | | THE JAMES CENTER is not the sort of place Marino used to visit when he was a cop in Richmond, and he never bought his Marlboros in the fancy tobacco shop or in any tobacco shop.

He never bought cigars, not any brand of cigars, because even a cheap cigar is a lot of money for a single smoke, and besides, he wouldn't have puffed, he would have inhaled. Now that he hardly smokes anymore, he can admit the truth. He would have inhaled cigar smoke. The atrium is all glass and light and plants, and the sound of splashing water from waterfalls and fountains follows Marino as he walks swiftly toward the shop where Edgar Allan Pogue bought cigars not even three months before he murdered little Gilly.

It is not quite noon yet and the shops aren't very busy. A few people in stylish business suits are buying coffee and moving about as if they have places to go and important lives, and Marino can't stomach people like the ones in the James Center. He knows the type. He grew up knowing the type, not personally, but knowing about the type. They were the type who didn't know Marino's type and never tried to know his type. He walks fast and is angry, and when a man in a fine black pinstriped suit passes him and doesn't even see him, Marino thinks, You don't know shit. People like you don't know shit.

Inside the tobacco shop the air is pungent and sweet with a symphony of tobacco scents that fill him with a longing he doesn't understand and immediately blames on smoking. He misses it like hell. He is sad and upset because he misses cigarettes, and his heart hurts and he feels shaken somewhere deep inside his very soul because he knows he'll never be able to smoke again, not like he used to, he just can't do it. He was kidding himself to think he might sneak one or two now and then. What a myth to think there was any hope. There is no hope. There was never hope. If anything is hopeless, his insatiable lust for tobacco, his desperate love for tobacco, is hopeless, and he is suddenly crushed by grief because he will never light up a cigarette and deeply inhale and feel that rush, that sheer joy, that release he aches for every minute of his life. He wakes up aching, he goes to sleep aching, he aches in his dreams and he aches when he is wide awake. Glancing at his watch, he thinks about Scarpetta, wondering if her flight has been delayed. So many flights are delayed these days.

Marino's doctor told him that if he keeps on smoking he'll be carrying an oxygen tank around like a papoose by the time he's sixty. Eventually he will die gasping for air just like poor little Gilly was fighting for air while that freak sat on her and pinned her hands, and she was under him and panicking, every cell in her lungs screaming for air as her mouth tried to scream for her mommy and daddy, just screaming, Marino thinks. Gilly was unable to make a sound, and what did she ever do to deserve a death like that? Nothing, that's what, Marino thinks as he looks around at boxes of cigars on dark wooden shelves inside the cool fragrant rich man's tobacco shop. Scarpetta should be boarding the plane right about now, he thinks, noticing the boxes of Romeo y Julieta cigars. If she isn't delayed, she may already be on the plane, heading west to Denver, and Marino feels a hollowness around his heart and somewhere in an off-limit part of his very soul he feels shame, and then he feels very angry.

"Let me know if you need some help," a man in a v-necked gray sweater and brown corduroys says from behind the counter. The color of his clothes and his gray hair remind Marino of smoke. The man works in a tobacco shop full of smokes and he has become the color of smoke. He probably goes home at the end of the day and can have all the smokes he wants while Marino goes home or back to a hotel alone and can't even light up a smoke, much less inhale smoke. Now he sees the truth. He knows it. He can't have it. He was kidding himself to think he could have it, and he is filled with grief and shame.

He reaches inside a jacket pocket and pulls out the receipt Scarpetta found on the bone-dusty floor in the Anatomical Division of her old building. The receipt is inside a transparent plastic bag, and he places it on the counter.

"How long you worked here?" Marino asks the smoky-looking man behind the counter.

"Going on twelve years," the man says, giving him a smile, but he has a look in his smoky gray eyes. Marino recognizes fear and does nothing to allay it.

"Then you know Edgar Allan Pogue. He came in here on September fourteenth of this year and bought these cigars."

The man frowns and bends over to look at the receipt inside the plastic evidence bag. "That's our receipt," he says.

"No joke, Sherlock. A short little fat guy with red hair," Marino says, doing nothing at all to ease the man's fear. "In his thirties. Used to work at the old morgue over there." He points toward 14th Street. "Probably acted weird when he was in here."

The man keeps glancing at Marino's LAPD baseball cap. He is pale and uneasy. "We don't sell Cuban cigars."

"What?" Marino scowls.

"If that's what this is about. He may have asked, but we don't sell them."

"He came in here asking for Cuban cigars?"

"He was very determined, more so last time he was in here," the man says nervously. "We don't sell Cubans or anything else illegal."

"I ain't accusing you and I ain't ATF or the FDA or the Surgeon General or the goddamn Easter Bunny," Marino says. "I don't give a rat's ass if you sell Cuban shit under the counter."

"I don't. I swear I don't."

"I just want Pogue. Talk to me."

"I remember him," the man says, and now his face is the color of smoke. "Yes, he's asked me for Cubans. For Cohibas, not the Dominicans we sell, but Cubans. I told him we don't sell Cuban cigars. They're illegal. You're not from here, are you? You don't sound as if you're from here."

"I sure as hell ain't from here," Marino replies. "What else did Pogue say? And when was this, when he came in here last?"

The man looks down at the receipt on the counter. "Probably since then. Seems like it might have been in October when he came in last. He came in here maybe once a month. A very strange man. Very strange."

"In October? Okay. What else did he say when he came in?"

"He wanted Cuban cigars, said he would pay what he had to for them, and I told him we don't sell them. He knew that. He'd asked me before when he came in here, but not so insistently, not like he was when he came in last. Strange, that man. He'd asked me before and was asking me again, but very insistent. Seems like he said Cuban tobacco is better for the lungs, some nonsense like that. You can smoke all the Cubans you want and they won't hurt you, in fact they're good for you. They are pure and better for the lungs and actually have a medicinal quality, something silly like that."

"What did you tell him? Don't lie to me. I don't give a shit if you sold him Cubans. I need to find him. If he thinks the shit's good for his screwed-up lungs, he's buying it somewhere. If he's got a thing about it, he's getting it from somewhere."

"He's got a thing about it, at least last time he was here, he was adamant. Don't ask me why," the man says, staring down at the receipt. "There are plenty of good cigars. Why they had to be Cuban, I don't understand, but he wanted them. It reminded me of sick people desperate for some magic herb or marijuana or people with arthritis who want gold injections or whatever. Obviously a superstition of some sort. Very strange. I sent him to a different store, told him not to be asking me about Cubans anymore."

"What store?"

"Well, actually it's a restaurant where I hear they sell things and know where to get things. In the bar they do. Anything you want, I guess. That's what I've heard. I don't go in there. I don't have anything to do with it."

"Where."

"Down in the Slip," he says. "Just a few blocks from here."

"You know any places in South Florida that sell Cubans? Maybe you recommended a place in South Florida to him."

"No," the man replies, shaking his gray head. "I don't have anything to do with that. Ask them in the Slip. They probably know."

"Okay. So here's the million-dollar question." Marino tucks the plastic bag back inside his jacket pocket. "You tell Pogue about this place in the Slip so maybe he could find his Cubans?"

"I told him some people buy cigars in the bar there," the man says.

"What's the name of this place in the Slip?"

"Stripes. The name of the bar is Stripes, just down Cary Street.

I didn't want him coming back. He was very strange. I always thought he was strange. He'd been coming in here for years, every few months. Never said much of anything," the man says. "But the last time he was in here, in October maybe, he was stranger than usual. He was carrying a baseball bat. I asked him why and he never answered me. He didn't used to be so insistent about wanting Cubans, but he was just bizarre about it. Cohibas, he kept saying. He wanted them."

"Was the bat red, white, and blue?" Marino asks, thinking about Scarpetta and grinders and bone dust and everything else she said when she was leaving Dr. Philpott's office.

"It might have been," the man says with a strange look. "What the hell is this about?" he asks.

56.

|||In the woods around the town homes the shadows are deep and cold around patchy white and gray aspen trees. The trees are bare but thick in the woods. To get through them Lucy and Henri have to duck and push branches and winter-dormant saplings out of the way. Their snowshoes don't stop the snow from coming up to their knees with each step and wherever they look the smooth white surface is unmarked by the tracks of humans.

"This is a crazy thing to do," Henri says, breathing hard smoky breaths. "Why are we doing this?"

"Because we need to get out and do something," Lucy replies as she steps into snow that comes almost up to her thigh. "Wow! Look at this. Unbelievable. It's beautiful."

"I don't think you should have come here," Henri says, pausing and looking at her in deepening shadows that tint the snow blue.

"I've gotten through it and had enough and I'm going back to Los Angeles."

"It's your life."

"I know you don't mean that. Whenever you say flip things like that your nose grows."

"Let's just go a little farther," Lucy says, forging ahead, making sure she doesn't let any branches or tender young trees snap back into Henri's face, although maybe she deserves it. "There's an old fallen tree, I'm pretty sure. I saw it from the path when I was coming up to see you, and we can brush the snow off and sit."

"We'll freeze." Henri says, lunging into a deep step and blowing out a cloud of frozen breath.

"You're not cold now, are you?"

"I'm hot."

"So if we get cold, we'll get up and move again and go home."

Henri doesn't reply. Her stamina is noticeably diminished from what it was before she got the flu and then was attacked. In Los Angeles, where Lucy first set eyes on her, she was in superb physical shape, not big but very strong. She could bench-press her own body weight and do ten hand-over pull-ups unassisted, when most women can't bench-press a third of their weight or do one pull-up. She could run a seven-minute mile. Now she'd be lucky to walk a mile. In less than one month's time, Henri has lost it and she loses more every day because she has lost something else that is more important than her physical conditioning. She has lost her mission. She has no mission. Lucy worries that Henri never had one, only vanity, and the fires of vanity are quick and hot and soon enough gone.

"Just up there," Lucy says. "I see it. See that huge log? There's a little frozen creek beyond it, then the health club is over that-a-way." She motions with a ski pole. "Perfect scenario would be end in the gym and then the steam room."

"I can't breathe," Henri says. "Ever since I got the flu, my lungs feel half the size they were."

"You got pneumonia," Lucy reminds her. "Or maybe you don't remember. You were on antibiotics for a week. You were still on them when it happened."

"Yes. When it happened. Everything is about it. It." She keeps emphasizing the word "it." "I guess we talk in euphemisms now." She steps where Lucy has stepped because she is slowing down and sweating. "My lungs hurt."

"What would you like us to say?" Lucy reaches the fallen tree, and it was once a large tree but is now just a hulk, like what is left of a great ship, and she begins to brush deep snow off it. "What would you call what happened?"

"I'd call it almost being killed."

"Here. Sit." Lucy sits and pats a cleared-off area of log next to her. "It feels good to sit." Her frozen breath rises like steam and her face is so cold she can barely feel it. "Almost being killed as opposed to almost being murdered?"

"Same thing." Henri is tentative as she stands beside the log, looking around the snowy woods and the deepening of the shadows. Through dark cold branches the lights of town homes and the health club are a buttery yellow, and smoke rises from chimneys.

"I wouldn't exactly call it the same thing," Lucy replies, looking up at her, noticing how thin she has gotten and aware of something in her eyes she wasn't aware of in the beginning. "Almost being killed is a detached way of saying it. I guess I'm looking for feelings, real emotions."

"It's better not to look for things." Henri reluctantly sits on the log, keeping her distance from Lucy.

"You didn't look for him and he found you," Lucy says, staring straight ahead into the woods, her arms resting on her knees.

"So I was stalked. Half of Hollywood is stalked. I guess that makes me a member of the club," she replies, and seems rather pleased to be a member of the star-stalked club.

"I thought that too until a little while ago." Lucy's gloved hands reach into the snow between her feet and she picks up a handful of powder and looks at it. "Apparently you gave an interview about my hiring you. You never told me."

"What interview?"

"*The Hollywood Reporter.* It quotes you."

"I've been quoted saying a lot of things I didn't say," she replies, bristling.

"This isn't about what you didn't say. This is about your giving an interview. I believe you did. The name of my company's in the story, not that the existence of TLP is a deep, dark secret, but the fact that I relocated my headquarters to Florida is secret. That I've kept very secret, mainly because of the training camp. But it ended up in the paper, and once something runs, it is picked up again and again."

"You don't understand rumors and bullshit stories, apparently," Henri replies, and Lucy won't look at her as she talks. "If you ever worked in the movie business, you'd see. You'd understand."

"I understand plenty, I'm afraid. Edgar Allan Pogue found out somehow that my aunt supposedly works for me in my new Hollywood, Florida, office. Guess what he does?" She bends over and scoops up more snow. "He comes to Hollywood. To find me."

"He wasn't after you," Henri says, and her tone is as cold as the snow. Lucy can't feel the snow because of her glove, but she feels Henri's coldness.

"I'm afraid he was. It's hard to tell who's driving those Ferraris, you know. You have to get up close to look, and they're easy enough to follow. Rudy's right about that. Very easy. Pogue somehow tracked me down. Maybe he asked enough questions and found the camp and followed a Ferrari to my house. Maybe the black Ferrari. I don't know." She lets the snow fall through her black-gloved fingers and scoops up more, refusing to look at Henri. "He found my black Ferrari, though. Scratched the hell out of it, so we know he found that car when you took it without permission after I told you never to drive it, as a matter of fact. Maybe that's the night he found my house. I don't know. But he wasn't after you."

"You're so egotistical," Henri says.

"You know, Henri"—Lucy drops the snow from her open black glove—"we did an extensive background check on you before I recruited you. There probably isn't an article written about you that we didn't find. Sadly, we're talking very few. I wish you'd stop the star shit. I wish you'd stop the I-got-stalked-so-I-must-be-something shit. It's really boring."

"I'm going in." She gets up from the log and almost loses her balance. "I'm really tired."

"He wanted to kill you to pay me back for something that happened when I was a kid," Lucy says. "As much as one can assign logic to a nutcase like him. Thing is, I don't even remember him. He probably doesn't really remember you, Henri. All of us are just a means to an end sometimes, I guess."

"I wish I'd never met you. You've ruined my life."

Tears sting Lucy's eyes, and she stays seated on the log as if frozen there. She scoops up more snow and tosses it and the powder floats down through the shadows.

"I've always been into men, anyway," Henri says, stepping into the trail they made when they snowshoed to the log just a little while ago. "I don't know why I went along with it. Maybe I was just curious to see what it was like. I guess a lot of people would find you very exciting for a while. Not that experimenting is unusual in the world I come from. Not that it matters. None of it matters."

"How did you get the bruises?" Lucy asks Henri's back as she takes high, exaggerated steps into the woods, stabbing her poles and breathing hard. "I know you remember. You remember exactly how."

"Oh. The bruises you took pictures of, Miss Super Cop?" Henri answers, out of breath, stabbing a ski pole into the deep snow.

"I know you remember." Lucy looks after her from the log, her eyes swimming with tears, but she manages to keep her voice steady.

"He sat on me." Henri stabs the other pole into the snow and lifts a snowshoe. "This freak with long kinky hair. At first I thought he was the pool lady, thought he was a she. I'd seen him around the pool a few days earlier when I was upstairs sick, saw him, only I thought it was a fat lady with kinky hair, skimming the pool."

"He was skimming the pool?"

"Yes. So I thought he was a second pool lady, maybe a substitute or something, a second pool lady skimming away. And here's the funny part." She looks back at Lucy, and Henri's face doesn't look like her face. It looks different. "That fucking drunk of a neighbor was taking pictures just like she does of everything that happens on your property."

"Good of you to pass along the information," Lucy says. "I'm sure you didn't mention it to Benton after all this time, all this time he's spent trying to help you. Nice of you to let us know there might be pictures."

"That's all I remember. He sat on me. I didn't want to tell." She can barely breathe as she steps, then stops, and turns around, and her face is white and cruel in the shadows. "Found it embarrassing, you know." She breathes. "To think of some fat ugly wacko showing up at your bed. Not to have some. You know. But to sit on you." She turns around and trudges ahead.

"Thanks for the information, Henri. You're quite the investigator."

"Not anymore. I quit. I'm flying back," she gasps. "To L.A. I quit."

Lucy sits on the log, scooping up snow and looking at it in her black gloves. "You can't quit," she says. "Because you're fired."

Henri doesn't hear her.

"You're fired," Lucy says from her log.

Henri steps high and stabs her poles through the woods.

57.

||| INSIDE THE Guns & Pawn Shop on U.S. 1, Edgar Allan Pogue walks up and down the aisles, taking his time looking as his fingers stroke the copper-and-lead cartridges deep inside the right pocket of his pants. He takes one holster at a time off the rack and reads the package, then neatly hangs each holster back. He doesn't need a holster today. What is today? He isn't sure. Days have passed with nothing to show for them except vague memories of changing light as he sweated on his lawn chair and stared at the big eye staring at him from the wall.

Every other minute he starts coughing a deep dry cough that leaves him exhausted and wheezy and more upset. His nose is running and his joints are aching and he knows what all of it means. Dr. Philpott was out of flu shots. He didn't save any vaccine for Pogue. Of all people who should have had a dose saved for him, he should have, but Dr. Philpott never gave it a thought. Dr. Philpott said he was sorry but he didn't have any vaccine left, nobody in the entire city did as far as he knew, and that was that. Try back in a week or so, but it doesn't look good, Dr. Philpott said.

What about down in Florida? Pogue asked him.

I doubt it, Dr. Philpott replied, busy and hardly listening to Pogue. I doubt you'll find influenza vaccine anywhere unless you're lucky, and if you're that lucky, you ought to play the lottery. There's a severe nationwide shortage this year. They just didn't make enough and it takes a good three or four months to make more, so that's it for the year. Truth is, you can get vaccinated for one strain of flu but catch another. Best thing is to avoid sick people and take good care of yourself. Don't get on airplanes, and stay out of gyms. You can get exposed to a lot in gyms.

Yes sir, Pogue replied, although he has never been on an airplane in his life and he hasn't gone inside a gym since he was in high school.

Edgar Allan Pogue coughs so hard his eyes water as he stands before a shelf of gun cleaning accessories, fascinated by all the little brushes and bottles and kits. He won't be cleaning guns today, and he strolls along the aisle, noticing everybody in the store. A few minutes later, he is the only customer, and at the counter he looks at a big man in black who is replacing a pistol in the showcase.

"Can I help you?" the man asks, and he's probably in his fifties, has a shaved head and looks like he could hurt someone.

"I hear you sell cigars," Pogue replies, stifling a cough.

"Huh." The man looks at him defiantly, then his eyes drift up to Pogue's wig, then back to Pogue's eyes, and there's something about the man that taps Pogue on the shoulder. "Oh really? And where'd you hear that?"

"I heard it," Pogue says, and something taps his shoulder, asking for his attention, and he starts coughing and his eyes tear up.

"Sounds like you don't need to be smoking," the man says from the other side of the glass showcase. He has a black baseball cap stuck in the back waistband of his cargo pants, but Pogue can't tell what kind of cap.

"I'll be the judge of that," Pogue replies, trying to catch his breath. "I'd like Cohibas. I'll pay twenty apiece for six of them."

"What the hell kind of gun is a Cohiba?" the man says with a straight face.

"Twenty-five then."

"I got no idea what you're talking about."

"Thirty," Pogue says. "That's as high as I go. They'd better be Cuban. I can tell. And I'd like to see a Smith and Wesson thirty-eight. That revolver right there." He points at one in the showcase. "I want to see it. Let me see the Cohibas and the thirty-eight."

"I hear ya," the man says, looking past him as if he sees something, and his tone changes, his face changes, and something about him taps Pogue's shoulder, keeps tapping it.

Pogue turns around as if something might be behind him, but nothing is, nothing but two aisles crowded with gun equipment and accessories and camouflage clothing and cases of ammunition. He fingers the six .38 caliber cartridges in his pocket, wondering how it will feel to shoot the big man in black, deciding it will probably feel good, and he turns back to the glass showcase and the man behind it is pointing a pistol right between Pogue's eyes.

"How ya doin', Edgar Allan," the man says. "I'm Marino."

58.

||| SCARPETTA SEES BENTON coming down the shoveled path
that leads from his town home to the newly plowed road, and she
stops beneath dark green fragrant trees and waits for him. She hasn't
seen him since he came to Aspen. He quit calling her very often after
Henri moved in, something Scarpetta knew nothing about at the
time, and he didn't have much to say when they talked by phone. She
understands. She has learned to understand and doesn't find it all that
hard to understand, not anymore.

He kisses her and his lips taste like salt.

"What have you been eating?" she asks, holding him tight and
kissing him again outside in the snow beneath the heavy branches of
evergreens.

"Peanuts. You should have been a bloodhound with that nose

of yours," he says, looking into her eyes and wrapping an arm around her.

"I said I taste something, not smell something." She smiles, walking with him up the shoveled path toward the town home.

"I was thinking about cigars," he replies, pulling her close, both of them trying to walk together as if their four legs are two legs. "Remember when I smoked cigars?"

"That didn't taste good," she says. "Smelled good but didn't taste good."

"Look who's talking. You smoked cigarettes back then."

"So I didn't taste good."

"I didn't say that. I sure as hell didn't."

He holds her tight and her arm is tight around his waist as they walk toward the lighted town home that is halfway in the woods.

"That was really smart. You and cigars, Kay," he says, digging in a pocket of his ski jacket for keys. "If I haven't made that clear, I want to make sure you know how smart that was."

"I didn't do it," she replies, wondering what Benton feels like after all this time and checking on her own feelings to see what they are. "Marino did."

"I'd like to have seen him buying Cuban cigars in that fancy tobacco shop in Richmond."

"That's not where they sell the illegal stuff, the Cuban stuff, and by the way, how stupid is that? Treating Cuban cigars like they're marijuana in this country," she says. "Someone in the fancy tobacco shop had a lead for him. Then the leads went on and on right down to that gun-and-pawn shop in Hollywood. You know Marino. He's something."

"Whatever," Benton says, and he isn't particularly interested in the minutiae. She feels what he is interested in and isn't sure what she wants to do about it.

"Give Marino the credit, not me. That's all I'm saying. He's been through it. A little credit would be a good thing for him right now. I'm hungry. What did you cook for me?"

"I've got a grill. I like grilling in the snow on the patio out by the hot tub."

"You and the hot tub. In the cold in the dark with nothing on but a gun."

"I know. I still never use that damn hot tub." He stops at his front door and unlocks it.

They stomp snow off their feet, and there isn't much snow to knock loose because the walk is shoveled, but out of habit and maybe a little self-consciousness they stomp their feet before going inside. Benton shuts the door and holds her close to him and they kiss deeply and she doesn't taste salt anymore, just feels his warm, strong tongue and his smooth-shaven face.

"You're letting your hair grow," she says into his mouth, and she runs her fingers through his hair.

"Been busy. Too busy to get it cut," he replies, and his hands are on her, all over her, and her hands are on him, but their coats are in the way.

"Busy shacking up with another woman," she says, helping him off with his coat as he helps her off with her coat, kissing, touching. "I heard."

"You did?"

"I did. Don't cut your hair."

She leans against the front door and cold air seeping in around the door frame doesn't bother her. She hardly notices it, and she holds him by the arms and looks at him, at his mussed-up silver hair and what is in his eyes. He touches her face as he looks at her, and what she sees in his eyes gets deeper and brighter at the same time, and for an instant she can't tell if he's happy or sad.

"Come in," he says with that look in his eyes, and he takes her hand and moves her away from the door and suddenly it is warmer. "I'll get you something to drink. Or to eat. You must be hungry and tired."

"I'm not that tired," she says.